RAID
ON
TRUMAN

RAID
ON
TRUMAN

a novel

John T. Campbell

LYFORD
B O O K S

The *Kiss of Death* symbol portrayed in this work was first seen by the author while serving aboard the USS *Shangri-La* during its final cruise to the Tonkin Gulf in 1970. The symbol was used by attack squadron VA-l2, which was engaged in combat operations over Vietnam.

All the vessels portrayed in this work are real except for the USS *Truman* and the USS *Lansdale*. The U.S. Navy did have a ship with the name *Lansdale*, but its construction was never completed, and it was scrapped in the '50's.

All characters in *Raid on Truman* are fictitious. Any resemblance to actual persons, living or dead, is purely coincidental. Nothing in this book should be construed as expressing the views of any department of the United States government or any branch of the United States military service.

A glossary at the back of the book defines naval terms and acronyms mentioned in the text with which the reader may be unfamiliar.

LYFORD BOOKS
Published by Presidio Press
31 Pamaron Way, Novato, CA 94949

Library of Congress Cataloging-in-Publication Data

Campbell, John T.
    Raid on Truman / John T. Campbell.
      p. cm.
    ISBN 0-89141-386-3
    1. Korean War, 1950-1953--Fiction. I. Title.
PS3553. A469R35   1991
813' .54--dc20   90-27902
                                           CIP

Typography by ProImage

Printed in the United States of America

This one is for the Snipes.

snipe (snīp) *n., pl.* **snipe** or **snipes. 1.** Any of various long-billed wading birds of the genus *Capella*, esp. the common widely distributed species *C. gallinago*. **2.** A shot, esp. a gunshot, from a concealed place. **3.** Naval slang for a ship's engineer.

The author wishes to thank many people who had a hand in bringing this work to fruition. My wife, Carol, must be first and foremost. She always believed in me and provided unending encouragement. My brothers, Chris and Bob, along with my father, Christopher, provided much needed data and valuable criticism. My mother, Mrs. Mary Campbell, typed the initial versions of the work and to her I am deeply indebted.

A host of others have helped in various ways. Phil Hatfield, Dick Kopey, George Wood, Joe Winner, Mrs. Claire Han, Chuck Bixler and his son Commander Charles Bixler, USN, Tom Yurick, Rikk Wolfs, Cedric Taylor, David Lopez of the Smithsonian Institute, and Mrs. Dawn Engleman and her husband all had their hand in bringing this work to fulfillment. To all of them I offer my heartfelt thanks. I want to also thank Ed Murphy for providing details on the Medal of Honor citations.

A special thanks is given to Bob Tate of Presidio Press for nudging me along to produce a better work, and to my agent, Elizabeth Pomada, for being the first one in the industry to give me a chance to get this work published.

John T. Campbell

Prologue

NORTH KOREA, 1950

P ilot to navigator." His eyes anxiously scanned the sky above for enemy formations, but the sky was clear. He let out a sigh and relaxed a bit while remembering that this war was quite different from the last one.

"Yeah, Skipper." The electronic rendition of the navigator's voice sounded clear but distant, even though he was only five feet from the pilot.

Captain Thomas Reynolds, USAF, took a hand off the yoke, which guided the huge bomber, and touched his throat mike. "Give me an ETA, Harry," said Reynolds.

The reply was immediate. "Twelve minutes to target, Skipper."

Reynolds's eyes flicked over the array of gauges and controls in front of him. Everything was all right; nothing amiss. He looked out the left side window first at the two wing engines veiled by the blur of their rotating propellers, and then at the other B-29s in the formation. They looked like a huge flock of graceful silver birds gliding through the sky instead of the death-dealing war machines they really were. Their skin was smooth, flawed only by an occasional bubble, the telltale sign of a gun turret. They were sleek and shiny and already obsolete as they thundered through the skies of North Korea. The advent of the jet airplane would relegate them to the scrap heap or some deserted airfield in some obscure part of the United States.

The bombardier-navigator, "bombigator" as they called him, shuffled past Reynolds and squeezed his way between the pilot and copilot's consoles to take up his position behind the Norden bombsight, which was located in the nose of the plane. He quickly settled himself in place and hunched over to set up the bombsight for its minute or two of operation. After a few moments of examination to ensure that his equipment was operating properly, the bombardier began to stare at the clock on his instrument panel.

He glanced back over his console, then activated the bomb bay door control. Pneumatic machinery flung the bomb bay doors open as Reynolds instinctively compensated for the extra drag by tugging at the yoke.

"Bombardier to pilot. Bomb bay doors open."

"Roger, Harry."

After the briefest of pauses the bombardier spoke again. "Ten seconds to IP." Another few seconds and the bombardier's voice floated over the plane's intercom. "IP on my mark . . . MARK!" After a short pause, "Bombardier to pilot. I've got it, Skipper."

His voice sounded tense to Reynolds despite the roughness added by the intercom. Reynolds glanced quickly over his instruments one last time before switching to the autopilot and gingerly lifting his hands away from the yoke.

"Pilot to bombardier. You've got it, Harry."

The yoke continued to sway back and forth, to and fro, as if the autopilot had imparted some rudimentary life to it. Reynolds stared at the yoke for a moment until he was satisfied with its operation, then looked across the cabin toward the copilot. He also seemed tense, and for good reason. They had just begun their bombing run and therefore were in the most vulnerable phase of the flight. They had to fly straight and level with no maneuvering as their bombigator made minor adjustments and aligned the plane with the target.

Reynolds let his eyes sweep the console in front of him and then encompass the skies around his huge bomber. No opposition yet, he thought. It'll be like the last mission. Simple. Drop the bombs and go. It's a lot different from the last war. He half expected to see a "Nick" or a "Tony" shoot by his aircraft with guns blazing in a vain attempt to stem the advancing tide of B-29s. Reynolds had been a copilot on a few missions over Japan in the waning days of World War II. He had remained in the air force, and most of the peaceful years after the war were spent training in the B-29s. He pulled himself upward as far as the seat harness would permit and stared at the horizon for a glimpse of the city they were about to destroy.

Pyongyang, the capital of the Democratic People's Republic of Korea, lay below in the early morning light. The Korean War had begun a bare two months before. In June 1950, Communist North Korea invaded South Korea in an attempt to take over the entire peninsula by force. The invasion proceeded smoothly for the North Koreans and began to slow down only when the United States reinforced its torn army in Korea. As a result United States and South Korean forces occupied only a 150-mile perimeter around the port city of Pusan in the southeastern corner of Korea. The North Koreans were making a tremendous effort to smash the forces at Pusan by sending reinforcements and vast amounts of war materiel to the south with all possible speed. The job of the Far Eastern Air Force, or FEAF, was to stop the flow of Communist ammunition, armor, and men from augmenting the North Korean forces around Pusan.

During the previous month, formations of B-29 Superfortresses had been striking at enemy formations and marshaling points in North and South Korea in an effort to stem the Communist tide. The Pyongyang rail yards were a major artery in the flow south and had quickly become a prime target for the virtually unopposed American bombers. This was the second mission this month for Reynolds and his crew over Pyongyang. They had nervously anticipated fierce opposition from the North Korean Air Force on this second raid, but it was becoming apparent that the Communist Air Force was not up to the challenge.

"One minute to target."

The bombardier's voice sliced through the constant drone of the plane's engines in the background, and his announcement immediately heightened the tension. Reynolds stared at the bombardier's back and mentally reviewed the bombardier's procedures. He would be aligning cross hairs on the target and then he would wait until a second set of cross hairs, which indicated where the bombs would hit, were superimposed upon the first set, then—

"OK, OK, here we go . . . ," said the bombardier to no one in particular. Reynolds held his breath.

"Bombs away!"

Reynolds thought he heard the click of the solenoids that released the bombs and sent them whistling down to their ultimate destination. He could feel the plane lighten as the bombs dropped, but he could sense that something was wrong in the bomb bay. The plane didn't lighten enough.

"Damn!" The bombardier's oath confirmed Reynolds's suspicion.

"We've got a hung bomb rack, Captain!" shouted the bombardier. Reynolds's stomach muscles knotted.

"Hit the bomb release switch again while I inform the boss." Reynolds felt some satisfaction at the apparent calm in his voice. If he panicked, the rest of the crew would most likely follow his lead. And that wouldn't solve the problem. Reynolds picked up the microphone used for plane-to-plane communications and pressed the transmit button.

"Cobra Leader, this is Cobra Five. We have an emergency. We've got a hung bomb rack. Over." His earphones crackled with low-level static for a few seconds as he impatiently waited for a reply.

The static suddenly was replaced by a booming voice. "Cobra Five, this is Cobra Leader. We will maintain course and speed while you rectify the problem, but be quick about it. Over." Static again.

"Roger, Cobra Leader," replied Reynolds.

"Bombardier to pilot, I've recycled the release switch and tried the emergency release, but it's no go. Someone will have to manually release it."

The seriousness of the situation made Reynolds sweat despite the relatively chilly air in the cabin. A hung bomb rack meant that there were still bombs in the bomb bay. At best they might be neatly tucked away undisturbed in the rack, and at worst the first bomb or two might be dangling half out of the bomb bay. Worse yet the bombs might be armed. Any pressure on the nose of the bomb and the entire crew would be sent to kingdom come. Reynolds didn't dare try to close the bomb bay doors for fear of detonating a bomb.

All this meant no changes in course, speed, or altitude until the rack was cleared by someone entering the bomb bay and manually releasing the rack. That necessitated crouching on an all too narrow catwalk and dangling from the bomb rack brace while actuating the bomb release unit by hand. It was an exceedingly dangerous procedure: If the bombs didn't detonate from the vibration, there was still the danger of falling out of the bomb bay.

Reynolds took a deep breath to settle himself and felt the copilot's eyes on him as he touched his throat mike with his left hand. "Pilot to waist. Sergeant Wood, get in the rear bomb bay and release the rack."

Wood's voice came back from the inner recesses of the aircraft. "Roger, Skipper."

Just behind the cabin containing the pilot, copilot, flight engineer, bombardier, and top gunners were the two bomb bays, with the waist gunner compartment behind the second bomb bay. A tube just big enough for a crew member to crawl through ran lengthwise above the bomb bays and connected the gunners' compartment with the forward cabin. Both compartments and the crawl tube were pressurized but the bomb bays obviously were not. The aircraft had to be depressurized before anyone could enter the bomb bays.

"Pilot to crew. Everyone get on oxygen and prepare for depressurization." Reynolds put on his oxygen mask, which had been dangling just under his chin, while he listened to the crew members acknowledge one by one that they also had their oxygen masks in place.

"Pilot to engineer. Let 'er go."

His ears felt the change in pressure as the air was slowly exhausted out of the cabin. The tone of the engines took on a faraway note, and the cabin suddenly became much colder than before.

"Pilot to waist. Get on with it," said Reynolds.

Wood mumbled something that sounded like an acknowledgment and got to work on the hatch. A few moments later Wood's tense voice came over the intercom.

"Skipper, one of the bombs is hanging by its rear support from the shackle. It's the bottom bomb in the rack and the wind is really knocking it around. The rest are OK."

Reynolds ground his teeth. This was bad news. "Wood, is the bomb armed?"

Seconds passed as Wood shifted his position to get a better look at the bomb's nose. "The pin is out, Captain. I can see it hanging from the release unit. I think the propeller arm is gone, too."

As each bomb fell from the rack, a pin on a wire connected to the release unit would be pulled from the nose of the bomb. This would let a propellerlike device spin until it came off the nose of the bomb, and thus arm the bomb as it fell toward the target. This bomb had fallen enough to have the pin pulled, and the blast of air passing by the aircraft unscrewed the propeller arming device. The bomb was now fully armed.

"Wood, can you release the rack manually?" asked Reynolds.

"Geez, I don't think I can get to it, sir."

Reynolds gave his copilot a pained look.

"Skipper, it looks like the shackles opened partway, then closed—" began Wood.

The flight engineer spoke up. "Wood, check for a loose connection on the cable going to the rack release unit."

After a few seconds Wood came back. "I've got the unit in sight, but it doesn't look like anything's wrong with it."

Reynolds started to review in his mind the bailout procedures. Air-sea rescue would pick them up, if the Communists didn't get to them first and assuming they could make it to the sea.

"Wood," said the engineer, "wiggle the cable while the bombardier hits the release."

Reynolds nodded in an exaggerated fashion to show his acceptance of the suggestion.

"OK. Hit it," said Wood.

The bombardier shifted slightly and pressed the release button. His arm suddenly shot up to give the thumbs-up sign. "Bombs away!" he shouted.

Wood was only a second behind the bombardier. "There they go!"

Reynolds muttered a prayer of thanks and waited until Wood was out of the bomb bay and got the doors closed. He picked up the mike and pushed the transmit button.

"Cobra Five to Cobra Leader. Situation corrected. Let's go home."

PYONGYANG, NORTH KOREA, 1950

Kang Chung Kwon was in the field helping to gather his family's livestock when the bombs struck. He was home from the fighting near the Pusan perimeter and was already a war hero of the Democratic People's Republic of Korea. The propaganda machine of the Communist government had needed a hero to parade before the masses in its exhortations to the people to greater war effort, and Kang was selected for his courage during combat.

Kang was young, almost too young for the role, but he was "of the people," having been a peasant before joining the army the year before. Kang was disappointed to be pulled back so quickly from the fighting, which he found to be exhilarating; he had performed brilliantly in his country's swift drive southward. He particularly distinguished himself in the Kum River offensive and was in one of the advance units of the third division that crossed the river and annihilated the U.S. 63d Field Artillery Battalion. That combat had heightened his senses and had given a drive and a direction to his life; it was a truly glorious undertaking for him. He had participated in the greatest war in Korea's history, the war that would unite the entire peninsula under one government, his government.

Kang was doubly disappointed at his assignment behind the front lines due to his belief that the war would not last much longer. The Pusan perimeter would collapse quickly and his comrades-in-arms would experience the exhilaration of the final surrender of the South Korean and American troops that opposed them. The war would then be over, and he would be hundreds of miles away when the final moment of glory came.

The Americans puzzled him. Why were they in Korea? He had only the vaguest idea where the United States of America was located, but he knew that it was very far away from his country. He had decided that his government must be right about the American intention to subjugate all of Korea. Why else would they leave their distant land to fight the forces of Korean unification? The Americans and their influence must be eliminated from Korea when his government assumed control of the peninsula—of that, Kang was sure.

Kang was short and wiry and he had an easy manner about him, as if he was enjoying every moment of his life. His manner changed greatly, however, when conversation centered around politics or the war. His quiet grin would shift to an intense, passionate expression, and he would speak swiftly and forcefully on the need for a Communist Korea and the absolute necessity for the fighting in the deep South. Their ultimate victory was never questioned by Kang, and he was becoming prepared for the rebuilding of the South after the war was concluded. He had decided he would play a great part in the rebirth of Korea and he dedicated his life to that purpose.

He had heard the thunder to the south and west and gazed over the green and brown landscape, past the straw huts with their overhanging roofs, only to see clouds of smoke rising from the city. It was the second time in a month that Pyongyang had been bombed by American planes. The first air raid had been described to him by his mother, sister, and brothers, and Kang had thought that they had exaggerated the noise and the smoke in order to impress him that the workers behind the lines were making sacrifices along with the soldiers at the front.

As he looked at the flames and smoke and listened to the countless explosions, he had to marvel at the destructive power of the enemy planes and wonder how many of his countrymen would lose their lives on that day. He lifted his gaze and squinted in order to make out the high-flying planes, which he saw as seemingly motionless specks of black against a clear sky.

They were coming in his direction, he decided after a moment, and suddenly he was afraid for his life. He shrugged off the fear after remembering the words of one of his officers. The officer had said that the American planes drop their bombs all at once and that most of their raids were confined to cities, which have the highest concentration of industry. Kang remembered the derision in the officer's voice when he told his troops that the Americans thought they could win the war by bombing North Korea's industry. They did not know, the officer had said, that North Korea's greatest industry was its people, and that the warmongers would have to kill every man, woman, and child in North Korea in order to win the war.

The planes were about overhead when Kang caught a glimpse of movement in the direction of his family's house. His mother was standing in the doorway and waving to him to come inside the house. He yelled to her that he would be right there, and turned to see how scattered the farm animals had become during his few moments of inattention.

The bombs struck with terrifying rapidity. Kang had just started to react to the first explosion when the second one came. He whirled to see the third bomb turn the road near his house into a huge vertical column of dirt, smoke, and flame. The fourth bomb made a direct hit on his house.

Kang opened his mouth to scream with rage, but the sound was lost amid the roar of exploding bombs. He began to run toward the shattered home and was promptly knocked on his back by yet another explosion. He staggered to his feet and lunged toward the bomb crater that had replaced his family's house, unmindful of the dirt that covered him or the open wound in his side. He got within ten feet of the crater and fell face down in the mud. He felt his strength ebb away as the pain in his side grew in intensity, and he quickly realized that he no longer had the strength to stand. He pushed himself forward with his feet and one arm, the other being useless, and with great effort he made it to the lip of the crater. One final thrust with his legs and he was suddenly over the edge and rolling down the side of the crater. He landed on his stomach on the bottom and immediately recoiled from the heat and fumes of the recent explosion. After a few moments he managed to open his eyes and gaze about.

The crater was fairly shallow, only about four feet deep. Kang looked about quickly, but there was no sign of his family. Hope rose within him—maybe they had escaped the house and were hiding in the field. He pushed himself over on his back and lay panting for a moment, then dug his heels in the ground and began inching up the side of the crater. He pushed with his legs and gripped the ground with his good arm to prevent sliding back to the bottom, and after a few moments he was on the lip of the crater.

He lay still and summoned enough energy to call his mother's name. There was no answer. He tried again and again, but still no reply. He heaved himself over onto his stomach in order to get a better look at the fields surrounding what used to be his home, and was immediately greeted by a ghastly sight. Not five feet from him was his mother's body. She was covered with mud and the remains of the house, but a blood-covered arm extended out from the pile of rubble and announced her death to him.

Kang squeezed his eyes shut and began to weep. Great sobs wracked his torn body as his remaining strength ebbed away. He dropped his head into the mud and wished for death. The wish was a fleeting one, and thoughts of vengeance filled his mind as he began to lose consciousness. The excited voices of peasants reached his ears as he slipped into a coma.

PYONGYANG, NORTH KOREA, PRESENT DAY

The flashes of jagged white light had made a gash across his vision and seemed to cut a path into his mind. The bomb blasts that had taken his family's lives were forever seared into his memory. Whenever he would shut his eyes for a while he'd see those same gashes of light, rending, tearing at his loved ones, and he would relive the agony of their loss decades ago.

Kang shuddered at the memories. So long ago and yet so fresh in his mind. He leaned back in his chair and rubbed his eyes, an uncharacteristic gesture for him. Memories of how his family died seemed to surface periodically and push him on with his plans. Did he hate the Americans because they killed his family so long ago? Yes, that was part of it. He used their death to shore up his hate and determination whenever he suspected it was losing its intensity. He used every opportunity to embarrass the United States.

During the war he had volunteered to be smuggled into Koje-do, the island prisoner of war (POW) camp southwest of Pusan that the United States had set up for North Korean and Communist Chinese prisoners. He was smuggled in to create havoc. In order to avoid feeding fuel to the Communists' propaganda machine, the United States had a hands-off policy on the Communist POWs prior to the kidnapping incident. With no one controlling them, the Communists organized themselves, manufactured some crude weapons, stole gasoline, and with it fashioned Molotov cocktails. Matters grew worse as Communist agents, such as Kang, were smuggled into the prison camp, and the situation culminated in the kidnapping of Brig. Gen. Francis Dodd.

The Communists then used their hostage to force the United Nations command to "admit" to certain atrocities, which resulted in a huge propaganda victory for the Communist forces.

Kang came out of the war as a major and was repatriated to North Korea in 1953 in Operation Big Switch. For his service during the war he was awarded the Order of the National Flag first class, and their highest award, the Order of Hero of the Korea Democratic People's Republic.

After the war his goal in life had become crystal clear. He would do whatever it took to avenge his family's death. His hero status had helped greatly in establishing his credentials as a good Communist. He had sought and obtained membership in the Liaison Bureau, the North Korean equivalent of the KGB. From there he could lash out at his enemies and take the revenge he had always sought.

His chance came unexpectedly when the North Koreans established an agent in the federal government of the United States. The agent had access to war records and did the research necessary to establish what had happened on that fateful morning in 1950 when Kang's whole family had perished at the hands of the American bombers. A dispassionate review of the events of that day had revealed some inconsistencies as to why the Americans had bombed the area around Kang's house. There had been nothing of military value there and the Americans weren't known for arbitrarily bombing civilians.

A search of the air force's records of that bombing mission unearthed the written reports of the aircraft commanders. All were routine with typical, almost boring, bombing reports, site damage assessments, and the like. Except for one. Captain Thomas Reynolds and his crew had dropped a rack of bombs late due to equipment failure.

Kang remembered the analysis he had done with the information given to him by the agent. The course the Americans had been flying was on a direct line between the Pyongyang rail yards and his house. Recorded airspeed multiplied by the amount of time the drop was delayed gave the ground release point. That spot was a few miles distant from his house, but he figured in the altitude of the bombers, the wind speed and direction, and the drag on the bombs. And there it was, staring him in the face. He had found his family's killers.

The hatred that had been simmering in him boiled anew now that he had a specific target. He would track down the ten-member crew of that bomber and make them pay the price his family had paid. It was a daunting task. America was a huge country and it didn't control or monitor its citizens' whereabouts as North Korea did.

Kang dispatched five agents to America. He would have liked to send many more, but he had to keep his mission a secret from his superiors. His hero status had served him well in this instance. They did not supervise a war hero very closely. His agents performed well. They put an ad in the newspapers of most of the major cities in the United States hinting that some compensation was still due the crew of that particular bomber. Kang figured that nothing appealed to Americans more than money.

Four of the ten crew members answered the ad and three more were found through the initial four. A series of calamities befell each of them in turn. Car crashes, falling out windows, and chemically induced heart attacks were his agents' favorites.

The last three crew members were the most troublesome to find. After ten years of searching, two more were located. A clean, simple boating accident took Captain Reynolds's life, but the attempt at Sergeant Wood's life was messy to say the least. The ex-sergeant fought like a wildcat when Kang's agents tried to make his death look like an accident by having him fall off a cliff. They wound up shooting him twenty times, then dumping his body in a ravine. Kang had been extremely angry at the botched job and had both agents involved executed while still in the United States.

Flight engineer Brett Gray took the most time to find. Five years after Wood's death the agents traced Gray to a cemetery in Tacoma, Washington. The dates on the tombstone indicated that he had died in 1956, only a few years after the war had ended.

That anticlimax had left Kang off balance and without the fierce satisfaction he had expected and craved. He hadn't seen any of them die, and although he believed his agents, he would have derived great satisfaction from seeing the fear race through their quarry. The realization that they were going to die in the next few minutes would wash over them like a wave, their eyes blinking quickly with panic. Kang had relished that sight when he had executed some of his country's enemies and would have greatly enjoyed seeing it in that barbarous American bomber crew.

Now in the next few weeks he would come face to face with the Americans again as he had so long ago at the Kum River and at the Koje-do prison camp. He would see fear repeated on thousands of faces and the fierce satisfaction of revenge for his family's lives would be his.

He told himself that there was more than just personal vengeance. The American arrogance—thinking that they could push around all the small countries of the world—was part of it. If the South wanted to lick their boots, so be it. His country would never do that. Far from it. There was great satisfaction to be gained in bringing the most powerful country in the world to its knees. His personal revenge would run hand in hand with that goal and he would accomplish both with one brilliant stroke.

Kang stood abruptly and walked to the window. He pulled back the curtain and searched the skyline until his eyes met the statue of Ch'ollima, the winged horse. Ch'ollima was the legendary flying horse who performed heroic deeds in Korea's past, and it was the name of the North Korean economic movement in the 1950s. The hero of North Korea that had provided much inspiration in the economic sector would also be used to inspire his troops to glory.

Ch'ollima was the key.

Chapter One

ALAMEDA, CALIFORNIA

The water seemed almost alive, with the glow from the opposite shore reflected in sprinkles of light that danced on the tips of the waves. The lieutenant stared, a bit mesmerized by the random bouncing of the small waves next to the pier.

Here and there he saw a miniature rainbow on the shimmering water, the telltale sign of fuel that always seems to leak in traces from large ships. The multicolored streaks and intermittent blocking of the sparkling light by refuse reminded him of just how polluted the water really was.

A cold, impersonal feeling slowly came over him; the twinkling lights from the water were just a phenomenon of nature. The merry flickering was illusory, and created a warm feeling for no reason.

A distant thrumming came to him, along with the attendant odor of diesel exhaust that floated on the evening's breeze. Some portion of the massive ship behind him was being powered by diesel generators. He heard footsteps, and marveled at their regular beat, in contrast to the random lapping of the waves against the pilings beneath him. The two sounds mixed almost pleasantly until the footsteps grew louder and gradually came to a halt. Someone waited patiently behind him.

His attention lingered on the sparkling waves in spite of the presence; he was in no hurry to acknowledge it.

"Lieutenant?"

Paul Simmons sighed. Apparently the patience of the man behind him wasn't inexhaustible. He seemed respectful, though. Simmons turned and eyed the young sailor who was shifting his weight from one foot to the other and back again. The sailor gave a relatively sloppy salute, which Simmons returned. The sailor's gaze dropped to the ribbons that formed two rows just above the officer's left breast pocket. Standard procedure, thought Simmons. First they look to see if they have to salute, then they check out where you've been.

The enlisted man seemed suitably impressed. A peacetime navy doesn't give out many medals.

"Help you with your things, sir?"

Simmons nodded. "Yes, thank you." He couldn't help sounding weary. It had been a long flight from Norfolk.

The sailor dutifully picked up two suitcases, and looked around to see if the officer was coming. Simmons picked up the garment bag and the other suitcase, and they both started in the direction of the officer's gangway. The drumming of the diesel generators droned on, punctuated periodically by the popping noise that the waves made against the sides of the ship. The familiar smells of a U.S. Navy ship floated to him, but there was one slight odor that he couldn't identify. He placed it after a moment—JP-5, jet fuel. They must have spilled some recently.

The ship seemed in a hurry to leave its berth even though there was no activity on board or on the pier this late at night. There were far too many stores alongside the ship and on the aircraft elevators that lined the side of the ship for the USS *Truman* to stay in port. Simmons had a bad feeling that the ship was about to take off for parts unknown.

As they walked up the forward brow Simmons felt dwarfed by the mammoth aircraft carrier. His eyes swept over the gray metal and lingered briefly at a familiar outline on one of the forward sponsons. The upright tubular shape, looking like a large version of the tubes that expensive cigars come in, was the telltale sign of a Phalanx close-in weapon system. His previous ship, a light cruiser, had had the same weapon system, nicknamed R2-D2 after the famous robot in the *Star Wars* saga. It was designed to shoot down low-flying cruise missiles.

He leaned back to get a look at the island, the ship's superstructure. The flat sides near the bottom of the island disappeared into a labyrinth of antennas of all sizes and shapes, from long, narrow whip types to the large dish antennas for the radars that were the eyes of the fleet. He scanned the edge of the flight deck and saw several tail sections with the peculiar double vertical surface and massive twin jet engines that were the trademark of the F-14.

Navy gray filled even his peripheral vision as he shook his head; he was sure he'd get lost. He reached the top of the gangway where the quarterdeck was, dropped the suitcases, faced the ensign who was watching him, saluted, and said, "Lieutenant Paul Simmons reporting for duty."

The sailor didn't bother to salute but stood patiently by for the officers to take care of the formalities. Simmons guessed that he was part of the quarterdeck watch.

The ensign returned his salute and said, "Welcome aboard, Lieutenant. Your orders, please?"

Simmons unzipped a side pocket on one of his suitcases and produced a manila folder containing copies of his orders. He gave a copy to the ensign, who began to log the lieutenant aboard.

"You're assigned to a stateroom with Lieutenant Cooper, Mister Simmons. It's on the 02 level just aft of frame 44 on the starboard side. You can dump your stuff there and report to the engineering officer tomorrow."

"Thanks," replied Simmons. He picked up his bags and started off, only to stop again. "Uh, which level are we on now?" he asked sheepishly.

The ensign grinned. "We're on the main deck, or the hangar deck. The 02 level is two decks above."

The lieutenant nodded and mumbled, "Thanks again."

The sailor took off at a brisk pace; he seemed in a hurry to complete his errand. Simmons followed. As they swung out into the hangar bay, which was fairly well lit, the sailor headed straight for an F-14 to get to an access trunk on the other side of the aircraft. Simmons's eyes wandered up to the stark red and black squadron logo painted on the aircraft's vertical tail surface. It was a black circle with a white skull on it with blood red kiss marks—as a woman with a lot of lipstick would leave on a man's cheek—coming from it. Underneath the circle were the words *Kiss of Death*. His mind froze. More reminders, he thought. Everything seems to remind me.

Only a few planes, along with the yellow trucks for moving them about, were visible in the hangar bay. Maybe the *Truman* isn't going anywhere for a while, he thought. Then he remembered that aircraft carriers pick up most of their aircraft after the ship is at sea. The aircraft fly out from the naval air stations and land on the carrier while it is underway.

Simmons sighed. More sea duty. . . . He forced his thoughts to stop there and tried instead to memorize the route back to the quarterdeck. He followed the sailor into a dark passageway that led off the hangar bay, then through a series of rapid turns, then up two levels and more quick turns, until Simmons abandoned his effort.

Ten minutes later, Simmons stood inside his so-called stateroom. It had two bunks, one above the other against one wall, and a navy standard stainless steel sink against the opposite wall. A combination chest with locking drawers and a desk were provided along with a six-foot-high locker. Several extra drawers were located below the bottom bunk, but when Simmons checked them he found them all occupied. He would have preferred the bottom bunk, but it was obvious that his roommate had the same preference.

Simmons threw his suitcases in the corner and decided to unpack later. He took off his jacket and tossed it at the foot of the upper bunk, while simultaneously yanking at his tie and unbuttoning the top button of his shirt. Fatigue came over him, making him wonder if he was going to have a bad night. This was different, he thought hopefully. A change of scene, new people—it was a new start. He rubbed his left arm instinctively, as if hit with a sudden memory. Even his arm was beginning to heal. Time *is* the great healer, isn't it?

Simmons tried to keep those thoughts and even create some new ones as he struggled to analyze what he had seen of his new ship. He climbed up into his bunk and sat at one end while vaguely wondering who would win the war for his mind—his intended thoughts, or fatigue, or . . .

The USS *Truman*, the name of this aircraft carrier, was ninety-some thousand tons of home to six thousand–plus sailors, pilots, and airmen. And engineers; let's not forget the engineers, he thought with almost a smile.

Yeah, that's what I am, an engineer, a snipe; that's what everyone calls us, snipes. That's the bird that makes its nest in a hole in the ground. Just like us engineers. We nest in the bowels of the ship.

His gaze was automatically drawn to the left side of his jacket above his row of ribbons and the gold device portraying crossed swords with a ship in the middle. He picked it out in the meager light that came from under the door to his stateroom, and which lit the drab interior in shades of fuzzy gray.

The gold tone of the surface warfare device made it through the dim interior of the room and seemed to penetrate into Simmons's mind. He began to sweat. Close to the device, almost touching it, was the ribbon signifying the award of the medal. I got a medal, he thought in a near panic. I'm a hero, aren't I? A goddamned hero. Heroes aren't supposed to *feel* like this.

He knew he should get up and turn on the lights, read a book, anything to keep his mind busy until fatigue would overcome him in a rush. But then he might dream.

Let's see, President Truman was the thirty-third President of the United States, from 1940 something or another to 1952. He presided over most of the Korean War. Simmons gasped. His mind was being dragged back.

I'm an engineer, an engineer! I stand watch in the engineering spaces, main control. As M division officer, I'm responsible for the engine rooms.

He could go no further. Weariness pressed in on him and melted his resolve. The slit of light from underneath the door seemed far away, as if at the end of a tunnel, and he groaned as his eyes slipped out of focus and a wave of vertigo passed over him. He could almost feel the engine room heat and humidity that were now so familiar to him, and he knew that it was going to be one of the worst nights he had known.

The stateroom turned into a brightly lit engine room, the sailors at their watch stations, some of them with headphones on, others just staring at the myriad array of gauges that had to be monitored constantly. The far bulkhead was in his peripheral vision; it took on a fuzzy texture that moved frantically in all directions at once. The overhead lights in that section of the engine room were rapidly blotted out by the advancing horror. A roaring, now distant but coming nearer at a terrifying rate, overwhelmed his mind with the searing knowledge of what was going to happen. The sailors turned—it seemed in slow motion—their minds not comprehending the enormity of the advancing wall of death. He saw the open mouths and he heard the screams, and cried out in agony as pain shot through his left arm. Darkness closed in about him and he began to choke.

And he heard the sailors' voices. *Did you see them? Oh, my God! Did you see what happened to them?*

Chapter Two

PYONGYANG, NORTH KOREA

Darkness had begun to settle in on the city as the sharp details of the buildings faded into the fuzz of deep twilight. The city was never known to be noisy, except when there were mass parades or demonstrations, but on this particular night it seemed more still than he had ever known it to be.

The streets of Pyongyang were familiar to Lim Chul Min from his childhood, along with the city's many monuments to the state and its workers. Huge statues and universities named after the leaders of the state were commonplace, as were the ubiquitous museums and statues to the workers and their efforts. Lim was familiar with them all; he had been paraded past them and through them innumerable times during his education and training.

The monuments seemed especially still tonight, as if in anticipation of the far-reaching changes that would result from his mission.

Lim turned slightly and let his gaze sweep the streets and buildings before him. He tried to make his observations as casually as possible. It was a habit he had developed over the years he had spent in the South. There was no reason for anyone to be watching him, but it didn't take much for the president's bodyguards to become suspicious. Even

19

now he might be under surveillance by the elite agents from the State Political Security Department, who reported directly to North Korea's head of state. They didn't need a lot of excuses to start blasting away. That wouldn't do for his mission. It wouldn't do at all.

His men were all in place, and even he was having a hard time picking them out in the rapidly advancing night. He felt a swell of pride within him; he had had his pick of the best agents available and he had made the most of it. Lim silently hoped that most of his men would survive. There would be need for such good men in the future.

His gaze wandered up the small hill to the structure that was their objective. Here in Pyongyang, in a rather austere mansion, lived the North Korean president. Hemmed in by surface-to-air missile (SAM) sites and surrounded by gardens and smaller structures containing bodyguards, the North Korean dictator ruled the lives of 21 million North Koreans. He had brought them a long way, but he was now an anachronism, the real power having passed to a committee made up of the leaders of the various factions within the North Korean government. And they were impatient for change.

Lim had to look at his watch, but he knew just how to play it—a man impatient for the arrival of a colleague and a ride home. Two minutes to go—two minutes before a momentous change in his country's history. He squinted into the darkness. Yes, there he was, right on time. A man sauntering up to the main entrance of the president's house, a man obviously lost and in need of directions.

Lim shot an anxious look up and down the street. The timing was what he worried about. His mind froze with the possibilities if their split-second coordination failed.

A white-yellow flash lit the sky behind him and an instant later the sound reached him, crushing him with its intensity. He whirled about to see the explosion die to a reddish glow, only to be replaced by another white-hot flash and thunderous sound, and another and another.

The First Guards barracks, thought Lim savagely. And *ahead* of schedule. He hoped that the others would take the cue. Lim shot a look at his man near the entrance. He was cowering effectively while staring in apparent astonishment at the explosions. The guards were looking dumbfounded at the rising balls of fire in the nearby sky.

Lim squinted and just picked out a glint of metal in the man's hand. Relief flooded him—Chang would go ahead as planned. More explosions muffled the gunshots and both guards fell lifeless to the ground. Lim caught Chang's swift arm movement near the door to the guard building. Chang threw himself to the ground a second before his grenade blew the windows out of the building.

Lim took his eyes off Chang—the man had done his job—and worried about the next step. Now, thought Lim. *Now!*

Muffled explosions came from many directions simultaneously, and their arrival one on top of another caused the earth to shake beneath his feet. His men *had* taken the cue and had blown the tunnels at the right time. Now the president was trapped; he couldn't go underground to escape. He would have to take an above-ground route, and Lim and his men had all the exits covered.

The noise from the explosions died away and was replaced by shouts of astonishment and sporadic automatic weapons' fire. The whine of incoming shells prefaced explosions on the far side of the hill. Powerful lights flooded the area, but the incoming smoke rounds made things impossible for the defenders.

The shouts from the far side of the hill and the responding automatic weapons' fire increased dramatically, until it became an unceasing din. Lim knew that his men were assaulting the other side of the stronghold.

His plan was simple enough, and it included some second-guessing of the defenders. The grenade in the entrance to the guard building, then the quick assault on the other side, were meant to look like a diversionary attack on the entrance, with the real assault coming at the rear of the stronghold. It was actually the opposite: Lim would lead the real attack on the entrance with a select group of men.

He glanced at his watch. He wanted to launch his attack precisely a minute and a half after the diversion started, to give the defenders time to concentrate most of their resources on the far side.

Lim looked at Chang. He had his back pressed to the front of the guard building and was looking in Lim's direction. Lim picked up his radio and counted off the last seconds. He said one word into the microphone.

"Kaja!"

Seconds later, automatic weapons' fire slammed into one of the four tall buildings that stood at the corners of the base of the hill. The fire would keep the guards ducking until Lim and his men could get up there with explosives. The lights on this side of the compound were shot out quickly and expertly. That was his cue.

Lim glanced right and left, then ran out into the wide street and headed directly for Chang, with his men following suit. Machine guns in the guard tower opened up and got a few stragglers, but most of the fire was directed at Lim's men who were left behind to keep firing on the tower.

Lim grabbed a satchel charge from one of his men and sprinted the thirty yards from the guard building to the base of the tower. He knelt next to the armored door, feverishly pulled the arming pins from the explosives and shoved the satchel against the bottom of the door, then he leapt to a safe spot around the corner.

Five long seconds later, the charge blew the door off its hinges. Lim tossed a grenade into the now open door. The explosion occurred quickly. Lim's men, led by Chang, charged the smoking doorway. Seconds later they were locked in close combat with the president's bodyguards.

Lim heard three explosions muffled by the thick walls of the guard tower and a few screams of agony, which were brutally silenced by automatic weapons' fire.

Lim waved to the rest of his men who had gathered at the outside wall to follow him up the driveway. His men joined him and together they sprinted up the hill toward their ultimate destination, the palace and its chief occupant. The darkness caused no problem for them; they had memorized photographs for months on end. They knew every turn, every bush, every feature of the driveway.

The next obstacle in the layered defense of the compound occupied Lim's thoughts. The house itself was formidably defended, but he and his men were relying on speed, cunning, and the diversion.

The air suddenly throbbed around him and he looked about panic-stricken to find its source. An intense light cut through the night sky and illuminated Lim and his men in the glare of an electric sun.

Helicopter gunship! Lim dove for cover as the palace's defenses and the helicopter gunship opened up simultaneously. Half of his men were caught in the open and cut to pieces in the first five seconds.

Lim yelled to his men who had taken cover to hold their fire—any counterfire would invite a wall of lead from the gunship. He glanced at the dead and dying in the harsh circle of light from the helicopter, and it was then that he saw an incredible act of bravery.

Chang, who had been racing to catch up with Lim's group, ran into the light and picked up a Stinger—a shoulder-fired, antiaircraft missile—from a dead comrade. It took a few seconds for the crew of the gunship to react, and Chang was heading full tilt for the shadows as the gunship sent a hail of bullets in his direction.

Lim instantly knew what Chang had in mind and ordered the men on either side of him to open fire on the helicopter. They knew it meant almost certain death, but they obeyed orders. Lim joined them as the three sent a burst of fire at the helicopter, many of their bullets bouncing harmlessly off the armored sides of the gunship. The helicopter rotated toward them, abandoning its search for Chang, and began to stitch a furious line of lead toward Lim and his men. Now, Chang, while you can see its turboprop exhaust, thought Lim.

Lim caught a flash from the shadows, and suddenly the helicopter was a flaming ball falling from the sky. Chang had done it! Lim felt a few seconds of relief, until the palace's defenders opened up on them again.

Bitter thoughts filled him as he surveyed the situation. His diversion hadn't worked and the helicopter gunship had slaughtered more than half his men. Now the palace defenders were alerted and he didn't have the strength to assault them. But there was a backup—one desperate gamble left.

Lim raised his radio to his lips and issued a guttural order. He positioned his men as best he could and waited the expected minute and a half. The rumble of a diesel engine floated above the crashing sounds of the diversionary attack that was still proceeding on the other side of the hill.

An armored personnel carrier (APC) appeared going full speed up the hill as Lim and his men braced themselves for what was to come. The driver wheeled around the flaming remains of the helicopter and lifted one side of the vehicle off the ground in the process.

The noise of the diesel increased as the driver pointed the APC straight at the palace. The defenders blazed away with everything they had, and a furious amount of fire slammed into the APC. The driver was undeterred and kept his accelerator foot to the floor until the APC smashed into the center of the palace's defenses, sending stone, mortar, wood, and human flesh in all directions. A heartbeat later, the dying driver flipped a switch on the dashboard that detonated the ton of TNT that was crammed into every corner of the vehicle.

The enormous explosion sent a fireball two hundred feet into the air and shattered half the front wall of the palace, exposing the three floors and connecting staircases.

Now! Before they can reorganize their forces! Lim leaped from behind his cover and shouted to his men to follow him. Together they dodged falling debris as they raced toward the palace. Lim looked about wildly—

they would need grappling hooks. As if in response to his unspoken wish, one of his men ran past him waving a grappling hook and its launcher.

They raced to the base of the palace wall and his man fired the launcher, putting the hook expertly on the second floor. Half the men waited to climb the one rope—originally there were to be five ropes—and Lim led the others over the rubble into the first floor.

There was no opposition, a fact that surprised Lim, and hope rose within him. The president's offices were on the second floor, but at this point the president could be anywhere in the building. Lim instantly decided to work his way up to the second floor and converge with his other party on the president's personal offices.

Lim and his men were halfway up the stairway when they heard machine gun fire erupt on the second floor. Many different weapons spoke at once until only the peculiar rattle of the defenders' machine guns were heard. Lim had the sinking feeling that his men on the second floor had met their end.

He raced up the stairs and onto the landing, determined to avenge his fallen comrades. He and his men were in luck—they had come up behind the president's bodyguards. Thirty seconds of automatic weapons' fire left a host of corpses in the corridor.

Lim raced down the hallway and made the turn that led to the president's offices, a turn he had made countless times in training. It took him a full two seconds to react to the hastily prepared machine gun nest at the entrance to the offices. The machine gunners were equally surprised, and they all stared at each other for an instant.

Lim fell to the deck and swung his weapon around as he yelled to his men. Too late, they crowded into the area just as the machine gunners opened fire. His men grunted, screamed, and died.

Lim fired an ineffective burst into the sandbags in front of the machine gun as the bodyguards swung the barrel of the machine gun in Lim's direction.

A dark object flew over Lim's head, careened off the office door, and landed neatly at the feet of the gunners. The explosion blew sand and flesh all over the walls and ceiling of the entranceway.

Suddenly there was someone next to him, pulling him out from the debris caused by the blast. It was Chang, the incredibly brave man who had shot down the helicopter gunship. Their eyes met and they exchanged brief looks of surprise at their survival. Lim looked past Chang—there was no one. They were the only two left.

Chang flicked his eyes toward the mangled doorway, a clear invitation to charge through. Lim started to shake his head, but Chang had already leaped over the bodies of the gunners and was in the doorway. Shots rang out; Chang grunted in pain as the bullets tore into his abdomen. Chang's weapon spoke in a reflexive action and Lim heard a body hit the floor inside the office.

Lim peered over Chang's huddled figure and into a room of bookcases and exquisite figurines. The president of North Korea sat at a massive solid wood desk in all his corpulent elegance. In front of the desk lay the body of his heir apparent, the minister of defense.

A stroke of luck, thought Lim. I don't have to chase all over the building looking for him. He gave a quick look around; the president had run out of bodyguards. Lim strode into the room and walked around to the side of the desk. The president's eyes followed him and he turned in his chair to face him. They spoke not a word; they both knew what was next.

There was no ceremony; there were no speeches, no trumpets blaring, no banners waving. Lim merely emptied the clip of his weapon into the president's chest and stomach, and true to his strict instructions was careful to leave the face intact. He ejected the empty clip onto the floor and shoved in a fresh one. He emptied that one too into the quivering mound of flesh that used to be North Korea's president.

His eyes went to Chang, and concern welled up within him. Lim would have left any one of his men behind but Chang. He went over to him and gently turned him over. The wound was the kind that produced excruciating pain and a slow death.

Lim stood, turned off the lights, and walked purposefully to the window. There in the glare of spotlights were units of the North Korean Army summarily executing the remainder of his men. Lim looked out another window and saw several men machine-gunning the bodies of his men who had fallen to gunfire from the helicopter gunship.

He was almost amused at the thought that the officer responsible would get his ass chewed royally. The government would want some prisoners. If they didn't get any, there was almost no purpose to the mission.

Lim thought about the final phase of his mission and glanced at Chang. Would he carry it out, or would Chang die before he "talked"?

Lim's duty lay before him and he knew what he must do, yet he shrank from it. Was there another way? He thought feverishly—there was little time. He was surprised they weren't here by now.

His thoughts ended with one course in front of him, idealistic and shining. At least he'd be a hero of the new government.

Lim pulled out thin gloves from a pocket and quickly slipped them on. He went over to the dead minister of defense and picked up his automatic. He called softly to Chang.

His friend lifted his head. When he saw the automatic, realization filled his eyes. He nodded in an abrupt motion, and Lim put one bullet through his heart.

Lim would hide until cooler heads prevailed, and then let himself be captured. They would torture him unmercifully, and he would resist, until with eyes gouged out, testicles smashed, and arms pulled out of their sockets he would "confess." Confess that he was an agent of the South Korean government and he led the mission to kill the North Korean president.

Events would then take on an insurmountable momentum.

Kang Chung Kwon stared at the report in front of him and a feeling of satisfaction ran through him. As head of the Liaison Bureau, the espionage agency of the North Korean government, he was one of the first to get the report: 57 agents killed, one captured—Lim Chul Min. The president and the minister of defense assassinated, along with 152 bodyguards, and 426 in the First Guards barracks killed.

Lim had done his duty. He and his men had been covertly brought back from deep cover assignments in the South by the Liaison Bureau, given South Korean weapons, and trained in a secret base in North Korea. Their South Korean identities could easily be traced by army agents, but their real identities as Liaison Bureau agents would be jealously guarded by Kang.

Another step was completed, this one a complex, dangerous hurdle but a necessary one. The former president had always moderated Kang's thirst for revenge. Now he was unbridled.

Except for Kim Woo Chull. He had become a thorn in Kang's side, opposing him at every opportunity. The president had always listened to Kim's moderating tone. Now, with the inevitable chaos in the North Korean government, Kim could be ignored. It wouldn't do to kill him outright—the army would be suspicious enough of Kang due to the president's murder. Kang couldn't count on everyone buying the story of a South Korean force assassinating the North Korean president. Time enough to deal with Kim later, after Kang's secret plans had become a reality.

Kang smiled; it was a twisted jerking of his mouth and it conveyed no mirth. He picked up another report. The gas had been delivered by his Russian friends. Since the advent of their infant democracy, the KGB was trying to come up with a more policemanlike image. Kang and his Liaison Bureau got more and more "subcontract" work in the area of assassinations, so-called "wet work" by the KGB. The gas could be relatively easily purchased on the open international market, but it would attract attention, even within his own government. Instead, Kang had called in a few favors to get a surreptitious shipment of anesthetic gas for his use.

Along with the helicopters they had purchased last year and the modified crop-dusting planes they had commandeered from the agriculture ministry, the gas would provide a nasty surprise for the American navy. He thought of the capture of the USS *Pueblo* by his country in 1968. That glorious victory over the United States had taught him an important lesson about the limits of power. The United States had incredible military power at their disposal, but they could use it only in very restricted circumstances.

The *Pueblo*, a so-called oceanographic research ship that was actually used for intelligence gathering, was captured by North Korean boarding parties. One American sailor was killed and the remaining eighty-two men were held in captivity for almost a year, until the United States confessed its "guilt." Kang, a young colonel then, was at first fearful of an attack by the United States. He was flabbergasted when the United States did nothing.

Then why not go after something bigger? Why not the biggest the United States had? More complicated certainly, but not impossible. Kang had been planning ever since.

The details had slowly fallen into place over the years as his rank and power increased. The American ships were totally open to the atmosphere—powerful fans pumped outside air into the lower decks. In the event of chemical, biological, or nuclear warfare, the air vents would be shut, thus sealing the ship from outside contamination. Kang's gas would therefore have to be a surprise to the American crew.

Then the last piece had fallen into place. Colonel Pak Myung Jo, a young, brilliant, dedicated officer, had come under Kang's command. Kang had found to his delight that Colonel Pak hated the United States almost as much as he did. Pak had read the history of the Korean War and had formed a loathsome picture of Americans. Kang used Pak's hatred to full advantage and enlisted him in the plan. Pak had come up with a way to surprise the Americans. It was nothing elegant, just a lot of good, hard work.

Think of it! An entire carrier crew, captives of the People's Republic!

After Kang's seizure of the carrier, his country would then be in a position to embarrass the United States through a media barrage. The Democratic People's Republic would eventually destroy the carrier as "punishment" for the capitalists. The crew would not be killed, lest the temptation to attack North Korea become too strong for the Americans. The crew would be used to prevent attack by the United States and would be used to attack the American ego.

The crew would be kept until no longer useful, then let go in an agonizingly slow process that would take years. They would not be in good physical or mental condition when they returned. The emotional toll on the Americans would be devastating.

The carrier had nuclear weapons on it and his country would suddenly be vaulted into the exclusive club of nuclear nations. Kang grunted in amusement at the thought of how relations with the South would change when they found out that their brothers to the North possessed nuclear weapons. If there was any bootlicking to be done, the South would do it. In addition to licking American boots, they would add the boots of the Democratic People's Republic.

Kang gave his twisted rendition of a smile once again. With the president out of the way there was no stopping his plan.

Chapter Three

The room gradually slid into focus as Paul Simmons kept his eyes open until they began to water. He blinked furiously and rubbed his eyes, then forced them open again. The room came into focus more quickly this time.

He was alone—his roommate was still nowhere to be found. Maybe he was married and living ashore with his family. Simmons thought that it was just as well; he had no desire right at the moment to exchange pleasantries with a total stranger.

He ran his hands through his hair and leaned his head back as far as he could. The whole day stretched before him with nothing to do but exchange pleasantries with strangers. God, he hated that, and the navy as well.

His father popped into his mind. This last leave had been a bad one for their relationship. He revised that thought. It was bad all around. He supposed that medical leave to recuperate from injuries was never fun, but this one seemed to leave some very unpleasant undertones in his relationship with his family.

His older brother, older by two years, normally teased him unmercifully, but he was unnervingly reserved and seemed almost to care. Simmons grunted in amusement. Can't have that between brothers. His sister seemed afraid to talk to him at first. What the hell had his father said to all of them?

His sister had opened up after awhile when she found that he wouldn't fall apart if she questioned him about what had happened. He'd told her the barest of details and left out all of the emotional aspects. Without knowing it she gave him support and strength. She was so straightforward and honest. It was a refreshing change from the abnormal behavior of the rest of his family.

His mother gave him sad looks and always seemed to be about to ask something but then would bite her tongue.

"Go ahead, Mom. Say it," he had said.

She was obviously in a quandary. "Oh, . . . but your father," she stammered.

There it was again. His father.

His father, Joseph Simmons, had been on river patrol boats (PBRs) for the navy in Vietnam. Thank God it was before the military started to defoliate the riverbanks with Agent Orange, among other chemicals. Otherwise, God only knows what he'd be like now. His father had been a lifer and a chief petty officer when he retired after twenty years in the navy. He had the medals he earned during two tours in Vietnam in a glass case in a small room he used as an office.

Simmons smiled to himself. He remembered looking at those medals for hours on end and dreaming of becoming a hero someday, as only a naive child would. He had those medals memorized. Navy Cross, Bronze Star, two Purple Hearts, Presidential Unit Citation, Combat Action Ribbon, Vietnam Service Medal, Vietnam Campaign Medal—Republic of Vietnam, and the National Defense Medal. After twenty years he had other assorted ribbons for marksmanship, good conduct, and the like, but they weren't displayed.

The Navy Cross was the biggest award, second only to the Congressional Medal of Honor. His father had spoken about the action in what Paul suspected were very simplified terms. On a routine mission to pick up some marines in the Mekong River valley, BMC Joseph Simmons ran into a full-scale firefight with Vietcong (VC) forces who were set up on the riverbanks to ambush his small force of PBRs. A horrendous battle ensued as the PBRs slugged it out point-blank with their stubborn enemy. The battle carried on for hours, with Chief Simmons eventually calling in an air strike on his own position. The Vietcong (VC) body count for the week took a tremendous upturn after the battle.

His father never mentioned the U.S. casualties, or how many were killed or wounded by our own bombs. Paul had wanted to ask him a dozen times during this last leave but couldn't bring himself to do so. What about the survivors? When they sleep do they dream about it? What about the memories?

Simmons tried to imagine his father's answers but his mind went blank. He couldn't imagine answers to those questions. He groaned to himself. This was too much mental exercise for his sluggish mind. He'd give it up for now.

Half an hour later, he inspected himself in the mirror over the sink and grunted in semiamusement. At least I'm clean shaven, he thought. Maybe the uniform really does make the man; his blues lessened the effect of the bags under his eyes and the general weariness he felt.

He picked up the folder with his orders in it and inspected himself a last time. While I still wear the uniform I'll do the best job I can. It's only for another year, then I'll get out and try to put all this behind me.

A steward arrived, introduced himself, and asked if he could be of any assistance. Simmons asked the location of the wardroom; his last meal had been on the plane from Norfolk and it wasn't very substantial. If he didn't get some food in himself quickly he felt as if he'd keel over. The steward offered to guide Simmons to his destination and started aft with the lieutenant following behind him.

Simmons kept his eyes on the back of the steward's head for a moment and wondered why anyone would want to wait on the U.S. Navy's officers. Imagine serving meals in the wardroom and cleaning officers' staterooms. After a few moments of thought he knew why.

Most of the stewards were Filipino nationals who were recruited in the Philippines. They become actual members of the U.S. Navy even though they are not citizens of the United States. Stewards receive the same pay and allowances as the other sailors, which more often than not is a strong inducement for joining the American navy. To earn the equivalent pay in the Philippines is impossible for most of the population, and the navy jobs represent a rare opportunity to break out of the poverty that grips many Filipinos.

Simmons disliked the idea of one human being acting as a servant to another. He just didn't feel so important that he should have servants scurrying about at his command. This is the navy, he thought, not some goddamned fiefdom in the Middle Ages. But most of his fellow officers didn't seem to mind, and a lot of them rather enjoyed the idea.

The steward led Simmons to the second deck, one deck below the hangar deck, and after winding his way through a labyrinth of passages and spaces, he finally indicated their destination.

After a lethargic meal in the generally vacant wardroom, Simmons managed to find his way topside for morning quarters, the obligatory ceremony that starts off the working day aboard ship. Morning quarters consisted of a formation on the flight deck of all personnel not on watch. A muster is taken, and the men salute the raising of the flag at the aft end of the ship and listen to the orders of the day.

At the close of morning quarters Simmons managed to get directions to the engineering logroom, his first stop in the check-in procedure. After fifteen minutes and several wrong turns he found the office. The room contained several desks, which belonged to the engineering officer and his assistants. All but two were empty, and both men who were seated at the desks looked up as he entered.

"Well, you must be Paul Simmons," greeted one of the men, a lieutenant commander.

Simmons managed a smile and replied, "That's right, sir."

"I'm Larry Champlain, the MPA, and this is Commander Adamson, the chief engineer." Champlain put out his hand and gave Simmons a warm handshake. Simmons turned to Commander Adamson and shook his hand while exchanging pleasantries.

"Looks like you'll be going to M division, Mr. Simmons. I hope that suits you," said the chief engineer.

Simmons nodded. "That'll be fine, sir." At least it's something I'm used to, he thought. He forced his mind to go no further.

The chief engineer waved Simmons to a chair and asked to look at his service record, which the lieutenant had brought along with him. Simmons handed it over and the commander began to thumb through the pile of papers attached to each side of the folder.

Lieutenant Paul Simmons was a product of the nuclear age. He was an unrestricted line officer who was also nuclear power qualified. After graduation from college with a bachelor of electrical engineering degree, he joined the navy in the reserve officer program. After nineteen weeks of training at the Naval Officer Candidate School, Newport, Rhode Island, he was commissioned an ensign in the naval reserve. He then entered training to qualify as a nuclear power officer.

Upon completion of his nuclear power training, he received a regular commission in the navy and was required to complete an additional three years of active duty. He was then assigned to a new nuclear-powered guided-missile cruiser home-ported in San Diego, California, and served with distinction while receiving the Navy and Marine Corps Medal for his handling of a severe main steam leak in one of the engine rooms. He had spent two years on his first ship and had become a qualified officer of the deck underway, combat information center watch officer, and engineering officer of the watch.

"That's quite an impressive record, Mr. Simmons," said the chief engineer. Adamson's eyes lingered at the notation in the lieutenant's record of a month's medical leave to recover from injuries received during the engineering accident in the engine room. Simmons's previous ship had suffered a total main steam line rupture. Adamson remembered looking for a pinhole leak in a main steam line years ago by passing a broom handle near the suspected areas. The broom handle had shattered—he had found the leak. Simmons hadn't contended with a pinhole leak; he had handled a total rupture.

Adamson's eyes flicked up to Simmons. "How's the arm?"

Simmons instinctively touched his left arm. "Coming along, sir."

Adamson's eyes dropped down to the records once more. This must be a surprise to him, thought Simmons. Handling an accident like that was almost equivalent to combat experience in a peacetime navy. He could feel the undercurrent of respect building in Commander Adamson.

When Adamson spoke, his voice was quiet with sympathy. "Lose anybody?"

The question surprised Simmons. He opened his mouth to speak, but nothing came out. Simmons clamped his mouth shut and tried again.

"Fifteen." His voice was hoarse.

Adamson's eyes were on him again. There's the sympathy again, thought Simmons. It would make his life here a bit easier. He glanced at Lieutenant Commander Champlain, who had a puzzled look and was about to ask a question. One look at Simmons's face and he evidently thought better of it. Simmons felt he'd better change the subject before the inevitable barrage of questions.

"By the way, Commander, are we going anywhere soon?"

"Oh, I guess you haven't heard," said Adamson with mild surprise. "The North Korean president was assassinated last night, and that coupled with the bombing of the *Briscoe* last week by the North Koreans says that we have to be ready for anything. So we've been ordered to Korean waters." Simmons's heart sank.

"We leave in two days, so you'll have your hands full trying to get up to speed," added the commander. After noting the disappointment on the young lieutenant's face, he said, "I know. Just think how we feel. We just came back from there about a month ago."

A pause followed as Simmons digested the bad news and Commander Adamson considered Simmons's unusual service record.

Lieutenant Commander Champlain broke the silence. "Well, I guess you'd better get up to personnel and get checked in. I'd give you a check-in card, but our yeoman is on liberty. You can pick one up in personnel."

Champlain launched into a flurry of instructions directing Simmons to the personnel office, but Simmons only half listened. He hadn't expected a long deployment, and with the worsening situation in Korea, the cruise did not sound like an enjoyable one. It sounded like the kind with a maximum of operations and a minimum of liberty.

". . . so all you have to remember is port side and around frame 130 or so. OK?"

"Yes, sir. Thanks," Simmons replied.

Simmons spent the next several hours checking in. He received a card listing all the different offices he had to visit in order to let them know he had reported aboard. He had always been annoyed by this procedure, and had the feeling that the personnel office should have handled the check-in instead of wasting his time with it. He went through it, however, consoling himself that he had only a year left of these petty irritations and then freedom after nearly four and a half years of navy life.

He had his mandatory interview with the executive officer, the second in command of the ship. The executive officer, or XO as he is known to the crew, manages the day-to-day running of the ship and handles the administrative details for the commanding officer. Again the brief questions regarding the accident, again the sympathy.

Simmons came away from the interview with a very favorable opinion of the XO. He was surprised at the geniality and candor of the man. Many naval officers in similar positions seemed to think that they had to be the captain's hatchet man. As a result, they had a decided lack of humor and seemed to impose punishment with relish. Commander Richard Wyatt seemed to be quite different from the stereotype Simmons had built up in his mind.

Hours later, Simmons hovered over a drink at the officers' club while lamenting the fact that he would have to put off seeing San Francisco for several months. It was probably good for him, he thought. New ship, new people, he could immerse himself in learning about the different systems; it could be a significant distraction.

He had just decided to get thoroughly inebriated when a woman entered the room and sat down on a stool at the bar. Talk about distractions, he thought with a smile. From the vantage point at his table in a dark corner of the room, Simmons busily studied her attributes. She had a beautiful figure, which was highlighted by a provocatively low-cut dress, and her hair flowed back on either side of her head with lots of curls in the middle. She had her back to Simmons, which heightened his curiosity to the point where it became almost unendurable.

He satisfied himself with studying what he could see and immediately noticed the zipper in her dress, which ran down to the small of her back. He grinned to himself. It was a good thing he noticed it now, rather than have to fumble around for it later when every moment would count. He automatically took the thought one step further. He studied her back for the telltale lumps and ridges of a bra. The wider the strap, the more hooks to undo; it might mean the difference between a one-handed or a two-handed approach later on. He chuckled while thinking there was no substitute for planning to achieve a goal, no matter what the goal was. He was surprised to discover that her back was smooth; she apparently wasn't wearing a bra. His eyes immediately flicked below her waist in order to determine if her lack of underwear was complete. It wasn't—she had panties on.

At that moment, she turned sideways on the stool and crossed her legs in a most enticing manner. Her skirt slid halfway up her thighs with her movement and revealed a stunning set of legs. A vague memory stirred in Simmons's mind as he continued to inspect her, but he couldn't quite bring it to the surface.

She fumbled in her purse and after a moment or two she produced a cigarette. Another naval officer who was seated at the bar had been watching her out of the corner of his eye. He slid over to the seat next to her and quickly lit her cigarette. She seemed receptive to his company and Simmons cursed his decision to sit at a table. He shook his head. Something about her was familiar.

He couldn't place it—a flip of the head or the way she was poised on the bar stool. Something. Any movement on her part that suggested revealing her face quickened his pulse. He strained to see her face but she was leaning forward and turned toward the bar. It wasn't until she threw back her head and laughed that Simmons got a good look at her.

He recognized her with surprise. Eva Manning. A host of memories came flooding into his mind. He had met her at a beachside officers' club dance at the North Island, San Diego, Naval Air Station. He remembered the fantastic number of people that used to crowd into that small building on the beach. She had been backing up trying to escape the gyrations of some of the dancers when she ground her heel on Simmons's foot. After he howled with pain and she apologized profusely, they quite naturally struck up a conversation, which was one of those elementary getting-to-know-you things that no one seems to remember afterward.

She was beautiful and Paul Simmons had been instantly fascinated. She was the model type, tall and slender with alluring, ultrasophisticated features. Long brown hair curled softly around her face. Her pale blue eyes were the type that made men wonder if they would become irretrievably lost.

Whenever Simmons could tear his eyes from hers, he had delighted in her high cheekbones, which conveyed the impression of refined ancestry. Her nose was a bit too long and sharp, and her lower lip had the habit of protruding out beyond her upper lip, but those slight imperfections were easily overlooked as he basked in the light of her smile. He often returned to her eyes, whose beauty was subtly enhanced by a minimum of makeup.

He remembered meeting her at the dances at the Marine Corps Recruit Depot Officers' Club in San Diego, the MCRD, or M Crud as they humorously referred to it. All the marine officers made a point of telling the ladies that they were marines and not naval officers, as if the latter were some kind of disease. It seemed to Simmons that the ladies preferred the navy men. Every Sunday night they would go to the beachside North Island O Club, and every Friday night would be M Crud night.

Mental pictures flitted through his mind like single frames from a movie. A walk on the beach, a kiss in the shadows, her face reflecting orgasmic pleasure were the images he saw as he stared down at the drink in front of him. Theirs was a conventional affair—a few dates and some easily won sex, with the end coming as he went out to sea.

He never wrote, although he promised he would, and she was gone when he came back from his first deployment as a naval officer. That was two years ago, two very long years in the life of a young man. He took a last look at her, intending to finish his drink and quietly leave unnoticed, but Eva seemed to be ignoring the man next to her and was staring intently in Simmons's direction.

Their eyes met and after a second or two her eyebrows shot up in surprise and a smile filled her face. The officer sitting next to her turned around on his stool to see what had caused her reaction. He saw Simmons and his face fell with disappointment. She stubbed out her cigarette and made apologies to her companion, then picked up her drink and walked over to Simmons's table. Simmons's heart beat faster with every step she took toward him. He berated himself for getting nervous; after all, she didn't look like she was going to make a scene.

"Hi, Paul," she said softly. Simmons studied her face and decided she was just as beautiful as ever, but the beauty seemed tempered with a hint of sadness or regret, he didn't know which.

"Hello, Eva," he said with a smile.

She sat down in the chair next to him and said, "Well, how have you been?"

"Fine, and you?" He began to get nervous again. Was she going to ask a lot of embarrassing questions, questions that had no answers?

"Just fine. I thought we might talk over old times," she replied.

Simmons gestured in the direction of the morose officer seated at the bar and forced a grin. "He won't mind, will he?"

She laughed and Simmons's nervousness diminished.

"Maybe he will, but he hasn't got anything to say about it," she said while tilting her head back and giving him an impish grin.

Their eyes met again and she put on her most beguiling look. Soft music floated in from the main room of the officers' club. It was drowsy and romantic and sung in a sultry voice, which did everything to contribute to his fascination. A whiff of perfume entranced him, her eyes captured him, and Paul Simmons was lost.

"Mrs. Hastings."

Her eyes shifted with surprise and she looked up, breaking the spell on Simmons. The bartender was standing next to the table with an apologetic look on his face. She stared at him at first, then her face softened a little in resignation.

"Mrs. Hastings, there's a phone call for you," said the bartender.

"Who is it?" she asked.

"Mrs. Arnold, your neighbor."

"Well, tell her I'm not here," said Eva with a note of finality in her voice.

"She said she was supposed to meet you here tonight," the bartender persisted.

"I know. Just tell her I'm not here," she said with exaggerated patience. The bartender shrugged and walked away. She gave Simmons an embarrassed look and started to sip her drink. Simmons glanced down at his drink and said the obvious.

"I didn't know you were married."

"Oh, yes," she said breezily. "Just after you went out to sea. You know, when we were in San Diego." She nearly choked on the lie.

She's back to her old self, thought Simmons—confident, assured, relaxed, now that her little secret is out in the open.

"Congratulations," he said. She thanked him.

"Any kids?" he asked after a pause.

She suddenly seemed nervous. "Yes, one, a boy," she replied and then started to fumble in her handbag for a cigarette. When she finally produced one, Simmons picked up a book of matches from the ashtray on the table and lit her cigarette. She took a long drag, inhaled the smoke deep within her, and blew it out in a large cloud directly in front of her.

"Where are you stationed, Paul?" she asked after a pause.

"I'm on the *Truman*," he replied.

"The *Truman*!" She seemed surprised. "That's leaving in a couple of days for Japan, isn't it?" Now she seemed disappointed.

"Well, it'll be based in Japan, but we'll be operating near Korea." He smiled. "Apparently the North Korean government is in a mess, with the North Korean president being murdered and all, so we have to go over there and intimidate them. They think there might be a lot of trouble over there."

She watched him steadily as he talked, and it was immediately evident that he had changed. He was subdued, the brashness of youth gone out of him. But there was something else, something deep within him, holding him back, something he's constantly aware of.

She had been falling for him two years ago in spite of being married, but she resisted it. You know what they say about sailors, and in his case it seemed true, at least at the time. He went to sea and there wasn't a word from him. She had to do a lot of talking to herself, convincing herself it wouldn't have worked anyway. She was married and Paul was her only affair, but it had come at a time of desperate need, a need she successfully hid from Paul. Then Ron came back from his deployment. . . .

Eva bit her lip and felt the tears that were about to fill her eyes, and wished she hadn't had that drink at home. She blinked furiously and the feeling began to pass. Am I slipping again? Could I be falling for him again? Is he what I need?

Eva studied him as they made small talk for the next half hour. He seemed to keep his eyes away from hers, but once in awhile their eyes would lock together, and his talking would slow perceptibly, which made her smile in amusement. Same as before, she thought, except his eyes are different. Whatever it was, it gave him an irresistible allure and Eva felt drawn to him. Drawn to something in him, she didn't know what.

Realization came in a rush of incredibly accurate intuition, which made her instinctively reach across the table to touch his hand. Pain. Not the physical kind, but some pain that lurked in the recesses of his mind, waiting for an unguarded moment, waiting to twist and destroy.

She half expected him to pull his hand away, but instead he gripped her hand tightly. Emotion raged within Eva as she tried in vain to fight the overpowering urge to help him. He needs me, she thought. Can I make him forget? Can I take away the pain just for one night?

On impulse, she leaned closer to him and whispered, "Why don't we go somewhere else?"

Simmons had been surprised at the warmth in her manner while they talked, but he was flabbergasted at her thinly veiled suggestion of intimacy. He was the one who treated her badly, wasn't he? The minimum he had expected was a slap in the face. Her skin was soft and smooth under his hand and her touch began to arouse some of his old feelings for her.

His heart beat with excitement, but he forced himself to look at her with detachment. She was fast approaching her mid-thirties, but there wasn't a telltale sign; she still smiled and acted like a girl just graduated from college. Whatever weight she had gained having the baby she had lost afterward, and her figure was as stunning as ever. She was married and that should have made a difference, but Paul Simmons felt himself weakening.

He avoided her eyes and glanced over her body, which was hardly concealed by the tight-fitting dress, while remembering their sexual exploits of two years ago. His blood began to pound in his veins and he blushed slightly.

"Well, where can we go?" he asked.

"My place."

"And your husband?"

"He's got the duty tonight."

"Your son?"

"Little Ronnie is with a neighbor," she whispered softly as she slid closer.

He could smell her perfume and sense her breath on his cheek. She put her hand on his leg and began to rub the inside of his thigh. Simmons rapidly lost control of his body.

"It's going to be a long cruise," she purred.

He looked into her eyes and became lost.

The light flickered through the thinly curtained window and slid across the wall of the darkened room, eventually to disappear as the slowly passing car moved down the street. Paul Simmons sat on the edge of the bed and dumbly stared at the misty light from the window.

"What's the matter, Paul?" Eva was next to him, her naked body against his side. He should have been excited, but he wasn't. She seemed genuinely concerned and not at all insulted at his sexual nonperformance.

"I don't know—I guess I'm different."

She began to stroke his hair in a soothing manner and felt more drawn to him than ever. "Is it because I'm married?" She knew the answer to that one.

"It's supposed to matter, isn't it?"

She didn't answer but kept stroking his hair. She thought she had better back off and not push him. Suddenly his body tensed and she heard him inhale, and when he spoke he was almost in a panic.

"Something's happened."

She became alarmed. This wasn't one of life's everyday upsets. This was real, and dangerous. "What?" she asked.

He turned away from her. The voices started. *Did you see them?*

"Something's happened to *me*!"

She gripped him by the shoulders. "What?" she repeated, then decided again not to push.

He began to talk after a few moments in a voice that was low and far away. He talked quickly in an attempt to drown out the voices. *Did you see . . . ?*

"I was involved in an engineering accident on my last ship. A main steam line ruptured in an engine room. The steam comes out at over 400 psi and over 500 degrees Fahrenheit. It's saturated steam. That's the worst. It took five seconds to fill the space."

She was scared. Her scalp felt as though there were a thousand needles in it. "The steam—what does it do?" She was afraid of the answer.

His reply was quick. "It cooks you alive in seconds."

She gasped and leaned her head on his back in an effort to stem the mental image of what it would do to the human body. "The scars on your arm?" She felt weak at the question.

"Yes."

He began to talk, his words picking up speed as if he had to get them out in a rush. "There were eighteen men in the engine room. I was standing with two enlisted men on the upper level near the ladder when the line went. As soon as I figured out what was happening, I shoved the two men up the ladder and ran up myself. I didn't even yell to the others. There was no time. I don't think they would have heard me anyway, the steam made so much noise. Fifteen of my men died." He stopped talking suddenly and left a queer vacuum in the room. *Oh, my God! Did you see them?*

"Sounds like there was nothing you could have done."

"I could have yelled to them."

They sat motionless for several minutes as Eva absentmindedly began to stroke his hair again. He asked the question that she had been afraid to even think about.

"Do you know what that kind of steam does to the human body?" He didn't wait for her to answer. He talked in a rush. "The bodies shrivel. They *shrivel*! Most of the men died where they stood, but a few made it partway up the escape ladder and were overcome by the fringes of the steam." His words came in a panic. "They weren't shriveled—"

"Paul!"

". . . their bodies were swollen and . . . and their skin had ripped in places with cooked muscle tissue sticking out—"

"Please, Paul!"

She was in tears, but he heard only the voice of the sailor who had put all their feelings into words. *Did you see them? Oh, my God! Did you see them?* The words ran round and round in his mind, then gradually faded and were replaced by Eva's sobbing.

"They gave me medical leave after questioning the crap out of me about the whole incident. They found that I acted in an exemplary fashion." He sounded sarcastic. "Then I went home. . . ." His voice trailed off.

Eva sniffled a bit and waited patiently for him to continue.

"There was a question I wanted to ask my father when I was home on leave," he said.

"What was that?" she asked.

"You see, he went through something very similar in Vietnam. At least I think it was similar," he continued, not hearing her question. "He got into a big firefight and lost a lot of men just like I did, but . . . he never talked about that part."

What about all those men, Dad? All those guys who'll never see the light of day again. They gave you a medal, too. Just like me. . . .

He suddenly seemed to hear Eva's sniffling. He turned toward her and put his hand on her cheek. "Have you ever been close to death?" he asked as he stared into her face.

"My grandparents died, but nothing like—"

"I feel . . . ," he began and turned away to stare into space. "I don't know. I guess I feel guilty I didn't do more to save them. They were my men. What made it worse was that they gave me a medal . . . for heroism." He shook his head.

"Do you think you're a coward?"

"No—I don't know. I feel *guilty*."

"Guilty of what?" A pause. "Being alive?"

He turned slowly and looked at her. Then he looked away and his voice floated to her in the darkness.

"Should I have died with my men?"

So much pain, she thought as she gripped him in an emotional embrace. They laid in each other's arms until dawn.

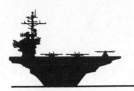

Chapter Four

N ow the officer of the deck is shifting his watch from the quarterdeck to the bridge."

Commander Ron Hastings lay on his bunk while listening to the announcement over the 1MC, the ship's public address system. It was the navy's way of announcing that the ship was about to get underway. The USS *Harry Truman* would soon stir from its berth and its huge gray mass would slide under the Bay Bridge and the Golden Gate Bridge to begin the return journey to the Western Pacific.

Hastings was glad he was on board this time, glad he could immerse himself in his career in an attempt to forget what had occurred just a day ago. He briefly considered going up to the flight deck to see if his wife would be watching the ship depart. Of course she wouldn't be, not after what had happened. He stared up at the metal ceiling and didn't see it; his vision was turned inward, observing scenes from his past that flitted through his mind at random as if they were ghosts in a graveyard.

He saw his own smiling face when he graduated from Annapolis. He had been so confident, so relaxed. With a ready-made career in front of him and a beautiful girl waiting to marry him, he was on top of the world. He thought of Eva; she was twenty then, and had a fresh, sunny smile. They were terribly in love, with a yearning and a passion that only the young possess.

The events of yesterday came into his mind unannounced and uninvited. They had had the confrontation that they both knew was coming. Was it all over? Is this how marriages end?

He forced himself to trace where they had gone wrong, starting with their euphoric honeymoon in Florida. After graduation from the naval academy, he was assigned to flight training at Pensacola, Florida. After the grueling months of flight training he had been assigned to a relatively inactive fighter squadron in Mayport, Florida. He and his wife made good use of the bountiful liberty available by taking an extended honeymoon. They had gone sight-seeing all over Florida, and he remembered that time as the happiest in his life. He decided that it must have been just after flight training that he began to think about having children. They had never talked about the possibility of children before they were married, and Eva automatically started taking birth control pills during his last year at the academy.

After several years of marriage they decided to have a baby, and his obsession began. Eva had called it an obsession and she was probably right. He knew now that he had fallen into the trap in which many new parents find themselves. He was obsessed with making everything just so. This baby had to be perfect. There was that word again—*perfect*. Eva had used the word on him like a weapon.

And the baby was perfect—for a while. That was when things started to go wrong, he decided.

It soon became apparent that his son was slower than the rest of the children his age. The doctors explained it—an IQ of 90, not enough to be retarded, but . . . *Retarded* was the only word he had heard. He used to pamper and spoil the child before he found out, and he used to glory in the boy's curly blond hair and blue eyes.

Arguments with Eva followed as she instinctively fought for her son, fought for some love for the child from his father. Their sex life trailed off until they barely indulged themselves. Then he left on a deployment for eight months to WestPac and felt that she secretly desired him to go. He almost expected her to be gone when he came back, but she was there, smiling and happy to see him home. The days and months that followed rejuvenated his life with her.

Eva seemed as happy and relaxed as she did during those balmy days in Florida when they were both so young and so much in love. It was as if they were getting to know each other for the first time, and their lovemaking took on a passion and excitement that they scarcely

knew was possible. He attributed this renewal of devotion to his prolonged absence and their mutual desire to start anew.

He had tried, really tried to be the loving father that she wanted
him to be, but in the end he just couldn't pull it off; it was just an
act. He knew now what had bothered her; she had made it perfectly
clear. *Perfectly.*

The events of the previous day roared through his mind, causing
him to open his eyes quickly in an attempt to hold back the thoughts.
He jumped out of his bunk and stepped over to the stainless steel sink.
After running some water in the basin he let the faucet handle automatically
snap shut, then he bent over to splash some water on his face. He
straightened and was startled by his appearance in the mirror above
the sink.

He gazed at himself in disgust, noting the bags blossoming under
his bloodshot eyes. Thirty-four years old and you look fifty, he thought.
He had been extremely flattered to have married a girl as beautiful as
Eva, and he was particularly sensitive to the fact that he wasn't attractive
to most other women. He was not a handsome man: He had a receding
chin, his eyes were set wide apart, and the recent pressure in his family
life had given him a sagging, depressed demeanor.

He walked over to his locker and pulled out a bottle of scotch from
underneath a pile of underwear. He took a glass from its position on
the sink, splashed some whisky into it, and quickly drank it down. The
liquor warmed him and consoled him, offering him numbness from
painful memories. In spite of the whisky, he was losing his battle to
forget yesterday's scene; he had spent a sleepless night replaying it a
hundred times over in his mind.

His pain turned to anger in an instant as he thought of what he had
sacrificed on previous deployments so that he could remain faithful
to his wife. He had refused all sexual encounters with women in the
foreign countries he had visited ever since his marriage to Eva. The
effort required of him increased with the years, but he had always hung
on. Now he felt terribly wronged after all those years of fidelity.

It's strange, he thought, how events just seem to come together in
a peculiar pattern to produce disaster. He had pulled up to his house
after having the overnight duty as command duty officer for the air
wing on the *Truman*, and had stopped to talk to his neighbor, Lt. Comdr.
Tom Arnold, his squadron's XO.

Arnold had a twinkle in his eye and came up close to him to exchange a confidence. "Back so soon?" he said with a knowing look. His face didn't change even in the light of Hastings's puzzlement.

"What are you talking about? I was CDO last night, you know that."

"Right," said Arnold with a wink. "Well, rank has its privileges, RHIP, you know." Arnold got in his car. "Then that wasn't you I saw leaving early this morning." It was a statement he clearly didn't believe. He waved, ignoring Hastings's frown. "See you later on the ship."

Thoughts of his wife's infidelity raced through his mind, but he immediately dismissed them. Things like this had happened before, and there was always a logical explanation. Like the time he had seen Eva with another man in a bar. Shook him to the core. It turned out to be her brother.

His mind ran on with possible reasons why someone would be leaving his house in the early morning. Maybe he wasn't leaving at all. Maybe he had just come to the door to see him, or drop a message in the mailbox.

Hastings walked the few steps to his front door and gave a quick look in the mailbox. Nothing. He quickly reasoned that Eva might have gotten the mail already. He shoved the key in the lock and opened the door.

Eva was seated on the living room sofa enjoying a cup of coffee and watching a quiz program. She looked at him, then quickly looked away.

"Hi, hon," she said. She seemed normal, happier than usual, but a little wistful. That would be something new.

"Did you bring in the mail?" he asked. She didn't take her eyes off the TV set. "No, he didn't come yet."

He studied her for a moment, then decided on the direct approach. "Was anyone here this morning?"

Eva glanced up, then back to the TV again. What just crossed her face? He studied her some more. The look had gone.

"Who?" she asked.

"I don't know. Anyone."

"Not that I know of."

Am I making too much of this? he asked himself. He mentally shrugged it off and went over to give her a short kiss. "Where's little Ronnie?"

"Oh, he slept over at one of the neighbor's."

Perfectly natural, he thought as he walked into the bedroom.

It was the bed that sent a shiver through him. Normally when he came home after a night's duty on the ship his side of the bed would be undisturbed, the pillow still nicely rounded, the covers straight. Eva just didn't roll around that much. He stared at the mussed covers that apparently had been quickly thrown flat in an effort at straightening up. He went over to the bed and lifted the covers over the pillow. The pillow had a round depression in it, as if someone had been lying there.

A rustle behind him made him turn; Eva was standing near him with her eyes fixed on the pillow. She glanced at him. His eyes demanded an explanation. Another unfamiliar look passed over her face and this time Hastings felt it was guilt.

"Oh, little Ronnie—" She abruptly stopped.

He was beginning to feel weak. "What about little Ronnie?"

"Nothing."

"Were you going to say that he slept here last night? That he had a nightmare and crawled in with you?"

She knew she was doing a bad job of covering up; she was nervous and acting as though she had something to hide.

"Ronnie slept over at a neighbor's house last night, remember?" he said. He knew where this was going to lead, and his emotional world came crashing down around him. Maybe not, he thought quickly; maybe she has a logical explanation. His eyes involuntarily flicked over to the two pillows. Hers had one corner depressed, the corner nearest his pillow. The depression in his pillow was much too large to be a child's. Maybe she had caused it. He stared at her and waited for a logical explanation.

Why didn't I straighten up, she asked herself bitterly. What an idiot I am. I knew he was coming home this morning, and I spent the time mooning over Paul and his problems. Did I really *want* to get caught?

"Well?" said Hastings.

She knew he was waiting for an explanation. She offered none. Eva turned her back on him and walked into the living room. Hastings was stunned. Eva had not even attempted an explanation beyond her abortive first try. He composed himself with a substantial effort and followed his wife into the living room.

"Well, I guess it's over, then, isn't it?" His voice was not the steadiest it had ever been. "What I want to know is, why?"

"The ironic part is that nothing happened."

"I don't believe it!" he said.

She dismissed his remark with a wave of the hand. "You're so damned perfect, Ron. So sophisticated! Is this how the perfect male reacts to his wife's infidelity?"

"What the hell are you talking about?"

"You badgered me for a child and we had little Ronnie. When you found out he wasn't perfect you ignored him. You couldn't just love him for who he was, an adorable little boy. He looked up to you so much, Ron. But he wasn't perfect, was he? What was he for? Just to prove you're a man?"

He bristled but contained himself.

"What's the matter, Ron? Doesn't the perfect male fight back these days?"

Hastings pressed his lips together and said nothing.

"You wanted the perfect family—I was supposed to be the perfect wife. When you found out I wasn't perfect either, you began to shut me out of your life, too. You even had to make love to me perfectly, always taking such great pains—the music had to be just right, the timing of your orgasm had to coincide with mine." Her voice turned bitter and sarcastic. "We didn't do it often, but, God, we were *perfect* when we did!"

His mouth dropped open in surprise.

"Don't gape at me. Don't act so surprised," she shot at him.

He clamped his mouth shut as Eva started again.

"What was that you used to tell me? You were doing something that only a handful of people could do—be a fighter pilot for the navy. You're so proud of that, that it has blotted me out completely. What do you think you've made me feel like? You're perfect. Me? I'm something so far below you in capability that you've totally shut me out of your mind.

"I want a man, not a god! Someone who makes mistakes once in awhile, someone who needs forgiveness—someone who needs me."

She stopped talking but stared at him with an intensity he had never seen before. He had to say something.

"Who is he?"

"What the hell does it matter?" she retorted.

"Tell me!"

"Paul Simmons," she said defiantly.

"Navy?"

"Yes."

He didn't know what to say next, and they stared at each other for a few seconds. "Why?" he finally asked.

She rolled her eyes in frustration. "Haven't you been listening?"

"Why him, then?"

Her intensity broke as her eyes began to cloud over. "He *needs* me," she said softly.

Commander Ron Hastings's eyelids drooped as he felt the scotch take effect. He was on his third glass of the brew and had every intention of finishing the bottle. The hideous scene began to replay in his mind; he automatically started to fight it but wearily gave up the effort. The events would rerun through his mind until the liquor blurred his thoughts and the blessing of unconsciousness overtook him.

The 1MC blared a brief message. "The ship is underway."

"Now relieve the watch. Relieve the wheel, the lookouts, and the life buoy. Lifeboat crew of the watch on deck for muster. On deck the second dog watch."

Paul Simmons smiled. He had come to like that particular piece of navy tradition, although he had always wondered if the lifeboat crew of the watch really did exist. When the end of the watch was due, the bo'sun would recite that little speech over the 1MC as if he were ordering all the various watches on the ship to change. In reality, the change of watches had probably taken place fifteen to twenty minutes earlier. It was customary for the ongoing watch to show up early and be briefed by the off-going watch on the status of their respective watch stations.

Simmons began to think about all the people he had met in the past few days, especially the people under his command. The personnel in Simmons's division were excellent, and the chief petty officers were talented professionals who were dedicated to their jobs. The senior enlisted man in the division was Senior Chief Machinist's Mate Alvin Taylor, a black man who stood six feet, four inches and weighed well over two hundred pounds. Simmons instantly liked the big man and was resolved to listen to his advice concerning the running of the division. The chief was dedicated to the navy and seemed to enjoy his job.

"Mister Simmons."

Simmons looked up from the stack of paperwork to see Chief Taylor standing in the doorway of the office. He caught a glimpse of a sailor standing behind the massive chief.

"Yeah, Chief," replied Simmons.

"I've got Fireman Apprentice MacKenzie here, sir. You said you wanted to see him," said Taylor.

"Yeah, Chief. Send him in," said Simmons. A new man had reported to the division just before the ship sailed and Simmons wanted to welcome him aboard personally. MacKenzie walked past the chief and nervously stood in front of the officer. Simmons tried to put him at ease with a grin.

"Have a seat, MacKenzie, and relax. I don't bite," said Simmons.

The young man sat down in a nearby chair and attempted to return the smile, but the effort resulted only in a nervous twitch of the mouth. He was a short, skinny youth who hadn't started shaving yet. The recruiters must be having a hard time filling their quotas, thought Simmons. Now they're beginning to rob the cradle.

"You came to us right from boot camp, I understand," said Simmons.

"Yes, sir, that's right," replied MacKenzie, who proceeded to noisily clear his throat.

"Well, welcome aboard the USS *Truman* and welcome to M division. I imagine you're pretty much settled down by now." It was more of a statement than a question.

"Yes, sir, I'm all set." MacKenzie finally managed a smile.

"Good," replied Simmons. He paused, considering the next question. "Why did you join the navy, MacKenzie?" queried Simmons.

The question seemed to take the young sailor by surprise and he scratched his head in an effort to find an acceptable answer. "Well, sir, I guess I didn't have anything else to do at the time," replied MacKenzie after a moment or two. He gave Simmons a downcast look that admitted his answer was frivolous.

Simmons saw his discomfort and said, "Don't worry about it, sailor. A lot of people have joined the navy for worse reasons than that. By the way," Simmons continued, "how old are you?"

"Seventeen, sir," was the reply. It was Simmons's turn to be surprised.

"Seventeen! Did you graduate from high school?"

MacKenzie's melancholy expression spoke for itself. "No, sir," he mumbled, "I dropped out in the tenth grade."

Simmons couldn't resist the next question, although he suspected that the conversation was turning into an interrogation. "Why did you drop out?"

"I don't know, sir. I guess I just couldn't hack it."

"And you expect to hack it here?" asked Simmons in disbelief. "High school is nothing compared with what you're expected to do here. Everybody on this ship is extremely important. If you fail in your job on this ship, then we might fail to meet our mission. If that happens, the people depending on us could lose their lives. You've got to be heads-up all the time. Out here you're expected to perform, and perform you will or you'll suffer the consequences." Simmons's tirade left the sailor with a more depressed look than before.

"I'll do my best, sir," he said while staring down at the deck.

"I hope your best is good enough, sailor," replied Simmons. He suddenly began to feel compassion for the miserable sailor who sat in front of him. He remembered his first few weeks on a ship and the bumbling about that he had done. MacKenzie was no different. It would take some time for him to get used to navy life.

"Look, don't worry about it, MacKenzie," Simmons said in a softer tone of voice. "Just relax and do what your petty officers tell you to do and you'll be all right."

"Yes, sir," replied MacKenzie.

"If there aren't any questions, then you can get back to work," said the lieutenant.

"Yes, sir, I mean aye, aye, sir," said MacKenzie, and he ran from the office, sideswiping the chief along the way.

A long pause followed as Simmons thought about the confused young sailor. Finally, Chief Taylor spoke. "You were a little hard on the kid, weren't you, Lieutenant?"

Simmons looked up and frowned slightly. "Yeah, I suppose so, but there are no kids on this ship, Chief. Everyone from the lowliest seaman to the captain does a damned important job, a man's job. If he's a kid then it's up to us to see that he grows up in a hell of a hurry. Especially now, when there's all this trouble in Korea," said Simmons. Chief Taylor nodded his head in thoughtful agreement.

"If there's nothing else I'll be heading back to the chiefs' lounge," he said.

"One more thing—I'd like to see Johnson about this early liberty chit," said Simmons.

"Yes, sir. I've been meaning to talk to him about that myself," replied Taylor.

Simmons swung his attention back to his desk and the mound of request chits he had been thumbing through. Virtually every man had requested early liberty when they arrived in a few days in Yokosuka, Japan. The morale on the ship was at an all-time low, due to their quick redeployment to WestPac. Quite a few sailors never made it back to the ship when it sailed from Alameda.

Simmons's division was not as hard hit by desertions as some divisions—M division had only five sailors missing out of more than a hundred. Simmons shook his head; in days gone by that would have been a horrendous percentage, but now it seemed about average. The ship's crew had also received the familiar series of bomb threats that always seem to accompany the sailing of a large ship on an extended deployment. Demented minds trying to stop the inevitable sailing of the ship, thought Simmons.

"You wanted to see me, sir?"

Simmons glanced up at Machinist's Mate Third Class Johnson, a tall, lanky, affable sailor.

"Yeah, Johnson. I've got a question," replied the officer. Chief Taylor also had entered the office and sat down at the division yeoman's desk.

"Now I've been going through this pile of request chits for early liberty, and on the form there's a block where it says 'Reason.' Most people filled in R & R, meaning rest and recreation. However, yours is different." He paused and picked up Johnson's request form, with the feeling that he was being the straight man in a burlesque act. Johnson's grin confirmed his suspicion. "Yours," he continued, "instead of R & R, has I & I." Johnson could hardly contain himself as Simmons delayed asking the obvious question.

"I give up. What on earth does I & I mean?"

Johnson glanced first at Chief Taylor, who had a twinkle in his eye, then looked back at Simmons. "Why, sir, that means intoxication and intercourse," replied Johnson with a smile.

Simmons tilted his head back and roared with laughter, with Chief Taylor joining him. "Pretty accurate, if you ask me," managed Taylor between guffaws.

Their laughter subsided and Simmons said with a smile, "OK, Johnson, you can go."

"Is the chit going to be approved, sir?"

"Most likely it will be," said Simmons.

"Thank you, sir," said Johnson and left the office.

"I can't believe you hadn't heard that before. It's standard navy tradition," said Taylor with a grin. Simmons shook his head. His smile slowly faded. He had missed that little tidbit, probably because of all the chaos of his previous duty station.

The chief noticed the lieutenant's shift in mood and decided to change the subject. "Well, sir, how do you like the *Truman* so far?"

Simmons glanced at the chief and smiled. "The *Truman* is impressive, all right. It's the sheer size of it that gets me. I didn't know anything this big could float," he said in exaggeration.

The chief grew serious and stared off into space. His voice was low and soft. "It's the weapons that get me. We've got nuclear weapons on board this ship that you wouldn't believe. No one talks too much about them, but they're there. Ready. Waiting. Enough power to devastate almost any country in the world, and we're sitting on it, sleeping with it, working around it. I just hope we don't have to use it on anybody."

Simmons had to agree with the chief. It was in the back of everyone's mind. How many hydrogen bombs were on board? There were probably enough to flatten half of the Soviet Union, not that that was very likely anymore with the way democracy was breaking out all over the world. The United States still had its enemies, and they were sailing toward one at the moment. He fervently hoped that they wouldn't ever have to use anything nuclear on anyone, even the North Koreans. He shook the thoughts from his mind.

Chief Taylor lifted the mass of his body from the chair and walked to the door. He turned and had a pleasant smile on his face. "I heard a rumor that they're just about to give out some mail that we picked up from the last UNREP. I don't know about you, but a letter from my wife would sure raise my morale."

Simmons nodded in agreement. The mail from the underway replenishment, or UNREP, was something to look forward to.

"Well, I guess I'll have to stroll over to the wardroom. Thanks, Chief," said Simmons. Chief Taylor waved and disappeared through the door.

If I have to endure a deployment I'd rather do it with people like Al Taylor around, decided Simmons. Another thought struck him and he laughed out loud. I & I. What a clown!

The 1MC sprang to life, causing Simmons to jump. "Mail call! Mail call!"

Commander Ron Hastings sat at the table watching the mob of officers cluster about the mailboxes that lined one wall of the wardroom. He had faint hope that his wife had written him. Even if it was to tell him that their life together was over, the letter would have been welcome— anything to end the silence between them. For the past week and a half he had replayed the scene with Eva in his mind while searching for answers to her actions. He had found none.

The crowd began to thin and Hastings pushed his way past the remaining officers to get to his mailbox. It was empty.

A khaki-clad figure jostled him, then immediately stepped back and apologized. "I'm sorry, Commander. I didn't see you there."

Hastings lifted his gaze to stare at the figure in front of him. His gaze got no further than the name tag on the left side of the man's shirt—Lt. Paul Simmons, Engr. His mind froze.

Hastings dragged his eyes away from the name tag and carefully looked over the lieutenant. He was about six feet tall, maybe a hundred ninety pounds, and looked thoroughly capable of defending himself. Hastings had fantasized about how he would act if confronted with "the other man." He had even gone so far as to conjure up a fight, a fight that he would win, but he knew it was only to salve his ego.

"Are you feeling all right, sir?" asked Simmons.

Hastings brought his eyes level with Simmons's and saw not a concerned, pleasant face but a monster's visage. What do I do? he thought furiously. What do I say to him?

"I'm . . . all right," mumbled Hastings.

"You didn't look well," responded Simmons. When it became evident that Hastings was not going to acknowledge his remark, Simmons shrugged his shoulders and walked away.

The call to action came quickly to Hastings—men were supposed to fight over their women, weren't they? He ran from the wardroom to see Simmons just rounding a corner and passing out of sight. He was after him in a flash but quickly became hindered by the traffic in the passageway.

Simmons proceeded at a swift pace along the second deck, then up a ladder on the port side to the hangar bay. He made his way zigzagging between aircraft to another ladder at the forward end of the hangar bay. Hastings followed him, his resolve growing with every step.

Suddenly they were in a deserted passageway on the 02 level and Hastings made his move. He took a hose wrench from its cradle on the bulkhead and ran to catch up to Simmons. Simmons heard the footsteps approaching and half turned to glance back in curiosity. His heart skipped a beat as he saw Hastings swing the wrench toward his head. Acting on pure instinct, he ducked below the trajectory of the wrench and stepped forward under the arm of his attacker. He reached up and placed his hands on Hastings's chest and pushed him away. Hastings staggered back until he hit the bulkhead. The look on his face surprised Simmons

and at the same time made him cringe. The hatred on Hastings's face
was made all the more terrifying because Simmons knew no reason
for it.

"What the hell's the matter with you?" asked Simmons in a shaky
voice.

Hastings's breath came in gasps as reason slowly returned to him.
Simmons had shoved him back easily, and now the element of surprise
was gone. Another feeling flooded him: The feeling was completely
foreign but he recognized it instantly. Fear. Simmons was bigger, stronger,
and younger. Simmons could beat him soundly. That wasn't the way
his fantasy fight ended.

Simmons was astounded by the commander's actions toward him.
The man was a perfect stranger. As far as he knew they had met for
the first time in the wardroom just minutes before.

Hastings struggled with himself. He couldn't feel fear. He wasn't
supposed to feel fear. Yet it was there and it was very real. He studied
Simmons's face as the young officer looked at him with disbelief, his
eyes seeking some answers on the older officer's face. Simmons's gaze
settled on the commander's name tag. Hastings saw a hint of uncer-
tainty in the young man's face, then recognition—and yes, fear.

Now! Now, while Simmons is still thinking about it, thought Hastings.

Hastings charged, swinging the wrench in front of him. Simmons
ducked again but was not fast enough this time. He took the full force
of the blow on his left shoulder. The blow knocked him sideways and
made him cry aloud with pain. Hastings swung the wrench again, this
time aiming for Simmons's head. It was a vicious sideways thrust that
was designed to knock Simmons off his feet. The young man jumped
back and the wrench missed his nose by less than an inch.

Simmons's quick backward flight made him stumble, and he fell
to the deck, landing heavily on his right side. He glanced upward in
horror to see the wrench held high above him, poised for the fatal,
slashing blow to his head. Below the weapon Hastings's face hovered,
a mask of rage.

Simmons rolled to his left just as the wrench began its downward
plunge. The wrench just missed his head and hit the deck behind him,
sending a shower of tile about the passageway. Simmons rolled onto
his back and desperately grabbed for Hastings's arm before he could
swing the wrench again. He grappled with the commander and swiftly
thwarted a move by Hastings to shift the wrench to his free hand. Simmons

rolled to his left and dragged Hastings on top of him until he had the commander pinned against the bulkhead.

Simmons positioned his body on top of Hastings and the fight seemed to come to an end. He ripped the wrench from Hastings's hand and threw it down the passageway. Simmons expected the commander to settle down, but he fought back furiously. He scratched and clawed his way toward Simmons's face. Simmons tried to fend him off, but the commander squirmed and twisted until his legs came free. He began to kick savagely in an effort to get out from under the lieutenant.

Simmons knew he had to stop the enraged officer before he got on his feet again. The blow he received on his shoulder had left him weak, and the punches and scratches on his face left his vision blurry.

He shaped his hand in the form of a knife and hit Hastings in the crotch as hard as he could. Hastings's eyes opened wide as he quickly sucked in his breath, then he jammed his eyes shut and let out a drawn wail of agony.

Simmons got to his feet and watched with revulsion as Hastings rolled about the passageway, retching with pain. He gripped his throbbing left shoulder and staggered backward until he rested against a bulkhead. Other officers began to show up and looked on the scene with astonishment.

The executive officer arrived and pushed through the rapidly swelling crowd, only to look in amazement at Hastings, who was sobbing and gingerly holding his genitals as he lay on the deck. The XO looked at Simmons in fury.

"What the hell is going on here?" The crowd that had been murmuring suddenly quieted down.

"He attacked me with a wrench," said Simmons in a hoarse voice. Amazement emanated from the crowd, and a look of incredulity filled the XO's face. He opened his mouth to speak, then thought better of it. He glanced at the crowd.

"Did anyone call sick bay?" A voice in the crowd answered in the affirmative. On cue, the personnel from sick bay arrived and began to strap Hastings into a stretcher. The XO ordered the crowd to disperse while a doctor confronted Simmons.

"What happened here?"

"He attacked me with a wrench and I stopped him the only way I could. I hit him in the balls," replied Simmons, to the same look of disbelief.

The doctor noticed the way Simmons was holding his left arm and asked, "Are you all right?"

"I took a shot in the arm with the wrench."

"You come with me to sick bay. I want to take a look at that shoulder," said the doctor.

"Where is this wrench that Commander Hastings supposedly hit you with?" demanded the XO. He sounded as though he would be difficult to convince.

"I think it's down the passageway somewhere," said Simmons as he gestured with his right hand.

"I want to talk to you immediately after the doctor releases you from sick bay. You understand me, mister?"

"Yes, sir," mumbled Simmons and turned to follow the doctor as the XO strode down the passageway in search of the wrench.

Simmons's thoughts turned inward. Eva's husband had somehow found out about their night together and in a fit of vengeance had attacked him. Simmons cursed his luck. He *had* to be stationed on the same ship as Eva's husband. It would be extremely difficult to avoid him in the future.

He had noticed the same squadron symbol on Hastings's name tag that he had seen in the hangar bay the night he had reported aboard the ship.

Black circle, skull, blood red kisses.

Kiss of Death.

Chapter Five

C aptain Ralph Sturdevant stared down at the message lying in front of him. It's very easy for them to order ships around like pieces on a chessboard, he thought. But what about the men who man them? What about their attitude and effectiveness? Did that bunch in the Pentagon ever consider the men's feelings?

In theory, when a man joins the military, his superiors can give him any legal order without regard to the man's emotions or motivation and that man must obey it. It just doesn't work that way in reality. For men to fight and die, for men to be effective at all in combat they must be motivated. Vietnam had taught every military commander that lesson. So, the people in the Pentagon did all the ordering and the field commanders worried about motivation.

Sturdevant thought about the *Truman*'s crew, his crew. How could they be any less motivated after what had happened in the last month? With one extended deployment after another, no wonder the desertion rate was so high, he thought bitterly.

"Captain, bridge."

Sturdevant looked toward the intercom at one end of his desk. He had expected the call. He pushed the lever on the front of the box. "Captain here."

The reply was delayed a few seconds as if the officer of the deck (OOD) had something else on his mind. "We're on station, sir."

"Thank you." Sturdevant took his finger off the intercom lever and gazed down at the message he had received the day before. The *Independence* had had a fire and had put into Yokosuka instead of the *Truman*. It wouldn't do to have two carriers in the same port with the North Korean government in chaos, so the *Truman* had to stay at sea. The *Nimitz* was steaming north from the Indian Ocean toward Korean waters with all possible speed, and the *Kitty Hawk* was ordered to WestPac from the West Coast to pick up the slack in the Indian Ocean.

Sturdevant was in command of a pretty thin task force at the moment. Normally he'd have at least a half dozen escort vessels, deployed in sectors along each threat axis. One of the escort vessels would be an Aegis cruiser; it would be deployed on the major threat axis, in between his carrier and the North Korean mainland. The Aegis cruiser would handle a myriad of threats to the task force and would coordinate all radar data from every vessel in the task force along with data from its own highly capable phased-array radar.

At the rear of the task force he should have had a destroyer or a frigate with a towed sonar array to detect underwater threats that might sneak up on him from the rear. Helicopters with dipping sonar would be deployed between the carrier and his screen of vessels in order to detect any underwater threats that might breach that ring of vessels.

The North Koreans had a number of submarines procured from the Soviet Union and Communist China, as well as those built by the North Koreans themselves. Most of the submarines were deployed on North Korea's east coast and operated in the Sea of Japan. The four ex-Soviet Whisky class diesel boats were stationed on the west coast at the Pipagot naval base. These subs were pretty old, but Sturdevant was not about to underestimate their capability. They were quiet and hard to detect when they were submerged and running on batteries. They could still put a torpedo into any ship in the task force if Sturdevant's people were lax enough.

Fortunately, the North Korean submarine fleet was in port at the moment, except for one boat that was in the Sea of Japan. Or at least that's what the latest intelligence report said. The report was four hours old. In four hours those Whisky boats could be in the Yellow Sea knocking on his door. He hoped the report was accurate. His antisubmarine warfare (ASW) capabilities were limited at the moment.

To complete his task force, he should have had two auxiliary vessels, an oiler and a stores ship, and an ammo ship if they got into some real combat. They would be deployed outside the normal operations area, where they would be out of danger but close by so that the task force wouldn't have to go far to be replenished.

Two auxiliaries were on their way from Japan, but it would take at least two days to get near the *Truman*'s operating area. While the *Truman* and the *Truxtun* were nuclear powered and needed no fuel, the *Oldendorf* used fuel at a prodigious rate and would need refueling very soon.

The USS *Philippine Sea*, an Aegis cruiser, was on its way from Pearl Harbor but wouldn't get there for about a week. Sturdevant shook his head. He really would have felt better if the Aegis cruiser was around. That class of cruiser provided sub defenses as well as wide area air defense. For the time being he'd have to rely on his Hawkeye, the funny-looking radar plane that gave him early warning of airborne threats.

Sturdevant had been ordered to steam into Korea Bay periodically to send a message to the North Koreans that there was massive destructive power at their doorstep. Sturdevant glanced at a chart on one wall. The Yellow Sea narrowed down in the north to only about a hundred miles across, with the Shantung Peninsula on the west and the jutting coastline of North Korea and some South Korean islands on the east. The People's Republic of China claimed an area that extended twelve miles off their coast, and the North Koreans claimed about fifty miles off their coast. That left a corridor about forty miles wide. Inside Korea Bay, international waters widened to about one hundred eighty miles in a northeast-southwest direction, but he'd have to be on his toes not to violate North Korean or Communist Chinese territorial limits.

The *Truman*'s presence off the coast of North Korea was supposed to make the North Koreans think twice about creating any incidents. Sturdevant and his crew were supposed to intimidate them. Sturdevant wondered just how well it would work. Were the North Koreans intimidated by anything?

The captain thought about his crew. He only hoped that they would deliver when the time came. Desertions had riddled his ship, and he had thought that morale couldn't possibly go any lower after they left Alameda, but he was wrong. When the crew discovered that they wouldn't be docking in Yokosuka, disciplinary problems, which were rampant prior to the announcement, then became epidemic. Captain's mast, at which Sturdevant would issue penalties for misconduct, began to take most of his time, and the conduct of the sailors at mast was surly at best.

Then there was this horrible business of two of his officers fighting in a passageway, like a couple of dogs in an alley. He had tried to keep it under wraps and so far he was successful, but he didn't know how long it would last. If the crew ever found out . . .

His glance dropped down to the message he had been reading over and over again. One line caught his eye.

BORDER INCIDENTS RISE IN KOREA

He eyed the second word, *incidents*. In incidents people get killed. What an impersonal word for what really happens. People get shot at, people die. He quickly decided that the word did not adequately reflect the wrenching terror of battle, or the pain of a wound, or the drained, empty feeling after seeing a good friend die a terrible death. Those faceless, brainless people in the Pentagon had the knack of choosing the most nondescript words for their messages in order to take as much horror out of the situation as possible. It would not do to remind the front-line troops of the horrors that could spring up at any moment.

Captain Ralph Sturdevant sat and brooded as the *Truman* ran through Korea Bay.

Fireman Apprentice Jeff MacKenzie lay in his bunk, his heart pounding and his breath coming fast. He had just gone through a horrendous day at sea. He was known as the new kid and, as such, he was the butt of every practical joke sailors had ever dreamed of to play on new recruits. The worst jobs had always migrated downward in the power hierarchy, and he was at the bottom of a long command structure.

So this is the navy. The third class machinist's mate he was assigned to was a total idiot and treated the men under him like they were dog shit. What was that stupid expression these lifers always use? Lower than whale shit at the bottom of the sea. Yeah, that's the way he was treated. After spending a morning wiping out the bilges in the forward engine room, he was sent back to the shaft alleys, the compartments that contained nothing but a rotating propeller shaft, to scrupulously clean the cramped space. He had to dodge the enormous rotating shaft all the while.

The day before that he was cleaning heads. God, couldn't those sailors aim straight when they took a piss? Other more experienced head cleaners had told him it was ten times worse the day after liberty in a port.

MacKenzie's stomach churned. He thought he was done with all that after basic training. Now his job was doing it again almost all the time. And they wonder why nobody reenlists.

He had overheard one of the first class machinist's mates talking about sending someone to the mess decks. Each division was required to supply a number of people to the division that prepared food. Typically each division supplied sailors just out of boot camp. Someone had mentioned that he might be the one to go to the mess decks. That would be all right with him. It would get him away from that third class jerk. Maybe if he was handling food he would be prohibited from cleaning heads for sanitary reasons. He resolved to stay on the mess decks forever if that was the case. It would get him away from the filthy jobs and the practical jokes.

The other sailors did everything they could to embarrass him. His third class sent him to Senior Chief Machinist's Mate Taylor to get a bucket of relative bearing grease. What the hell did he know? So he went, and got a royal ass-chewing from the senior chief himself. The chief started yelling that he didn't have time for childish games, which totally puzzled MacKenzie. The third class had been working on a lube oil pump at the time and had taken a set of bearings—at least he said they were bearings—and told him they were relative bearings and needed a special kind of grease. Only the senior chief in the division had access to this very expensive grease. They didn't even trust the officers with it.

MacKenzie returned to the engine room in despair at his failure to get the grease and expected to get another ass-chewing from the third class. What happened was totally unexpected and worse than an ass-chewing. He returned to the derisive laughter of the entire engine room crew. That was the humiliating end to his workday. Later, an older, more sympathetic sailor said that the relative bearing grease joke was the oldest in the book. It had been pulled on the uninitiated for at least the past hundred years. He patiently explained that relative bearings had nothing to do with pumps. They were the location of objects at sea measured in angles from dead ahead, or simply the angle off the bow.

MacKenzie squirmed in his bunk at the memory. Why do they take so much time humiliating people? And why do they enjoy it so much? Don't they remember when they were on their first ship?

The memory of his interview with Lieutenant Simmons ran across his mind. At least the officer seemed sympathetic for a while, but he wound up chewing ass as well. This wasn't what he had expected. He had joined the navy to get respect. People would see the uniform and right away they would have a different feeling about him. He wasn't just another dumb kid. He was navy.

But the real navy wasn't like the one portrayed in the advertisements on TV. There all the sailors were laughing and having a good time in exotic ports of call, or doing important jobs like launching and recovering aircraft. What the hell was so important about scrubbing shaft alleys so clean that you could eat off the bilge bottom?

All his life he felt he had been at a disadvantage, compared with everyone else in the world. In elementary school and later in high school he was always at the bottom of the class, always on the outside. Everyone else seemed to know what was happening. He was always playing catch-up, and never quite caught up. He never had any friends, unless you could call Moose a friend. He was the only one who seemed slower to catch on than MacKenzie. Hell, he was the only one who would have anything to do with MacKenzie.

High school was intolerable, suffocating; he felt he just had to get away. He dreamed of the day when he would drop out and be free. No teachers would scream at him to pay attention; no parents would scream at him to do homework. In fact, there would be no homework at all.

MacKenzie had gotten his wish, but it came in a form he hadn't expected. Moose and he, on one unbelievably boring Saturday night, took a neighbor's car for a joyride. It was a neighbor his parents were feuding with over some of the dumb things that neighbors find irritating about each other. The neighbor reported the car stolen, and the cops picked up the two wayward teenagers. The neighbor refused to drop the charges and the judge gave Moose and him two choices, jail or the military. Moose took jail; MacKenzie took the navy.

He had heard that basic training was a lot of crap, and it was, but he was prepared for it. He knew it wouldn't last forever. Once it was over he'd get the respect that was accorded his new status in life.

Only that didn't happen. Being aboard the *Truman* was more of a nightmare than basic ever was. He had the same problem as before. Everyone else knew more than he did and jammed it down his throat every chance they got. Determination built up within him. Sometime, somewhere, things would be different.

When he got the advantage over someone else, he'd jam it down his throat.

Paul Simmons's thoughts drifted as he stared at the paperwork in front of him. The pain in his shoulder had subsided somewhat as the painkiller administered to him in sick bay began to take effect. X rays had shown no broken bones, but the blow had left the shoulder severely swollen and restricted in movement. The only good news was that he had been hit above where he had been burned in the engine room accident. He sighed and felt his insides quiver, and vainly attempted to concentrate on the formulation of a training plan for his division.

His thoughts ran over the past few weeks and lingered over his encounter with Eva. Beautiful Eva. He had told her more about himself in one night than he had ever told anyone. Was she right? Did he feel guilty about surviving because so many others had died?

He had heard about survivors of plane crashes and Nazi concentration camps remembering people they knew—family, friends, even strangers— and wondering why all those people had died and they had lived. They felt that they should have died also. The engine room accident wasn't the same magnitude as those disasters; besides, two other sailors had survived. It didn't fit the formula, so why should he feel guilty about being alive?

It was there, though. Eva had put into words exactly what he felt. He wondered if recognizing the feeling would help in dealing with it. He wondered also if his father had felt the same way after seeing all that death in Vietnam. Maybe it was worse for him because he was making decisions and people were dying because of them. He couldn't think of anything more horrible than someone dying because of a decision he had made.

He thought of Eva again. Her face floated in a twilight world in Simmons's mental vision. She was alluring and provocative in his memory, and she drew him into herself even though she was more than five thousand miles away. Euphoria suffused his being as he remembered the touch of her body on their last night together. There was a straining need in her; what it was he didn't know. That much had gotten through his self-indulgence.

His arm began to throb again as if to remind him of the distressing realities of the situation. Utopian thoughts quickly ebbed as memory of the fight with Eva's husband intruded. He had never bargained for that. Everything in life has a cost, and Eva's love was no exception. Would Commander Hastings try again? Simmons shivered slightly at his last thought, and then gratefully directed his attention to Chief Taylor, who had just entered the M division office.

"I heard you had an accident, Mr. Simmons," he said with concern in his voice.

Simmons turned to face Taylor and winced with the effort. "Yeah, I fell down a ladder," he replied.

"Right," said Taylor. "You gotta watch out with those ladders. Mighty dangerous things, those ladders. Why, I wouldn't be surprised if on the new ships they don't put elevators all over the place. That way nobody will get hurt the way you did."

Taylor looked askance at Simmons with such a knowing, amused glance that the lieutenant almost laughed out loud.

"I should know better than to try to slip something past you, Chief," said Simmons.

Taylor took a step closer and said in a low voice, "I heard you got into a fight with a pilot."

"Have you ever considered working for the CIA?" asked Simmons in an effort to make light of the affair. "That's supposed to be hushed up."

"Well," said Taylor slowly, "one of the chiefs overheard a couple of pilots talking about it, and he knew I was in the same division as you, so . . . " He left the rest of the sentence unspoken. "What was it about? Is he a jealous husband or something?" Taylor asked with a grin.

Simmons's jaw dropped with astonishment, but then he quickly realized that Taylor had meant the remark as a joke. Taylor's grin vanished at the sight of Simmons's reaction.

"I'm sorry. I didn't mean—" Taylor began.

"He's the jealous type all right." Simmons lowered his voice. "I just didn't know how jealous." He looked at Taylor and then stared down at the desk in front of him. "I knew his wife a couple of years ago when I was stationed in San Diego. Then I met her again just before we sailed." Simmons sighed. "One thing led to another and . . . " He couldn't bring himself to say anything more. An uncomfortable pause followed, with Taylor breaking the silence only after several minutes.

"How's the arm?"

"It'll be all right in a couple of days," Simmons replied.

Taylor stared at the space over Simmons's left breast pocket, the space where his ribbons would appear if he had been wearing a dress uniform instead of his wash khakis.

"You know it's all over the ship."

"About the fight?" asked Simmons.

Taylor hesitated. "About the engine room casualty."

Simmons averted his eyes from Taylor and nodded slowly. "I guess that kind of stuff gets around."

"Yeah." Taylor stared into space and asked a question softly and quietly, and with a certain sadness to his voice. "When you joined the navy, did you ever think you'd be involved in anything like that?"

Simmons shook his head. "Join the navy and see the world, and all that shit."

"You believed the ads?" asked Taylor. He was incredulous.

"Yes," Simmons replied with embarrassment.

Taylor shook his head in disbelief. "Yeah. 'Be all you can be! It's not a job, it's an adventure!' And they show some fuzzy-faced kid learning electronics. Only they don't tell you that all your training is aimed at one thing—to kill people." Taylor stopped abruptly. He continued after a few moments with his voice taking on a wistful tone.

"The saddest part about it is that sometimes that's necessary for our country to survive, and brother, let me tell you, if the United States goes down, the rest of the lights will go out in the free world. But what most people don't realize is that there's a price to everything we do. The reaction is never what we expect." He gave Simmons a sideways glance. "I'll bet you never expected to fight a commander, either."

Simmons tried to give Taylor a dirty look, but he wasn't quite up to it.

"Like the kids who joined the navy for the adventure of it," continued Taylor, "they never expected to go into combat, yet it might happen, with the tensions with North Korea. I just hope none of them get killed."

Taylor lapsed into silence for a few moments and they both listened to the thrumming of the ship's engines, instinctively checking on its health while letting their thoughts run free.

Taylor spoke first. "The ads never mention the memories, either. That's the worst part, the most subtle part about it all. Memories can cause so much pain."

Simmons gave Taylor a quick look of surprise.

"Memories like you have of men dying in an engine room," said Taylor.

Simmons stared at the deck. "How would you know about memories like that, Chief?"

"As a black man who joined the navy eighteen years ago, I've got a few, man. Don't kid yourself." He grunted. "It's an adventure, all right."

Chapter Six

PYONGYANG, NORTH KOREA

Colonel Pak Myung Jo swallowed nervously and shifted his weight from one foot to the other. He berated himself for being nervous, but when he was in the presence of General Kang it was always the same. His mouth would go dry and his hands would get moist. His superior and most ardent supporter was still getting settled. He steeled himself for the wait.

General Kang Chung Kwon focused his eyes on Colonel Pak and the huge wall chart that hung behind him. "You may begin your briefing, Comrade Colonel."

It seemed to Pak that Kang's voice hissed a bit, somewhat like the sound of a snake. This was a strange briefing, just the two of them, with Kang half hidden in the shadows cast by the lights that illuminated the wall chart and the one doing the briefing. Pak swallowed again.

"The American carrier *Truman* and its two escort vessels are currently in an operating area in the center of Korea Bay. At times they have intruded on our territorial limits, but they haven't lingered there and have immediately returned to international waters. Their location in Korea Bay means that any air support from the South or from Japan would have a longer flight time and also have reduced time over the task force's location."

Kang eyed his tactical commander. Pak had one hundred sixty-five pounds of muscle packed into a five-foot, nine-inch frame. At thirty-five years old, Pak was one of the youngest colonels in the North Korean Army. He was a tough commander, devoid of any compassion for the weak or incompetent, and he constantly pushed his men to their breaking point. He ruthlessly punished any hint of undisciplined behavior in his men until he had them functioning with mindless precision. His loyalty to his country and his superiors was unsurpassed, and he obeyed all orders without question. He expected his men to do the same. He was the ideal commander for this extraordinary mission.

"We have at our disposal twenty helicopters, a squadron of MiG-23s, a squadron of MiG-29s, and a missile battery of Silkworm cruise missiles. We—"

"I know very well what you have at your disposal, Comrade Colonel. I am the one who provided it all." Kang's face cracked into the briefest of smiles.

Pak swallowed again. He fervently hoped his nervousness didn't show. He plunged on. "The helicopters will carry fifty soldiers each—"

"These helicopters can carry sixty-five soldiers each. Why have you decided upon a smaller number? Would it not make sense to get as many soldiers on the flight deck as soon as possible?" Kang looked at him closely.

The question left Pak wondering why Kang had ordered this last-minute briefing. If he knew all these details, then why go over them just hours before the attack was to begin? Was Kang nervous also?

"Tests were conducted during training on off-load time. Fifty soldiers were found to be optimum to minimize off-load time and thus maximize the number of soldiers ready to attack if necessary." Pak hoped that his explanation would put an end to that particular issue. Kang settled back a bit in his chair as Pak continued.

"Our gas planes will approach the carrier from the west; the Americans will most likely have their early warning aircraft airborne east of the carrier and near the North Korean mainland. The planes will have to fly slowly only feet off the waves to avoid detection by the Hawkeye radar plane, and get close to the Chinese mainland to get west of the carrier."

Kang shifted in his chair. "Our Chinese friends won't know what's happening until it's over."

Pak nodded. He hoped Kang was right. The unarmed gas planes would be easy targets for any Chinese fighters.

"The gas will be delivered by fifteen modified crop-dusting planes, each with one thousand cubic feet of gas. They will pop up to an altitude of five hundred feet and fly in a straight line and in such a formation that the invisible gas cloud will be one thousand feet in depth." Pak grabbed a pointer and indicated on the wall chart a blue curved arrow that represented the track of the gas planes.

"Then comes the tricky part. The American ship has to keep going straight through the gas cloud and not turn away or otherwise become suspicious, or else the attack will fail. To allay the Americans' suspicions, the gas planes will fly without fighter escort. If the Americans have a combat air patrol aloft, then we will use the squadron of MiG-23s to draw them off. That same squadron of MiGs will provide the final coordinates of the American task force to the other units, most importantly to the helicopter assault force."

Kang's face remained impassive even when Pak used the word *fail*. Pak decided he'd better quickly continue and not give his superior a chance to further question his plan.

"The squadron of MiG-29s will overfly the ship to cover the helicopter landings. This squadron would also have the responsibility of downing the American radar plane."

"What about the cruise missile batteries? When do you employ them?" Kang arched an eyebrow as he waited for Pak's answer.

The Silkworm missiles were a recent addition to the plan, and Pak chalked up their presence in his forces to paranoia about the capabilities of the American navy. Would extra ships appear out of nowhere? The Americans took time to get their ships into the vicinity of Korea. They had to obey the laws of physics like anyone else.

"The cruise missiles would be used only as a last resort to fight off any other ships that would come to the rescue of the carrier."

Kang gave him a hard look. "Let me remind you of your orders, Comrade Colonel. You and your forces will keep the killing of Americans to a minimum. I want prisoners, not corpses!"

Pak put on an air of deference and almost snapped to attention. "Yes, Comrade General."

Kang settled down and nodded to Pak to proceed.

"I have separated the helicopter forces into two sections, an attack section and an intelligence section," continued Pak. "The attack section, consisting of eight hundred men, will go in first and secure the ship.

This section will be needed only if the gas takes partial effect; our men will crush any opposition from the ship's crew."

"And where will you be, Comrade Colonel?" asked Kang.

"I will be in the first wave to hit the ship," replied Pak. "My helicopter will land on the aftermost part of the flight deck, then I will proceed immediately to the hangar bay to direct operations."

"Is that wise, Comrade? A commander normally is behind the front-line troops." Kang's voice betrayed no emotion.

Pak knew that Kang wasn't concerned for his safety for any altruistic reasons. He just didn't want his tactical commander killed in the first few minutes of the battle.

"I must immediately assess our opposition, if there is any, to better direct my troops." Kang said nothing, and after an appropriate delay Pak continued.

"The intelligence section of two hundred specialists will board the ship immediately after it has been pronounced secure by me. The specialists' mission is to ensure that nothing of value is destroyed and no sabotage is committed, and to supervise the sailing of the ship to port. Intelligence personnel will be placed in critical areas of the ship, namely the bridge, combat information center, or CIC, flight deck, hangar bay, armory, engine rooms, and the enclosed operating stations in the reactor rooms. Key U.S. naval personnel will be revived and forced to sail the ship to Nampo."

Kang leaned back in his chair as Pak went on with detail after detail about the plan. Concentration camps, demolition units to destroy the carrier, and the like were presented by Pak. The colonel went over the code names for the units in the assault: Ch'ollima 1 designated the helicopter force, Ch'ollima 2 was for the fighter squadrons of MiG-23s and MiG-29s, and Ch'ollima 3 was for the cruise missile units on the North Korean coast.

Kang's thoughts ran on. And Ch'ollima 4 and Ch'ollima 5. They are the units you don't know about. They are for contingency purposes in case you, Comrade Colonel, somehow fail. But they would not fail, resolved Kang.

The chance of a lifetime presented itself today and Kang would fulfill his dream of many years. He had spent most of his adult life trying to embarrass the United States, starting with the capture of that American general on Koje-do years ago. This operation required much more planning and many more of his country's resources. He had even murdered the president to eliminate his constant veto of his plans.

Kang thought over the plan again and carefully looked over the man who would carry it out. He had the resources and the people, and, yes, they had thought of everything. He would come to glory at day's end.

Hours later, Col. Pak Myung Jo sat in his headquarters at the training area, which was on the northwest side of a four-thousand-foot mountain just south of the Nam-Gang River. The village of Koksan lay at the base of the mountain and on the opposite side of the training area. Located to avoid arousing the curiosity of the town's inhabitants, the training area was about midway between the port of Nampo on the west coast of Korea and Wonsan on the east coast. This was to make the flight time to either port equal, in case the *Truman* was either to the west of North Korea or in the Sea of Japan.

A helicopter coughed to life just outside Pak's hut, and its huge five-blade main rotor gradually started to revolve. In a few seconds the rotor was at idling speed and kicking up a cloud of dust, which began to filter through Pak's window. Pak could hear other helicopters start up as his airborne force got ready.

Pak glanced at his watch again. Would the signal to attack ever come? Maybe his feeling about today was wrong and this was just a false alarm. He walked over to his locker, opened it, and lifted a heavy clip belt off the inside shelf. After a minor struggle he had the belt fastened around his waist. He picked up the automatic weapon that was leaning against one wall of the locker and looked it over. It was an AKR submachine gun, one of the newer Russian-made infantry weapons. It was stubby, with a folding stock and a thirty-round banana magazine. A little more than sixteen inches long with the stock folded, it had a bell-mouthed barrel tip and a firing rate of eight hundred 5.5mm rounds a minute. Pak and all his men had gotten the very first ones that North Korea had acquired, but Pak had misgivings.

Their Russian comrades had praised the weapon to the skies and had extolled its potential field performance, but in Pak's own field tests he found that the weapon had a tendency to jam. He had gotten the feeling that the Soviet Union had given the weapons to the Koreans to find out how effective they were under actual combat conditions, and not because of any altruistic motives. Pak would rather have had an AK-47, or the newer AKM, derived from the AK-47; the AK-47 had been proven very reliable in Southeast Asia years before. Pak was overruled, however, and he suspected that the decision was made in favor of the AKR because of some vague fear that his superiors had about the capabilities of the sixty marines aboard the *Truman*. His superiors had made the point that the AKR had a higher rate of fire than the AK-47.

Pak looked the weapon over with some satisfaction, however. He had spent the night cleaning and oiling it so that there would be no jamming on this most critical day. He hesitated before closing the locker door as he decided whether or not to take his pistol. He decided against it; he had enough weight around his middle. He would be burdened further when he added the hand grenades to his uniform.

The men were ridiculously well armed—submachine guns, hand grenades—plus they all had to struggle with the gas masks. Some of his men were even taking their bayonets. Pak sighed in resignation. His superiors were taking no chances with this extraordinary operation.

Pak thought about the significance that Kang had attached to the name of the American carrier. The name *Harry Truman* had angered Kang. The attack that Pak would launch today seemed an almost personal thing to Kang, an act of revenge upon a man long dead. Pak grunted to himself. They could just as easily be attacking a ship named *Independence*, except that it was in Japan. Pak thought that the *Truman* represented bigger fish, not because of its name but because it was nuclear-powered, and it was the American navy's newest vessel.

Pak sensed excitement in the next room and went to the door. He questioned his second in command with his eyes. The officer spoke only one word. "Ch'ollima!"

Ch'ollima, the legendary winged horse from Korea's past, who performed incredible deeds of heroism, was the code word ordering the attack. The symbolism was not lost on Pak; a hero's name was being used to order heroes into battle.

Pak strode out the door of his hut and into the daylight, and left his second in command to scramble toward his helicopter. Pak entered the hangar and jumped into the open hatch in the side of the waiting helicopter. The rotor blades increased speed as Pak radioed the attack signal to the rest of his men. The helicopter lifted off the ground amid a cloud of dust and an unbelievable amount of noise.

A moment later the helicopter was high in the sky, rendezvousing with the nineteen other helicopters in the group. In unison, they turned westward and headed out to sea.

# Chapter Seven

"G eneral quarters, general quarters, all hands man your battle stations." More than six thousand men jumped to the call, their hearts thumping, and scrambled to their GQ stations.

Then came the disclaimer, "This is a drill, this is a drill."

The men slowed their flight to their stations and shook their heads in disgust. It was just another useless drill.

Captain Ralph Sturdevant, observing the flight deck crew from the bridge, was furious. He really should learn to expect that kind of thing, he thought, but, damn it, couldn't the men respond as if it were the real thing? Commanding officers of combat ships had long fought the problem, only to have it end in frustration. Captain Sturdevant was no different. The American military man is the best fighter in the world but the worst trainee. It takes shots fired in anger to make American men put forth their best effort.

Sturdevant stared at two sailors who were sauntering across the flight deck and hoped they would glance up at the bridge so he could hurry them along with an icy look. The men continued their slow journey and ignored the beckoning of their shipmates who were already at their GQ stations.

Sturdevant resisted the impulse to shout to the OOD to put the men on report; above all he didn't want to seem like a Captain Queeg. He had toyed with the idea of sounding general quarters and not announcing it was a drill, but after a few times the crew would catch on. Their response would then be diminished if he had to call the real thing.

He tried to settle down and wait for the report from damage control that the ship was set for maximum watertight integrity, called condition Zebra. The report finally came, fifteen minutes into the drill. That's not satisfactory, thought Sturdevant, not satisfactory at all. He sighed as he pushed the 1MC switch.

"This is the captain speaking." He heard his voice echo throughout the ship. "It took us fifteen minutes to button up the ship. That's not good enough. We should be able to do it in half that time. At the next GQ drill I will expect nothing less than perfection or we will keep doing it over and over until we get it right." He waited until the echoes died away. "That is all."

Captain Queeg again, he thought. Maybe he was a little too hard on them; after all, they hadn't had a whole lot of time with their families between deployments. Well, neither did he. He felt inquiring eyes on him and glanced up at the OOD. The expectation in the officer's eyes was unmistakable.

"Shall we head into the wind, Captain?" he asked. Sturdevant grumbled assent and then asked about wind velocity.

"Three knots, sir. It hardly seems worthwhile," the OOD said with a smile.

"Do it anyway, mister," Sturdevant snapped. The smile vanished.

A helmet was timidly offered to him by one of the telephone talkers. Sturdevant snatched it out of his hand and growled at him. "A little late with that, aren't you?"

The sailor mumbled, "Yes, sir," and fumbled nervously with his sound-powered phones.

Sturdevant mentally berated himself. He didn't want to cause the ship's morale to sag further. Two long deployments with only a month off in between was enough to destroy the morale of even the best crew. He wondered what the brass really had in mind. Oh, he knew all the official reasons, but his superiors didn't know what they had done to the ship's efficiency by sending her out again unexpectedly.

"Captain, flight deck control says we have thirty-two knots of wind down the flight deck," declared one of the telephone talkers.

Sturdevant nodded. Three knots of natural wind and twenty-nine knots due to the speed of the ship. Sturdevant knew that it was sufficient for launch. More than sufficient actually; they could launch planes while dead in the water, but he, like every other aircraft carrier CO, wanted to give his pilots every advantage. He automatically went into the wind prior to launching or recovering aircraft and went to flank speed to obtain as much lift on the wing surfaces as possible. During World War II it was a necessity, or the planes would have crashed for lack of airspeed. During Vietnam most of the carriers had to resort to this tactic even though they had powerful catapults. He knew; he had made enough launches from those now-obsolete carriers.

Sturdevant took one last look at the flight deck. The first four aircraft were attached to the four powerful steam catapults that lined the bow and the angle deck of the carrier. Launch control on the *Truman* was located in a shelter that rose partially above flight deck level during launch operations. The shelter, humorously referred to as the cathouse, due to its location between the catapults, or "cats," resembled a blockhouse in shape, with sides tapered outward at the base. Windows lined the sides for maximum viewing of the flight deck by the launch personnel.

He pressed the lever on the intercom. "PriFly, bridge. Launch planes."

In a matter of seconds, a curiously flat-sounding voice repeated the command to the flight deck personnel over loudspeakers hidden somewhere in the island. It didn't seem to matter who gave the command or which ship it was on—there was always that same quality imparted to one's voice by the flight deck loudspeakers. It was as if the voice of the flight operations officer was filtered to let only authority through and reject all of the emotional and tonal quality that goes into making the voice human.

Sturdevant watched the red-shirted sailor arm the missiles under each plane by pulling a red tag from each weapon. Then all the flight deck personnel stepped back to await the launch. A blast deflector slid up behind the aircraft. The pilot, anticipating the launch, went to afterburners, and the plane seemed to crouch down as if it were a wild animal about to pounce. After a delay of a few seconds, the catapults were activated by the cathouse personnel, and the huge aircraft was flung into the air with seeming abandon.

Sturdevant gazed down at the planes as they were hurled into the air one by one, and felt a twinge of nostalgia. He relived all the feelings that a pilot experiences just before the jolt of the catapult, and he was flooded with the anxiety and sometimes outright fear that weighs down a pilot's insides. He remembered it all and still wished he was behind a stick again.

He wondered what it was like to be in an F-14. From its appearance it seemed unlikely that the plane could outfly anything he had flown in his career. The aircraft seemed large, too large for it to be an agile fighter. Two huge jet engines were set just aft of the wings, with their air intakes extending forward and stopping just aft of the radar intercept officer's cockpit.

The *Truman* had just received the newest model of the now-venerable F-14 line of aircraft. It had updated avionics and displays and also was lighter and more maneuverable. It was capable of exceeding Mach 2.5, more than 1,800 miles per hour. As a dogfighter and long-range interceptor it was unexcelled. The F-14's radar could track a multitude of targets at ranges up to 120 miles and launch six Phoenix missiles simultaneously at as many targets. That represented quite an advance from Sturdevant's days as a Phantom pilot. The captain wondered what air combat over North Vietnam would have been like if he had been flying an F-14. Imagine shooting down six MiGs at once, he thought to himself and smiled. Presto—instant ace.

His thoughts returned to the pilots in the line of planes strung out across the flight deck awaiting their turn to be catapulted into the sky. One plane in particular caught his attention. It was Commander Hastings's plane. His squadron's logo, with its skull in a field of black, stood out among the other relatively restrained squadron symbols. Kiss of Death indeed, thought Sturdevant. Let's hope it's only the enemy that gets kissed.

Sturdevant had reminded the air wing commander, CAG, to keep an eye on Hastings for any decrease in his squadron's efficiency. That was one of the reasons why Hastings's squadron was scheduled for launch today—it would be an opportunity to evaluate him. Sturdevant had become convinced that some serious problem was troubling the commander. Hastings's fight with that snipe lieutenant—what was his name? Well, the fight was just a symptom of something beneath the surface. He couldn't let it impair the efficiency of the ship.

Sturdevant walked back to the intercom, spun the selector switch, and pressed the lever. "DC central, bridge. Are you finished with all your drills?"

"Bridge, DC central. That's affirmative."

Sturdevant turned and glanced down the flight deck. They were finished launching planes and his combat air patrol was on its way. No sense in keeping the crew at GQ, he thought. He gave the OOD the command to secure from general quarters.

As the watch changed, Sturdevant began to brood again about the generally low morale of the crew and what it might mean if they were needed in Korea. His thoughts were jolted by one of the intercoms.

"Bridge, this is combat."

The CO spun around and stabbed his finger at the intercom lever. "Bridge, aye." Sturdevant lifted his finger and immediately the voice returned with a hint of tension.

"Hawkeye has ten bogies, bearing 105 degrees relative. Altitude 15,000. Range 120 miles. Speed 300 knots."

A shiver went up Sturdevant's spine, as it had always done after the reception of similar messages, even though there was a lot of such traffic along the North Korean coast.

"Combat, this is the captain. What is their course?" Seconds passed. Sturdevant started to review in his mind the procedure to be followed in the event of radar contacts. A message had to be sent—

"Bridge, combat. Hawkeye has them heading 165 degrees, sir."

Sturdevant sighed with relief. No need to sound general quarters yet. Those contacts, probably North Korean MiGs, were headed away from him to the south. To attack South Korea? Or to make a rear attack on his task force? Or was it just a routine patrol? They would bear watching.

He quickly thumbed the intercom lever again. "Combat, get Blackline flight into the area to see what they're up to."

"Combat, aye."

Sturdevant nodded to himself. The E-2C Hawkeye, nicknamed the Stoof with a Roof, was a strange-looking aircraft and seemingly out of place among the quick and agile jet fighters that the *Truman* carried. It was a prop aircraft of a relatively ancient variety, with a radar antenna in a large mushroom-shaped rotodome protruding above the midsection of the aircraft. Screwy design, he thought, but absolutely indispensable for early warning of threats to his task force.

Communications called back, cutting across his thoughts, and confirmed that the contact report had been sent. It was routine to send a message to the commander of the Seventh Fleet (COMSEVENTHFLT) in Japan in the event of a possible unfriendly radar contact, whether surface or air, even though he had the rest of the task force on emissions control. It was imperative that he keep the Pentagon and the Seventh Fleet informed about North Korean activity.

The CIC came in a few seconds later to inform him that the MiGs had moved far to the south. It was evidently not an attack on the ship, but a routine patrol.

Sturdevant thought over the situation; the idea of his combat air patrol moving off far to the south to chase after a routine patrol suddenly struck him. Are they being drawn off? He turned toward the aft bulkhead of the bridge and eyed the GQ alarm button underneath its metal cage.

"Bridge, combat!" There was no mistaking the urgency in the voice.

"Bridge, aye."

"Hawkeye has fifteen bogies, bearing 350 relative, altitude 500 feet, speed 120, range 8 miles, heading 095." The voice sounded apologetic.

Sturdevant was furious. Morale be damned. "Sound general quarters!" he shouted to the bo'sun's mate of the watch. The bo'sun's mate jumped to the task and the alarm rang throughout the ship.

Sturdevant hit the intercom lever. "How the hell did they get in so close?!"

After a short delay the CIC officer came back. "Hawkeye says they're small, slow-moving targets, and they must have hugged the water until a few seconds ago, when they popped up."

What the hell was this? They certainly didn't sound dangerous, and they were headed almost directly away from the ship. "Anything else in the area?" demanded the captain.

"No, sir, nothing at all." Then, after a small hesitation, "How about a radar ID, Captain?"

Sturdevant thought quickly. The *Truman* was equipped with the latest advances in shipboard radar, one of which was the ability to identify targets by radar signature. The contacts had all the earmarks of an intelligence mission; was it wise to turn on the ship's radar with intelligence planes about? But if it was an intelligence mission, why fifteen planes? It didn't make sense. One thing he was sure about—he had to know what he was up against.

"Combat, bridge. Permission granted for radar ID."

"Combat, aye."

It was a calculated risk, but that's what he got paid for. He suddenly had second thoughts—the powerful radar would announce the *Truman*'s location to all the world.

"Combat, bridge. Did you track them long enough to get any identification?" the CO asked. He suddenly seemed to be out of breath.

"Bridge, combat. Computer has an almost positive ID—85 percent confidence factor. They're a Russian-Polish M-15 chemical utility plane. These planes are normally used for spraying crops."

Spraying crops? Sturdevant wondered what such a plane would be doing offshore. He fought a feeling of dizziness. "Where are they now?" he asked.

"Range 40 miles and rapidly increasing. Speed 150 knots. Course 095. They're putting some distance between us, Captain."

Sturdevant nodded to himself. "Secure from general quarters," he told the bo'sun's mate. The man gave the order over the 1MC.

The term *chemical utility plane* had struck a discordant note in Sturdevant's mind. He didn't know why; he couldn't place it, but the North Koreans were up to something. After mulling it over he shrugged his shoulders. He couldn't figure it out; he just didn't have enough information to come to a conclusion.

He hadn't been paying much attention to the situation on the bridge; the ship was still traveling at flank speed. His task force was approaching the claimed territorial waters of North Korea. He didn't particularly want a confrontation just yet. Better to wait until the rest of the task force got there.

Sturdevant told the OOD to slow to fifteen knots and swing the ship on a southerly course, then he turned his back on the bridge personnel to gaze out the starboard window. The OOD hesitated, then stammered out the orders quickly, as if he'd forget them if he didn't repeat them as fast as possible.

The CO wondered what that was all about as he thought over the strange contact. The clanging of the bells on the engine order telegraph sounded muffled, as if someone had put a wall between them. He suddenly felt tired. A wave of nausea passed over him; he felt light-headed and put a hand on the bulkhead to steady himself. He looked toward where the helmsman should have been, but the helmsman had disappeared. Sturdevant tried to force his mind to understand where the helmsman was. He heard a thump next to him and swung around to discover that the OOD had hit the deck.

Chemical utility plane. Spraying crops. The words went round and round in his mind as he fought for consciousness. Finally the words hit home, and he knew why those planes were out at sea.

A gas attack!

He must warn the crew! He struggled to remember where the chemical warfare alarm was. That alarm had to be activated—the GQ alarm was not good enough. If the crew responded to general quarters they would only close hatches and watertight doors, but the ventilators would still be open, allowing the gas to invade the ship. He had to get the crew to set Circle William!

His eyes focused briefly on the aft bulkhead where the alarm controls and the intercom were located. He pushed himself away from the starboard window and lunged for the controls.

He never made it.

USS *TRUXTUN*

Captain Lawrence Degan's gaze swept the horizon and he marveled at the feeling of being so isolated from the rest of the world. Everywhere he looked he saw nothing but water, except when he looked off the port bow and saw the stern of the largest warship afloat, the USS *Truman*. His ship, the USS *Truxtun*, was in a plane guard position, at 165 degrees relative to the *Truman* and about a thousand yards away from the huge carrier. In the event of a plane or an aircrew going into the water, the ship would be in position to pick them up; hence the name of the position.

The captain lingered with the view and the feeling until his signal bridge got a *speed 15* signal from the *Truman*. When they got the *execute* signal they would slow down to fifteen knots. That would ease the worries of the ship's engineers, who bit their nails to the bone whenever the *Truman* went to flank speed to launch planes. The almost-thirty-year-old ship had to be pushed to its limit every time to maintain station on the carrier. The *Truxtun*'s pride was at stake; if they couldn't keep up with the carrier they'd never hear the end of it, especially during port calls, when the carrier sailors would make things miserable for the cruiser sailors.

Degan's eyes wandered over the water, which seemed to cover the entire earth. No land could be seen anywhere. It gave him a curious feeling of peace and comfort and isolation, like that of a man hidden away from the world in a mountain cabin. Degan sighed and closed his eyes.

The *execute* signal arrived and the OOD gave the proper order. Engine order telegraph bells rang. Main control answered the new change in speed and more bells rang. Degan could almost hear the engineers in the depths of the ship exhale with relief.

The signal bridge received a signal indicating that they should prepare to turn to starboard, such that they wind up on the *Truman*'s starboard beam rather than just follow in a line behind the carrier. Degan made sure that the OOD knew what to do. It was an elementary maneuver, one that was taught early in an officer's training, but if the OOD screwed it up the ship would get one royal ass-chewing. He closed his eyes once again and waited for the *execute* signal.

And waited.

"Captain." It was the OOD. Degan dragged his eyes open and looked at the concerned face of the lieutenant. "Sir, the *Truman* seems to be drifting to starboard."

Degan stared at him, waiting for the young officer to say something else. When the OOD just stared back, the captain cleared his throat. "What do you mean, drifting?" he asked.

The OOD looked puzzled. "Well sir . . . ," he hesitated, "we're keeping station on her all right, but the course was originally 095, and now it's 100."

Degan smiled. "Maybe Captain Sturdevant has to kick his helmsman in the ass." The OOD smiled and there was muffled laughter from the rest of the bridge crew.

"Helmsman, what is our course now?" asked Degan.

"105, sir."

The OOD's mirth was replaced by concern. "We didn't get the *execute* either, Captain."

Degan's smile vanished also. He rubbed his chin and slid from his chair to stand on the deck. After staring at the stern of the *Truman* for a few seconds, he shook his head. All seemed normal. He looked at the OOD.

"Tell the signal bridge to contact the *Truman* by light and ask them their course." The OOD gave him a crisp "aye, aye" and proceeded to carry out the order.

That should wake them up, thought Degan. He could imagine the straightlaced Captain Sturdevant getting that message and checking on their course. Sturdevant would be furious enough about the Hawkeye letting those planes in so close, but a helmsman wandering all over the ocean would be too much. He should be puffing with rage about now and screaming at the helmsman. Let's see, thirty seconds of screaming, then the hapless sailor would be relieved of his duties and kicked off the bridge—Degan glanced at his watch—right about now. Degan would relish teasing Sturdevant about this at the next port call. He'd have to be diplomatic about it, of course, since Sturdevant was senior to him and was already an admiral selectee. Degan smiled to himself once again. They should be correcting their course any second now.

"Captain, the signal bridge says the *Truman* doesn't acknowledge the message," the OOD said.

Sturdevant really has his problems with that crew, thought Degan. "Keep sending the message until she answers up," he replied.

"Aye, aye, sir," answered the OOD.

"What's our course now, helmsman?" asked the captain.

"It's 108, sir. It's getting hard to keep station on her, sir." He sounded apologetic. Degan shook his head in disgust and picked up a set of binoculars. He centered them on the superstructure of the carrier, located the 010 level, and stared for a while, trying to pick out the sailors manning the carrier's signal bridge.

Something doesn't look right, he thought. The *Truman* had gone to GQ, he mused, then secured from it a few minutes later. That had to be due to those slow-flying planes that had surprised the Hawkeye. Degan was about to go to GQ himself when the *Truman* went back to a normal watch as the planes moved off. That happened sometimes when there was a lot of air traffic around. But still . . .

A vague feeling of uneasiness ran through him. He let the binoculars scan the flight deck, the fantail, the sponsons. Something was damn peculiar. He looked over the flight deck and the island once again. He was making his third pass over the normally busy flight deck when the realization hit him like a thunderbolt.

No one was moving! He looked for some movement, any movement, but it was in vain. None of the crew was visible.

"What the hell kind of game is Sturdevant playing now?" he mumbled under his breath. He turned and looked at the puzzled OOD.

"They still don't answer up, Captain," the OOD stated flatly.

The captain shook his head as if to clear it. Well, he'd give them the once-over before he'd break radio silence. "Right standard rudder. All ahead flank. Let's see if we can get their attention if we come up on their starboard beam." The OOD nodded and relayed the orders to the bridge watch. Degan knew he had to open up some distance between the carrier and his ship. If he just increased speed without changing

course, he'd wind up less than five hundred yards awa
on its starboard beam. With the *Truman* wandering
his ship on the *Truman*'s starboard side, that few hund
disappear in a hurry. Degan waited until he had the head
then ordered, "Rudder amidships."

The *Truxtun* proceeded at a forty-five-degree angle to the *Truman*'s
slowly changing course until Degan felt that he had enough distance
between his ship and the carrier.

"Left standard rudder," he ordered. The *Truxtun*'s course became parallel
to the carrier's. "Rudder amidships." Then, "Make turns for fifteen
knots." The bridge sailors answered up in response to their orders and
got an individual "Very well" from their captain. Then they all fell
silent as they slowly slid by the huge gray ship on their port beam.

Degan's heart began to race as they passed the *Truman* and inspected the aircraft elevator aft of the island on the starboard side of
the vessel. No movement at all. They could see into the hangar bay,
where normally figures could be seen scurrying to and fro, but now
there was no one. This is incredible, thought Degan. He inhaled deeply;
it seemed as though he couldn't get enough air into his lungs. I'm probably
hyperventilating, he thought disgustedly.

The *Truxtun* pulled up alongside the elevators forward of the island.
The forward elevator was all the way down at the hangar bay level.
The scene on the elevator electrified Degan. There was a distinctive
yellow aircraft tractor used for hauling aircraft around the ship, and
there was an unconscious sailor draped over it!

Something had caused him to pass out, but what? Was the rest of
the crew unconscious? The thought of his imminent danger didn't occur
to him at first. There is a certain sense of being in totally separate
worlds when two ships pass each other at sea, and Degan fell victim
to that perception. His feeling was that the crew members of the *Truman*
were somehow unfortunate victims, but that he and his crew were immune
to their fate.

The sound came from behind him. It was a rasping, guttural moan
that sounded less than human. He whirled in surprise; the resulting
dizziness spun his mind seemingly in all directions. Degan's vision
cleared briefly—his OOD was hanging onto the engine order telegraph.
His mouth was wide open in a grotesque distortion of his features.

"C a p t a i n ! G a a s !"

Degan opened his mouth to speak but could not. He realized how wrong he had been—his crew was suffering the same fate as that of the *Truman* and he couldn't do a damn thing about it. Degan gagged, more with his helplessness than with the gas that was invading his body. Darkness advanced in on him and he found it irresistible. He fell backward striking his head on the forward bulkhead, and settled into a heap on the deck.

USS *TRUMAN*

Simmons swore under his breath. This was going to be one of those watches; the kind where everything takes a turn at going wrong. He was on watch in the forward enclosed operating station and, along with other watch personnel, stood in front of a large status board containing a vast array of indicators and gauges that monitored points in the engineering plant.

They had just gone back to a normal steaming watch from GQ and had gotten most of the sailors back into the forward engineering spaces for a major cleanup, called a field day. Simmons went back to mulling over the fight with Hastings and the CO's decided lack of action when a warning buzzer interrupted his thoughts. A row of indicators turned from green to red. The buzzer was manually turned off by Chief Taylor just as it was becoming annoying.

"It's number one switchboard, sir," he said to Simmons. "Looks like a complete electrical failure." The indicators went from red back to green as electronic switching circuits automatically transferred the critical electrical loads carried by number one to various other switchboards in a predetermined arrangement.

One indicator stubbornly refused to turn green. Great, just great, thought Simmons, all the loads switched except the one for ventilation. He held his hand up to the vent in the vain hope that the indicator might be wrong. Oh well, he sighed, he had a feeling that something was going to go wrong. It might as well be the ventilation as anything else. The electrician on watch hung up the phone.

"Number one board is completely down, all right. Murphy is checking into what caused it. He's a good man, sir. He'll have the answer in no time."

Simmons mumbled assent, then asked, "What parts of the ship don't have any ventilation?"

"Mostly this deck and below, sir. Just about all the forward engineering spaces."

Bells rang. The pointer on the engine order telegraph shifted to a new position, indicating a change of speed.

"How long before we get some ventilation?" asked Simmons.

"We could switch the circuit to a new switchboard manually, sir, but I hate to take anybody off the damage assessment of number one. The OOD will probably want to know what's going on in a hurry."

"I agree," said Simmons, "but as soon as the damage assessment is made, have them switch the circuit manually. It's going to get awfully stuffy in here before long." The electrician gave him an "aye, aye" and returned to his status board.

Simmons picked up the telephone and punched the three-digit number for the bridge. After the fifth ring he began to suspect that something was wrong. The phone was usually answered quickly. His eyes fell on the emergency number for the bridge, but he resisted the impulse to use it. He turned back to the electrician.

"Could the telephones be affected by the switchboard failure?" he asked.

The electrician kept his eyes on the status board and answered over his shoulder. "It's possible, sir, but they've got batteries for backup power, so all the phones should be working even if all the switchboards are out."

Simmons persisted. "How do you know the batteries are all right?"

The electrician turned to face the lieutenant. "I had a man check those batteries yesterday, sir." After a pause he said, "What's the matter, you don't get any dial tone?"

Simmons shook his head. "I don't get any answer."

The electrician shrugged his shoulders. "Maybe they're busy up there." Simmons shook his head again.

He lifted the phone one more time and dialed the bridge. No answer. He dialed the emergency number. That would bring them running. The phone rang and rang. No contact with the bridge, he thought nervously. How often does that happen? He hung up the phone and tapped the shoulder of the nearest sailor who was wearing a sound-powered phone set. "Are you on the bridge circuit?" he asked.

"Yes, sir, the 1JV, sir."

"Ask the bridge what's wrong with their telephones."

The sailor immediately pressed the talk button and tried to raise the bridge. The sailor tried repeatedly with no success, then raised his eyebrows as he looked at Simmons.

Simmons muttered an oath. What was wrong with the communications on this ship? He was getting nervous at the thought of what might cause a total communication breakdown, and almost leaped over to the intercom. He quickly set the selection dial to the bridge and pressed the lever.

"Bridge, this is forward EOS." No answer. He repeated the call three more times, each time his voice louder than the time before. Silence answered him. What the hell was going on here?

Chief Taylor walked up next to him. "Shall I send a runner up to the bridge?"

"Yeah, that's a good idea, Chief," said Simmons. "And get an electrician to find out what's wrong with the communications on this ship," he added in disgust.

Something told him that this was no simple equipment failure, otherwise not all methods of communication with the bridge would fail simultaneously. He had better tell the chief engineer. He dialed the engineering logroom and waited to hear the familiar voice of Commander Adamson. The phone kept ringing. Are they all asleep up there? He looked up the number for the E division office and dialed it quickly. No answer.

He had just come to the conclusion that the entire telephone system was out when he looked up and saw the runner they had sent to the bridge. He was staggering toward them and looked about to collapse. Simmons rushed over to him and threw an arm around him for support, then gently eased him down to the deck. The sailor was speaking incoherently and Simmons felt a flash of alarm rising within him.

In an instant Chief Taylor was next to them and immediately began to interrogate the ailing sailor. The sailor swallowed hard and made an intense effort to speak.

"Mr. Simmons, everybody . . . third deck . . . dead. . . ."

"Everyone is dead on the third deck?" asked Chief Taylor in disbelief. The sailor weakly nodded assent.

Simmons looked at the chief as he felt his scalp start to tighten. "Chief, is that possible?" He couldn't keep his voice from wavering.

Chief Taylor gave Simmons an intense look. "There's only one way to find out. I'm going up there."

Simmons felt he should object, but the big man was halfway up the ladder before Simmons could stop him. Seconds later, Taylor was back. The look on his face told Simmons the worst.

"There are bodies in the passageway up there! My God, Mr. Simmons, what happened?"

Simmons momentarily froze with panic. He pushed himself past the initial shock and forced his mind to think. He now had the reason for the lack of communication between this deck and the bridge. The implication of that conclusion hit him all at once with devastating impact. Everyone on the bridge was dead! Panic gripped him again, but he forced it down. He couldn't panic, not now! He and the few men on this deck might be the only crew members alive at this point. He glanced at the chief, who was shaken and waiting for him to speak.

"What could have killed those men, Chief?" asked Simmons.

Taylor answered after a pause. "Could it have been the food? Maybe there was something in the food that killed everybody."

Simmons thought for a moment. "If that was the case then why are the men on this deck all right and only the people above affected. No, I don't think it was the food."

The same idea occurred to both of them at the same time, and they gave each other a shocked look.

"The ventilation!" Simmons shouted. "Of course! There must be some kind of gas in the ship that affected everybody. The ventilation was cut off only to this deck and below, but everywhere else it was OK. That's why we're all right and everybody—"

He broke off the sentence in horror and ran back to the electricians. "Kill all ventilation to the entire ship! Do it now!" he shouted at the electrician. The electrician's eyes widened in amazement.

"Hurry, damn it, or we'll all be killed!"

The electrician gave him a crisp "aye, aye" and Simmons hurried back to Chief Taylor.

"Call sick bay," he said to Taylor, "See if they're still functioning. If they are, tell them what's happened and get them moving." Simmons thought furiously. The ship had chemical warfare equipment on board, including gas masks, but where was it? He had no idea. Better to go with what you know, he decided. The orders came quickly.

"Break out every OBA you can find. We might need them if the gas starts to seep down to this deck. Also, close all the hatches and vents on the unaffected decks. Better yet, make every man put on an OBA as soon as he gets one."

Chief Taylor started rattling off orders to some of the watch standers who had gathered around them. Simmons decided that despite the situation Taylor would be all right. Whatever happened, the big man would do his duty.

Simmons looked down at the sailor who had brought them the first hint of their terrifying situation. He was sitting on the deck with his head in his hands. He seemed very young, and very scared. Simmons tried to reassure him by putting his hand on the young fireman's shoulder. "How are you feeling?" he asked quietly.

"I'm OK now, sir," he said. Simmons knew he was stretching the truth.

"Just take it easy, buddy," Simmons told him. The sailor glanced up at Simmons and searched his face for some sign of hope. The look made Simmons feel a sense of responsibility as he had never felt it. The outcome of this situation and their very lives could depend on his actions in the next few minutes.

"Mr. Simmons, the whole crew . . . they're not dead, are they?"

The young man badly needed reassurance, but Simmons could give none. He looked away from the sailor and tried to sort out the details of their hellish predicament. Moments later, a sailor handed Simmons an OBA.

The oxygen breathing apparatus, or OBA, used chemicals to convert carbon dioxide to oxygen, and was used aboard ship as a self-contained supply of air during firefighting and other dangerous situations. Simmons started to strap on the equipment when another sailor arrived with his arms full of the chemical canisters used in the OBA. The sailor bent down and managed to drop a canister without spilling the rest, and rushed off to attend to his shipmates.

Simmons felt he had to make a survey of the ship to see what sections were functioning and, he thought grimly, discover how many casualties the crew had sustained.

He pulled off the metal cap from the top of the canister and inserted the canister into the bottom of the OBA, which lay across his stomach and chest. With his left hand he pushed the canister stop, which allowed the canister to be fully inserted, then turned the handwheel to force the canister all the way up into the front of the OBA.

He put on the facepiece, pulled the straps tight, and squeezed both hoses leading from the facepiece to the rest of the OBA, then inhaled to test for airtightness. Above all, he needed a good, airtight fit—it could save his life.

The facepiece collapsed as he inhaled, indicating a tight fit. He pulled a lanyard on the right side of the OBA, which initiated the supply of oxygen and as a by-product sent some harmless smoke into the facepiece. He took a few deep breaths and, to his relief, he felt a cool wisp of oxygen on his face. Simmons set the timer on the upper right side of the OBA to sixty minutes, then backed it off to forty-five minutes.

Chief Taylor came up to him in a rush. "Sick bay doesn't answer. Looks like second deck is knocked out also. The aft EOS doesn't answer up either. It's a good thing we had a lot of our people in the forward engineering spaces for the field day. I'll have to get some people back there to man the aft reactor and main engines."

Simmons pulled the OBA mask off his face. "That leaves only the hangar bay and the island in doubt," he said. He shuddered at the next thought. "If it is a gas attack, then they'll be knocked out also, but if the gas came from someplace inside the ship, then they'll be OK." He tried to hang on to the last possibility; a gas attack from outside the ship was too grim to think about.

"Chief, I'm going to make a survey of the ship and assess damage. You take charge of everything down here. If I'm not back in thirty minutes, then you'll know I'm dead and you're free to proceed on your own initiative." His words chilled him. They had never prepared him for this in any of the training he had ever taken.

Their eyes met, the white lieutenant and the black chief petty officer. Chief Taylor gripped Simmons's hand. "Good luck, Paul," he said softly.

Simmons pulled the mask down over his face and climbed the ladder.

Chapter Eight

Embarrassment subsided slowly in Lieutenant Majewski. He sought to hurry it along by concentrating on the tactical situation, but his thoughts kept returning to this business of the crop-dusting planes from nowhere. How had they gotten around this flying radar platform, their Hawkeye?

They could have approached the ship from the west, the side away from the bulk of the Hawkeye's radar coverage. The crop dusters were capable of very slow speeds, and by hugging the wave tops they just might have been able to sneak in close to the carrier. Maybe the signal processing in the Hawkeye's radar was a little *too* optimized for detecting fast, low-flying cruise missiles over water.

Majewski ground his teeth at the thought of letting planes wander all over the area in the vicinity of the carrier. Good thing they weren't fighters.

"Mr. Majewski."

He turned in his seat to look at the radar operator.

"I've got many targets, bearing 180 degrees, speed 110, course 270 degrees . . . uh, can't get the altitude yet. They're headed right for the task force."

Majewski glanced over his shoulder at the fuzzy green dots on the right side of the radar display. He frowned as his mind raced. What now? Something clicked in his mind. "Helicopters. See if you can get a count."

The radar operator nodded and turned toward the screen. Majewski's thoughts ran on. He'd better get Blackline flight up closer to the task force. He had vectored them to their current station to the south to keep an eye on the MiG-23s, but the enemy planes had gone back into North Korean airspace.

"Bogies! I've got twenty bogies, bearing 180, speed 750, course 270, angels 45!"

Majewski shot a look at the radar screen and caught a glimpse of multiple targets in close proximity to the helicopters just before the right side of the screen lit up with a solid green color.

"We've got jamming!" said the radar operator.

Majewski instantly keyed his transmitter. There was only one interpretation of the situation—the North Koreans were attacking! "Blackline flight, this is Eagle One! New vector 345, max speed! We have jamming prior to attack!"

He listened for a response and was greeted with a loud growl in his headphones. "Damn! They're jamming our comm!"

The throbbing of the turboprops increased to a scream and the plane banked over as the pilot tried to run from the attack. Majewski glanced at the radar display again and saw it suddenly clear as the North Koreans dropped their radar jamming. A series of small blips moved rapidly toward them.

"Kill the radar, now!" he yelled to the radar operator. If they were antiradiation missiles they would follow the radar signal back to its source, their aircraft. He thought of trying to contact Blackline flight, the *Truman*'s combat air patrol, but the growl in his headphones was unceasing. The 300-mph Hawkeye didn't have a chance against Mach 2 fighter aircraft.

He thought of his wife and children as an air-to-air missile slammed into the port engine and sheared off three quarters of the wing.

Eagle One fell cartwheeling into the sea.

Pak's mind raced along, keeping pace with the charging helicopter force, as he and his men flew only twenty feet above the waves of Korea Bay. They were attacking at last! His long wait was over and his country was about to come to glory. Adrenaline surged through his body and he fought the emotions raging within him. He had to remain calm and supervise the attack dispassionately or he was likely to make mistakes.

He gazed out the open side door unmindful of the rotor wash whipping his upper body. Just feet below the water raced by at a dizzying speed and the noise of the helicopter engines drummed and vibrated the crew until they became numb. His helicopter was in the first wave of four, with the other four waves of four helos each spread out in a rough rectangle behind him. Twenty helicopters, one thousand men, brave men to take on the most powerful navy in the world. Emotion welled up in him once more.

Pak shook it from him and glanced at his watch. He had the digital display on the timer function instead of the normal time of the day to facilitate recognition of the various milestones in the mission. They had been in the air just about ten minutes now. In five minutes they would don gas masks. Five minutes after that they should spot the task force. And then . . . Pak tried to concentrate his thoughts on the present.

One of his men stirred next to him. He excitedly pointed out the door into the distance. Pak's eyes flicked over to a streak of smoke high up and miles away. He brought his binoculars up to his eyes and centered them on the smoke. He saw nothing but the streak in greater detail. He quickly searched below it and a bit toward the North Korean coast. Pak went by it at first—it seemed like a piece of tinfoil driven by the wind—then went back and got a good view of the whirling, rapidly falling object. It was a peculiar-shaped object rolling end over end, and it took Pak a few seconds to recognize what it was.

Electricity shot through him. It was the American radar plane, that strange-looking aircraft with the mushroom on its back, now minus one wing! Their comrades in the air force had shot it down just as planned! He let the man next to him use the binoculars, and word spread rapidly among the fifty soldiers in the helicopter.

Pak turned to his men, his face filled with pride and determination. "Ch'ollima!" he said in a guttural voice.

His men took up the cry. Ch'ollima! Ch'ollima! Ch'ollima! They chanted it over and over. Their voices rose above the drumming of the helicopter blades and picked up volume until they were shouting at the top of their lungs, led by the ragged emotion of their leader, Col. Pak Myung Jo. Their feelings poured out and filled the inside of the helicopter.

Ch'ollima! Ch'ollima! Ch'ollima!

USS *OLDENDORF*

"Surface contact!"

Captain Anthony Mendicino whirled about to face the lookout on the starboard wing of the bridge. His ship, the USS *Oldendorf*, was performing task force screening duties and as such was far ahead and off the starboard bow of the USS *Truman*. The lookout started to give more information as all eyes fell on him.

"Belay that! *Air* contact! Helicopters! A lot of them! Bearing 020!"

Now, what the hell, thought Mendicino. First, some sort of weird, slow-flying planes that fly off immediately, and now helicopters in the middle of Korea Bay. The North Koreans were up to something, but he couldn't fathom a guess.

The captain got his own glasses on the helos and tried to estimate their course and speed. They seemed to be heading directly for the *Truman*. He'd have to cut them off, and fast!

"General quarters! Battle stations air! Right full rudder. All ahead flank!" He turned to the intercom as his men scrambled to follow his orders. "Combat! Give me an intercept course!"

CIC came back quickly. "Permission to turn on radar, sir."

Mendicino moaned under his breath. That was stupid. He should have remembered that they were under radio and radar emissions silence. Damn Hawkeye should have alerted them. Damn airdales!

"Permission granted." He looked up at the OOD.

"095 should do it, sir," the OOD offered.

"Come to course 095!" ordered the captain. He peered through his binoculars once more. The OOD was right on about the course—095 is what he would have recommended.

"Prepare to launch Sparrows!" he ordered. One of the telephone talkers on the bridge repeated his order twice into his microphone.

Mendicino pressed the talk lever on the bridge's intercom. "Combat, got a solution yet?"

There was a brief hesitation. "Bridge, combat. Negative, sir. They're at too low an altitude. They keep popping in and out of the sea returns."

Mendicino shook his head in frustration. Seasparrow was a surface-to-air missile with semiactive homing. It used the ship's radar to send electromagnetic pulses and the missile itself to receive them in order to home in on a target. If the ship's radar wasn't getting good returns, then the Sparrow's wouldn't either.

"Let's get 'em with Phalanx, then," ordered Mendicino. "Don't fire until my order."

"Aye, aye, sir. Phalanx on manual."

Mendicino turned and eyed the rapidly approaching helicopters. "They're coming up on the port bow." The Phalanx amidships on the port side would have to handle the initial engagement, but first he'd have to attend to the "amenities."

He walked over and picked up the handset of the bridge RT, the radiotelephone. The speaker issued static. He was forced to break radio silence. He pushed the talk button.

"Unidentified aircraft, this is the U.S. Navy warship on your 195 at three miles. State your intentions!" Mendicino let the talk button go. The static out of the speaker was unceasing. He pushed the talk button once again.

"Unidentified aircraft, understand that we will open fire if you proceed on your current course. State your intentions and change course!"

The port lookout spoke up. "They're heading straight for the *Truman*!"

"Raise the *Truman* on the RT and tell her the situation," Mendicino ordered. The thought occurred to him that the huge carrier might not know exactly what was going on. That was why his ship had taken the "point." They were to find out what was up ahead and protect the carrier if necessary.

He looked through his glasses one more time. The helicopters were obviously North Korean, but they didn't seem to be gunships. That puzzled him. If they weren't gunships, then what were twenty helicopters doing in the middle of Korea Bay?

"Any course change?" he asked the port lookout.

His reply was immediate. "No, sir."

That was it, then. He couldn't let them get any closer. "Port Phalanx open fire!"

The order was relayed, and seconds later the close-in weapon system let fly with a barrage of depleted-uranium-cased bullets. The gun made an incredibly rapid puffing sound as it threw a wall of slugs at the low-flying helicopters.

Mendicino ran his hand over his face as fatigue suddenly swept over him. He looked across the bridge. The men were all weaving at their posts as if drunk. The starboard lookout was nowhere to be seen; he had fallen to the deck as the gas overcame him. The sailor at the screw pitch controls fell over on top of the console and slid heavily to the deck, knocking the screw pitch setting to zero. The ship would go dead in the water even though the engines were still running. A wave of intense dizziness passed over Mendicino. Panic ran through him as he fought to remain conscious.

What was happening?

Lieutenant Roger Lorenz stood among a host of displays and electronics equipment in the combat information center of the USS *Oldendorf*. As the tactical action officer, or TAO, he was responsible for operation of the combat systems on the ship. He viewed most of the equipment surrounding him with some disgust. Most of it was of no use right at the moment, except for one display that teased the CIC crew with glimpses of the oncoming North Korean helicopters. The North Korean jamming had been especially severe—Lorenz had never seen it so intense—and it had rendered the radar equipment useless. But then the jamming had lifted, and they intermittently got a good set of returns even though their targets were too distant and too low in altitude, and the radar returns from the targets were mixed in with the returns from the sea. They were using these glimpses to direct the Phalanx, along with their own guesses as to where the helos were at any one moment.

The intermittent returns weren't enough to light the firing indicator on the Phalanx control console. The lack of the light meant that the Phalanx's computer was unable to calculate the proper aim for the targets. Lorenz also had an inkling that maybe the Phalanx didn't recognize the helos as a threat; the aircraft were too slow.

The CIC crew's success or failure with the Phalanx would be due directly to any evasive action the enemy would take. Even the most elementary evasive tactics would be enough to escape most of the Phalanx's lethal barrage.

It was almost impossible to tell whether or not they got a hit; he needed lookouts above decks to guide him. He was standing between radar displays, where he could scan them all in a second if necessary, and was wearing sound-powered phones with a long cord to enable him to move around freely. He fingered the sound-powered phone button to speak to a phone talker on the bridge.

"Ask the captain for permission to put Phalanx on automatic." Maybe the gun system itself would have better luck if he took the man out of the loop.

A few seconds went by with no reply. Lorenz repeated his request.

Again no reply. He glanced at the radar screen. The helicopters would be out of range soon.

He felt the ship suddenly slow down. Alarm ran through him. He raced over to the intercom.

Pak and his men were grim now, their emotion spent by the chanting. They all had gas masks on, and they nervously fidgeted to get a glimpse out the open side of the helicopter. Pak swallowed hard as he stared at the lead vessel in the American task force. The gas should have knocked out the entire crew by now, but the American warship had turned to intercept them. Did it catch the fringe of the gas cloud? Or did it miss it completely? Pak suddenly knew what was missing from his attack force. Helicopter gunships! If he had some, he could engage the ship with them and go on to attack the *Truman* with the rest of his men.

The helicopter pilots, without orders, increased speed to outrun the ship and its weapon systems, and the drumming of the engines and rotor blades became unbearable.

The helicopters could outrun any ship, but Pak knew they would never outrun a missile traveling at Mach 2. He stared intensely through his binoculars at the horizontal box at the aft end of the ship just above the five-inch gun mount on the stern. That was where the missiles would come from—the Seasparrow octuple launcher. The launcher began to move, sending adrenaline coursing through him.

Pak shoved his way through his men and got up between the pilot and copilot. He shouted through his gas mask. "Break radio silence! Contact Ch'ollima 2. Get an air strike on that ship!"

Both pilot and copilot nodded. They both tried several times without success. Pak could see the grimaces through the gas masks.

"Are we still jamming?" he asked his men. They shook their heads. The jamming from incredibly powerful transmitters located on the coast of North Korea was carefully timed to occur at the onset of the operation, so that communications would be cut between the American radar plane and the combat air patrol, between each ship, and from ship to shore. If an alert got out he and his men were as good as dead. Pak cursed in an explosion of frustration. The jamming wasn't long enough! What had happened to his air support?

A glance back at the U.S. Navy ship sent a shiver up his spine. The missile launcher was pointed in their direction, but it hadn't launched yet. There was a rapid flashing and puffing of some smoke near the middle of the port side of the ship. The Americans were firing their Phalanx gun system at them—20mm rounds at three thousand a minute. His attack force would be shredded to pieces!

Pak gasped in despair as he saw flame out of the corner of his eye. He craned his neck out the side of his aircraft and saw one of the helicopters in the last wave explode into flame and immediately crash into the sea.

"NO!" he screamed into his gas mask. He couldn't sit by and see his men slaughtered even before they got into battle! His men deserved much more than that! He turned back to the pilot's cabin and grabbed the copilot in desperation.

"Contact Ch'ollima 3! Give them these coordinates! Tell them to launch now!"

The copilot shouted acknowledgment and immediately got busy over his radio. Pak cursed to himself and watched the distance between the American warship and his helicopter force start to slowly widen. It was too slow—he needed Ch'ollima 3's land-based cruise missiles to take out the American warship. He was taking a great risk by giving Ch'ollima 3 their coordinates. The missiles could attack his helicopters as well.

Pak looked back at the remainder of his helicopter force. Before his eyes he saw the side of a helicopter in the last wave collapse inward as the wall of lead from the Phalanx found another target. The landing wheels folded upward at the same time as the rotor blades tilted over to an almost vertical position. Bodies spilled out and fell like rag dolls to splash into the sea and be immediately left behind. The helicopter's insides turned red and went nose down, hitting the sea and sending a geyser of water into the air.

The Phalanx pounded away as Pak groaned in despair.

PYONGYANG, NORTH KOREA

Kang sprang from his chair. The call was loud and clear through the comm system. Pak was requesting a cruise missile launch on his own position!

The colonel who ran the headquarters staff had his back to Kang but sensed the sudden movement behind him. Some of the more junior members of the staff glanced at the general, then looked expectantly at the colonel. The colonel slowly turned and looked at his superior. He saw in Kang's eyes something he had never seen before. Indecision and fear of failure had never been part of Kang's nature. The colonel slowly turned back to the staff hovering near the status board.

"Contact Ch'ollima 1," the colonel ordered in a somber voice. He would have to remind the helicopter force that the coordinates they had just issued were their present location.

Kang's mind raced. Pak's helicopter force was still about three miles from the *Truman*. Pak had just called for an air strike from Ch'ollima 2, his air force, but had gotten no reply. Pak's force never said what the target was, but the air strike was probably intended for the lead ship in the task force. What was happening? Why didn't Ch'ollima 2 answer up? Except for Pak's desperate call, his strict orders on radio silence were being obeyed to the letter and were creating a great deal of confusion at headquarters. Pak must have called for the cruise missile strike because he got no response from the squadron assigned to fly cover. Pak would never do anything like that unless he was in dire straits. Kang was stunned. His forces had been attacked before they even got close to the carrier!

Kang suddenly became aware that every eye in the room was on him. He had to make the decision. Countermand the order or let the strike happen. Pak was an outstanding officer and knew the operation inside and out. He did not make rash decisions. It was time to trust the officer in tactical command.

"Contact Ch'ollima 3," he ordered. The colonel turned to his staff to ensure that they obeyed. He needn't have worried. When the orders came from Kang personally, the staff was unusually quick to comply. The colonel turned back to Kang and swallowed hard. The general gave him the order he dreaded.

"Tell Ch'ollima 3 I want a five-missile launch on those coordinates."

If Pak had failed, there were Ch'ollima 4 and Ch'ollima 5, thought Kang grimly.

NORTH KOREAN COAST

The colonel in command of Ch'ollima 3 looked over the line of mobile radar trucks and missile launchers that were strung out over the North Korean coast. He had just received a panicked call from Pyongyang ordering him to launch five missiles at an American warship at a given set of coordinates. The coordinates told him that the target was about fifty miles offshore, and as such it was at the limit of the Silkworm's range. It made it easy for him and his men—just point the missiles and fire away—but he didn't like it.

He grumbled to himself. His missiles were the active homing type; that is, they had a complete radar system within them and did not need to receive radar pulses from any outside source. By the time his missiles got within the radar range of the coordinates he was given, the target could be somewhere else. All the American ship would have to do is travel away from shore two to three miles and it would be beyond the range of the missiles.

He abruptly got word back from the radar platforms on the trucks that they couldn't detect the ship. He could have told them that. With his radar antennas about six hundred feet above sea level, the radar horizon was about forty-five miles away; beyond that the radar signals just kept traveling straight out into space. The American ship was fifty miles out—well over the horizon—so it couldn't be seen by his radar.

The American ship could very well hear his radar, though. Sensitive equipment could pick up enough of the signal refracted by the atmosphere to register on their screens. It was stupid for his forces to turn on their radars, but procedures were procedures, and he didn't dare change them. His career could be on the line.

He mused for a moment on the panicked nature of the order. He hadn't been briefed on the whole mission, just that his missile batteries might be used. Launching missiles to a point in the middle of Korea Bay at the limit of their range seemed a desperate measure. Someone must be in trouble. Still, orders were orders.

One missile battery came back over the comm net and declared that they were ready to launch. The other four ready reports came tumbling in over the now-chaotic comm net. He gave them the sequence of launch and ordered the launches in five-second intervals so that each missile's radar wouldn't get confused by another that was too close behind. His men were excited. They knew that these were the first shots of an upcoming battle, and they had the honor of making them. The colonel just worried that everything would go well. He looked expectantly at the first missile launcher.

Seconds later, the launcher flung the twenty-foot-long, fifty-five-hundred-pound missile into the air, an enormous cone of fire shooting out behind it. The colonel followed it out to the horizon with his field glasses. The radio altimeter in the missile came on and brought the missile down to a hundred feet above the water. All seemed well. They only had to fly six minutes, then end their mission in a flash. That is, if they detected the American ship.

The other four missiles leaped into the air at five-second intervals and rocketed out to sea.

USS *OLDENDORF*

Lorenz's race to the intercom was halted by the beeping of equipment nearby. He recognized the sound and immediately went cold. The electronic countermeasures (ECM) equipment was alerting the operator that it had detected a possible threat. He got to the equipment in a flash and peered at the green symbols against the black background that was the ECM equipment display.

The display had three concentric rings, the innermost for friendly emitters, the next ring for emitters classified as threats by the equipment, and the outer ring for enemy missile launchers, such as aircraft or ships. Lorenz saw one symbol in the outer ring; it had a bright square around it, indicating that it hadn't been evaluated by the operator yet. The operator maneuvered his joystick, and the bright square around the symbol in the outer ring was replaced by a circle.

Lorenz looked at the upper left side of the display. The cryptic numbers and letters told him of a situation for which he had trained many hours. His eyes focused on the designation HY-2G. They were being scanned by a Silkworm radar on the coast of North Korea. The ECM gear also told him that there was a high probability that missiles had been launched.

A butterflylike symbol suddenly appeared in the middle ring. The ECM equipment beeped again until the operator assessed the threat. The symbols in the middle ring suddenly went from one to five. The *Oldendorf* was in real trouble.

"We've got Silkworms . . . incoming at bearing 040!" Lorenz gasped for breath. His eyes wanted to close. He forced them open. The ECM console operator began to cough violently.

Lorenz remembered to push the talk button on his phones. "Incoming! Vampire! Vampire! Five at 040!" The last sentence was a whisper. He swung his body around and viewed the ship's CIC. Most operators were slumped over their consoles. Lorenz staggered, grabbed an overhead equipment box handle, and almost fell.

The North Koreans had done something to them, he was sure of that. Gas, biological warfare, something. His vision started to fade and he knew he had only seconds of consciousness remaining. Lorenz flung himself at the ECM console and set the chaff dispensers to automatic launch. He slid to the deck and crawled to the Phalanx console. Gasping for air he turned the key that set the Phalanx gun system on automatic. Then he fell to the deck and slipped into unconsciousness.

Four and a half minutes into the flight the five Silkworm missiles reached the radar horizon between them and the American vessel. Their radars easily detected the huge return from the starboard side of the *Oldendorf*. They automatically went into their terminal attack phase and dropped down in altitude to roar in at the USS *Oldendorf* at more than five hundred miles an hour and only fifty feet above the water.

The *Oldendorf*'s starboard Phalanx radar detected the incoming missiles and wheeled the multiple-barreled weapon around to face the oncoming threat. The *Oldendorf*, its gas turbine engines still turning at a high rate of speed, but with its screws at zero pitch, went dead in the water.

The ECM computer calculated the optimum point and optimum tube from which to fire chaff and automatically fired the charge into the space between the oncoming missiles and the ship. The chaff went off with a popping sound and spread tinfoil strips in a wide arc that slowly fluttered down to the sea.

The first two Silkworms gained altitude to follow the radar return produced by the chaff. They plunged into the middle of it and detonated in an airburst a mile short of the ship. The explosions scattered the chaff, punching a hole in it.

The remaining missiles weren't fooled by the scattered chaff; they relentlessly bored in on the now-stopped ship. The Phalanx opened up on the lead missile, the gun's computer constantly adjusting the aim by measuring the miss distance between the bullet's trajectory and the incoming missile. Seconds later, the high-density slugs found the Silkworm's warhead and turned it into a ball of flame.

The radar automatically went to the next perceived threat—the next inbound missile. It opened fire, its multiple barrels spinning and throwing slugs at an incredible rate. The Phalanx caught the tail section, shearing it off and leaving the warhead to fall and detonate harmlessly in the sea. The *Oldendorf* fired more chaff, but it went behind the last on-rushing missile.

The Phalanx ripped at it all the way up to five hundred yards away. The gun system got a few slugs into the body of the missile, causing the nose to tip up and the missile to gain some altitude. The missile radar, suddenly not seeing a target, detonated the thousand-pound warhead short of the ship, and the resulting blast rolled the ship to port.

The *Oldendorf* rolled back upright and settled down, its engines churning, its crew asleep.

Pak squinted in the distance at the rapidly retreating American destroyer that was in the process of being swallowed up by the thin mist that hung over the sea. He had seen a flash but couldn't tell if the ship was damaged. His binoculars weren't much help; they only brought the haze on the horizon closer. Word of the explosion got around the soldiers in the helicopter and they cheered. Pak let them. They didn't have to know that he suspected that the American warship was undamaged. If they thought that their country had struck back, then morale would go sky-high, and it would get them up for the attack that was to come. But would the destroyer survive and come after them in spite of the cruise missile attack?

Pak bit his lip and felt his stomach churn. He worried so much about his men that it would be the death of him, he thought. He lifted the binoculars to his eyes once again and scanned the sea for the remains of the two helicopters that the destroyer had shot down. He found them after a short search. There wasn't much to see. One tail rotor was sticking up from the sea and there was some debris nearby, but that was all. No sign of the hundred men who died in the helicopters.

One hundred men! His men! Trained for months on end for this day and they died before they could get to fight. Pak gritted his teeth. The Americans would pay for this. Their weapon systems were all they had; they let machines do their fighting. It would be a different story when he met them face to face. Man against man they would be grossly inferior to Pak's men.

What effect would his loss of those hundred men have on his mission? He thought for a bit as stoically as he could. The two helicopters were in the last wave, the one that contained his intelligence section. They were supposed to supervise the sailing of the carrier to Nampo, but now the intelligence section was cut in half. He shook his head in frustration. He would have to supplement their numbers with other soldiers.

The pilot turned and waved to him through the hatch leading to the pilot's cabin. He shouted something through his gas mask, but Pak couldn't understand him. Pak got over to the excited pilot as he gestured out the windshield. Pak got his binoculars to his eyes. Electricity ran through him. The men knew without being told. Pak could hear them raising the chant once again even though it was muffled by their gas masks. Ch'ollima! Ch'ollima! Ch'ollima!

The USS *Truman* lay on the horizon.

Chapter Nine

Hastings shuddered slightly as he remembered the "cat" shot. In all his years as a jet fighter pilot, that was his single most terrifying moment. The tension, the dryness in his mouth, the knot in his stomach were familiar feelings just before a huge invisible hand hurled him and his fragile aircraft into the air to fly . . . or crash if everything didn't go exactly right.

Commander Ron Hastings sighed and shifted his weight for the second time in less than a minute. His shoulder harness restricted his movement as he squirmed more than usual while remembering his fears of the catapult launch. The next tense moments for him would be his landing on the flight deck. He had prayed on more than one occasion during the suspenseful seconds just before the tailhook catches the wire. A sensation of relief would flood through him after feeling his plane jolt to a stop. He had never crashed, at least not when he was still in the aircraft. Once he had to "punch out" during a training flight near Pensacola, Florida, when he was an ensign. He was on one of his initial solo flights and he had had a flameout. That was an experience he was in no hurry to repeat. He had been lucky to get his wings.

His eyes scanned the instruments for the ten thousandth time since the launch, and his mind once again unconsciously noted that all was well. He thought of his flameout again and instinctively was reminded of the ejection seat handles above and behind his head.

He had come to hate the thought of those handles and was glad they were out of view. The handles' existence intimated that men and machines are not perfect, and that their imperfection might be the cause of the handles' use someday. Hastings's eyes scanned the instruments again as he forced his thoughts to take a more optimistic turn.

There were compensating factors for all the anxious moments that a pilot faces. A man could experience exhilaration known only to a few while flying for the United States Navy. A well-designed fighter aircraft, such as his F-14 Tomcat, put through its paces was a fantastic experience. The anticipation of flight after launch made bearable the anxiety of the rough handling of the catapult. Once in the air, a sense of freedom would inundate Hastings—the reward for having suffered at the hands of the ship. A feeling of power would slowly suffuse his being, and he would long to shed his discipline and slash through the sky at the limits of the aircraft. Power to defy gravity, to climb, to roll and dive, power to race through the sky at more than twice the speed of sound—all constituted an exhilaration beyond description. Upon landing, the feeling would fade as he was reintroduced to the role of a mere mortal.

Hastings shifted his weight again while idly wondering when the TACCO, or the tactical coordinator, on the Hawkeye would come on the communications net to give them a vector to their new position. It was a restricted world he was in, a world of computer-generated displays, gauges, flight procedures, and, above all, very tight discipline. Even with the discipline, he wouldn't have traded his job for any other in the world.

He glanced out the side of his bubble canopy at the world thirty thousand feet below. The sun glinted strongly off the sea, giving it the appearance of wrinkled tinfoil. On the horizon to his left he could barely make out the shape of the landmass of the Korean peninsula. It was an ideal day for flying; there were very few clouds and the visibility was almost unlimited.

Hastings's mind began to wander, his thoughts eventually returning to his fight with Simmons. He had made an ass out of himself and had very nearly ruined his career. He resolved not to let it happen again. With considerable effort he put any thoughts of Simmons out of his mind. It wouldn't do to get distracted, not while flying this kind of aircraft. The least little mistake and you're dead.

"Commander." The voice over the intercom belonged to his RIO, radar intercept officer, Lt. (jg) Rick Norris.

Hastings turned and gave a half look to the rear in an attempt to catch Norris in his peripheral vision. "Yeah, Rick," replied Hastings.

"Commander, we got jamming on the comm net."

"Try to raise Eagle One."

"I've tried, sir, and it's no go."

"How about Kingpin?"

"Trying now, sir." Norris gave it five iterations, then got back on the plane's intercom.

"No contact with Kingpin, sir." Before Hastings could reply, Norris added, "Jamming's lifted." There was a hopeful note in his voice. "Shall we contact the ship, sir?"

"We'll give Eagle One a few more minutes," said Hastings, wondering whether some of the enthusiasm of youth had in Norris's case turned into the anxiety of youth. Periodic jamming was commonplace near North Korea.

Hastings smiled to himself. He had had quite a few RIOs, but Norris had to be the youngest. He was out of flight training just about six months when he was assigned to Hastings's squadron.

The commander thought of the RIO's role in aerial combat and hoped that Norris had stayed awake during his training classes. The RIO selected the various modes of the aircraft's radar, and during combat could determine priority of attack on multiple targets while controlling the launch of the plane's Phoenix missiles.

He had Norris check their position, but they were still far from their next turn. His squadron was flying combat air patrol about seventy-five miles south of the *Truman* near the DMZ. They had chased some MiG-23s toward the south, then broke off as the MiGs fled toward North Korean airspace. Eagle One then told them to fly a standard "racetrack" pattern, extending about fifty miles in the north-south direction and twenty miles in the east-west direction. They had just made a turn to the south and had six minutes to go before they turned eastward.

The TACCO was supposed to give them a new vector to their next position; this southern leg, which they were flying at the moment, was supposed to be their last. However, they still had plenty of time for the TACCO on the Hawkeye to contact them. If he didn't give them a new course in time, they would continue to fly the racetrack pattern, he decided.

Hastings switched himself from the plane's intercom to the communication net, which put him in radio contact with the other planes in the flight. It seemed to Hastings that half the squadron was engaging in small talk, but after a few sharp words the squadron quieted down. He shook his head. He would never know why fighter pilots flapped their jaws so much. Nervousness, maybe. Chatter on the comm net was a constant problem.

Two minutes to go before the eastward turn, noted Hastings. Maybe young Norris was right. Maybe he should contact Eagle One, or Kingpin, which was the rather obvious code word of the day for the *Truman*.

"Eagle One, this is Blackline flight. Over." Silence greeted Hastings's ears. Now what? he thought.

"Eagle One, Blackline flight, do you read? Over." No response.

"Blackline Leader to Blackline 103, how's my transmission? Over."

The answer came immediately. "Blackline 103 to Blackline Leader, receive you five by five, Skipper."

What the hell, thought Hastings, if it wasn't radio failure, then why didn't the Hawkeye answer? Did the jamming have something to do with it? One minute to go before their turn, the one they weren't supposed to make. TACCO was never this late, he thought. He tried the Hawkeye's auxiliary frequencies and the ship's communication network frequencies with no success. There wasn't any jamming. Not only were the Hawkeye and the *Truman* silent, but he couldn't raise the escort vessels either.

He ordered some of the other planes in the flight to try to contact either the Hawkeye or the *Truman*. He still had the thought that maybe his transmitter was defective. Another idea struck him. Why hadn't the Hawkeye or the ship tried to contact them? His receiver was operating properly.

The other planes concluded their attempts to raise the task force, with no success. Maybe they were in trouble. Could they be under attack? What would cause complete lack of communication? There was nothing to do but head back to the *Truman* and assess the situation.

"Blackline flight, this is Blackline Leader. Make a 180 to the left on my mark. Acknowledge."

"Blackline 101, roger."

"102, roger."

"103, roger."

"106, roger."

"107, roger."

"109, roger."

"110, roger."

"Blackline flight, this is Blackline Leader. Ready . . . mark!"

They had been flying along in two groups of four planes each, the leader of each group the leftmost plane, and the other three aircraft to the right and slightly behind the leader. Hastings led one group and the squadron's XO the other.

At their squadron leader's command the flight executed the turn in perfect formation. Hastings took a quick look around and noted with satisfaction that everyone was in proper position. He had a young squadron—the XO wasn't much older than his RIO—but they were all highly trained professionals. If it came to a combat situation, he couldn't have wanted better pilots flying with him.

Norris's voice cut across his thoughts. "Commander." He sounded tense.

"Yeah, Rick."

"I have twenty bogies, 10 degrees to starboard, angels four five. Range 125 miles."

NAVCOMSTA YOKOSUKA, JAPAN

Ensign Frank Clagett started slightly as he came out of his reverie. He opened his eyes and gazed at his surroundings as he gave a bored yawn. He decided that a naval communications station, a NAVCOMSTA, was one of the most depressing places to be during the spring in Japan. It was a gorgeous day outside, but he wasn't going to enjoy it because he was the communications watch officer for this particular eight-hour period. He felt doubly cheated because the building had no windows; he couldn't even gaze outside to enhance his daydreams.

"Contact report!"

A first class petty officer, one of the several controllers under Clagett, jumped to his feet and ran over to the fleet center side of the room. He and a radio operator studied a busy printer.

"Damn, it's garbled. ZDK them when they're finished. I'll tell QC," said the controller.

The radio operator nodded and the controller went over to QC, the quality-control area, which contained monitors on all the communications circuits in the COMSTA. After being informed of a possible malfunction they would begin elaborate fault isolation procedures to check the questionable circuit. The radio operator had just typed his retransmit request for the second time when the controller returned and waited to check the text of the received message. They waited several minutes in vain for a response.

"Log out the circuit, switch to the backup frequency, and try to raise 'em," the controller said finally. The operator nodded his head and the controller walked over to the QC area again.

Clagett watched the controller return to the radio operator after having an animated conversation with the QC personnel and wondered when the controller would retransmit the contact report. They were almost always flash messages, the highest priority of any message in the system, and they had to be retransmitted immediately.

Clagett yawned disgustedly and lifted himself out of the chair. He would have to hurry these people along. As he walked up to the controller and the radio operator, their voices were transformed from a murmur among the general noise of the room to intelligible speech.

" . . . but the crypto gear is still locked on," protested the controller.

"What the hell do you want me to do? I still can't get anything," responded the operator.

"Well, log the damn thing out. I guess we'll have to go to HICOM to reach them," said the controller.

"What's going on here?" demanded Clagett. "Let's get that contact report retransmitted now."

The controller looked up with a start—he hadn't heard the officer approach. "I was going to wait for a clear copy, Mr. Clagett," he said.

"What's the matter with it?"

The controller gave his mouth a twist. "It's garbled."

"Then get them back and have them retransmit it."

"We can't. They don't answer up on the RATT circuit." He hesitated— the mockery in his voice gone and only puzzlement remaining.

"We got the garbled message, then we had some brief jamming, but it's gone now. And we can't raise 'em. The crypto gear is still locked on, sir. I don't understand it. If they lost their transmitter, the gear would lose lock. So, it can't be that. It's as if the transmitter is on but they're not sending anything." He gave the young officer a puzzled look.

The controller was right, Clagett thought; it was strange. Maybe the ship had lost only its receiver and that was the reason they didn't answer the retransmit request.

"All right, go to HICOM to reach them. I'll check QC to see if our transmission is all right." The enlisted men nodded and Clagett went over to the QC area. After satisfying himself that their transmitters were functioning properly, Clagett returned, only to face consternation on the controller's face.

"They don't answer up. We've tried all the frequencies, sir, and we get nothing." He paused. His eyes took on a new look—fear. "I hope you're ready for this."

"What now?" demanded Clagett.

"I tried to contact the other ships on every circuit available to us." Again he hesitated. "Nobody answers. None of them. The whole damned task force has disappeared!"

The sense of urgency in the enlisted man's voice sent a chill up Clagett's spine. His mind raced. How could that happen? He thought about trying to contact the aircraft from the carrier, but lack of contact with aircraft that far away was normal—they didn't have the range. But the ships? One ship maybe, but a whole task force? What the hell was going on out there? He had to inform his superiors. With a curt word over his shoulder to the controller to keep trying to establish contact, he hurried back to his desk.

He got the command duty officer's phone number from the plan of the day and with shaking hands he quickly dialed the phone. The U.S. Navy doesn't lose contact with a carrier task force every day in the week, he thought. Could this be the opening shot of another war? His chill deepened. Possibly, ground troops were already engaged on the Korean peninsula.

The phone rang several times before a woman's voice answered. Clagett guessed she was the wife of the CDO, the command duty officer. When Clagett identified himself she attempted to make small talk until he cut her short. She sounded very much offended as she told him to hold the line for her husband.

After an irritating delay, the CDO was on the line. "Lieutenant Commander Shark." He seemed out of breath.

"Mr. Shark, this is Ensign Clagett, the communications watch officer." His voice rose a little at the end as if he was asking a question.

"Yes, Mr. Clagett," was the reply.

Clagett took a deep breath. "We've got problems, sir. I think your presence is required."

"What kind of problems?" was Shark's surprised reply.

"It's not anything I can discuss over the phone, sir," said Clagett.

"All right, I'll be there in ten minutes," said Shark in resignation.

"Thank you, sir," replied Clagett and hung up. He felt as if an enormous weight had been lifted from his shoulders. Shark would know what to do.

Clagett looked up as the controller approached. "Any luck yet?" Clagett asked.

"No, sir, it's the same as before, except that the *Truman*'s transmitter just timed out."

Clagett nodded. The timer was used to protect against inadvertent radio transmission during combat conditions. A radio transmitter was like a lighthouse to navigators; the transmitter's signals could be used by the enemy to locate the ship. The timer turned off the transmitter after a brief period if no messages were being sent.

"I thought you might need this," said the controller.

For the first time Clagett noticed the paper in the controller's hand; it was the garbled message from *Truman*. He took it from the controller and read it.

ZAATZYUW RUDDMAX 7321 127 1005-T T T T RUKKDAA ZNY T T T T T
Z 070115Z MAY
FM CTF 78.1
TO COMSEVENTHFLT
BT
T O P S E C R E T
1. RADAR CONTACT FIFTEEN BOGIES, APPROX. ALT. 500 FT. QZFKE . . .

The rest of the message was illegible. The obvious conclusion was that the *Truman* had been attacked just after the message was sent and while they were being jammed. But the jamming was brief, too brief for an attack on a task force. Besides, it was normal these days to get periodic jamming from North Korea.

Clagett wracked his brain for a possible solution. The only possibility that fit all the information was that all the radio operators on all the ships were out of action but the radio equipment wasn't. That didn't make any sense at all, he decided, especially if three ships were involved.

He glanced up from the message as he heard the outside door open and watched Lieutenant Commander Shark enter the COMSTA. A few seconds later he was standing next to Clagett.

"What's up, Frank?" he said in a low voice.

Clagett handed him the message from the *Truman*.

"We received this message at 1015. When we requested a retransmit on it we got nothing. No answer at all. The worst part is that we don't get any answer from any of the ships in CTF 78.1."

"Jamming?" asked Shark.

"Only briefly after we lost contact with the task force. It's been all clear for about twenty minutes now. Our transmitters are all right, also," replied the ensign.

Concern mounted on the lieutenant commander's face. "Any ideas, mister?" he asked.

"I can't figure it out, sir," Clagett replied. He paused while staring off into space. "Another thing, sir, the crypto gear was locked on until the transmitter timed out. That means their transmitter was still working, but they weren't transmitting any messages."

Shark screwed up his face as he replied to Clagett's last remark. "There's nothing much we can do except keep trying to contact the task force. We'd better tell COMSEVENTHFLT so he can get some planes out there to see what the hell's going on." Shark lowered his voice. "Damn, I hope they're all right."

Clagett swallowed hard and followed Shark over to the row of offices behind his desk.

"What are the other two ships with the *Truman*?" asked Shark as he fumbled in his pocket for the key to the office.

"The *Truxtun* and the *Oldendorf*, sir," replied Clagett. Shark nodded acknowledgment and quickly disappeared into the darkened office. The light came on, allowing Clagett to see Shark sit down in a swivel chair and start dialing one of the several multicolored phones atop the desk. That would be one of the secure telephone circuits he was using, thought Clagett, the ones with voice scramblers on both sides of the line.

COMSEVENTHFLT HQ, JAPAN

Rear Admiral Ernest O'Connor dropped the phone back in its cradle. He raised his bushy eyebrows and glanced at the status board through his office window. "OK, what do we have available?" he asked his aide.

The commander seated near him shifted in his seat. "Well, we've got almost nothing, other than the task force itself. The *Nimitz* could be ordered to go to flank speed. It won't reach the area until late tomorrow, but its planes will be within range sometime tomorrow morning. The *Independence* is still in Yokosuka being repaired, but we could order her escort vessels to the area; however, they'll take a better part of a day to get there." He scratched his head.

Admiral O'Connor stood explosively and seemed to rocket away from his desk. He was through the door and next to the status board in a few seconds. His aide scrambled to keep up. The admiral was talking before his aide got next to him.

"Closest air base is Osan. Get ahold of Seventh Air Force and see if they can scramble some fighters." He stabbed a finger at a symbol on the electronic status board. "What's this?"

"ELINT mission. USS *Lansdale*, sir. She's currently east of Luta, south of the Liaotung peninsula on mainland China."

"Let's get her over into the *Truman*'s operating area," ordered O'Connor.

"Aye, aye, Admiral. At flank speed she ought to be there in three hours," replied his aide, and together they went over to the communications people. After setting up the required messages they returned to the admiral's office.

Admiral O'Connor picked up the phone on his desk. He glanced at his aide. "I've got to tell the boss." He was referring to the commander of the Seventh Fleet. "By the way, what do they have at Osan?"

"Squadron of F-4s on alert," his aide replied.

O'Connor grimaced. "I sure hope those North Korean MiG-29s don't show up," he said through his teeth. "I wish they hadn't pulled the F-16s out of Kunsan."

"Fifth Air Force is getting a squadron of F-15s up from Kadena on Okinawa," offered his aide. "But they won't show up for at least two hours." He turned away to look at the status board once again. "Seventh Air Force is also getting their AWACS up from Taegu air base. It's a good thing it was moved up from Kadena a couple of weeks ago." He turned back around. "How about our ROK friends?"

O'Connor frowned. "Would you have them think we don't know how to run our navy?"

"Just a thought, Admiral." He fell silent for a moment. "What if those MiG-29s do show up?"

O'Connor looked his aide straight in the eye. "The F-4s are expendable."

*   *   *

Twenty minutes later, Clagett was bending over the radio operator, who was still trying to contact the task force, when the message came in over landline. He read it as the COMSEVENTHFLT printer quickly spit it out.

```
ZAATZUY RUHKDAA 2476 127 1126 - TTTT - RUHPBLA ZNY TTTTT
Z 070158 MAY
FM COMSEVENTHFLT
TO CINCPACFLT
BT
TOP SECRET
1. COMMUNICATIONS INTERRUPTED BETWEEN THIS COMMAND AND CTF 78.1
070115 Z MAY. NO RESUMPTION OF CONTACT USING AUX. AND EMERG. FREQUENCIES.
BRIEF JAMMING AFTER LOSS OF CONTACT.
2. RADAR CONTACT 15 BOGIES INDICATED BY CTF 78.1 JUST PRIOR TO IN-
TERRUPTION.
3. SCRAMBLED CAP FROM OSAN AND KADENA.
4. ALL SURFACE VESSELS IN VICINITY ORDERED TO CTF 78.1 OP AREA.
BT 2476
NNNN
```

He eyed the telltale leading *Z* in the message header. It was a flash message. He'd have to get it transmitted to CINCPAC in Hawaii in a hurry. Here's where the shit hits the fan, thought Clagett. The word is going up the line—the *Truman* is in trouble.

Chapter Ten

Disbelief crowded in on Lt. Paul Simmons as he walked along the passageway leading away from the ladder he had just climbed from the fourth deck. Three people were in that passageway, two face down and the other on his back. He had almost expected Taylor to be wrong, or maybe it was wishful thinking.

Simmons gingerly stepped over the bodies and went through a door to his right. He found himself in an enlisted men's lounge, its bulkheads covered with Marine Corps insignia. The lounge was empty, for which Simmons was grateful. The thought flashed through his mind that he would feel damn silly if suddenly a group of marines entered the lounge as if nothing had happened. What a ribbing he would take when they saw him wearing the OBA. He'd suffer along gladly; it would be quite a relief from the present situation.

He made his way across the lounge to the starboard side and entered a passageway. He went over to an access trunk and looked down at the hatch leading to the fourth deck. It was dogged down in accordance with his instructions. The safety of the fourth deck beckoned him, but he fought off the feeling. He had to press on.

He climbed the ladder to the second deck, dreading what he might find. The area was familiar to him—it was sick bay—but he was unprepared to deal with the horror of the scene before him. There was a string of bodies extending from the sick bay doorway along the passageway through the aft watertight door and around the corner. The sailors must have been in line for sick call when they were struck down. The confined atmosphere of the OBA made the scene distant and unreal.

He sucked in oxygen as he stared disbelieving at the bodies in the passageway. He felt light-headed, and a wave of dizziness swept over him. The scene shimmered and shifted as the mists crowded around him and dragged him back to the hellish world of the recent past. The roaring of the escaping steam filled his mind, mixing with and finally drowning out the sailors' screams. After shoving the two sailors next to him up the ladder, he had scrambled up behind them, only to hesitate over some sense of duty to the already doomed men. He turned and took a step back down, and received the image that would stay with him for the rest of his life.

One of his men, with his skin melting from the incredibly hot steam that swirled about him, was staggering in the direction of the ladder. He had his arms uplifted in supplication to the young officer. Simmons stared in horror at the man's efforts and shrank back as the man's eyes, devoid of eyelids or any surrounding skin, suddenly found him. The steam swirled up near one eye, boiling the fluid within, leaving one seemingly disembodied eye locked onto the one man who might save him.

The entire incident took less than three seconds; then the steam intruded between them and the man was gone forever. Simmons stood frozen at the man's fate as the killing steam rushed toward him. The front edge of the steam, only a wisp really, touched his arm and set off incredible pain within him. The physical shock released him to frantically scramble up the ladder, as much to escape the steam as to get away from the nightmarish vision. The picture was forever seared into his mind.

His arm began to throb and his lungs began to grope for air as his mind slowly returned to the reality of the *Truman*. His mind searched for a thought to push away the feelings—anything, any thought to shove back the horror in his mind. The crew needed him—he couldn't fail them now. He had failed his men in the engine room, hadn't he? Now he was failing the *Truman*'s crew. Not again! He wouldn't have those feelings again! Not now! Not ever!

He suddenly realized that he was breathing very deeply. He could just barely feel the oxygen waft up to his face; before, the sensation was much stronger. Something was wrong with his apparatus; it was becoming more difficult to exhale with every breath. Panic rose in him as his breathing became more labored. He couldn't pull off the OBA or the gas would get him, and he couldn't get to the safety of the fourth deck before he passed out.

He fell to his knees, groggy from the lack of oxygen, his hands flying over the harness of the OBA frantically trying to find out what was wrong. He felt a sensation of warmth through the breastplate—the canister was working. His fingers ran over the outside of the OBA apparatus. His right hand touched the air bag near the canister compartment. The air bag somehow was the key to his dilemma. He grabbed the bag in desperation to jog his memory. The bag was hard with oxygen in it! Then he remembered—the OBA was saturated with oxygen and this was the reason he had difficulty exhaling!

Simmons put his hand on the air bag to keep pressure on it and pressed the exhaust button with his other hand. The button actually opened the OBA to the outside atmosphere, but with the internal pressure higher than the external, there was no chance of the gas getting inside the OBA. Simmons kept his finger on the exhaust button until he felt the air bag sag a little.

After a few breaths, he felt a cool draft of oxygen again. He sat on the deck, gratefully recovering from his narrow escape, and concluded that he must have been breathing too quickly for the OBA to keep up. Mental discipline is in order, he thought. The time for self-indulgence is past. Concentrate on the situation at hand or die with the rest of the crew. Or, even worse, survive and *feel*. . . .

He cut the thought short and idly looked over the sailors lying near him. He blinked his eyes a few times and wondered if he was imagining things.

Was the sailor next to him breathing? It had never occurred to him to check any of the bodies he had discovered. He had just assumed they were all dead, as Taylor and the young sailor had told him. He reached out with trembling fingers to touch the man's neck over the carotid artery. There was a definite pulse. Simmons exhaled quickly into the OBA mask as hope swelled within him. He ran from sailor to sailor and checked each man's pulse. They were all only unconscious!

Feelings surged within him; he felt as a swimmer feels after a long haul underwater. With lungs bursting the swimmer's head breaks the surface and he drinks in cool, sweet air. Suddenly the world is a better, less desperate place. Now, it was the *entire* crew that was relying upon him, not just the survivors. The increased numbers proportionately increased his resolve.

His next thoughts were how to revive them, but he had no idea how to do so. He finally decided that the first crew members to be revived should be the men on the bridge, no matter how it was done.

He ran to the nearest ladder that led up to the hangar bay. After entering the bay forward of the aircraft elevator nearest the bow, he ran aft toward the base of the island. The scene in the hangar bay was much the same as the one below decks, with men lying where they had fallen, some of them in awkward positions, as if they were the discarded dolls of some giant child. Simmons slowed his pace to take it all in, and mentally noted that the gas must have come from sources external to the ship.

He quickly reached the passageway leading up into the island, but he started gasping for breath due to the limitations of the OBA. It was either slow down or pass out. He stood with both hands on the bulkhead, his head hung down as he concentrated on controlling his breathing. After several minutes his breathing returned nearly to normal and he began his climb into the island.

He reached flight deck level and peered out the open doorway. Some trucks were scattered about and a few of the flight deck crew were lying on the deck. He looked back into the island and saw a welcome sight, a personnel elevator, which would convey him to the upper levels of the island. The elevator had a directory on one wall. His eyes stopped at the line: 09 LEVEL—Bridge, Ops Plot, Chart Rm, Commanding Off State Rm, Navigator State Rm, Air Off State Rm.

That was what he wanted, the 09 level, and he immediately pushed the button. The door closed automatically, and after several seconds and only a hint of motion the door opened at the 09 level. He left the elevator and cautiously went to the right, around a corner to the passageway that led to the bridge.

Unconscious sailors were heaped on top of one another and strewn around the deck in the now-familiar scene. Simmons spotted the captain after a moment. He was sprawled face down on the deck near the aft bulkhead. He noticed a small pool of blood near the CO's face and bent down to assess the extent of the injury. The blood seemed to be coming from his nose. Probably hit it when he fell, thought Simmons.

Simmons stood and let his gaze sweep the bridge. Now what was he going to do, he wondered as apprehension built up within him. His gaze reached the inboard windows of the bridge, then through them and beyond, where he noticed something moving on the horizon. He walked over to the window and stared intently at the moving objects at the limit of his vision. Could it be help on the way, he wondered, and so soon?

He suddenly had a sense of foreboding. Someone had spread the gas that had struck the crew unconscious. It was a question he had put off asking until now. Who would want to knock out the ship's crew and for what purpose?

The objects were larger now, and he could distinguish their outlines with better detail. They were helicopters and coming on very fast. He counted them—eighteen in all, four across and four-and-a-half rows deep. The markings were strange, not at all like those on U.S. Navy helicopters.

His heart began to pound and his sense of impending doom grew stronger than ever. He glanced quickly around the bridge for a pair of binoculars. He immediately found them and nervously attempted to look through the OBA mask and the field glasses at the same time.

The helicopters were bigger than any Simmons had ever seen. He estimated the rotor diameter at one hundred feet, and the length of the fuselage to be about the same. Two tubular-shaped appendages were located above the cabin; Simmons guessed they were air intakes for the engines, which were probably turboprops. An ominous blood red insignia caught his attention. It was a red star in a field of white. A red circle enclosed the star, with a blue circle concentric with it.

Realization flooded in on him. They were North Korean! It was they who had attacked the ship with gas! And now they were going to land on the flight deck and hijack the ship! Simmons froze with fear. He tried to shake the fear loose and force himself to think. They had to be stopped. But how?

He thought of all the radars that the ship had to detect threats; the Phalanx gun system should be pumping lead all over the sky by now. Had it been activated? That was always done during general quarters. They had gone off GQ just minutes before. At any rate it wasn't working and he had only minutes to come up with some defense.

The ship had marines on it; he thought of possibly reviving some of them and organizing some kind of defense. A quick look at the approaching helicopters dispelled that idea. They were closing in too fast. He would have to use whatever engineering personnel he could find, but what about weapons? The ship had an armory, but where was it? And what kind of weapons did it have in it? Would they be effective against a boarding party of that size? He put these last questions out of his mind for the moment and concentrated on a way to buy time.

He spotted the engine order telegraph and instantly rushed toward it. He rang up flank speed and fervently hoped that the engineering crew was still answering all bells. He suspected it would be difficult to land a helicopter with more than thirty knots of wind down the flight deck. After a delay of about ten seconds, the response came back from the depths of the ship. The indicator swung around with its attendant ringing of bells to match the flank speed order.

Simmons nodded to himself in satisfaction. That ought to slow them down a little, he thought. He spotted the helm and went over to it. The rudder was set three degrees to starboard. He set the rudder amidships and glanced at the course—210, southwest, almost directly away from the North Korean peninsula. At thirty knots he would rapidly put some distance between the North Korean mainland and the *Truman*. If any enemy reinforcements were on the way, it would take them longer to get here. Now he had to get down to the fourth deck and start arming his men for the inevitable attack.

Simmons rushed from the bridge and elected to take the ladder instead of the elevator. He ran out into the hangar bay and retraced the route he had taken just moments before. He was gasping for breath by the time he reached the ladder leading past sick bay to the decks below. He flew down to the third deck, leaping down three and four steps at a time.

His vision began to blur as he staggered over to the hatch leading to the fourth deck. He began to pound on it with his fist, and screamed for the crew to open the hatch. Panic rose in him. They weren't hearing him. He tried unsuccessfully to open the hatch himself, but he was too weak from lack of oxygen. He collapsed on top of the hatch and rolled over on his back while despairing at the thought of having to remove his face mask. The gas would knock him out, but at least he would still be alive.

He stared straight ahead and his eyes focused briefly on an object hanging on the bulkhead. It was a fire extinguisher. Despair faded as he dragged himself to his feet and unhooked the metal bottle from its holder. He lifted it as high as he could and dropped it on the hatch. After repeating it several times, he saw the handwheel on the scuttle move. *Thank God!*

The scuttle was suddenly open, with Simmons slipping and sliding through it, and landing on his rump on the deck below. With shaking hands he ripped off the OBA mask and inhaled deeply several times. His vision began to clear enough for him to recognize the faces that stared at him through the plastic windows of their OBAs.

"There's an attack coming!" he said in a hoarse voice. "The North Koreans are going to land on the flight deck and try to hijack the ship. We've got to stop them! Chief, get every available man and let's get to the armory." He paused for breath. He could see the chief's incredulous look even through the OBA.

The chief slowly took off his facepiece and stared at the lieutenant. "What?" was his simple reply.

"You heard me, Chief. The North Koreans launched a gas attack on the ship to knock everyone out so they could board and take it!"

The chief seemed unconvinced despite the lieutenant's agitation. "The crew isn't dead," Simmons explained, "they're just unconscious. Come on, Chief, we've got to move fast. Get everyone out of the main engineering spaces and let's get to the armory!"

Taylor thought it over briefly and concluded that Simmons's statement was the only possible explanation for their situation. He swung into action, bellowing orders at the top of his lungs. The sailors under his command scurried to and fro in response to the chief's instructions. Although the sailors had to go to the third deck to go forward or aft, Taylor had thirty men assembled in the forward reactor room in a very short time.

"That's not all of them, sir. We had about sixty men in the forward spaces because of the field day we were having," explained Taylor.

Simmons nodded. "Let's get them to the armory to get weapons, then I'll take a group topside. You get the rest of them back here to defend the engineering spaces as best you can."

Taylor gave him a crisp "aye, aye."

Simmons briefly explained the situation to the disbelieving sailors. Simmons knew he had to move them along before they began to think about the upcoming battle. They seemed to be following orders automatically and he didn't want to give them a chance to refuse to fight the North Koreans. He quickly led the group up the ladder in search of the armory.

Simmons thought the armory was in the vicinity of the marine spaces, because they were the only ones who handled any kind of weapons aboard ship. He stepped out of the access trunk and into a crew living space. He ran across the living space, stuck his head into another passageway, and saw that the armory was directly in front of him. He gave thanks that he had found it so quickly.

The next problem was how to gain entry. There was a door of expanded metal on the outside with a padlock on it, and inside there was a solid metal door with a combination lock on it. He grabbed the nearest sailor, pressed his OBA mask to the young man's ear, and told him to get something to get the padlock off. The sailor nodded quickly and was gone. Simmons then ran over to the marine office. One marine was lying on the deck and another one, a sergeant, was slumped over his desk. Simmons grabbed the sergeant by the shoulders, pulled him off the desk, and let him drop unceremoniously to the floor.

Simmons frantically searched each drawer of the desk, with no success. He had to find the combination! Then he noticed a row of filing cabinets lining one wall. His heart sank. It would take several hours to go through all the files, and he had only minutes before the enemy helicopters landed on the flight deck.

The sergeant of the guard office popped into his mind. He vaulted over the prostrate marine and reentered the passageway. Which way? He ran to his left and into a marine living space. On the opposite side of the space was a narrow corridor, at the end of which was a sign proclaiming the sergeant of the guard's office. Simmons ran through the space, stepping on a half dozen marines lying on the deck in various states of dress. Within seconds he was inside the office and rummaging through desks and cabinets. In one filing cabinet there was a locked metal box.

Simmons snatched a huge ring of keys off the desk and tried every key that looked as though it would fit. He succeeded on the fourth try and could have cried with delight when he found an envelope marked COMBINATION ARMORY.

He grabbed the envelope, crushing it in his haste, and rushed back to the passageway in front of the armory. He pushed through the crowd of sailors and saw that the expanded metal door had been opened, leaving only the solid metal door with the combination lock.

Simmons immediately started to work on the combination. Tension mounted as he tried the door and it failed to open. He ran through the numbers a second time. He grabbed the handle of the door and gave it a shove. The door opened.

A vast array of weapons, mostly M16s, was clearly visible. Simmons stepped back and found the senior enlisted man among the group of waiting sailors. It was the electrician he had been on watch with, Electrician's Mate First Class Wright.

"Get each man an M16 and all the ammo he can carry," he shouted through the OBA face mask. Wright nodded and immediately proceeded to carry out the order. Simmons wondered how many of his men would remember the weapons drills they had undergone during boot camp. All of them should have been trained to use an M16, even if the training was brief.

Wright handed Simmons an M16 with a clip belt. He donned the belt, and silently motioned to the waiting men to follow him up the ladder past sick bay to the hangar bay. The shock among the men as they saw their unconscious shipmates in the hangar bay came through the OBA masks, and Simmons worried about their reaction. The sailors slowed their pace as they took it all in; Wright, who was in the rear, tried to speed them up by shouting through his mask.

The scene took on a sense of unreality for Simmons. The sight of thirty sailors running through the hangar bay with M16s chest high made Simmons wonder if he was locked in a nightmare. Within minutes they would be fighting and dying to repel the enemy from their insane attack on the ship. Not so insane, thought Simmons. They have every chance of pulling it off.

After what seemed like an eternity, Simmons and Wright got the men up the ladder to the island at the flight deck level. The beating of the helicopter rotors was very loud, and Simmons knew they were about to land.

Pak looked at the carrier with mounting anticipation. They were approaching the port side of the warship and the ship seemed dormant. It had been slowly drifting to starboard, as it might do when there is no one at the helm. There was no activity on the flight deck. He could see the yellow trucks mixed in with the huge gray planes, and strained his eyes to pick out small, dark-shirted figures scurrying about. There was no one.

Then suddenly he recognized one of the flight deck crew. He was lying on the deck! The gas had worked! There would be no resistance from this ship. It had evidently gone straight through the gas cloud.

Pak gave a worried look at the distinctive tubular shape of the Phalanx gun systems at the corners of the ship. The protective covers for their barrels were off but the radar wasn't activated. He held his breath, waiting for those deadly barrels to swing around at his helicopter force.

They remained motionless. He let his breath out in a puff and forced himself to relax.

They were close now, only a thousand yards from the flight deck, and there was no reaction to his force at all. Pak had a peculiar feeling run through him. He recognized it—disappointment—and was surprised. He almost wished that the Americans would resist so that he could experience the glory of combat. He and his men deserved to at last get into the fight, but unless the U.S. Marines were waiting for them, the fight, if it happened at all, would be quick and one-sided. His men would crush any sailors waiting for them.

Pak stared at the huge vessel below him. Had it sped up? His eyes flicked over to the stern and beyond. The main engines were churning the water into a frenzy, and there was much more foam. It had increased speed! Someone was still conscious on the bridge! He got his glasses up to his face and examined the bridge. He could see no one moving. Had they increased speed just before passing out?

The North Korean colonel shook his head and went over to the pilot, who saw him and struggled to talk through his gas mask. "They've increased speed to about thirty knots! It's going to be tough to land!"

"Just get us on the deck! Once down they can't stop us!" Pak shouted back to the pilot and copilot. They both nodded back enthusiastically. Pak went back to the open door in the side of the helicopter and boldly looked out at the flight deck of the largest warship afloat. It was now only feet below them as the helicopter pilots maneuvered to line up in their prearranged pattern. Four helicopters hovered in the wind caused by the movement of the ship. They kept their spacing well in spite of the wind and lowered quickly, just as they had practiced.

Pak stared at the deck, which was rapidly rising to meet them. They were only feet away from their objective. He looked up quickly.

Pak spotted movement in the island.

Simmons peered out the doorway to the flight deck. The helicopters were flying parallel to the ship, the first four of them maneuvering to select their landing spots. There was very little time left.

The lieutenant cautioned the men to hold their fire until he gave the order. He then distributed his men as best he could, sending five men to the 010 level, the highest deck in the island, to fire down on the invaders. He put the rest of the men in the various compartments that had doors leading out to the flight deck. They would have to fire through the restricted opening of the door; there was no better way to do it, even though only three or four men could fire through a door at a time.

Simmons took a last look at his men; they all looked scared, very scared, as scared as I am, he thought. He glanced quickly through the door again. It would be only seconds before the helos touched down. One helicopter was hovering over the flight deck just aft of the island. Another was maneuvering into position aft of that. Simmons's mind raced—there was nothing left to do. The North Korean markings were plainly visible now; there was no doubt who they were. And there was no doubt as to their intention.

Simmons gripped his M16 with his left hand and stepped back from the doorway. He raised his face mask. "Fire . . . *FIRE!*"

There was a moment of hesitation among the sailors of the USS *Truman*, a moment that seemed to last forever. Suddenly a cacophony of sound shook the passageway and reverberated up the island. It seemed as if all the sailors had opened fire simultaneously, after hesitating slightly as though they were guided by some common mental accord.

A tremendous volume of automatic weapons' fire issued from the island, directed mostly toward the helo just aft of the island. It was hovering ten feet above the flight deck when its engines failed. It crashed to the deck and exploded upon impact, killing its crew and most of the North Korean soldiers within. Flaming gasoline spewed in all directions, igniting most of the flight deck aft of the island.

Muffled expressions of surprise went up from the sailors in the island, but Simmons's thoughts were already on the other helicopters. They had shot down only one helicopter out of eighteen.

Most of the crew in the passageway stopped firing and looked with horrified fascination at the burning spectacle on the flight deck. Some enemy soldiers, their bodies soaked with flaming gasoline, ran screaming from the doomed helicopter and collapsed on the deck to burn in silence.

The thirty knots of wind down the flight deck rolled the flaming helo aft until it was stopped by a truck. The flames immediately engulfed the vehicle and the unconscious sailors within it. The truck exploded, sending pieces of metal and human flesh in all directions.

Simmons cringed at the thought of unconscious sailors dying just because they were in the way. He pulled his eyes from the sight and noticed a sailor drop his weapon and turn to run. The horror and disgust mirrored on his face showed clearly through the breathing equipment he wore.

Simmons grabbed him and shook him as hard as he could. The man seemed to notice Simmons for the first time. "Pick up the weapon!" Simmons shouted. It was MacKenzie, the young high school dropout turned sailor.

MacKenzie complied with the officer's order but acted in slow motion, as if he was coming out of a dream. The officer then dragged the reluctant sailor back to the open doorway and told Electrician's Mate First Class Wright to keep an eye on him. The petty officer nodded and Simmons shifted his attention back to the flight deck. He cautiously stuck his head out the doorway and looked aft.

A second helicopter had landed near the aft end of the flight deck. The men in the aft compartment of the island were firing in the helo's direction, but they were hampered by several trucks that were partially in the line of fire. The sound of another helicopter made Simmons jerk his head in quickly. He cautiously peeked out again but this time to look forward. A third helo was hovering to land forward of the island. Simmons quickly decided that he needed a better look at the flight deck. He raced up the ladder through the inside of the island to the 010 level and got out on the aft surface lookout station, where he got a view of the situation on the flight deck.

Helicopters had landed forward of the island and their men were just beginning to discharge onto the deck. Simmons's gaze swept aft, past the burning helicopter to the helo on the aft flight deck. Men were unloading onto the deck and running toward the aircraft elevator aft on the port side. The North Koreans were obviously going to use the elevator to get below decks.

A chill had gone through Pak just as he dove through the open side of the helicopter to land on the deck of *Truman*. He had no sooner landed than automatic weapons' fire exploded from the island. His worst fears were confirmed! The helicopter in front of them exploded in a shower of flaming gasoline and knocked him flat on his back. The heat seared him but he ignored it. Another fifty of his men killed!

Pak crouched low to the deck as his men crowded around him. He angrily cursed at them to spread out; should the Americans detonate the gas tanks in the helicopter behind them, he would lose yet another fifty of his men. He looked over the situation and cursed again. Their plan was to get below decks by using the island. But now he was effectively cut off from the island by the Americans and the flaming helicopter. He had to find a different way to get below, and it had to be fast. More men would be landing minutes from now. He had to get his men out of the landing zone.

Pak leaped to his feet and ran over to two trucks that were between him and the island. He clambered up on one and surveyed the scene on the flight deck. The Americans were firmly in control of the island, judging by the amount of fire his helicopters were receiving. Automatic weapons' fire seemed to be coming from every orifice in the steel structure. He caught a glimpse through a doorway of different shades of blue. Navy? He and his men were up against sailors?

Pak shook his head. These American sailors were fighting a fine defensive battle, at least until now. He felt a pang of regret—he couldn't help it—that he wasn't up against U.S. Marines. He berated himself. Don't think about that now. We've got to get below decks! He looked over the aircraft elevator aft of the island; that would be the quickest way, but his men would get cut to pieces by the Americans in the island. Pak searched his memory of the layout of the flight deck of the carrier. There was an aircraft elevator on the port side.

Pak scrambled off the truck and waved to his men to follow him over to the port side. He saw with satisfaction that the elevator was at flight deck level and ordered his men on it. They had been trained to use the aircraft elevators and immediately took up positions inside. They formed a defensive perimeter and began firing through the flames of the downed helicopter at the island. One of his men got to the elevator control station and with a nod from Pak sent the elevator on its journey to the hangar bay. A Klaxon sounded and a wire fence arose from a recessed position in the flight deck to form a lifeline around the hole left in the deck by the elevator.

Pak nervously licked his lips. They were on their way.

Simmons grabbed the nearest phone and dialed the forward EOS. He put the phone up against his face mask just as the phone was answered.

"Cut the power to number four aircraft elevator! Do it now!" He hoped the sailor could understand him through the OBA and would obey the order without question. The surprised sailor gave an "aye, aye" and Simmons hung up the phone.

The elevator ground to a halt. Pak looked around in panic. What had happened? He shoved aside his men and got to the edge of the elevator deck. They were about fifteen feet above the hangar bay and at least that much below the flight deck. The Americans had cut the power to the elevator to trap them there!

Would nothing in this operation go easily? He had already lost 150 of his highly valued men and he hadn't even engaged the enemy! He looked above and below and to each side. No way out except to jump for the hangar bay deck. He summoned his courage and leaped into the air.

Pak landed and rolled onto the deck. He kept alert for any of the enemy and searched the hangar bay with his eyes. His men followed suit, and in a few seconds they gathered around him. The sounds of battle raged on above them in the direction of the island.

Pak was undecided. This unit's objective was to take the engineering spaces, leaving him and his staff behind to coordinate things in the hangar bay. Should he change plans and flank the Americans in the island? That would ease the pressure on his troops on the flight deck. He suddenly made up his mind—he would not change plans. He had two units dedicated to taking the island. They would just have to perform as expected. He would have to immediately assess what they were up against, though, to better plan the rest of the mission.

Pak made his decision. He would go along with this unit to see what kind of resistance the Americans would be mounting throughout the ship, then return to the hangar bay to coordinate the rest of the operation. All of his decision making took less than five seconds, and was not noticed by his men. He gave the appropriate orders, and his men moved to comply. As they made their way down the ladders to the deck below, Pak paused to listen.

The chatter of automatic weapons' fire echoed throughout the hangar bay. The American M16s had a distinctive sound, much different from the rushing sound of his AKRs. There was an incredible amount of M16 fire mingled with the fire from his soldiers. This wasn't going to be easy.

Chapter Eleven

The reactor room was 100 degrees Fahrenheit and getting hotter by the second. With the ventilation cut off, no fresh air was being pumped into the space, nor was any hot air being exhausted. Senior Chief Machinist's Mate Alvin Taylor and the rest of the men were sweating heavily from the heat and the fear of imminent combat.

Chief Taylor strained his ears to catch any noise from the upper decks. The sound of steam rushing through the huge main steam pipes drowned out whatever noise reached him. He ordered the rest of the nervous sailors behind him to keep quiet, then put his ear near the steel hatch above him.

A rumble from above, its ferocity diminished by the intervening structure, met his ears and shook him to the core. The ship seemed to be indifferent to the sound, but Taylor knew better. It could only have been an explosion, and a big one at that. There really *was* fighting above them. *We're in a firefight!*

What next? Would the order "Repel boarders—flight deck!" come over the 1MC? My God! "Repel boarders, flight deck!" This was straight out of the 1920s, when the navy ran drills to repel boarders on their ships.

Taylor put his finger in one ear and pressed his other ear to the hatch. He could just hear the staccato sounds of small arms' fire above the sounds of rushing steam generated by the nuclear reactor behind him.

Taylor took his ear away from the hatch and nervously looked over his men. They all had on OBAs, their facepieces dangling in front, ammo belts around their middles, and M16s by their sides. They were all scared, and they were looking to him for some hope out of this situation. He had to say something.

"Gunfire" was Taylor's simple statement. He knew it was the wrong thing to say. The men's eyes widened with despair.

Taylor glanced around quickly. If they broke past Simmons's force, they would descend upon the engineering spaces with a vengeance. That was probably one of their main objectives. A few grenades or a flamethrower and his men would die before they had a chance to fight. The engineering spaces were designed without any doors going fore and aft, so that the forward and aft reactor rooms and engine rooms were cut off from one another. The men he had in those spaces were likewise cut off from one another. As individual forces they were easy prey for the North Koreans, but together they would be a formidable fighting force. He had to get his men out of the engineering spaces and up to the second and third decks, where they had room to maneuver.

Taylor refocused his attention on his men. They were mumbling to themselves in indecision and fear. One complained that the marines should have their M16s and do the fighting. If Taylor didn't act fast he could have a mutiny on his hands. He ran down the ladder and grabbed a first class machinist's mate.

"Get a head count and pick two guys to stay in the EOS. We might have to answer bells," ordered Taylor. The first class nodded quickly and went to obey his orders.

"What are we going to do, Chief?" one sailor asked. His voice shook. The rest of the men quieted down quickly. They wanted to hear what the chief had to say.

"All right, listen up. If we stay here we're dead. We've got to get up a couple of decks so we have room to maneuver." Their faces hardened. "If they break through, past Mr. Simmons, then we've got to stop them or they'll take over the entire ship."

"You think they'll break past Mr. Simmons, Chief?" asked another sailor.

Taylor immediately shook his head. "There's no way to tell. But we've got one advantage. There's only one way they can come at us, and that's through a hatch. That means we've got built-in choke points all over the ship. We're going to get up onto the second and third decks and form a perimeter around the engineering spaces. If we control the reactor and engine rooms, then we control the ship. We can stop it, reverse it, or even steer it using the engines—any damn thing we want to."

The first class came up to Taylor. "Twenty-one here, six in the aft reactor room, not counting two guys left in the forward EOS and two guys in the aft EOS."

Taylor nodded. "Tell the guys aft we'll meet them on the third deck." The first class ran to comply. "All right, a couple of you guys get some sound-powered phones. We ain't got any walkie-talkies, but the 1JV will do. One set of phones to each squad." There was a bustle of activity.

Taylor grabbed a third class machinist's mate and three men. "You're First Squad." He pointed to the third class. "You're First Squad leader. Second deck, sick bay forward." Taylor grabbed another petty officer and three more men. "You're Second Squad. Second deck, aft galley."

Taylor repeated the procedure. "Third Squad. Second deck, crew's mess forward. Fourth Squad, third deck near the photo lab, aft. Fifth Squad, third deck, ship's armory, forward. The Sixth Squad will be the guys from the aft reactor room and I'll hold them in reserve."

He looked over his men and prayed that his decision was the right one. Their faces were flushed with anticipation and fear.

"You guys on the second deck, close the hatches leading down to the third deck, but leave a hatch open near Third Squad. If it gets too hot we'll retreat to the third deck." Taylor racked his brain for details he missed. Three squads would be on second deck and two on third deck, with the remaining squad to go where the action was.

"Does everyone know his assignment?" They all nodded. "As soon as you make contact with the enemy, send word back to me over the 1JV, and I'll get some more men up to you right away. All right, OBAs on!" The men rushed to obey. "Check them out. Make sure your OBA is functioning. Anyone whose OBA isn't working raise their hand."

One obviously terrified sailor raised his hand. Taylor turned to the first class. "Square him away and get him moving!"

Taylor put on his OBA and moved up the ladder. He turned the handwheel on the scuttle and lifted the small round hatch in the middle of the larger square hatch. Cool air rushed at him and provided some relief from the torrid reactor room. He quickly glanced around the access trunk above him, then pulled his M16 through the scuttle and threw it on the deck. He crawled through the scuttle, picked up the M16, and peered up the ladder to the second deck.

Taylor redirected his attention out the doorway on his deck and scanned the small passageway that led to a crew bunk room to the right. His eyes lingered on the legs of a prostrate sailor in the bunk room. The rest of the sailor's body was hidden by a bulkhead. He hoped Simmons was right about the crew being only unconscious.

Taylor returned to the scuttle and motioned for his men to come up and deploy to their assigned areas. They struggled through the scuttle one at a time and cautiously departed to their areas. All of them were grim and scared, their face masks clouded with condensation from their rapid breathing.

The OBA lasts only sixty minutes, thought Taylor. He berated himself aloud for not thinking to issue extra canisters to each squad. With the way the men were breathing, the canisters would last only half an hour at best. He shook his head. He'd have to send out a search party for more canisters soon.

The first class and the terrified sailor who had had trouble with his OBA came out last. Taylor nodded to himself. They're all still functioning, even this terrified kid. The bravest men are the ones who are scared to death but fight anyway. The sailors of the *Truman* would do their duty.

The sailors fanned out across the ship to form a hemisphere of defense around the precious engine and reactor rooms. Chief Taylor followed them to make sure that they were positioned with plenty of cover so they could possibly take the North Koreans by surprise. He picked up the sailors from the aft engineering spaces and positioned them in the chief's quarters on the third deck midway between the ladders leading to the forward and aft engineering spaces. He told them to pick up any OBA canisters in the area from the nearest repair party station.

Then Taylor went up to the second deck and slowly worked his way forward. He could hear the gunfire clearly now that he was two decks closer to the flight deck. Simmons was in a real gun battle topside. That officer had a lot of guts, thought Taylor. The lieutenant didn't even think about surrendering. Arm the crew and fight seemed to be his only thought.

Taylor came upon the line of unconscious sailors that had been waiting to get into sick bay. Suppose there was a gunfight in this space. Would the North Koreans shoot unconscious sailors? He had to get his men to pull their sleeping shipmates to safe areas within the ship. He stepped over the bodies and came up behind the squad leader. He lifted one earphone of the sound-powered phone set that the squad leader was wearing and pressed the OBA facepiece to the third class petty officer's ear.

"Where have you got your men?" he asked.

"One in the scrub room, where he can cover the ladder opposite it. One down the passage, covering the forward crew galley. Two others on the port side in similar positions."

Taylor nodded. "Tell all squads to pull anybody who's unconscious to a safe spot. Cover them up with tables or anything that'll stop a bullet. Shove 'em into out-of-the-way spaces, if they have to."

The squad leader complied and Taylor went over the details furiously in his mind to pick up anything he had missed. One thought occurred to him immediately.

What do I do with the wounded?

Machinist's Mate Third Class Johnson peered out the door of the switchboard room toward the access trunk that led down from the hangar bay. His tall, lanky frame was stretched out on the floor; his M16 was by his side. He was careful to keep the gun barrel inside the room— he didn't want to tip off the enemy to his location. After a few minutes he rolled on his side. The OBA was extremely uncomfortable to lie on.

This wasn't exactly the I & I he'd been looking forward to. It was more like Die & Die, he thought and grimaced at the bad joke. His heart pounded in his chest, causing his hands to sweat and the OBA facepiece to become almost unbearably hot. His face was sweating profusely and the facepiece was beginning to slide around. He prayed that the seal between the mask and his skin would stay intact. If it didn't . . .

He jerked involuntarily at the noise at the top of the access trunk. Someone was coming down the ladder.

The lead North Korean looked at the closed hatch and was puzzled. Why was the hatch closed? He got to the bottom of the ladder, stood on the hatch, and looked up the ladder for instructions. A sergeant irritably motioned to him and two others to open the hatch. The three men gathered around in a semicircle and began undogging the hatch.

Johnson could hardly believe it. Three North Koreans were a mere ten feet from him! There was no mistaking them, with their green fatigues and strange gas masks. He quietly slid away from the door and brought his M16 up to his shoulder. He lined up the sight on the closest North Korean, took a breath, and held it. He closed his eyes and pulled the trigger.

Pak's head jerked around at the sound of automatic weapons fire in the access trunk just below him. *An M16!*

Johnson held the trigger down until the M16 stopped firing. The slugs ripped into the first North Korean, killing him instantly. A second enemy soldier was caught in the shoulder, spinning him around to fall on the hatch. The rest of Johnson's burst went wild but filled the access trunk with ricocheting slugs, two of which slammed into the third soldier's face.

The third class next to Chief Taylor suddenly stiffened and put his hands to his earphones. "Contact!" he said in a tense voice.

"Where?" shouted Taylor through the facepiece.

The man listened for a second. "Aft galley!"

Taylor jumped to his feet and ran at full speed down the passageway toward the galley. He passed Third Squad, who were glancing about quickly and gripping their weapons nervously. One of them pointed aft and shouted something, but Taylor continued past him without stopping to find out what he said. When Taylor got to the crew's mess, gunfire erupted in the galley—the next space aft.

Taylor dove behind a table, flipped it over on its side, and cautiously surveyed the situation. The crew's mess was a wide, open space with tables all over, in the manner of a cafeteria. One man was at the entrance to a port side passageway facing aft and looking about in indecision. The gunfire was coming from down the passageway. Taylor glanced over to the starboard passageway entrance to the messroom. There another sailor was nervously peering through the doorway down the starboard passageway. They could rush us from two directions at once, thought Taylor.

Pak quickly looked about the hangar bay. Directly across from where he was standing was another access trunk on the starboard side. He grabbed ten men and motioned for them to follow him.

Now it begins for the engineering spaces, thought Pak. A layered defense. Not bad for a bunch of sailors untrained in this kind of warfare. Who are they? How many? What kind of weapons? What kind of surprises will they have in store for us? He raced over to the starboard side. These Americans weren't going to roll over and die.

*　　　*　　　*

Taylor crawled on the mess deck over to the sailor near the port side passageway. The sailor pointed down the passageway.

"Johnson's in a space around the corner opposite the ladder." Taylor nodded and checked his weapon. Safety off, cocked, and on full automatic. He stepped into the passageway with the M16 out in front of him.

Johnson jammed another clip into his M16 and peered out the door. A stubby-looking automatic weapon was shoved around the access trunk bulkhead. Johnson immediately rolled away from the doorway. A burst of fire slammed into the door, shattering it and sending pieces flying around the prostrate sailor. He rolled back to the entrance and caught a glimpse of green hurtling out of the access trunk and down the passageway.

A long burst of fire from Taylor's M16 raked the two North Koreans and stopped them literally dead in their tracks. Johnson fired a short burst into the access trunk to keep them pinned down, then held his breath. A small object, almost unnoticed by Johnson, came out of the access trunk, hit the bulkhead of the room Johnson was in, and settled in front of the shattered door.

Johnson gaped at it. Grenade!

He dropped his M16 and scrambled on all fours to get deeper into the room. The grenade exploded behind him, part of the blast coming through the doorway and sending pieces of shrapnel into Johnson's back, legs, and buttocks. The rest of the blast was funneled along the passageway.

Taylor didn't see the grenade, and luckily he had retreated around a corner, with his back facing the crew's mess. The explosion took him by surprise and knocked him to the deck, but he immediately sprang to his feet and ran back toward the crew's mess. He knew what was coming—the North Koreans would be right on the heels of the explosion.

Taylor shouted to the sailor in the messroom to cover him, but the man already had his M16 to his shoulder. The chief got into the room and around a bulkhead just as the other man opened up with his automatic weapon. Taylor whirled around and put a burst of fire up the passageway. Neither man hit anything but it made the enemy cautious. Another grenade wouldn't be far behind.

Taylor stepped back and motioned to the sailor with him to close the watertight door leading to the messroom. The sailor nodded and quickly slammed the door. He grabbed the lever and rotated it, which closed all the dogs on the door simultaneously. Taylor had his answer as to what to do with the wounded. Johnson would have to be left behind, if he wasn't already dead.

The sound of gunfire erupted from the starboard side. Damn! They were coming at them from two sides. They needed reinforcements.

"Get on the sound-powered phones! Tell Squad Six to send three guys up here on the double, then tell Squad Three to get the hell over here, now!" The sailor immediately put on the phones and began to speak into the mouthpiece.

Taylor ran over to the starboard side, where two sailors were firing long bursts down the passageway. Any second a grenade would greet them. He grabbed one sailor.

"Slam the door!" he shouted through the OBA facepiece. The sailor nodded gratefully. The three of them got the door closed and partially dogged down when they heard something hit the other side. Taylor yelled, "Hit the deck!"

The grenade exploded outside the watertight door, but the door held. Taylor scrambled to his feet.

"Get up forward!" He motioned to the bulkhead on the other side of the messroom. That would be their next line of defense. Taylor and the three sailors ran through the forward doorways and turned to make a stand. A grenade went off in front of the port side door, but again it held.

Next they'll open the doors and throw grenades into the messroom, thought Taylor. But then they'll have to run across the sixty-foot-deep messroom to get to us, and if I can muster some firepower from both port and starboard forward doorways . . .

The sailors from Squads Three and Six arrived, and Taylor split them equally between port and starboard doorways. He cautioned them to expect grenades first, then to open up with short bursts at the charging North Koreans. Their eyes grew wide with shock but they rushed to obey.

The levers on the aft doors began to bang open. I should have jammed the door levers, thought Taylor. The doors opened simultaneously and grenades were thrown into the wide, open messroom. Taylor and his men cringed behind the forward bulkheads. Four blasts came in rapid succession, the thunderous explosions confined by the bulkheads in the space. The men's ears hurt with the overpressure that the blasts created. The overhead lights were blown out, and combined with the smoke generated by the grenades the mess area became a cloudy hell.

Taylor waited a few seconds for more grenades, then pointed his M16 into the messroom. Three enemy soldiers charged straight at him through the smoke. When they saw him they brought their machine guns up to fire.

Taylor and the sailors next to him fired a split second before the North Koreans, sending two of them spinning to the deck. The blast from the third soldier shot through the doorway, narrowly missing Taylor but catching one sailor in the head. The sailor was thrown back onto the deck and was killed instantly. The third North Korean died in a hail of fire from Taylor.

The sailors on the port side traded gunfire at point-blank range with four North Koreans. The enemy peppered the doorway with gunfire, killing three sailors who leaned around the bulkhead. The sailors managed to kill two North Koreans, but the other two took cover behind some overturned tables. The three surviving sailors hugged the bulkhead and didn't dare peek around into the messroom for fear of meeting the same fate as their shipmates.

One North Korean began firing at the doorway while the other threw a hand grenade through the opening. The grenade bounced off one sailor and landed in the middle of the three of them. One man realized what it was and rushed to pick it up. He got a hand on it when it exploded.

Taylor was thrown to the deck from the blast of the grenade on the port side. He knew instantly that the port side was open to the North Koreans and that this space was lost. He'd have to retreat quickly to save what few men he had left. He quickly bounced to his feet and yelled to the remaining sailors to move forward. His men had to reach the next space quickly or they would get flanked.

Taylor and his men got through the doorway leading forward just as the North Koreans sprayed the space they had just left with gunfire. The chief sent two men over to the port side to shut the door, then slammed and dogged down the door he had just come through. There was a rattle of gunfire from the port side, which was suddenly muted as the port watertight door was shut. Seconds later only one sailor came back.

Taylor shouted orders to the two remaining sailors. "We've got only a minute or two." He pointed to one man. "Get forward and tell First Squad we're retreating to third deck." He looked at the other man. The sailor was gasping for breath and had a fogged facepiece. "You and I are gonna hold them off until First Squad gets below. Go over to the port side. When they start throwing hand grenades, haul ass to the ladder we've got open on the starboard side here near the supply department office."

The sailor gulped nervously, nodded, and crawled off to take up his post on the port side passageway. Taylor glanced around him. They were on another mess deck, this one much smaller than the last. A grenade blast in here and . . .

His eyes rested on a spray nozzle about three feet long that was used for firefighting. He ran over to it and yanked it off its holder on the bulkhead, then he went to the door and jammed it into the door mechanism. It wasn't perfect but it would slow them down a little.

Taylor took up his position in the next space forward. He should have told the sailor on the other side to jam the door with something. He was about to get up and go over to where the other sailor was when the door lever was thrown back and caught on the spray nozzle. The lever clanged forward and was thrown back again, bending the nozzle. The North Koreans worked the lever back and forth, gaining more travel each time, until the crushed spray nozzle fell to the deck.

The lever on the door slammed back. Taylor got ready and brought his M16 up to his shoulder. With his gasping breath and the slamming of his heart against his chest, he barely heard First Squad run down the passageway behind him and scramble down the ladder to the third deck. An M16 opened up to his right. The other sailor was earning his pay.

The door in front of Taylor opened a crack. Taylor didn't wait for the grenade; he opened fire at the slit formed by the partially opened door. Part of his burst went through and found the arms and legs of two North Koreans, and ultimately found the grenade in the hand of one enemy soldier. The grenade kicked out of his hand and landed on the deck. The North Koreans scrambled after it in a panic.

Taylor's M16 emptied and he frantically pulled at his ammo belt for another clip while ejecting the empty. He found a full one and jammed it home. He peered around the corner to see the door swinging freely. The explosion caught him by surprise. The grenade blew the door wide open and killed the three North Koreans behind it.

Taylor stared through the smoke and could see more enemy soldiers gathering farther aft down the passageway. He fired a well-aimed burst up the passageway and saw two green-clad men fall to the deck. More green figures massed behind them. He had bought a reprieve, but it wouldn't last long. Taylor whirled around to get his man over to the ladder leading to the third deck but immediately collided with the sailor who was running in Taylor's direction. Taylor caught a glimpse of multiple blue forms on the deck in the aft part of the space. Unconscious sailors!

A grenade went off with a blinding flash of light and a thunderous roar, scattering tables and chairs, smashing the scullery, and sending utensils flying around the space. The blast knocked both men down, but they were saved by the intervening scullery, and the tables and chairs. Taylor glanced in the direction of the sleeping sailors. The blue forms on the deck were now a shredded mixture of blue and red. They never had a chance, thought Taylor.

They pulled each other up as Taylor shouted for them to get into the next space. They both ran for the doorway leading forward, with Taylor in the lead and the sailor following on his heels.

Taylor heard the North Korean automatics open up behind him. He ducked and threw himself through the doorway as enemy bullets pinged and ricocheted around him. The enemy fire caught the sailor across the back and sent him sprawling across the mouth of the door. Taylor scrambled to his feet and immediately saw that the sailor was dead and that there was no hope of closing the door in time to slow the North Koreans. In only seconds they would be filling his passageway with gunfire and grenades.

Taylor sprinted for the access trunk that led to the third deck. His men had the scuttle open, with one man partway through it to provide covering fire. Taylor veered to get out of the line of fire and the sailor opened fire down the passageway. When Taylor reached the access trunk the man dropped through the scuttle to allow Taylor room to get below. The chief tossed his M16 through the scuttle and leaped through just as he heard something hit the deck near him.

Taylor grabbed the scuttle and slammed it. He tightened the handwheel as an explosion shook the deck above him.

Pak slammed his fist against a bulkhead. Would they all fight like this? That black man in the khaki was either an officer or a chief petty officer and had his men fighting like demons. This unit alone had taken 40 percent casualties and they had secured only the second deck!

One more thing he had forgotten became clear to him. Body armor. He and his men had no bulletproof vests. Why had he forgotten that?

Was it some sort of warrior pride that caused him to overlook it? He knew the mentality well: His men were brave enough and they had enough disdain for the enemy to not protect themselves from the enemy's gunfire. That mentality should have disappeared with the end of World War I, but he and his men had fallen into that same old trap. The thinking in North Korean military circles was not to suggest anything that smacked of less than fanatical bravery under fire. His men had probably thought of it but were afraid to mention it. Now they were paying the price.

He knew now what they were up against. The Americans were making them pay for every space with North Korean lives. And the sailors were doing it! He might have expected that from marines, but sailors?

Pak ordered his men to wait until he returned, then proceeded to the hangar bay to get reinforcements.

Chapter Twelve

R ick, are there any targets other than those twenty bogies?" asked Hastings.

The answer came back quickly. "No, sir," replied Norris.

The bogies must have something to do with the lack of communication with the task force, thought Hastings. The enemy aircraft were very close to the *Truman*; they could have just completed an attack, leaving the ship helpless. Surely the carrier would have scrambled some fighters if it were attacked, but where were they? And where the hell was Eagle One?

The other aircraft in the squadron began to report the same radar contacts as Norris spoke again. "Bogies have changed course to head directly at us, sir. Their speed has increased to Mach 1.5."

To Hastings there wasn't much doubt as to their intentions. Their actions had all the characteristics of a bona fide attack. I'd better get my people up to speed, he thought.

"Blackline flight, this is Blackline Leader. On my mark increase speed to 1,600. Begin climb to angels four five. Ready . . . mark!"

In unison the eight fighters began their ascent to 45,000 feet while increasing their speed to just over Mach 2.

"Blackline Leader, this is Blackline 103. When do we get permission to fire, Skipper?"

"Blackline 103, you'll get permission to fire when they fire first," replied Hastings. He had strict orders to that effect. He supposed it was traditional for the American armed forces, but it didn't help to leave the first shot up to the enemy. He would have given a month's pay to launch his missiles now, before the North Koreans got their squadron in range. They're probably flying MiG-29s—that was the best plane in their air force. The Russians didn't let them have the new 31s. Even so the MiG-29 was a fairly even match for an F-14. He had also heard that the North Korean pilots were getting better every day. That plus the fact that the North Koreans outnumbered the Americans by better than two to one caused his insides to flutter.

Norris, meanwhile, had been concentrating on the displays in front of him. The tactical information display, a large one in front of him, showed all the targets within the field of view of the aircraft's radar, along with their altitudes, ranges, and speeds. On the right side of the target symbols was a number representing the computer recommendation of the missile firing order. That order was dependent upon the computer's analysis of which targets represented the most dangerous threat.

The target symbols suddenly began to flash on and off in a steady rhythm. "Commander," said Norris over the plane's intercom. "We're at the optimum firing point."

Damn it, thought Hastings. Damn those armchair sailors for giving him those orders. "What's their range and speed now?" he asked disgustedly.

"Fifty-five miles and Mach 2.1, sir. Intercept in 60 seconds." Seconds later, "We're in launch and leave mode."

Hastings thought of the words that the farmer had said to his companions at the Village Green in Lexington in 1775. "If they mean to have a war, let it begin here." It expressed his sentiments exactly. He flipped up a red-and-white–striped shield on his control panel and pushed the lever up. "Master arm on!" Hastings got ready.

Suddenly Norris was shouting over the intercom so loud that it hurt Hastings's ears. "Incoming! I've got six, seven, eight in the air! Impact twenty seconds!"

Hastings keyed his transmitter before the last sentence was finished. "Blackline flight, engage enemy! Evasive action at two seconds to impact!"

The next twenty seconds seemed the longest in Hastings's life as enemy missiles streaked across the sky toward them. Any break in concentration, any lack of attention, any detail missed and they were dead men.

Hastings adjusted his controls slightly as first one, then another Phoenix missile left its launcher rails and sped toward the targets. Norris was on the ball. The RIOs in the other planes in the flight duplicated Norris's action and a host of missiles sped toward the enemy planes amid a chorus of "Fox three!" calls over the comm net.

"Five seconds to impact," said Norris over the intercom. The tension rose in his voice as he spoke. "Four, three, two . . ."

Hastings reached down and jammed the throttles full forward and yanked back on his stick as the afterburners kicked in. The aircraft responded instantly to his commands by heading straight up into the sky as the chaff dispensers ejected an expendable jammer and spread aluminum-coated glass fibers where they had been. The blood pounded in Hastings's ears.

"One . . . ," came Norris's voice.

Hastings held his breath as his mind froze with a single thought. Was his timing right? The last second passed slowly as Hastings waited for the explosion that he believed would be the last thing he would experience in life.

His heart thumped once, then twice. The explosion never came. Suddenly time was back to normal and Norris was shouting again.

"They missed!" He sounded surprised. "Our missiles will hit in five seconds!" Norris declared.

Hastings came out of his blistering climb and leveled off to get the enemy formation back into the view of the plane's radar.

Norris was back on the intercom, sounding subdued with disappointment. "We got four of them, Skipper."

Only four? Hastings had expected a better showing than that. Their electronic countermeasures must be better than we thought. He replayed the maneuver his squadron had just completed and made a mental note to thank the intelligence people the next time he saw them. They had warned Hastings that the North Korean MiG-29s were equipped with radar-guided missiles and had suggested the evasive tactic.

The maneuver was the result of an embarrassing mistake made by an unknown Russian engineer. The enemy missiles were semiactive homing devices and were guided by the reflection of the plane's radar pulses from the target. As the missiles approached the target the reflected pulses grew in strength until the radar receiver became saturated, causing a permanent failure of the guidance mechanism. This failure caused the missile to fly in a straight path until it finally detonated.

The trick, therefore, was to permit the missile to get close enough to the pilot's own aircraft to let the guidance mechanism fail, and then make a hasty exit. Timing was the all-important factor; if a pilot pulled out too quickly, the guidance mechanism would still be functioning and the missile would home in on his plane. The maneuver was reminiscent of the evasive action American pilots had taken over North Vietnam. Whenever a SAM missile was launched the pilot would watch the missile approach, then calmly roll away when the missile neared his plane. The missile would then fly straight past the aircraft and detonate far above the intended target.

Hastings had added dispensing chaff and an expendable jammer called a POET to the maneuver as extra insurance that the missile would not follow his aircraft. The POET is a free-falling device that receives radar signals, amplifies them, and retransmits them back to the missile. The missile radar locks onto the stronger signal from POET and homes in on it rather than the aircraft.

In his most recent briefing on the subject, Hastings was warned that the Soviets had found the error in their missiles and were taking steps to correct it. Someone had joked that the first step had been to send the responsible engineer to Siberia for a free twenty-year vacation.

Hastings surveyed the situation below him. The other members of his squadron had broken formation in a prearranged pattern that they had been rehearsing for several months now. The North Korean squadron had broken formation also, and the result was a freewheeling dogfight.

Now is the time we earn our pay, thought Hastings as he rolled the aircraft over and sent them down toward the fight. Norris, anticipating a dogfight, switched the radar to a mode more suitable for close-in combat. Hastings noticed the change of symbols on his display with enthusiasm, and mentally promised to give his young RIO a "well-done" after the dogfight was over.

The aircraft screamed down out of the sky at more than Mach 2, with Hastings aiming at two MiGs that were trying to circle behind some F-14s. The pitch bar and artificial horizon line on his display dipped and rolled as he leveled off at the enemy planes' altitude.

"Shit," Norris said faintly at the effect of the g forces resulting from the pullout from the dive. One diamond-shaped symbol appeared, then another on Hastings's heads-up display.

The anticipation of the kill began to well up in Hastings as he maneuvered the plane to close in on his intended victims. His anticipation hit its peak as first one, then the other target fell within the steering circle on his display. "Centering up the T," he said.

Just at that point, the MiGs detected the F-14 coming up behind them and both initiated a hard, driving turn to the right. Hastings was flabbergasted that they both turned together rather than split up. He threw the plane hard over, putting more than six g's on the aircraft, and thundered after the MiGs.

Rapidly changing numbers flashed on his control panel, and symbols bounced on his heads-up display as Hastings bore down on the enemy planes. Within fifteen seconds he had the two target symbols within his steering circle once again. "Centering the dot," he said. Then, "I've got a tone!"

Hastings pressed the button, sending two Sidewinder missiles on their lethal missions. Simultaneously the North Korean pilot in the MiG on the outside of the turn decided to part company with his comrade by reversing his rudder.

"Fox two! Fox two!" exclaimed Hastings.

Norris's voice was tense. "Five seconds to impact."

Hastings kept his aircraft in the hard right turn and waited to see the results of the attack.

"Four, three . . . ," counted Norris.

Hastings watched anxiously as the target symbols moved quickly away from each other.

"Two, one . . ."

Hastings prayed that the damn MiG wouldn't get away. The MiG in front of him had just started a steep climb when the missile hit, turning pilot and plane into a ball of fire. The other MiG was still in its hard left turn when the second Sidewinder struck, dealing instantaneous death.

Hastings sighed with relief as the two target symbols on his display blurred, then disappeared as the radar lost lock.

Norris was shouting over the intercom again. "Damn! That's the way to get 'em! Scratch two MiGs!"

Hastings grinned. Like the gladiators in ancient Rome, the winner's reward was life. It didn't make any difference whether the weapon was a lance through the throat or an air-to-air missile blowing you apart, the loser was just as dead.

"What's the status, Rick?" he asked.

"They must have gotten one of ours, sir. I've got only five friendlies on the screen."

"Could he be behind us?" Hastings asked.

"Don't think so, sir. I've been watching ever since that last turn. Maybe he took a hit in his IFF equipment."

Hastings hoped that the young RIO was right. He increased speed to catch up with the rest of the squadron. Their encounter with the two MiGs had made them fall behind.

"How many MiGs left?" Hastings asked.

Norris replied with pride in his voice. "Five, sir. And they're running like hell for North Korean airspace. Do we pursue?"

"Damn right," replied Hastings angrily. "Now that the shooting has started, those bastards aren't going to get away from us."

He suddenly began to have second thoughts. What had happened to the ship? He decided he would have to forego another encounter with the MiGs and find out the condition of the huge carrier. "Blackline flight, this is Blackline Leader. Pursue, engage, and destroy the enemy aircraft." He hesitated. "Who bought it?"

"It's good to hear your voice again, Skipper. We thought maybe you caught one." It was the voice of his XO, Tom Arnold. "Wagner and Thompson caught a missile at the beginning. I didn't see a chute. Kauffman and DeLuca got it, but I saw two good chutes. I took a few hits, but I can still make it with the other guys. The rest of us are OK." Wagner was Hastings's "visual," or wingman.

"They were good men. It's a damn shame," said Hastings with feeling. "Take over, Tom, and get the rest of the MiGs. I'm going to see what happened to Kingpin."

"Blackline 102, roger. Be careful, Ron," came the reply.

Hastings changed course to head for the ship and settled down into his relaxed but alert flight mode. At least he tried to. Combat had heightened his senses, and his insides were in an excited turmoil. Relax, he commanded himself. That was just act one. He decided to try to contact the ship once again.

"Kingpin, this is Blackline Leader. Come in please. Over." Low-level static greeted his ears.

"Kingpin, Kingpin, what is your status? Over."

USS *TRUMAN*

Simmons stared down the passageway. Did he hear a voice? He walked toward the PriFly doorway then stood and listened at the closed door. The voice started up again and electricity ran through him. He wasn't alone. He grabbed the door handle and yanked open the door, expecting to greet someone.

Bodies of sailors and officers lay in disarray on the deck, and were slumped over consoles and pinned behind chairs. Was he going mad? He had heard a voice from this compartment and it was an American voice.

The battle raged outside, the sounds muffled by the thick glass in the windows that gave a view of the flight deck. The voice started up again and cut past the sounds of machine gun fire from the flight deck. "Kingpin, this is Blackline Leader. Answer up!"

Simmons jumped and whirled around. The voice was coming from one of the consoles that lined one wall. He ran over to it and hope welled within him. He picked up one of the handsets and squeezed the transmit button. "This is the *Truman*. We need help! We—"

The voice boomed again and Simmons realized that it was coming from the console next to the one he was using. He dropped the handset and picked up the one on the right-hand console.

"This is the *Truman*. We need help! We've been attacked by North Koreans!" He hoped that whoever it was could understand him through the OBA. He let the transmit button go and eagerly listened.

"Kingpin, what is the nature of the attack? Over."

"Gas attack knocked most of the crew unconscious. Helicopters are landing enemy troops on the flight deck. Over."

There was a short delay. "Yeah, sure, and my grandmother's an octopus."

"Damn it! It's true—maybe you can hear the gunfire." Simmons held the handset to the flight deck windows. The chattering of automatic weapons went on unabated.

"Who is this? Identify yourself," said the voice.

"Look, I'm from engineering—"

"Get someone from PriFly."

"Everyone's passed out!" shouted Simmons in frustration.

"Are you nuts? Identify yourself!"

Simmons took a deep breath. "I'm Lieutenant Simmons from engineering."

Hastings gripped the stick tightly. Simmons! He thought his voice sounded familiar. How did Simmons get into PriFly? Hastings shook his head. He'd have to answer that question later. The big problem was the ship and what condition she was in. At least now they knew what the North Koreans were up to.

"Please, who are you? Can you help us?" The voice from the *Truman* sounded desperate enough.

Norris replied after a respectful delay. "We're Commander Hastings and Lieutenant Norris, Blackline flight."

Simmons's jaw dropped open in surprise. He never thought that his salvation would depend on the man who hated him. However, Hastings's squadron could shoot down the helicopters! He might then be able to save the ship. "We need help! Are you coming?"

"On our way," replied Norris.

"Who would've believed it?" Hastings mumbled under his breath into the intercom.

"You mean about the North Koreans attacking the ship with gas?" asked Norris.

That wasn't what Hastings had meant. "Yeah," he said quickly. Simmons was in real trouble on the ship, judging from the amount of automatic weapons' fire he had heard over the radio. The prospect of his rival being in imminent danger sent a feeling of righteousness through him. Maybe there is justice in this world, he thought. Then he wondered, would Simmons still be alive when they got there?

 # Chapter Thirteen

USS *TRUMAN*

Simmons slowly put the handset back on its cradle. It must have been Hastings's backseater who had answered him. Evidently, Hastings couldn't bring himself to respond to Simmons's plea.

I don't believe what's happening! thought Simmons. First this attack, then when I locate help it's Hastings. He couldn't help the next thought. Would Hastings deliberately stay away to get revenge on me?

The sounds of battle interrupted his thoughts. Hastings or no, he had to deal with what was going on right outside, and he couldn't rely on Hastings to help him.

After a few moments' thought, a tenuous plan of action had formed in Simmons's mind. He would try to confine the North Koreans to the flight deck. Out there they were exposed to whatever fire he could muster from the island, which at times could be formidable. Failing that, he would certainly lose the ship. If the enemy got below decks it would take an army to flush them out of the thousands of compartments within the ship.

Another thought struck him and chilled him to the bone. There were seventeen helicopters left out there, all filled with men. How was he to prevent a helicopter from landing, unloading its men, and taking

off again, so that another helo could do the same, and then another
and another? The problem panicked him as he sought to solve it.

The solution came quickly enough, although he doubted whether
he could accomplish it. Then he was through the door leading to the
passageway and running to the forward lookout station. He quickly
found the men he had sent up there previously; they were leaning over
the side and firing inboard at the two helicopters that had landed forward
of the island. He went up to the nearest sailor and pressed his face
mask to the man's ear.

"Fire for the helicopters' engines. Try to hit their gas tanks and set
them on fire. Shoot to disable them. Fire at the soldiers only if they
try to rush the island." He gestured to the other helos waiting in the
sky. "We've got to keep them from landing," he shouted.

The sailor glanced in the direction of the other helicopters and quickly
nodded, then proceeded to tell the other sailors with him.

It was a simple plan. They had to disable the helicopters that had
already landed so there would be no room for the others to land. The
North Koreans would have to push them off the flight deck. Simple
enough plan, thought Simmons, if only I can pull it off.

The sailors resumed firing in accordance with their instructions as
Simmons glanced over the railing down toward the flight deck. Men
were pouring out of the helos forward of the island. The North Koreans
began to return fire and the fire from the island diminished. The soldiers
forward of the island were clustering behind the trucks between the
starboard side elevators in preparation for an assault on the island.
Simmons noted with satisfaction that the engines of one of the helicopters had failed and that the sailors next to him had shifted their
fire to the large group of enemy soldiers assembled below them.

Simmons suddenly noticed the two aircraft elevators at the starboard
edge of the flight deck. The enemy's path to the elevator just forward
of the island was blocked by trucks, and the automatic weapons' fire
from the forward compartment of the island was keeping the North
Koreans at bay. However, the enemy had easy access to the elevator
that was farther forward and could use it to get below decks, as the
other enemy soldiers had tried to do with the elevator on the port side.
But there seemed to be no attempt on the part of the enemy to use the
elevator, possibly due to the elevator being at the hangar bay level.
Or maybe it wasn't in their game plan, thought Simmons.

He immediately looked for a phone so he could cut off the power to that elevator also, but a new thought struck him. The value of the elevator cut both ways. Certainly the North Koreans could use it to get below decks, but he could use it to come up behind them. After casting a worried glance at the troops gathering for an assault on the island, he made his decision. A flanking maneuver would take the heat off the island defenders.

Simmons left the 010 level and ran down the ladder to the flight deck level. He ordered ten of his men to join him and then made his way to the hangar bay. Once there, they ran forward and found that the elevator was still down at the hangar bay level. Apparently the North Koreans had not caught on to its strategic location. On the elevator were an F-14 and a truck with an unconscious sailor draped over the steering wheel. The truck and the plane would provide excellent cover if they had to fight their way off the elevator, decided Simmons.

Simmons ordered one sailor to man the elevator control station in the hangar bay, ordered another man to get the unconscious sailor off the truck, and then positioned the rest of his men on the elevator behind the truck and plane. They were set up to fire inboard at the invaders as the elevator rose to meet the flight deck.

After a last look at the placement of his men, he pointed a finger skyward and gave the thumbs-up sign to order the sailor at the control station to send the huge elevator toward the flight deck. The sailor pushed the button, then ran onto the elevator.

A Klaxon horn suddenly sounded above the cracking of automatic weapons. Simmons berated himself for his forgetfulness. The horn was used to warn everyone on the flight deck and the hangar bay that the elevator was in motion. Now that it had sounded, the North Koreans would be expecting them. As the elevator slid smoothly into motion, the blast of the horn faded and was replaced by the ringing of a bell, which was barely heard over the sounds of combat above.

Simmons dropped to the deck in anticipation of the furious welcome they were to receive at the flight deck. His men started firing as soon as the flight deck came into view, but there was no return fire. There were only five surprised North Koreans, who immediately put their hands in the air in the international signal of surrender.

Simmons and his men were dumbfounded but relieved at finding only a few of the enemy. A terrific amount of noise was coming from the direction of the island, and they quickly realized that the bulk of the North Korean contingent was assaulting the island. Simmons and his men took cover behind the trucks that the enemy had used just moments before, and from that vantage point they could see the enemy fight their way into the two forward doorways in the island.

Fireman Apprentice Jeff MacKenzie cowered at the rear of the passageway, as far as possible from the doorway leading to the flight deck. The explosion of the enemy helicopter and resulting fire had shattered whatever little nerve he possessed. The one man whom he looked up to and who seemed to know what to do had just left with some of the men. Lieutenant Simmons was trying to outflank the North Koreans.

Maybe the young officer was his emotional blanket, thought MacKenzie; when the lieutenant was around you knew he was in command. Especially when he dragged you up to a doorway to fire at the enemy. MacKenzie had no idea what to do in any situation, and instinctively looked to Simmons, who seemed to know what to do in all situations.

MacKenzie looked at the backs of his shipmates who were desperately firing out the doorway. They seemed frantic and sometimes were shoulder-to-shoulder, filling the door opening with their bodies as they fired burst after burst onto the flight deck. MacKenzie tried to console himself with the realization that he couldn't have gotten near the doorway if he tried.

The passageway was filled with the searing sounds of automatic weapons' fire, most of it from the Americans' M16s, but another sound was rapidly becoming mixed with it. It was a combination of a rushing sound and a very fast rattle. MacKenzie was momentarily distracted from his fear by the emergence of the sound until he realized what it was. *Enemy gunfire!*

He glanced in terror at the doorway and compulsively sniffed; the sound was lost amid the ear-shattering roar of small arms' fire. His shipmates again filled the door opening as they sought the right angle to fire upon the invaders. A very loud rushing noise with an accompanying background rattle was heard, and a second later the three sailors who were standing in the doorway flew violently backward, their chests filled with North Korean lead. Two other sailors stepped up to take their places as MacKenzie gaped in despair at the three corpses.

MacKenzie tore his eyes from the dead and stared at the doorway. Beyond the desperate sailors he could see green forms moving quickly on the flight deck. One sailor's head involuntarily jerked back; his body suddenly relaxed and he fell to the deck, his head landing right in front of MacKenzie. A small hole was in the clear plastic facepiece of the sailor's OBA. MacKenzie gagged in horror at the sailor's face. One eye was missing and seemingly replaced by an oozing red hole. MacKenzie backed up until he hit a bulkhead, his eyes still riveted on the dead sailor's head. A pool of blood began to form beneath it.

MacKenzie squirmed to get his legs away, as if the ever-widening pool would burn him. He experienced a crushing realization. *That could happen to me!*

The din increased several notches and the enemy gunfire seemed very close by. Electrician's Mate First Class Wright, the leader of their group, turned away from the door and spotted the young fireman crouched in the corner of the passageway. He shouted something that was lost through the combination of the OBA facepiece and the now-constant gunfire. MacKenzie's gaze met his eyes. They were narrow with anger. Wright gestured quickly with one arm in an obvious attempt to get the young sailor to step up to the doorway. Another falling sailor distracted his attention and left MacKenzie staring at their leader. He was a first class petty officer whom MacKenzie had never met before. Was he going to be led to his death by a stranger?

MacKenzie's gaze dropped again to the dead sailor in front of him. Yes, step up to the door and die. He felt as if he were strangling; he longed to rip off his OBA and take a free breath again. He staggered to his feet and dropped his M16. He had to get away. *He had to!*

He ran to the access trunk and sprang onto the stairs. The rattle of gunfire increased in intensity, and it seemed to the terrified sailor that the whole of the North Korean Army was in hot pursuit. He took the steps two and three at a time, once stumbling and falling down an entire flight to land at the 03 level, the deck below the flight deck. He jumped to his feet once again, ignoring the pain in one of his shins, and heard all hell break loose above him. The enemy gunfire was insistent and devastating; the M16 fire sounded desperate and tentative.

The walls around MacKenzie suddenly shook as a grenade went off on the deck above him. He scrambled to the ladder and fairly flew down the steps. He could smell cordite and death. The scramble of feet and quick gunfire was very close behind him. He could hear the muffled shouts of despair and shock from his shipmates as they ran before the North Korean onslaught.

MacKenzie's mind worked furiously. He couldn't keep going down this ladder. The sailors behind him might follow, and the North Koreans after them. He got to the hangar bay, ran through the doorway, and turned aft. He got about twenty yards and twisted around while running to glance behind him. His foot suddenly became tangled in a tie-down chain for one of the aircraft and was yanked out from under him. He fell heavily on the OBA canister on his chest and ground quickly to a stop on the rough, nonskid surface that coated the hangar bay deck.

The sounds of battle came from the access trunk he had just left. He rolled under an F-18 and stared at the battle unfolding in front of him. American sailors spilled out of the access trunk and into the hangar bay. Half of them had no weapons and they were all running as fast as they could. Two North Koreans appeared in the access trunk entrance to the hangar bay and opened fire.

The two streams of gunfire caught the running sailors across their backs and sent them dead or mortally wounded to the deck. They seemed to fall very quickly and almost straight down, and they didn't move after they fell. It was over in seconds.

MacKenzie lay in shock at the brutality of the battle. His breath came in gasps—his OBA didn't seem to work. The two North Koreans came out of the access trunk and stood over the bodies. They began to hoot their victory through their gas masks. They were joined by several more enemy soldiers, who proceeded to kick at the bodies. Any twitch or movement from an American body brought a burst from an AKR.

The intermittent gunfire shattered MacKenzie's nerves. He began to shake uncontrollably. *Escape!* He had to escape. But there was no escape. There was no place on the ship he could go where they wouldn't find him. In a compulsive move he ripped off his OBA facepiece. Maybe they wouldn't shoot an unconscious man.

He lay gasping on the deck as the victorious shouts of the North Koreans filled the hangar bay.

Simmons raised his weapon to his shoulder and was about to give the order to open fire on the North Koreans entering the island when an automatic weapon opened up from one of the helicopters behind them. It was one of the crew members trying to fend off the Americans so they could get airborne. One sailor gripped his stomach and fell to the deck. Another was knocked down by the force of the bullet entering his chest. The others immediately scrambled for cover, and the North Koreans who had surrendered vaulted over an aircraft tractor and escaped toward the island.

The sailors returned the fire, shattering the windows above the nose of the helicopter and killing the pilot and copilot. Automatic weapons' fire erupted from the side door of the helo and a furious gunfight ensued. The enemy soldier and the sailors were only fifty feet apart and they began to slug it out at point-blank range.

Suddenly it was over, with the North Korean slumping down and hanging limply from the doorway. The sailors stood and cautiously approached the helo with their weapons ready. One man jumped through the door and after a few tense seconds indicated that the helicopter was clear of enemy soldiers. Simmons took count—four sailors killed, one wounded; the North Koreans had done their duty.

Simmons suddenly noticed that the crew members of the enemy helo weren't wearing gas masks as the assault troops were. The gas had apparently dissipated above decks, but the North Koreans who were going below decks weren't taking any chances of running into an isolated pocket of gas. Simmons reasoned that he was about out of oxygen anyway, so he removed his OBA mask and let it dangle in front of him. The sailors were surprised, but one by one they removed their masks as Simmons gestured at the dead enemy soldiers and their lack of gas masks.

Simmons quickly regained the cover of the flight deck trucks and took stock of the situation. He had come up on the enemy's rear but had lost the island as a result. However, he and his men had succeeded in disabling a third helicopter. He cautiously peered around the front of the truck and surveyed the island. A host of enemy bodies was piled on the flight deck in front of the doorways that led into the side of the ship's superstructure. He took grim satisfaction from the ghastly scene; his men in the island had taken quite a toll in enemy lives.

An explosion and subsequent shuddering of the flight deck beneath him jolted his senses. He quickly deciphered the meaning of the explosion and the direction from which it had come—the island. It could mean only one thing—the North Koreans were using hand grenades against his men in the island. His insides began to palpitate and he lost all strength in his legs. Fear enveloped him and turned his normally tough will to jelly. Thoughts of surrender swirled in his mind and the prospect of his ultimate safety beckoned to him with an irresistible appeal.

"Mr. Simmons," an excited voice whispered. Simmons turned and looked at the man next to him.

"Look what I found in that helicopter," he said while pointing toward several crates behind him. "Hand grenades." The sailor almost smiled as he said the words.

The equalizer, thought Simmons. Now they had a chance against their superior foe. He shoved thoughts of surrender from his mind. They would fight to retain the ship even if it meant their lives. He was certain that many more people would die if the North Koreans were successful at this brazen hijacking.

Simmons turned his attention toward the island and the bitter battle that was ensuing for that strategic area. It occurred to him that he might surprise the enemy by coming up on their rear. It would be dangerous—he might be shot by his own men in the island. He ordered his men to load up on grenades. After they had filled their pockets they prepared to run the short space of flight deck to the island.

Simmons's attention was distracted by a helicopter taking off from the aft part of the flight deck. He had forgotten about them! The smoke and flame from the burning helicopter had kept the aft flight deck from view. If another helicopter landed and more enemy soldiers were put on the flight deck, he would be compelled to surrender to save the lives of his men. He wondered if he could defend the ship against the soldiers who were already on the ship; with the additional soldiers that the next helicopter would bring, he could never hope to win.

Simmons estimated that each helicopter held fifty men. All the occupants of the first helo were either killed or wounded, but three other helicopters had landed and put one hundred fifty soldiers on the ship. He and his men had to work their way aft and attack the next enemy helicopter that was sure to land. That meant he couldn't give any support to the sailors defending the island; they would have to take care of themselves.

He gathered his men around him and told them what had to be done. None of them spoke a word; they seemed to take it for granted that he was in command, much to Simmons's relief.

One sailor finally spoke up. "What about Rodriguez, Lieutenant? What are we going to do about him?" Rodriguez was the one sailor who was wounded in the fight with the helicopter crew.

"There's no time to help him, even if we could do anything. Sick bay is knocked out; besides, we're cut off from those decks anyway. Make him as comfortable as you can, then let's get aft."

After a short delay, Simmons and his men threaded their way between the two disabled helicopters to reach the port side. Simmons worried about receiving fire from the enemy who now controlled the island, and he tried to give the island a wide berth.

Neither Simmons nor any of his men were paying attention to the skies above them when one of the remaining helicopters that were orbiting the ship opened fire with its nose machine guns. It took Simmons and his men completely by surprise. Machine gun fire hacked its way down the flight deck, leaving death and destruction behind. Writhing and screaming, the ambushed sailors sank to the deck. Simmons hit the deck and rolled under one of the disabled helicopters just as machine gun bullets streaked a path toward him. Two other men made it with him, but the rest were either lifeless on the deck or shrieking with pain.

Simmons could hear the machine gun slugs hit the disabled helicopter under which he had taken shelter. The bullets smashed and rended the helicopter with incredible fury. One hit in a gas tank and it's all over, thought Simmons. The circling helo continued to pound the disabled helicopter and the surrounding flight deck in an effort to get to Simmons and the men who made it under the aircraft with him.

Several explosions wracked the island but Simmons took no notice. The ferocity of the unexpected attack had shocked and panicked him. He forced himself to look up. The man next to him was crying; the other man had his head buried in his arms in a hysterical attempt to hide from the lethal bullets.

The helicopter finally stopped firing, allowing Simmons and his men a minor respite as it moved to the other side of the ship to get a better shot at them.

Simmons said a prayer of thanksgiving and let out a breath. His eyes feverishly searched the flight deck for an escape route before the helicopter started firing again. His eyes finally settled on another helicopter hovering over the aft flight deck. It was going to land and deal the *Truman* defeat in the form of a horde of enemy soldiers.

 # Chapter Fourteen

A squeal went off in Hastings's earphones. His threat warning receiver had detected that they were being scanned by a hostile radar.

"Where is he, Rick?" asked Hastings.

Suddenly an explosion rocked the aircraft. "What the hell was that?" Hastings exclaimed.

Norris was almost screaming. "MiG at six!" The explosion was an air-to-air missile prematurely detonated by the ECM equipment, which was integral with the F-14's flare and chaff dispensers.

Hastings jammed the throttles forward and simultaneously kicked the rudder over. The resulting hard left turn put more than seven g's on Hastings and Norris and drained the blood from their brains, so that it seemed to the two men that the sun was setting in midday. They both grunted and strained to tighten their stomach muscles in an attempt to stem the flow of blood from the upper parts of their bodies, as their G suits clamped down with a vengeance on their buttocks and legs.

The MiG pilot, having seen that his air-to-air missiles were ineffective, was clinging to the tail of the F-14, trying to take the inside track in the turn in order to bring his 30mm gun to bear. Norris turned to glance at the pursuing MiG. He was close, very close, and hanging desperately to their tail. Hastings suddenly reversed his rudder to swing the aircraft into a hard right turn in an attempt to shake off the MiG, and as a result Norris's head slammed into the side of the canopy.

Norris shook his head to clear it and glanced back at their pursuer once again. The MiG was still there. Of all the pilots in the North Korean Air Force, we have to get one of the best, he thought.

A series of malevolent flashes emanated from the MiG's port wing root. For a moment Norris thought he was launching another missile, but then he realized that the North Korean was firing his cannon. All he needed was one burst. . . .

Hastings's voice floated over the intercom to the still-groggy Norris. "Hang on, Rick. I'm going to stop the aircraft."

Hastings brought the plane out of its turn, yanked back on the stick, and backed off on the throttle. The nose pitched up and the aircraft suddenly decelerated. The MiG pilot, caught by surprise, roared by the F-14. Hastings expertly slid in behind the MiG and suddenly the roles of hunter and hunted were reversed.

Hastings closed in with a vengeance. He lined up the circle on the MiG, got a tone, and sent a Sidewinder on its way, but the MiG immediately dropped flares and rolled right. The Sidewinder went after the flares and detonated far away from its intended target.

Hastings cursed loudly and moved to close the distance between him and the North Korean. Hastings flipped the selector switch on his stick from missiles to guns and immediately began to line up the gunsight reticle on his display with the fleeing MiG.

The MiG pilot was not making things easy for Hastings. Just as Hastings would line up the enemy plane the North Korean would initiate some evasive maneuver and Hastings would have to begin again.

Finally the superiority of the training received by Hastings and the edge that his F-14 had over the MiG took its toll. Even a violent reversal of rudder by the MiG pilot couldn't keep Hastings from getting his boresight on the MiG.

Hastings slid his finger down over the button and with mounting anticipation he pressed it, producing a peculiar howling sound as a stream of cannon shells from the gunport on the left side headed toward the MiG. Norris could hear Hastings's nervous breathing and occasional muttering. An oath or two came through periodically as Hastings fiercely concentrated on keeping the gyrating MiG in his sights. Once he had the MiG lined up in the circle on his display, he grimly kept it there and fired burst after burst of 20mm shells.

Suddenly Hastings knew he had won. The enemy plane had slowed considerably, and pieces of its fuselage were being ripped off by the accurate firing of the F-14's cannon. The evasive maneuvering became less and less pronounced until Hastings began to fear that the North Korean pilot would punch out into the path of his aircraft.

He raked the MiG once more with his cannon, then took a position above and behind the vanquished aircraft to await the inevitable result. Smoke and fuel were pouring from the fuselage; Hastings wondered if the pilot would make it. He waited for the pilot to eject, but the plane began to dive and disintegrate. Probably dead, he thought. His eyes followed what was left of the MiG until it hit the water with a tremendous splash.

Hastings took a deep breath and felt a fluttering sensation as he exhaled. So this was combat. He'd never been exposed to the real thing before, but he couldn't stem the feeling of accomplishment that was rising in him. He had given an excellent account of himself—three MiGs in his first action. He'd probably get a medal for it and his career would receive a tremendous boost. He pushed the stick to one side and did the traditional victory roll. "We sure showed that bastard, huh, Rick?"

"You got it, Commander."

Hastings glanced at his fuel gauge. He was way off his fuel "ladder," the markers he had made up for this mission showing how much fuel he had left versus time into the mission. No problem if he could land on the ship. If he had to go to Osan he'd be running on fumes by the time he got there.

Hastings set a course for the *Truman* and worried at what he might find. Could Simmons be right? Had the North Koreans attacked the ship with gas and helicopters? If it was true it would explain a few things, such as no contact with any ship in the task force.

The thought again skittered across his mind that if he reached the *Truman* too late, Simmons would be dead or captured. He shook his head at the confused feelings the thought generated. He certainly would like to see Simmons get a comeuppance but not at the price of losing the ship. Memory of the fear that was on Simmons's face just before Hastings had attacked him in the passageway ran through his mind. He smiled. There was some satisfaction in that.

His smile was short-lived. Physically beating Simmons was no answer to the problems in his relationship with his wife and son. He had a decision to make—fight for them, not physically but emotionally, or back off and leave Eva and Simmons alone. But that decision was for later. Now he had to concentrate on this situation to ensure his survival as well as that of the *Truman*.

"How much farther to the ship?" he asked his RIO.

"A little more than three minutes," replied Norris.

"By the way, Rick, I'm proud of you. You were really on the ball back there. Couldn't have gotten those victories without you. You know that."

"Thanks, Commander."

"When CAG finds out what we did to those MiGs, man, is he going to be happy," said Hastings. "There'll be medals all around."

"As long as CAG is still around," was Norris's distant reply.

"Yeah." Hastings's enthusiasm faded.

They flew on in silence as Hastings scanned the sea below for any trace of the *Truman*. Norris alternated between trying to raise the task force and scrutinizing the radar screen in front of him.

Hastings finally noticed an indefinable object on the horizon and blinked his eyes several times in an effort to see what it was. It seemed fuzzy and dark and lacked definition. After a moment Hastings spoke over the intercom.

"Stay heads-up, Rick. We've got smoke on the horizon. See if you can get it on camera."

"Right, Commander." Norris's reply seemed far away, but then he came back in a tense voice.

"Skipper, I'm getting low-level radar contacts dead ahead. No response to IFF."

Hastings's eyes switched between the horizon and the TV monitor as he strained to detect the contacts to which Norris referred. Suddenly the contacts were in full view on the monitor; they appeared to Hastings like a cluster of flies hovering over some discarded piece of food. A few seconds more and he picked out rotor blades spinning at the edge of the world.

Helicopters! A lot of them. Simmons was right!

The superstructure of a ship peeked over the horizon and in a few moments the entire ship was in view. The *Truman*! She was still in one piece. Hastings followed the line of smoke from where it ended in the sky down to its origin on the flight deck. Something on the flight deck was totally engulfed in flames. As they drew closer they saw gunfire directed toward the flight deck coming from some of the helicopters orbiting the ship. The North Korean insignia on the side of the helicopters flashed boldly in the sun in seeming defiance of Hastings and his aircraft. He streaked by overhead and immediately put the plane in a sharp turn to attack the enemy helicopters.

God, the nerve of those bastards—trying to board a carrier, he thought. The *Truman* must have gone straight through the gas cloud. He wondered how the North Koreans delivered the gas. He shoved the thought aside and concentrated on the helicopters.

The helos were beginning to scatter all over the sea. He'd pay hell trying to catch all of them. They were smaller and much more maneuverable than his F-14, but they couldn't outrun him.

"How many 'winders we got left, Rick?"

"One."

Hastings shook his head. Nothing's ever easy. "It'll be guns then," he said.

"Roger."

Hastings eyeballed his round estimator. More than five hundred rounds left; it should be enough, but it might take him all day. He sighed and locked his wings full forward for low-speed flying, then he lined up the nose of his aircraft with three dots in the distance. In a few seconds the three dots turned into North Korean helicopters. They were hauling ass for the North Korean coast.

The helicopters were in staggered formation, the two trailing helos to the right and behind the lead helo. Hastings got an idea and jinked to the right. He'd come at them at an angle so that one burst from his Gatling gun would carry across all three of them.

He got the gun circle on the trailing helicopter and pressed the trigger. A howling sound started from the left side of the fuselage, and Hastings knew that his gun was throwing rounds at the targets at an incredible rate.

The initial fire went past the three helicopters and sent geysers of water into the air as each round struck the sea. Hastings made a minor correction, and the stream of cannon shells from the fighter found its mark with devastating effect. The three helicopters were shattered in quick succession as the F-14's flight took its stream of fire across each helo. The last two helos exploded in midair; the lead helo had its main rotor blades chopped off. It went nose down and crashed into the sea.

Hastings streaked by overhead as the North Korean soldiers fought in vain to get out of the sinking helicopter. Hastings had a brief thought of what it must be like inside the sinking helo, of what kind of hell the North Koreans were going through. He quickly dismissed it. He had a job to do; he couldn't get distracted now. The North Koreans hadn't seen him approaching. They hadn't taken any evasive maneuvers at all. That gave him a queer feeling. He put the aircraft into a sharp left turn.

"How many left, Rick? Did you get a count?"

"Twelve left, Skipper."

Hastings muttered in acknowledgment. Two helicopters appeared off to the left and were heading right at him. He got the gun circle lined up again and sent a burst their way. The helicopters made a quick evasive maneuver, but it wasn't quick enough for one of them. Hastings cut the enemy chopper in two, and he got a brief glimpse of bodies clad in dark green tumbling out of the two sections of the severed aircraft. The burst missed the other helo.

Hastings thought that the North Koreans hadn't done badly by that maneuver. Head directly at the oncoming F-14 to give the smallest target aspect possible, and close the distance between them as fast as possible. That would shorten the time he had to react and fire.

Hastings went into a left turn and the escaping helo crossed his nose. He fired a burst, leading the helo just enough, then held it as the nose of his aircraft swung the line of fire past the helo. Scratch another helicopter.

"Ten to go, Skipper," reported Norris.

Hastings got three more helos in individual battles, then gained altitude to spot the rest of them. All seven were in a line abreast and heading for North Korea. As Hastings flew toward them he had a feeling of foreboding. This was a bit too easy. They had something up their sleeve.

He swung around to their right and attempted to fly down their line so that one long burst would get most of them. He had just about gotten the gun circle on the rightmost helicopter when they suddenly wheeled to face him. Their noses lit up with intermittent flashes.

Nose guns! The helicopters had nose machine guns. Hastings fired a quick burst and shattered two helicopters in the middle of the line, then rolled left to evade the enemy fire. He had to hand it to the North Koreans. They didn't give up.

Lieutenant Hong shouted into the microphone. "Ch'ollima 2, this is Ch'ollima 1. We are under attack from a lone American fighter! Can you assist? Over." He repeated the call over and over and added in his position coordinates. It would take a miracle for them to shoot down the American plane with their machine guns. Ch'ollima 2 was their only hope, or one by one they would succumb to the American fighter plane.

Lieutenant Nam Hac Pil keyed his transmitter. His hand was shaking. "This is Ch'ollima 2. I'm on my way."

Nam had gotten separated from the rest of his squadron during the dogfight and had relaxed with the thought that the battle was over for him. His fuel was beginning to get low and he was out of missiles. All of his missiles either missed or detonated far away from the targets. They had to have better equipment to go up against the Americans. It was suicide to do it with what they had now.

He grumbled to himself. Now the helicopter force was in trouble, and duty was calling him back. He snorted in disgust. Duty would get him killed someday.

General Kang sat up straight in his chair. Now what was this? The message was mixed in with noise and dropped out several times, but it was repeated over and over. His helicopter force was again calling for help from his air force. He glanced at the elapsed time indicator. Pak should have had his men on the flight deck by now.

Tension eased in Kang. This must be the empty helicopters that were returning to base after unloading their men on the *Truman*'s flight deck. If they were shot down it didn't matter. Pak's men must be in control of the ship by now, and the American planes could do nothing to prevent it. What would they do? Attack their own ship? Absurd.

One word the helicopter pilot had used suddenly struck him. *Lone*. The lone American plane. Only one American plane left? Excitement ran through him. Kang smiled involuntarily, his face cracking and twisting in his rendition of mirth.

The *Truman* was his.

Hastings gave a disgruntled glance at his round estimator. A hundred rounds left and five helicopters to go. He swung the aircraft after the remaining helos. They were five abreast and flying at maximum speed toward the North Korean coast. Hastings lined up on one end of them and shoved the throttle forward. No sense giving them time to set up.

He fired a subsecond burst just as they started to wheel toward him in a repeat of their previous tactic. They fired machine gun bursts at him, but he was on them before they could adjust their aim. He shaved the tail section off one helicopter, causing it to spin helplessly end over end. Seconds later, it crashed into the sea.

The remaining enemy helicopters scattered before Hastings's onslaught, but one couldn't get out of the way fast enough. The F-14 slashed through the air overhead at something near Mach 1 and caught the helicopter in an enormous downdraft. The helicopter was shoved nose first into the sea, its main rotor blade shattering as it hit the water and the cabin crumpling into one tenth of its former size. The fifty North Korean soldiers inside were crushed to death instantly, their remains left to slowly sink to the bottom of Korea Bay.

Three to go. Hastings lined up behind another helicopter and dispatched it with a longer burst of fire than he wanted. He wheeled and sheared off the rotor blades of another, then went after the final helicopter. Fifty rounds left.

He lined up on the North Korean aircraft and squeezed the trigger just as the helo jinked to the left. Forty rounds left. Hastings cursed to himself as he swung by and went into a turn to get at the helo again. He got the gun circle on the target and squeezed the trigger again. The helo jinked to the right and Hastings's fire splashed harmlessly in the water. He lined up a third time, then swung slightly to the left and squeezed the trigger. The helo jinked to the left, directly into Hastings's stream of cannon shells.

The side of the helicopter was ripped open, exposing the shattered bodies of the soldiers on that side of the helo. They tumbled out the open side of the stricken aircraft and into the water. The helicopter flipped over onto its wounded side and dropped like a rock. The rest of its human cargo fell out the open side and dropped, writhing and screaming, into the sea.

Pak gaped in horror from his vantage point in the hangar bay. He had seen most of his helos shot down by looking out under the port side aircraft elevator. He had died each time a helicopter was shot down and was weeping uncontrollably by the end of Hastings's slaughter. Seven hundred fifty of his men had been killed before his eyes by a single aircraft!

He ripped off his gas mask and collapsed to the deck. To lose men in the heat of combat was one thing. At least they would have an honorable death. But *this!* They were slaughtered like dumb animals led to the chopping block. He sobbed for a minute, then forced his emotions under control. Suppose his men saw him like this? It wouldn't do.

He quickly counted. Four helicopters landed, one exploded. One hundred fifty men left in the three helicopters, of which about fifteen had been killed below decks and an unknown number had been killed taking the island. If he had a hundred men left he'd be lucky.

The excited shouts of his men came to him from the other end of the hangar bay. Pak dragged himself to his feet and carefully wiped his eyes. In any event his forces had all of the ship except the engineering spaces. He would see to that next.

Simmons heard another explosion but this time it didn't come from the island. He squirmed around to get a look behind him. All of the men cut down by the helo were still, except for one who raised a blood-soaked arm in a vain attempt to summon help.

He heard another explosion and suddenly realized that the helicopter that was keeping them pinned down by machine gun fire was gone. The only sounds that reached him were the horrible sounds of automatic weapons' fire from the island and the hangar bay. He glanced quickly aft and saw with surprise that the helicopter that was about to land had disappeared.

Now maybe he had a chance of saving the ship! He scrambled out from under the disabled helicopter and gazed up into the sky. The helicopters that had been hovering near the ship were now fleeing headlong before the onslaught of a lone F-14.

Simmons squinted into the distance. Is it Hastings? A cold feeling came over him. When he's done with the enemy helicopters, will he start on me? That's ridiculous, he thought. A fistfight in a passageway is a far cry from a navy pilot murdering another naval officer in the middle of a battle. Still, how many witnesses would there be? Could the RIO see what the pilot was shooting at?

He shook off the thought with some difficulty. I have to hand it to him—he turned the tide. A few moments before, he had been on the verge of surrender; now they had a chance. Simmons didn't know why he was so optimistic; he had more than a hundred North Koreans below decks.

He redirected his attention toward the dead and dying on the flight deck. As he knelt down next to the one man who was still alive he heard the scream of jet engines. He looked up quickly just in time to see the F-14 thunder by overhead.

He stared at the symbol painted on the tail: a white skull in a field of black with blood red kisses coming from it. He knew what the logo said underneath it. Kiss of Death.

Hastings put the fighter into a leisurely climb. That was Simmons on the flight deck. And he looked damned helpless. *I hope he feels that way. I hope he feels sick to his stomach, like I felt when . . .*

Lieutenant Nam saw smoke on the horizon. Dread ran through him. *What was waiting for him there? A lurking American fighter plane?* His eyes quickly scanned the skies above. He could see nothing. *Turn on his radar?* Nam resisted the impulse. The American planes had radar warning receivers just as the Koreans did. The ship did also, and there was no sense warning anybody on the ship that he was in the vicinity.

He had gone to the coordinates given to him by the helicopter force, but there was no one, no sign that the helicopters had ever been there. Wrong coordinates had been given under pressure before, and Nam suspected that that was what had happened. Or maybe he was too late and the helicopters had been shot down. If that was the case, the sea would leave no trace.

Nam took a deep breath to settle his insides and made a decision. He would fly by the carrier to see if he could aid his countrymen in some way. It would look good on his record that he had overflown the American vessel. He revised the thought. It might be indispensable to his future health to see what was happening on the carrier after getting that distress call from the helicopter force.

Nam approached the *Truman* by making a wide circle around the vessel so that he wouldn't be seen by anyone above decks. He slowed the aircraft to a near stall and stared at the flight deck. *A helicopter burning!* The attack had gone badly, even worse than the air battle. Three figures were on the flight deck and none wore the dark green of the North Korean attack force. One wore khaki and the other two had dark blue pants and lighter blue shirts. *Americans!*

A chill ran through him. The flight deck was the first objective of Pak's assault force and Americans were obviously in control of it. *The attack had totally failed!* Nam cursed the lack of any air-to-ship missiles. All he had were cannon rounds, but he resolved to use any means at his disposal to attack the ship.

Lieutenant Nam put his aircraft in a wide turn to approach the *Truman* head-on.

The whine of jet engines faded in the distance as Paul Simmons shoved Hastings from his mind and looked to his men. One man had a hole blown through his midsection; it looked as if some blunt instrument had gouged its way from one side of his body to the other. He was alive but not for long. The injured man raised his head to speak but finally settled down; he gave Simmons and the two sailors standing next to him such a look of despair and agony that Simmons had to avert his eyes.

Simmons turned to walk away and tried to eliminate the grisly scene from his mind, but the pitiful sight remained with him, a horrible reminder of the possible fate of any man on the ship. He looked back and saw his two men staring with mixed sympathy and revulsion at the man lying on the deck.

"Let's go," Simmons said.

"Can't we do something for him?" asked one of the men.

"No," Simmons replied flatly.

Something was wrong. A flag had gone up in Simmons's mind, something he could not ignore. There was a buzzing at some sublevel of consciousness, a warning of approaching disaster. He glanced around quickly. Everyone on the flight deck except him and his men was dead or wounded. Simmons gazed aft past the charred bodies of the North Korean soldiers who had landed in that ill-fated first helicopter. The remains of the helicopter still burned furiously and sent a pall of smoke high into the sky.

He shifted his gaze toward the island, noting that it was silent. The battle for the island was over and opposition to the North Korean onslaught had ended. Far away in the bowels of the ship he heard the chatter of automatic weapons' fire. Someone was still resisting. Probably Chief Taylor. He felt the urgent need to join forces with Taylor to continue to defend the ship, but the feeling was subordinate to his sense of impending danger. He shook it off and started aft to find a different way below decks other than the island, which he assumed was in enemy hands.

The buzzing in the back of his mind changed rapidly to the scream of jet engines. Simmons looked in the direction of the noise and saw a low-flying aircraft. Something about the approach of the aircraft confirmed his feeling of impending disaster. He squinted at the rapidly nearing dot in the sky.

Is it Hastings, or—

A tenth of a second later, the answer streaked through his brain, an unformulated, unarticulated flash of knowledge caused by a weak electrical impulse across his cortex.

MiG!

Simmons turned and ran for cover, his legs and arms pumping wildly. He caught sight of a yellow truck and headed for it at full speed. The scream of jets became modulated by a thumping sound, which Simmons knew was the plane's cannon.

The cannon shells began to shatter the flight deck behind him and sent pieces of men and machines flying in an orgy of destruction. He had only about a second left, he thought, maybe less. His thoughts turned to despair as he fought to reach the truck just ahead of the exploding cannon shells.

After what seemed like an eternity, Simmons approached the truck and desperately flung himself behind it. But the vehicle concealed a gaping hole left in the flight deck by the port side aircraft elevator. The waist-high safety line that surrounded the hole tripped him as he was going full speed for cover and he was somersaulted into space. He made a desperate grab for the line and got one hand on it, but his momentum wrenched his hand free and he fell to the surface below, landing heavily on his left side. Pain shot through him and he cried out in agony.

The truck above him exploded and its roar mingled with the thunder of the MiG as it streaked by overhead. Simmons was aware only of the sensation of pain, wetness on the side of his face, and the abrasive nonskid coating on the deck of the aircraft elevator. He opened his eyes and through blurred vision slowly focused on the climbing jet.

"You lousy bastard!" he gasped.

The MiG turned and made a wide circle to come up abeam of the carrier as if in response to Simmons's oath.

"How the hell did he get in there?" Hastings mumbled angrily under his breath. The MiG had sneaked in behind them as they climbed to thirty thousand feet to look over the *Truman*'s escort vessels and to survey the area for any remaining North Korean aircraft. The thought occurred to him that the MiG might kill Simmons. All he would have to do is hesitate just enough so that the MiG could get in another strafing run.

Hastings cursed himself for the thought. There were other people on the ship besides Simmons. He immediately put the F-14 into a screaming dive.

Norris came over the intercom. "He's making a turn for a beam attack on the ship."

"We'll get him," muttered Hastings.

Simmons stared at the circling MiG through a fog of pain and fear. The MiG came out of its turn and leveled off at a hundred feet off the water to streak in on the *Truman*. Simmons sat, commanding his body to move to no avail, as the MiG headed straight for the elevator and Simmons, closing the distance to the ship at an incredible rate.

Where the hell is Hastings? He's going to leave me to die!

Flashes appeared at the port wing root, and the ocean kicked up with savage pulses in a direct line to Simmons.

Another aircraft lined up behind the approaching MiG and sent what seemed like a blur of light toward the enemy plane. In a fraction of a second it was over. The MiG burst into a ball of flame.

"That's number four!" The young RIO's voice had a tinge of awe in it. "I've never seen anything like that before."

Hastings grinned. It was one for the books. Coming down from thirty thousand feet, leveling off at a few hundred feet, and simultaneously firing a Sidewinder wasn't in their training manuals. He had completely ignored the radar displays and had done some old-fashioned, seat-of-the-pants flying. A glance at his fuel gauge confirmed that he'd barely have enough fuel to get to the South Korean mainland. He let out a sigh of relief and gained some altitude to streak over the *Truman* once again before heading for Osan.

Hastings leaned over and stared at the flaming carrier. Someone was moving on the port aircraft elevator. It was Simmons. Well, I've saved the bastard's life. It's the right thing to do, isn't it? Is that the only revenge I'll get for the things Simmons has done to me?

He felt a sense of satisfaction run through him. Maybe it was enough.

Chapter Fifteen

S immons watched the flaming pieces of the MiG splash into the
water, then glanced up at the F-14 as it roared by overhead. He
tried to lift his right hand but couldn't find the strength. The aircraft
was already gone.

Hastings saved the Truman, *and now he's saved me. He could have
easily left me to die, but he didn't. How do I thank him when this is
over? What do I say?*

The realization weighed on him that although the *Truman* now seemed
safe from external attack, a large number of enemy soldiers were still
on board. The fight wasn't even close to being over.

He laid his head back on the hard surface of the elevator, closed
his eyes, and tried to deny the pain that was traveling through him.
He needed to rest if only for a second. The light that came through
his eyelids shimmered and faded, and his mind swam through time
and space. There was a figure standing in front of him.

How's the arm, Son?

Dad, what are you doing here?

Just thought I'd check up on you. Your mother's kind of worried.

The arm's OK, I guess. His father moved to go.

Dad, wait a minute. His father turned back around. *He doesn't look.*

at me directly—his eyes are off to one side. Why doesn't he look at me directly?

Yes, Son?

How did you get through it, Dad?

I guess I didn't have time to think about it.

Weren't you scared?

I never gave it a thought. I figured some other guys would get it but not me. If I had gotten shot, I'd have been really surprised.

So, that's the answer, then. You never thought about it even years after it all happened.

I've got to go, Son.

Why don't you look at me, Dad? Are you afraid you'll see in my face what you felt so long ago?

The figure faded and Simmons felt as though he was falling into an abyss. A cavernous nothing stretched out below him and he raced toward it, picking up speed, faster and faster until the nothingness sped by in a blur of motion. He fought for his breath, but it was being taken away by his headlong rush.

Suddenly he felt himself moving upward, and a great weight seemed to lie on him that increased as he moved. The light slowly returned.

He opened his eyes and looked about. He was lying on the port aircraft elevator. He had fallen or rolled to the aft end, away from the dripping, flaming gasoline from the truck on the flight deck that had exploded from the MiG's cannon fire. The elevator was presently stopped halfway between the flight deck and the hangar bay. Why was the elevator halfway down? His mind struggled. He searched his memory but gave up as the pain in his left arm blotted out his thoughts.

His left forearm had not fully recovered from the engine room accident and his left shoulder still hurt from his battle with Hastings. The fall onto his left side had only aggravated a bad situation into a worse one.

His face felt wet. He touched his left cheek and discovered blood; he had scraped his face on the abrasive surface of the elevator. He rolled over onto his right side, gasping in agony at the effort, and realized to his surprise that he still had the North Korean hand grenades with him. One of them had dug into his side when he fell. He dragged himself to his feet and staggered to the inboard edge of the elevator.

The answer to one of his questions flashed into his mind. He had called down to engineering to cut the power to this elevator to stop the North Koreans from getting below decks. His order had come too late. When the elevator stopped halfway down, the enemy had merely jumped from the elevator to the hangar bay.

Simmons's heart sank. There were about fifty soldiers in each helicopter and chances were that all the soldiers from one helicopter had made it to the hangar bay. The other two helicopters contributed a hundred soldiers, but about fifty of them had been killed as they assaulted the island. That made about a hundred enemy soldiers still left on the ship.

How many men did he have left? He had no idea. He had maybe fifty to start with, counting all the engineering personnel still conscious, but he had lost at least half of them on the flight deck and in the island. He held out hope that most of the sailors in the island had retreated below decks to defend the engineering spaces.

He quickly scanned the sky. At least Hastings had gotten rid of the rest of the North Korean helicopters and that MiG that had come out of nowhere. Were there more enemy planes above? If there were then he didn't have too much longer to live. Any one plane with the right weapons could blow this thing out of the water. He'd have to leave that part of the battle up to Hastings.

He pushed the thoughts from his mind and looked into the ship. It was about fifteen feet to the hangar bay level. After summoning up his courage, he gingerly jumped down to the hangar bay. He hit the deck and rolled to his right to protect his wounded left side, then froze immediately and listened intently to locate the remainder of the enemy. There didn't seem to be anyone in the hangar bay, at least not in the aft section.

The ship throbbed beneath his feet. The vessel seemed to go on living with ceaseless energy flowing from its nuclear reactors despite what might have happened to its crew or the enemy soldiers. Most of the crew was unconscious and the ship left unattended, and yet it still moved through the water as if the mortals were unnecessary to the ship's mission. The noise of the sea sliding by the hull, and the sound of an occasional breaking wave filled the hangar bay.

He looked forward and was greeted by rows of F-18s and F-14s, their wings folded back. Muffled gunfire erupted in the bowels of the ship. Taylor and his men must still be battling the invaders. A murmur of voices floated over to him across the space of the hangar bay, but it was a pattern of speech that sounded foreign to his ears. Simmons worked his way forward toward the sound of the voices until he got to an open area in the middle of the hangar bay. He gaped at the sight in front of him and horror ran through him.

There were bodies strewn on the deck. All of them were Americans; they had been shot in the back while running away. They were the men from the island who had opened fire on the helicopters as they landed on the flight deck. Under the North Korean assault they broke and ran, with the enemy in pursuit. Most of them made it to the hangar bay, only to be gunned down by the vicious foe.

Simmons fought back a rising tide of despair. His decision to resist the boarding of the ship had cost many lives. The men had followed him because he was in command, and he had led them to their deaths. He made an instant decision. He would surrender and stop the killing.

The murmur came to him again across the expanse of the hangar bay. The murmur changed suddenly into angry shouts, and Simmons realized that the language spoken was not English. He dove for cover under the nearest F-14 and cautiously worked his way forward on his hands and knees.

After crawling under the third plane in the row he finally got a clear view of the situation. Amid a host of trucks and planes scattered about the deck stood four North Korean soldiers with their guns trained on two terrified U.S. Navy sailors.

Simmons had just made up his mind to show himself when one of the North Koreans, who looked to be an officer, stopped the speech he was making and got a sadistic smile on his face. He unsnapped the cover on the holster at his side and drew out his pistol. He shouted a syllable or two at the other soldiers and they rushed forward to force the two pleading sailors to their knees. The officer walked around behind them and pointed his pistol at the neck of one of the sailors.

Simmons's mouth dropped open in horrified astonishment. The sailors were pleading for their lives and the North Koreans were not saying a word. Suddenly the North Korean officer tilted the gun away from the sailor's head and looked inquiringly forward.

Simmons then heard another steadily growing voice. A fifth North Korean burst into view. Judging by the deference paid to him by the North Korean officer, Simmons guessed that he must be their leader. He was a powerfully built man and stood with his arms slightly away from his sides as he shouted and gestured angrily toward the forward part of the ship. The other officer took the harangue with humility and hastily put away his pistol. In the middle of the senior officer's lecture he hustled his men and the two American sailors forward, with the senior officer following.

Simmons slowly let out his breath in relief. He would not have to witness the execution of his men after all. He quickly made another decision—he would not surrender. He would rather die resisting the enemy than get a bullet in the back of the head. He couldn't rely on that senior officer to stop every one of his soldiers from executing Americans.

He glanced about and was surprised to find an M16 just five feet away. He cautiously slid over and picked it up without making a sound. The senior officer was still in sight and Simmons had a clear shot at him. He hurriedly pulled back the T-shaped cocking bar and pushed the selector lever on the left side to full automatic. He put the weapon on his shoulder and quickly got the officer in his sights. The North Korean had his back to Simmons and his hands on his hips in disgust over the lack of discipline in his men.

Simmons centered the sights on the small of his back. All that was needed to rip the man's back open would be the pressure of one finger on the trigger. The burst would raise the barrel, the bullets stitching a line up his back, tearing him apart.

Simmons hesitated, then slowly lowered the weapon from his shoulder. He couldn't do it. To kill a man in the heat of battle was one thing, but to shoot a man in the back when he wasn't expecting it was something else. Simmons cursed his weakness. They were the enemy; he had to stop them from taking over the ship. He didn't pick this fight, they did.

The North Korean moved farther forward and disappeared behind a plane on the port side. He reappeared on the other side of the aircraft, preceded by the other North Koreans and the two captive sailors. They walked over to the starboard side and disappeared into a passageway in the forward hangar bay.

Simmons appeared to be alone in the hangar bay. He crawled out from under the plane and stared in revulsion at the scattered bodies. The sight of first class stripes on a blue work shirt caught Simmons's eye. The body was in a pool of blood, but he instantly recognized the face. It was Wright, the electrician's mate, who had been next to him in those first terrifying moments in the island. He turned away in utter disgust at the futility and waste of this small war they were fighting.

How could he stop the North Koreans now? Was Taylor still fighting? He listened intently and heard intermittent bursts of automatic weapons' fire. So, it wasn't over yet.

A telephone, he thought. He needed to make contact with Taylor. After quickly looking about, he spotted an office just off the hangar bay and ran over to it. He got behind the desk and with shaking hands dialed the number to the forward EOS. Tension mounted in him as the phone rang and rang. The receiver was finally lifted and Simmons held his breath in anticipation.

"Hello?" There was surprise in the voice.

Simmons almost jumped for joy. Whoever the speaker was, he was an American. "This is Mr. Simmons. What the hell is going on down there?" he shouted into the mouthpiece.

"Mr. Simmons! We thought you were dead!" the man replied. There was undeniable elation in his voice. "Thank God you're all right! We're fighting for our lives down here. So far we're holding them off, but I don't know how long we can last."

Taylor had done it! He had held out! Simmons exhaled with relief. "How many of them are there and where are they?" he demanded.

"I think most of them are still on second deck. We made first contact on second deck in the galley. We slowed them down some, but they started throwing hand grenades, so we ran like hell for third deck. They haven't gotten down here yet, at least not near the engineering spaces. I think we've got 'em stopped now." He stopped to take a breath.

"How many of them are there?" Simmons repeated his question.

"About fifty to sixty, I think, but it's hard to tell. You'd better get down here with some men, sir, or they might take third deck from us."

Men? What men? he thought bitterly. He looked out of the office toward the pile of corpses in the hangar bay. *There* were his men.

"I'll try to get down there as soon as possible," said Simmons in a lame voice. The sailor urged him to hurry and they both hung up.

The noise Simmons had been hearing subliminally finally registered in his mind and caused him to jump. Someone was in the hangar bay with him.

Lieutenant Commander Tom Arnold felt his aircraft slow suddenly. His nose began to dip. He had taken a burst from the 30mm gun of a MiG-29 that had gotten behind him. His visual had splashed the North Korean and had saved Arnold's life. Arnold adjusted the trim to get the nose up and looked over the gauges. The starboard engine was running hot and the aircraft had an increasing tendency to yaw to the right.

"Frank, this is Arnie," he said into his microphone. "Drop down and give me the once-over."

"Roger." His wingman took up a position fifty feet behind him and did a slow roll around Arnold's aircraft. "I can see through the center of the starboard wing and also through sections of the starboard vertical and horizontal tail surfaces."

The wingman stopped for a moment. Arnold could hear breathing over the comm net. "You've got vapor coming from the starboard engine exhaust," he continued.

Arnold nodded to himself. He had figured as much. He'd be losing altitude soon. "Teddy, what's the range to those MiGs?" he asked his RIO.

"Fifty miles and increasing," his RIO came back. "They're over North Korean airspace," he added.

The squadron's CO, Comdr. Ron Hastings, had given the rest of the squadron to him to get the remaining MiG-29s that had attacked them. As the squadron's XO he wasn't about to give up just because his aircraft had taken some hits. Arnold looked around and saw that the remainder of Blackline flight had formed up on him in a spread-out V.

"All right, how many of you guys got any Phoenixes left?" he asked.

"This is Blake. I've got one."

"I've got one, too. This is the Trapper."

Counting the one Arnold still had made three. Fifty miles was no sweat to a Phoenix missile. They would give those five fleeing North Koreans a surprise.

"OK. I don't want to chase these guys right into a shit load of triple A," he said to his squadron. "Arm the Phoenixes and let's get three of them at least."

"Roger," they all seemed to say at once.

"Launch sequence is Blake, Trapper, and yours truly," said Arnold.

Blake came back after only a second's hesitation. "Fox three!"

Trapper's rumbling voice came over the comm net. "Fox three! Go you mutha!"

Teddy launched Arnold's last Phoenix. "Fox three!" said Arnold.

The five aircrews watched the trails of the three missiles disappear into the distance. They switched to the TV and watched for a few more seconds as the Mach 5–plus missile sought its unsuspecting quarry.

Arnold's eyes flew over his instruments. The starboard engine was rapidly degrading—his wingman reported more vapor out the exhaust. He'd have to shut it down soon. He had to keep this heading so that they would know if they got the MiGs.

After what seemed like an eternity, Terry came over the comm net. "Splash one!"

"Way to go, Blake!" said someone.

"Splash two! Congrats Trapper!" Then, "Splash three!"

"Confirm all three kills," said Trapper.

Arnold shook his head. It was a curious, anticlimactic end to a furious, blood-pounding dogfight. It left him a little uneasy.

He started to lose altitude. "I'm shutting down the starboard engine," he said and pulled the throttle back. He locked the wings full forward, corrected for pitch, and increased power to the port engine, but he still continued to lose altitude.

His wingman came over the comm net. "Arnie, you've got vapor out of the port engine now."

"Frank, stick with me. The rest of you keep at angels three zero. All right, let's make the turn to get back to the ship."

They made the turn to port and Arnold settled down to a nail biter of a return leg to their floating home. Goddam KORCOM, thought Arnold. He really did a number on me.

"Teddy, give me range to the ship."

"Thirty-five miles."

Arnold did a mental calculation. At his present rate of descent, he'd just make it. Barely. Nothing to do but play it out. He thought of trying to contact the ship but rejected it. He probably wouldn't get any answer, and if any other MiGs were around it would only alert them to their presence. He didn't need another dogfight now. They were all very low on fuel; another battle and they'd never make the ship.

Arnold gave a worried glance at his altimeter. Twenty-five hundred feet and dropping fast. Below two thousand he couldn't eject. The aircraft was still controllable and he should be able to catch a wire if he didn't have to orbit the ship too many times. He'd have to catch the wire the first time; with one sick engine he wouldn't have enough thrust to get back up to altitude. His gaze centered on the horizon. Smoke! Please don't let it be the *Truman*!

"Vapor's increased from the exhaust, Arnie. Maybe you ought to punch out," said his wingman.

Arnold glanced at the altimeter. Nineteen hundred feet. "I can still put her on the deck," he replied.

His RIO was staring at his TV screen. "We got a flight deck fire on the *Truman*!"

Arnold looked at his screen with alarm but couldn't make out any details in the boiling smoke. One thing was certain, they couldn't land there.

"Ship must have been attacked. Cruise missile, I guess," said Teddy.

"Whatever it was doesn't matter right at the moment. Get ready to ditch," ordered Arnold.

"Roger." His RIO seemed calm enough.

"I'll jettison the canopy just before we hit. Hopefully we'll still be upright."

"Yeah, and alive," replied Teddy.

Arnold got on the comm net and told them what his plans were.

"We'll stay up and fly cover for as long as our fuel holds out, then we'll get some altitude and punch out," said Blake.

"That'll be about two minutes from now," grumbled Trapper. The rest chimed in with similar comments.

One hell of a goddamned note, thought Arnold. We kick some KORCOM ass and come back heroes, only to all run out of fuel and wind up in the drink. Well, maybe the *Truman* can get a helo up to pick us all up. Time to give them a call.

"Kingpin, Kingpin, this is Blackline 102. Mayday! Mayday! Will ditch on your port beam at seven thousand yards. Over."

Silence. "Mayday! Mayday! Answer up, Kingpin. I'm losing altitude fast. Will splash down in approximately thirty seconds. Over." Again silence. "Ah, shit," he said over the plane's intercom. "Let's get ready."

"Roger. Straps," said his RIO.

"Check."

"IFF."

"On emergency."

"SIF. 7700." Then, "Position."

"On transmit."

"Visor."

"Down."

Arnold grabbed the yellow-striped handle on the upper right side of his control panel.

The waters of Korea Bay rushed up to meet them. Arnold waited until they were ten feet above the water, then squeezed the canopy jettison handle and pulled. The canopy rocketed away and the handle came off in Arnold's hand. He dropped it, shut down his remaining engine, and put both hands on the stick. He got the nose up and prayed to get over a small wave that sped toward them. They were past it in a second and he felt the tail begin to scrape the water.

Suddenly it dug in and the plane slowed with a shudder. The tail shot into the air and pointed the nose down. Arnold yanked back on the stick, and the nose came up slightly. It wasn't enough. The aircraft hit nose first and dug into the water, flipping the huge aircraft over on its top. The plane bounced, then settled down into the sea upside down and with one wing in the air.

Arnold and his backseater, upside down and under the water, hit the harness release and scrambled to swim downward and to one side of the sinking aircraft. A minute later they broke the surface ten yards away from the wreckage, both thanking God for the underwater drills in flight school.

Arnold got his helmet off and scanned the skies for the rest of Blackline flight. He saw two chutes off in the distance. The rest of them would be joining them in the water in minutes. His gaze swung over to the massive carrier more than three miles away.

The *Truman* sailed away trailing a line of smoke.

Chapter Sixteen

Taylor got his breathing under control and shook his head to relieve the ringing in his ears. He scrambled to his feet and surveyed the space they were in. It was a bunk room just above the forward engine room.

He shook his head again and looked up at the hatch above. Several sailors had M16s trained on it in anticipation of the North Koreans. Taylor groaned to himself. They had lost second deck and a lot of men with it. The grenades had been a nasty surprise. Now he knew what military strategists meant when they said commanders used their men as expendable resources. They spent lives as you would gasoline, ammo, or food. It was the worst part of combat for a commander.

The North Koreans hadn't attacked right away. Maybe the prospect of fighting their way down a deck rather than across a deck had them worried. In any event it was up to Taylor to make the best use of the small reprieve. He grabbed a sailor near him and ordered him to find more OBA canisters and give them out. Taylor had no idea how long they had fought the enemy. It could have been five minutes or fifty minutes; he had totally lost track of time.

Had the North Koreans given up trying to take the engineering spaces? More likely they were gathering for the final assault. The fight on the second deck was just a warm-up for the main event, which would start any second now. He glanced about quickly and tried to decide how best to defend this space.

Fire zones popped into his mind. He had to set up some sort of fire zone. But where? He needed another wide, open space so he could get a lot of enemy soldiers into it, and then let fly with all the firepower he could muster. The bunk room was no good; there were too many rows of bunks that went from floor to ceiling to impede the line of fire.

Taylor worked his way aft on the third deck through two CPO living spaces and the post office, his mind working furiously. The ship was constructed to have passageways on port and starboard sides that ran pretty much the length of the ship. Firing through just two doorways would not give him enough firepower. How could he get more?

The answer hit him at once but he knew it would be extremely dangerous. The next space he stepped into was the machine shop. It was a fairly wide, open space with heavy metal lathes, presses, and cutting machines. He had his open space, and the machines would provide cover.

Taylor had read a book years ago on what a war in Europe would be like. He had been struck by a technique that the German Army would use. As they retreated they would leave behind some men, who would then come out of their hiding places after the Warsaw Pact forces advanced and harass the rear of the enemy. What were the German forces called? Jagd Kommando. The hunter-killer teams.

Taylor shook his head in frustration. He would either take a big chunk out of the enemy or get most of his men killed in the process. His mind quickly turned to planning his little surprise for the North Koreans. Fourth Squad was in the next space aft. He'd have to leave them there to show the enemy the same defense as on the second deck. The same for Fifth Squad up near the armory—they'd have to stay put in case the North Koreans came at them from the forward spaces. Who was left? Half of Squad Six and all of Squad One, plus the guys left in the enclosed operating stations, a total of eleven men.

Taylor counted the places that would cover a man. Six were good enough, maybe, to cover his people if a grenade were thrown in. To ask men to stay in a space when the enemy was likely to toss in hand grenades, no matter what the cover, was a tough order to give, to say the least. But he had to do something or the North Koreans would inundate the ship.

Taylor ran forward to get Squad One and the rest of Squad Six. He also pulled the sailors from the EOSs and silently prayed that no engineering casualty would occur that would need their attention. The *Truman* had the latest in automatic controls for the engineering plant, and the reactors and engines should be able to run for a while without human intervention.

Taylor got the men up to the machine shop and briefly told them what he had in mind, omitting the part about the grenades. One or two of them looked devastated, but the rest had the normal look of terror on their faces. Taylor singled out six men and tried not to look them in the eye. The rest he distributed in the next space forward between the port and starboard passageways.

The machine shop had a few rooms leading from its interior. He put one man in the electrical shop, one in an access trunk, one in the tool issue room, and another in the test lab. The remaining two men he put behind metal cutting machines. Taylor realized one disadvantage to the machine shop—it didn't extend all the way athwartships, or from the port passageway to the starboard passageway, as the mess decks did. He would just have to make sure that the North Koreans would come down the starboard passageway and into his little trap. And his Jagd Kommandos. That was some sophisticated-sounding name for a bunch of terrified sailors, he thought.

Taylor looked about. His men were all in position. His plan was to give ground until the North Koreans were bottled up inside the machine shop, then hold and let his Jagd . . . his terrified sailors do their job. The machine shop was right over the aft engine room; if the enemy came from aft he'd still be defending all the engineering spaces. But if they came from up forward, his plan would lose the forward reactor and engine rooms. What if they came from two directions at once?

There was no time to change plans. He'd just have to do the best he could with what he had. He went aft to the crew living space with Squad Four and waited for the enemy.

Pak's head swam with the events of the past few minutes. His attack force had been decimated! However, he still might fulfill his mission even with the few men he had left. Out of a thousand hardened troops he had seventy-some remaining. It was obvious to him that only a portion of the *Truman*'s crew was actively resisting. These sailors weren't trained for close-quarters combat, yet they managed to keep his men at bay.

He gritted his teeth with resolve to be true to his orders. He would take the *Truman*.

Pak went down to the second deck, where his men were silently waiting for new orders. He left thirty men dispersed on the second deck and took the rest aft to attack third deck horizontally. He had no desire to fight his way down ladders to attack third deck. He would lose many more men that way.

These Americans! How many more of them could there be?

Taylor heard movement in the narrow passageway that led aft from the space he was in. The next space aft was filled with a labyrinth of narrow passageways and officers' staterooms. The North Koreans would have to come at them almost single file. The passageway did a dogleg to the left, then to the right, and provided the North Koreans some natural cover from Taylor's gunfire.

Taylor eyed his men standing around the open doorway. They were nervously gripping their M16s and looking at him for a sign to start firing. Taylor took a deep breath and held it. He leaned around the corner and caught a glimpse of something dark green disappearing behind a bulkhead. Taylor pulled himself back from the opening and swallowed hard. Combat doesn't get any easier the second time around, and maybe it's worse, he thought with his heart pounding. This time Taylor knew what was likely to happen to all of them.

The timing is the thing, the only thing. Taylor forced himself to be patient; he had to wait until the North Koreans were in the passageway. Ten feverish seconds went by. Taylor swung his M16 around into the doorway.

He pulled the trigger and sent the full clip's worth of lead down the passageway. Most of the slugs ripped into three North Koreans, sending them sprawling onto the deck. They hadn't a chance to get off a burst in Taylor's direction. Taylor quickly got behind the bulkhead. He ejected the empty clip, inserted a full one, and pulled back on the T-shaped cocking bar. One of his men on the other side of the door leaned into the opening and fired short bursts to keep the enemy pinned down.

When does the hand grenade show up? wondered Taylor. On cue a small metallic object tumbled into the space and rolled to a stop at Taylor's feet. He dropped his M16, scooped up the grenade, and flung it back through the doorway, then fell on the deck. The two other sailors alertly slammed the door and leapt over to dog it down.

The grenade exploded just outside the door and flung it open with such force that one sailor was knocked unconscious; the other was flung on the deck and rolled groggily about.

Taylor got to his hands and knees and grabbed his M16. A rapidly approaching blob of green appeared in his peripheral vision and Taylor rolled frantically to his left. A burst of fire slammed into the space, riddling the two sailors and barely missing Taylor. The chief stuck his weapon around the bulkhead and fired blind up the passageway. Two bullets hit the charging North Korean in the midsection and he slumped over in excruciating pain.

Now! Taylor raced for the forward doorway that led to the machine shop before the North Koreans could set up to return fire. He got around the bulkhead and waited, his breath coming in gasps. He quickly glanced through the door and saw some green shapes moving in the passage beyond but got the sense that they weren't ready to fire. He made an instant decision to sprint for the next space forward, thereby setting up his surprise defense in the machine shop.

Taylor shouted to the sailors hidden in the space, "Don't shoot! It's Chief Taylor!" while praying they could hear him through the OBA facepiece, then he ran for the doorway leading forward. He made it before the North Koreans sent a halfhearted burst of fire in his direction.

Taylor slammed the door and dogged it down, then picked a fire ax from its bulkhead holder and jammed it into the door lever mechanism. He waved his men to the next space forward. If he had figured it right, the North Koreans would have seen him go past the machine shop and therefore conclude that he wasn't going to defend that space. Hopefully they wouldn't throw any grenades into the space. The North Koreans would then mass in the machine shop to cautiously open the door in order to assault the next space forward. Taylor's men hidden in the same space would then open fire and kill as many as possible.

"Oh, God, please!" implored Taylor as he stared at the closed door. Another thought struck him. He hadn't given his men explicit instructions on when to open fire. Would they be so scared that they wouldn't fire at all? Stranger things have happened in combat. One force with an advantage would inadvertently give it up and lose a battle they should have won. History was full of examples. Taylor bit his lip and waited.

The North Koreans cautiously approached the machine shop. Several fired into the space to invite return fire; when none was forthcoming they boldly stuck their heads in to search for Americans. All was silent, and the closed door at the other end of the space beckoned to them.

Two enemy soldiers sprang through the doorway and proceeded to the forward door in a crouched position. When nothing happened a North Korean officer waved the rest of his men into the space.

Colonel Pak was one of the last to enter and felt relief that one more space was theirs, this one without a fight. Maybe the black American was running out of men and he was busy consolidating another line of defense, probably around the forward engineering spaces.

Pak looked aft and decided to see how his men were making out on the port side. He stepped back out through the doorway of the machine shop and tiptoed around the bodies of his men whom Taylor had killed just moments before.

The sailor in the access trunk opened fire first. Duty didn't have much to do with it. He was scared they would see him and get in the first shot. His prolonged burst was joined by the rest of the hidden sailors in the machine shop. The noise of six M16s on full automatic filled the space and created an incredible din.

Bullets tore into the mass of North Koreans from six directions at once. They spun as the bullets slammed into them, and cowered to find some cover from the hail of death that assaulted them. The sailors moved their weapons from side to side to completely cover the forward area of the space and to evenly distribute the fire among the enemy. The few bullets that didn't find an enemy soldier ricocheted off the bulkheads and struck the invaders from behind.

The first layer of soldiers dropped instantly. The next layer squirmed and writhed as the bullets found them. The North Koreans next to the bulkhead started to return fire over their comrades until they too succumbed to the continuing fire from the Americans.

The overhead lights were shot out by the hail of lead coming from the Americans, creating shadows over the North Koreans. The sailors could see North Korean arms and legs flailing about as they intermittently entered the light, then retreated into the shadows. A water line and a low-pressure steam line were severed by the gunfire and further added to the chaos. The water and steam sprayed over the doomed enemy soldiers as if to further depress the survival efforts of the North Koreans. The combined effect was a ghastly, devastating scene of death and destruction.

One by one the American M16s fell silent as their clips ran out. The sailors stared dumbfounded at the brutal carnage. Twenty-five North Koreans lay dead or dying in a bloody heap in the forward part of the space. Water from the severed line collected under some of the bodies and allowed them to slide about as they twitched in their death throes.

Pak gaped at the oozing mass that had been his men. The Americans had perpetrated one of the most elementary surprises in tactical warfare and it had cost him many of his precious men. He flew into a rage and ran toward the machine shop.

The sailors tore their eyes from the North Korean dead and took stock of themselves. The brief enemy fire had taken a toll. The sailor in the tool issue room lay dead, and one of the men behind the machinery held a bleeding arm. They didn't hear Pak's approach until too late.

Pak's AKR fired toward the middle of the space, cutting down two sailors and sending the rest scrambling for cover. Pak ripped a hand grenade from the front of his uniform, and in a frenzy pulled the pin and tossed it behind the large machines near the port side. He fired a quick burst to keep the sailors ducking and took cover behind the passageway bulkhead.

The grenade detonated with a thud, instantly killing the two sailors behind the machines. Pak gazed into the space, his eyes searching for movement. Everything was still.

He backed away from the space and tried to catch his breath. He wondered who would run out of men first, the Americans or him. He slowly turned away and retraced his steps to get his men stationed on the second deck. He would need them for his final assault on the engineering spaces.

The lever on the door moved slowly and timidly, not at all the way the North Koreans threw open the doors. A fire ax held the door shut. It seemed that the person who was trying to open the door didn't have the strength to force it, as the North Koreans had before.

Taylor had been holding his breath since he heard the grenade blast, then let it out in a rush. He turned to the men around him and cautioned them to hold their fire. They all relaxed a bit. Taylor got to his feet and slowly approached the doorway. He took up a position next to the door and yanked out the fire ax.

The door swung open slowly and Taylor and his men let out relieved sighs at the sight of a blue-shirted arm holding an M16. Taylor's eyes flicked down to the pile of corpses in the space beyond. Their color was a mixture of dark green and blood red. His ploy had worked beyond all expectations. He also knew it wouldn't work again. The North Koreans would be expecting it next time, and to leave sailors hidden in spaces would be to sign their death warrant.

Taylor came to the aid of the sailor as he staggered through the door, and helped him back to where his remaining men were positioned. "Where's the rest?" asked Taylor. He already knew the answer.

"Dead, all dead," gulped the sailor. "I hid in the access trunk when they got us from behind. I—"

"OK, OK, you did a great job," interrupted Taylor. He jammed his eyes shut. Emotion rose in him. *I can't stand this! How can I spend lives like this?* He had just traded five American lives for twenty-five North Korean lives. Any commander anywhere in the world would love to have that ratio, five to one, but it was no consolation to the chief that so many of the enemy had died. The wives, parents, brothers, and sisters of these sailors wouldn't be consoled by that ratio. All they would know was that their loved one wasn't coming back, ever.

Gunfire from the port side roused him from his thoughts. He would lose more men if he didn't snap out of it. He got behind a bunk and looked over to the port side. More gunfire. Someone in a blue shirt fell to the deck. Someone in green ran into the space.

Taylor got his M16 to his shoulder and fired a burst across the space. Several bullets shattered the leg of an enemy soldier, who screamed and fell to the deck. Explosions shook the deck far forward. That would be Fifth Squad up near the armory.

Taylor saw more green across the bunk room and knew he was being flanked. He grabbed the sailors near him and shoved them forward. "Go!" he shouted. He was after them in an instant.

They ran into the next space forward, a CPO living space. The sailors hesitated but Taylor urged them on. He glanced across the space and saw more flashes of green. No gunfire at all from the port side. His men must all be dead over there.

They got through the doorway to the next space forward, another living space, and stopped in their tracks. They could see dead sailors, their blue shirts stained red and their OBAs shattered by North Korean gunfire. Taylor knew that his Fifth Squad was no more.

The North Koreans were in the adjoining space aft and in the adjoining space forward. The enemy had squeezed his men until there was no place left to go.

The enemy soldiers forward spotted them and set up to open fire. Taylor shoved two sailors aside and fired a wild burst that kept the enemy ducking. The sailors were right next to an access trunk that led to the forward engine room. Down there, there were no doorways leading forward or aft. The enemy would have to attack down a ladder, not across the deck as they had on second and third decks.

Taylor looked around in a panic. They were surrounded by North Koreans and cut off from the rest of the ship. He frantically waved to the rest of his men to get into the access trunk and get the scuttle open. He took cover behind a metal locker and fired some short bursts to keep the North Koreans at bay. He saw his men get to safety in the forward engine room, fired one last burst in the direction of the enemy soldiers, then ran for the access trunk.

The North Koreans opened fire and shredded the metal locker. With bullets whizzing by him, Taylor got to the scuttle and leaped through it. He landed on the ladder just missing one sailor's head with his feet, then he slipped off the rungs and fell heavily to the deck. Two sailors scrambled up the ladder to secure the scuttle.

Taylor got up shaking from the deck and looked about. He ripped off his OBA facepiece and took a deep breath while leaning heavily against a bulkhead. He took a head count. It didn't take long to count seven men. He had started with more than thirty men just half an hour ago.

This was it. They would fight and die here. There was no other place to go.

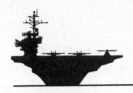# Chapter Seventeen

Major Scott "the Twink" Litwinko rolled his F-4E Phantom jet down the runway at Osan, South Korea. The aircraft picked up speed and in seconds he was in the air and heading into the open sky.

The scramble had put his heart in his throat and only now that he was in the air did he seem to be calming down. He took a deep breath and held it for several seconds, then let it out in a burst. It made a popping noise in his earphones.

"Yeah, I know how you feel, Major," said 1st Lt. Terry Wingrove, Litwinko's backseater. Litwinko put the fighter jet into a slow right turn and twisted around to eyeball the air base. The rest of his squadron was taking off. He could see one jet on the runway and one still waiting. They did a slow orbit of the base to allow the others to get in the air, then turned west toward the sea.

Litwinko adjusted his airspeed to something over three hundred knots and set his heading in a straight line for the intercept point where he would meet up with the rest of his squadron, who were now making a wide turn to the right. It made no sense to follow them around the curve when he could catch up with them by taking the inside of the turn. That way he wouldn't waste fuel.

He had a worried thought at the mission's fuel margin. They had only about fifteen minutes over the *Truman*'s operating area, and that would go quickly to zero if they had to do any evasive action or actual combat. A few minutes of afterburners and that would be it.

If the fuel concerned him, the mission itself worried him even more. The Pentagon, in their infinite wisdom, had moved the F-16s normally at Kunsan Air Base and left the Seventh Air Force with F-4Es, a capable aircraft but slow compared to some of the aircraft the North Koreans had arrayed against them.

"Red Knight Leader, this is Whisky Victor Three. How do you read? Over."

That was their guardian angel, the one who would look over them, the E-3 aircraft that was orbiting to the south. Called AWACS for airborne warning and control system, the modified Boeing 707 aircraft performed the same functions for the air force as the Hawkeye did for the navy. With a massive rotodome sprouting up over the fuselage, it looked like a giant cousin to the Hawkeye aircraft.

"Whisky Victor Three, this is Red Knight Leader. Read you five by five. Glad to hear you're up and about. Got us on the scope? Over." Litwinko sighed. At least they had some friends around.

"Red Knight Leader, this is Whisky Victor Three. That is affirmative. I've also got ten bogies in Indian country on your 110, angels 20, range 120 miles, just circling. Watch out for them. Over."

"Roger, Whisky, much obliged. Out."

So, the North Koreans had some planes aloft and in a position to jump them as they went to rescue the *Truman*. He shrugged. Maybe he was being too paranoid. The North Koreans always had planes up. Litwinko concentrated on meeting up with the rest of his squadron and setting the proper course for the silent task force. He gave a cursory order to form up on him and head 290. The eight planes joined up and formed a V-shaped pattern in the sky.

"Red Knight, this is Whisky Victor. Bogies have changed course to 245 and increased speed to Mach 1.5, still angels 20. Over."

Litwinko muttered an oath. He wasn't paranoid after all. The North Koreans were coming after them. "Whisky Victor, this is Red Knight Leader. Give me an intercept. Over."

A few seconds passed. The AWACS controller came back over a crackling radio link. "Red Knight, intercept is 045 at Mach 1.5. Bogies at angels 30 and climbing."

"Roger, Whisky. Thanks. Keep us informed. Out." Litwinko inhaled and held it once again. The *Truman* would just have to wait. The North Koreans were after them and they couldn't be ignored. He let out his breath in a burst, with the familiar popping noise in his earphones.

Litwinko gave the orders to get his squadron on the intercept course and tried to settle down. The sun bore in on him—they were headed directly into it. He flipped down his sun visor. Those North Koreans weren't any dummies.

The AWACS came back. "Red Knight, bogie ID estimate is Flogger Kilo. I say again Flogger Kilo. Over."

"Roger, Whisky Victor, copy Flogger Kilo as our opposition. Out." Flogger was the designation for the MiG-23, a powerful swing-wing aircraft that was more than a match for his F-4Es. Litwinko's squadron was at a significant thrust-to-weight disadvantage, which meant he'd also have to increase altitude to engage them. The MiGs would want to engage his squadron in the vertical plane, where their power advantage could be brought to bear. He, on the other hand, wanted to engage them in the horizontal plane to minimize his thrust disadvantage.

They began their climb to 45,000 feet in an attempt to get even with the MiGs. Litwinko grumbled to himself as he stared into the sun. They wouldn't get visual contact until it was too late.

His backseater spoke up. "Major, we've got ten bogies, dead on, angels 38, at Mach 2, range 85 miles."

Looks like they're attacking, thought Litwinko. But just maybe . . . He gave orders to jink to the right.

Wingrove came back on. "They've jinked to counter our move. They're coming head-on. Intercept in two minutes ten."

Litwinko thought of jinking again but rejected it. There wasn't much time and he couldn't let the mothers get behind them. Who shoots first? He had orders but he would have bet a month's pay that, should the brass know about this situation, they'd let it be up to him. He made his decision.

"Master arm on," he said over the comm net to the rest of his squadron. "Red Knight Leader to Red Knight flight. Engage enemy."

The AWACS broke in. "Red Knight Leader, this is Whisky Victor Three. You have permission to defend yourself. Over."

Litwinko mumbled to himself again. Nice that a higher authority had ratified his decision. "Thanks Whisky. Out."

Litwinko and his squadron went to afterburners and got their speed up to Mach 2 and held it. The North Korean and American planes raced at each other at more than four times the speed of sound. Litwinko knew what the North Koreans were doing. They were flying the "sunball" to his squadron. Sunballs looked like circular rainbows and were formed when a plane was between the sun and the clouds. All a pilot had to do was maneuver the sunball over his enemy and fly toward him. He'd automatically be coming out of the sun.

"Range 20 miles, speed—"

Litwinko got a tone in his earphones. That was it. He fired two Sidewinder missiles at the oncoming enemy planes. He caught a glimpse of shadows on the sun. The shadows stayed with the sun as the squadron's missiles rocketed away, leaving fragile smoke trails in the air. They curved slightly up and to the right toward the MiGs and the sun.

Litwinko strained his eyes, trying to pick out the explosions against the glare of the sun. He finally had to look away, his eyes watering. He blinked furiously to clear his vision and risked a glance at the sun. The shadows had disappeared. So, they knew that trick. The North Koreans had jinked away from the oncoming missiles. Litwinko knew where his missiles were headed. They were going toward the biggest heat source of all, the sun.

He gave orders for a sharp turn to the left, and stared to the left of the sun. What he saw nearly made him freeze with fear. The North Koreans had jinked to their *right;* the American and North Korean squadrons were still heading toward each other at nearly Mach 4. Only they were close, very close. There was no time to evade them. Litwinko wasn't worried about the North Korean guns or missiles; he was sure they didn't have time to react either. He said an instantaneous prayer and hoped they would miss them.

They thundered by in a blur of motion and a scream of engines. The air to his right was lit up by an explosion that flared with a blinding light. Somebody bought it. Midair collision.

Then Litwinko was by it, and he threw his aircraft into a tight left turn. He and his radar officer were thrown violently to the right against the straps. He could hear Wingrove's grunts against the g forces that sought to drain their brains of blood. He saw dots in front of his eyes, then the world turned gray. The lights started to go out and he could see only straight in front of him. He lost his sense of direction and dimly realized that he was at his limit. Then he pulled out and the lights went back on again.

"Damn!" he heard over the intercom. Wingrove was still up.

"C'mon, Terry, give us a heading!"

After a few seconds, "192 should do it."

Litwinko went back on the comm net. Everyone was talking at once.

"Zeke! Watch your six! Bandit on your tail! Roll out!"

"Red Knight Six, I've got two bandits climbing at 240. I'm after 'em."

"Red Knight Three, get the hell out of the way! I've got a tone on the bastard!"

"I've got a tone too, mother, so drop dead!"

A second later, "Scratch one MiG!"

"That was mine, you asshole!"

"Zeke! For God's sake, roll out!"

"I'm rolling, I—" they could hear grunting. "Must be pulling six—"

His radio went dead. Litwinko spotted a puff of smoke in the distance. Zeke was dead. Litwinko heard a shrill tone in his earphones.

"Oh, shit!" said Wingrove. Then, "One's in the air!" A second later, "Flares away!" and "Chaff away!"

A MiG had gotten behind them and the MiG's radar was detected by the F-4's radar warning receiver, giving a tone in Litwinko's earphones. The tone changed frequency, meaning that a missile had been launched. Wingrove had activated the decoy flares and chaff.

Litwinko took the cue; he shoved the aircraft into a six-g left turn and backed off on the throttles to get out of afterburners. The less heat the missile saw from his plane, the better. The enemy missile dutifully went after the flares and detonated far behind Litwinko's aircraft.

Litwinko dove and rolled to the right, and the tone went away. Back to afterburners and into a steep climb, then a roll to the left and the MiG's tail swung into view. He centered the steering circle on the enemy plane.

"Tone, tone, c'mon!" he said impatiently. He fingered the missile launch button. A little to the right. The beeping in his earphones went to a steady ring.

"I've got a tone!" He sent a missile up the MiG's tail pipe. It ripped off the rear of the single jet engine and sent the aircraft spinning down toward the water.

"I saw that one! The Twink's got a kill!" said an unknown member of his squadron.

"What's the count, Terry?" Litwinko asked as he leveled the aircraft and backed off on the throttle.

"I've only got three friendlies and six bandits on the scope. There might be some good guys behind us, though." He sounded concerned.

"All right. Let's get back into it. Gimme a vector," said Litwinko.

"105, Major."

"Roger." Litwinko put the aircraft on course, then lapsed into silence and considered his fuel gauge. All that time on afterburners had eaten up a lot of fuel. They could still make it to the carrier but they'd need midair refueling to get back.

A MiG-23 popped out of a cloud at the limit of his vision. "Tally one bandit!" Litwinko said over the intercom. The MiG looked to be in a hurry. Maybe I can sneak up on him, thought Litwinko. Then he saw why the MiG seemed to be moving with a purpose. A lone F-4 was fleeing in front of the pursuing MiG. The North Korean pilot was trying to get a bead on the F-4, but the American pilot had gone to afterburners and was making things difficult.

Then the F-4 pilot made his mistake. He started his aircraft in a sixty-degree climb in a panicked effort to get away from the MiG. The enemy aircraft was after it immediately, and Litwinko could see the wings of the MiG swing back as the North Korean pilot kicked in full power, the aft end of the MiG lighting up like a huge flare.

The comm net crackled to life. "Bud! Level off! Don't climb! Level off and roll out!" One of his squadron was trying to talk sense into the pursued American pilot.

Litwinko went to afterburners and swung after the MiG, who was about five miles away. He bit his lip in frustration. He'd never catch them at these speeds and the MiG would launch an air-to-air missile any second now.

The MiG had made up a large portion of the distance between him and the F-4, largely due to the better thrust that the MiG possessed. Litwinko was desperate. He had to try something. He jacked the nose of his aircraft up to anticipate where the MiG would be and launched his last Sidewinder. The missile obediently went off in the appointed direction, leaving a thin trail of smoke behind.

His eyes followed the smoke as the Sidewinder flew into the distance. He lost sight of it after a few seconds and shifted his attention to the MiG and the hapless F-4. Flame suddenly shot from under the wing of the MiG and hope surged in Litwinko that somehow his Sidewinder had found the enemy plane. A heartbeat later, his hopes were dashed as he saw an air-to-air missile leap from under the wing of the MiG. Litwinko's missile, if it hit, would be too late.

He got on the net. "Bud! Drop flares and chaff and roll out!"

Bud's backseater was on the ball. A flare popped out along with some chaff that fluttered down, and the F-4 finally began to level off and roll to the right. In the meantime the MiG had launched two more missiles. The first one was seduced away by the flare and detonated harmlessly. The second and third missiles homed in on the F-4.

Suddenly the MiG was transformed into a ball of flame as Litwinko's desperate Sidewinder did its job. Litwinko's eyes flicked back to the F-4. The missiles were horrifyingly close.

"Bud! Drop more flares and—"

The rear half of the F-4 erupted into a million pieces, shattering both engines and the entire tail section. The front half immediately tumbled out of control. Litwinko gasped into his microphone. He strained his eyes to see if the crew would punch out. He followed the wreckage down until he saw the canopy separate and two black dots fly away from the top of the fuselage. Their chutes unfurled and Bud and his backseater slowly sank down to the sea.

Litwinko gave a sigh of relief. He got on the comm net to tell the rest of the squadron that the crew was all right. "OK, I've got two good chutes."

Time to get back into the fray, he thought. After receiving a vector from his radar officer he set his aircraft on course and tried to settle down until the next confrontation.

Commander Ron Hastings glanced worriedly at his fuel gauge. He got on the intercom. "What's the fuel situation look like, Rick?"

His RIO came back, "We'll make it with two hundred pounds to spare. No sweat."

Hastings rolled his eyes. No sweat, he says. Two hundred pounds represented only a few seconds of flying time. If they had to make one pass around the field they'd crash.

His earphones came alive. "Tomcat, this is Whisky Victor Three, AWACS, on your 040. Please identify your mission and destination. Over."

Hastings got excited. The AWACS was the first contact he had from the outside world since being launched from the *Truman*.

"Whisky Victor Three, this is Blackline Leader. I'm what's left of a CAP from the *Truman*. There are some others around but they're up north chasing some Fulcrum Alphas. I'm very low on fuel and need to put down at the first opportunity—Osan, I guess. Any good guys up with us? Over."

"Blackline Leader, we'll get you down ASAP. We've got some Phantoms in a dogfight with Floggers on your nose. You'll have to swing wide to avoid. Do you know status of *Truman* and escort vessels? Over."

Hastings shook his head. There was a fight right in front of him and he was going to have to avoid it to save fuel. First he had to fill them in.

"Whisky, the *Truman* was attacked at sea by North Korean helicopters. Apparently they were trying to hijack the carrier. We splashed all the helos but some had already landed on the flight deck. It appeared that there was a hand-to-hand battle going on." He thought of Simmons's forlorn figure on the aircraft elevator. "*Oldendorf* and *Truxtun* appeared all right but *Oldendorf* was dead in the water. Neither escort vessel was resisting the helo assault. They could use air support. Over."

It took Whisky a minute to digest that one. There would be more than a few eyebrows raised on that AWACS.

"Blackline Leader, did you say KORCOMS are trying to *hijack* an aircraft carrier? Over."

"That's affirmative."

Another delay. "Are you shitting me, buddy?"

Hastings sighed in resignation. He knew what it sounded like. "Whisky, I wish I was."

"Commander," said Norris, "I've got six bogies mixed in with four friendlies, angels three five, range 40 miles, nose on."

And right in line with Osan, thought Hastings.

"Blackline Leader, vector 165, to avoid fight on your nose. Over."

"Whisky, how are the Phantoms doing? Over."

There was a delay. "Not good, Blackline. Can you assist? Over."

"Whisky, I'll run out of fuel."

"Roger, understand, Blackline. Vector is 165."

Well, he had to make a decision. He couldn't go around or he'd run out of fuel. Could he sneak through? He doubted it. What a spot. He had no missiles left and only twenty rounds of the six hundred fifty rounds he took off with in his Gatling gun. If he got into a fight, he wouldn't have much of a chance. He didn't have much of a choice either.

"Whisky Victor Three, forget the vector. I'm staying on course. Out."

"Roger, Blackline Leader. Good luck. Out."

Hastings thought the air controller had an undercurrent of admiration in his voice, as one man would greet another before he went into combat.

"Maybe if we stick to twenty thousand feet we'll get through," offered Norris.

"Sounds good to me, Rick," replied Hastings and descended to that altitude. He eyeballed the sky as they approached the dogfight. The MiGs and Phantoms sure were mixing it up.

*   *   *

Litwinko slammed the Phantom into a panicked roll, then went into a left turn. The seat straps bit into his shoulders as he desperately fought the effects of gravity. The seven-g turn could take the wings off a lesser aircraft; when he felt a flutter in the fuselage he knew it was time to back off. He straightened the aircraft out slightly and felt the heavy hand of gravity ease up.

"One's in the air!" gasped Wingrove. It was a miracle he was still conscious after that turn, thought Litwinko. "Flares and chaff away!"

Litwinko reversed his rudder and the aircraft responded by violently swinging into a right turn. Litwinko backed out of afterburners and rolled away. The MiG's air-to-air missile wandered off after the flares and detonated.

"Red Knight Leader, this is Whisky Victor Three. Look out for Tomcat on 295 true—"

Litwinko wasn't going to look out for anybody, damn it! He was busy!

Wingrove turned in his seat and saw flashes out of the belly of the MiG that was clinging to their tail. "He's using guns. He must be out of missiles!"

The MiG could still shred us to pieces with his 23mm gun, thought Litwinko just as part of a burst hit the Phantom's tail section, sending pieces flying. Control of the aircraft became sluggish.

This is it, thought Litwinko.

"One's in real trouble, Commander," said Norris. Hastings said nothing. "Commander?" asked Norris.

"I see him! I see him!" replied Hastings in an annoyed tone. He fell silent again and studied the one-sided dogfight above him. He couldn't leave him like that even if he was air force.

"Oh, what the hell." Hastings shoved the throttles forward, his wings automatically swinging back to form a swept-wing configuration. "I hope to hell you can swim, Rick," said Hastings in resignation.

"Let's get the sonofabitch!"

"Radar off. Maybe we can sneak up on him," said Hastings.

"Roger."

The F-14 shot through the sky as Hastings took a bead on the MiG. The MiG didn't see him—he was too enthralled with the anticipation of the kill. The Phantom pilot wasn't making out too well with pieces missing from his tail surfaces. In a matter of seconds the North Korean would shred the F-4 and the two Americans in it.

A fuel alarm went off. Going to afterburners had done it. Hastings had only seconds of fuel left. "There's the bingo alarm, Rick. I hope we can get the bastard before we flame out."

"Roge."

Hastings inhaled and held it. The MiG was in a shallow turn to the right, leisurely keeping up with the wounded F-4. Hastings got the impression that the North Korean pilot was gloating over his apparent victory. He's in for one hell of a surprise, thought Hastings.

"All right, Rick. Radar on."

"Roger."

Hastings's steering circle on his heads-up display came on and he got the enemy plane within it immediately. Hastings pressed the guns button and the peculiar howling sound of the Gatling gun was heard in the cockpit. It lasted less than a second, then Hastings was out of ammunition.

The first ten slugs missed but the next ten shattered the right wing of the MiG. The aircraft rolled to the right as the remnants of the wing flew upward. The largest piece slammed into the cockpit, shattering the windscreen and instantly killing the pilot. The MiG fell like a rock into the sea.

"And that's number five! Congratulations, Commander."

"Thanks, Rick. Congrats to you, too. We're a team." He looked at his fuel gauge. "Looks like a flameout in thirty seconds. I hope you've got a bathing suit with you."

Hastings positioned the F-14 on the right wing of Litwinko's F-4. Litwinko waved. "Sure glad to see you, even if you are navy," said Litwinko, then laughed.

"Glad to be of assistance. You guys going out to overfly the *Truman*?" asked Hastings. He could see the F-4 pilot shrug.

"Well, we were," replied Litwinko.

"They're going to need some air support. Right now they're bare ass naked out there," said Hastings.

Litwinko looked around. "Looks like the MiGs have taken off."

"How's your aircraft?" asked Hastings.

"Seems OK, just sluggish."

"I'd look you over, but I'm gonna flame out in about ten seconds," said Hastings.

"I'll give you an escort down," replied Litwinko.

The roaring of the twin jet engines in the F-14 suddenly ceased.

Hastings put the aircraft into a slow circle as the nose dropped to a sixty-degree angle of attack.

"Never mind us. Get after the *Truman*," said Hastings. He thought of Simmons again on the aircraft elevator. What was he doing now? Was he still alive? Damn funny. He would have cheerfully killed Simmons before today, and now he was concerned about him. Hastings's combat for the day was over, but not for Simmons. He would slug it out with the enemy face-to-face.

Litwinko watched the Tomcat rapidly lose altitude and felt compassion for this unknown navy pilot and RIO. They were going to take a bath because they had saved him.

"This is the Twink saying thanks and good luck. By the way, who are you guys?"

Norris spoke up. "America's newest aces."

Hastings chimed in. "See ya, Twink, on the beach." Then over the plane's intercom, "All right, Rick, checklist."

"Envelope," said Norris.

"We're there," replied Hastings.

"IFF/SIF." Norris answered his own query. "Emergency and 7700."

"Position."

"On transmit."

"Harness."

They both pulled them as tight as they could and locked them. "Lock," they both replied.

"Visors."

They pulled them down over their eyes. "Down."

"All right, Rick. You ready?"

"As ready as I'll ever be."

Hastings put his feet on the pedals and his head back, then reached up above his head and grabbed the yellow-striped cables. He pulled them down in one motion until his hands were in his lap. The canopy exploded upward and was immediately taken by the wind behind the falling aircraft. A split second later, Norris was shot out of the top of the fuselage, with Hastings following him in a terrific blast from the bottom of their ejection seats. They lost all orientation as they tumbled in free-fall. Their parachutes unfurled and yanked them upright, and they became reoriented to the world again.

Hastings looked upward to see the billowing chute above him and note that the rubber raft had deployed properly from the seat pan. He'd have something to get into when he hit the water. Off to his right he could see the plane dropping to the sea below. Seconds later, the F-14 hit with a tremendous splash. He hated to see the aircraft go. Funny how pilots get attached to their machinery, like it's a brother to them.

Both men hit the water within a few seconds of each other. The cold water immediately seeped into Hastings's flight gear and his life vest automatically inflated. He squirmed around and got into his rubber raft, then looked around for Norris. He was just getting into his raft. Hastings paddled over and they tied the two rafts together.

Hastings began to think over the encounter at the ship. He had found a side of himself that scared the hell out of him, a side that would have killed for revenge. Even worse, it was a side filled with cowardice. He couldn't take revenge on Simmons during the fight in the passageway, so he was going to let the MiG do it. He inhaled quickly and had a sick feeling in his stomach. Is this where his obsession had led? If he met Simmons after the battle what would he say? Could he somehow make amends?

Litwinko's F-4 rocketed by overhead. Hastings watched the Phantom and waved when Litwinko waggled his wings. Go, he thought, find the *Truman*.

And Simmons.

 # Chapter Eighteen

S immons cautiously peered out the doorway into the hangar bay.
The sound was coming from a row of F-18s on the starboard side.
He finally recognized it—someone was sobbing.

He crouched down to look under the wings of the planes and spotted
a sailor flat on the deck with his head buried in his arms. After a quick
look around to see if any North Koreans were about, Simmons crawled
underneath the plane to get to the weeping sailor. The man sensed someone
approaching and looked up in abject terror. The appearance of Simmons
shocked him even though he recognized the officer immediately. Mixed
blood and dirt lined one side of Simmons's face and extended down
the front of his uniform. His pockets, bulging from the captured hand
grenades, and the unused OBA dangling in front combined to give him
an almost extraterrestrial appearance.

"Get away from me! Get away from me!" the sailor shouted.

"Keep your voice down!" commanded Simmons.

"They're going to kill me! I don't want to die!" the man shrieked.

Simmons jumped on the sailor and put his hand over the man's mouth.
The sailor struggled to push Simmons off his chest, but the officer
wouldn't budge.

"Shut up, you idiot! Do you want every North Korean on this ship
to hear you?"

The sailor's struggles slowly diminished until he was calm enough for Simmons to risk getting off his chest. It was MacKenzie, the young sailor whom Simmons had prevented from running up in the island.

"Now you listen to me," began Simmons. "We're all in a hell of a fix on this ship, but we've got one chance. We've got to get to the engineering spaces and help Chief Taylor defend the ship. He's still holding out down there and he's relying on us. You and I have got to help Taylor."

MacKenzie avoided Simmons's eyes as the officer talked. Then he became agitated. "I can't do it, Mr. Simmons. I just can't do it."

Simmons's voice was firm. "Listen to me. We're all going to die if we don't fight these bastards off. Did you see what almost happened to those other two guys just now? The North Koreans were going to kill them."

"Yeah, but they didn't. That means we can surrender. We don't have to fight," countered the young sailor.

At least I've got this guy thinking, even if it's in the wrong direction, Simmons thought. He had backed himself neatly into a corner.

"Think man! Those guys are machinist's mates. The North Koreans need them to run this ship, to sail it to North Korea. What do you think is going to happen to all of us when we get there? They won't need us anymore, they'll have the ship."

MacKenzie listened to Simmons's words and after a few moments seemed less adamant. Simmons knew that the North Koreans would have to be insane to murder the rest of the *Truman*'s crew. They would have nothing to gain by it. On the contrary, six thousand hostages would provide a great lever for negotiations. He wouldn't let MacKenzie know that. He had to make the youngster want to fight.

MacKenzie brushed some of the wetness from his face, and Simmons sighed silently with relief. Apparently he had turned the tide. Simmons crawled out from under the plane and beckoned to MacKenzie. The young sailor reluctantly joined him.

"Pick up an M16 and a clip belt and let's go. We haven't got much time," Simmons ordered.

MacKenzie slowly obeyed and picked up a weapon that was farthest from any of the corpses in the hangar bay; however, he had to wrestle an ammo belt from around a dead sailor. Simmons tried to hurry MacKenzie along, but he had to content himself with the sailor's slow pace. At least he was moving.

MacKenzie's mind was numb. He had removed his OBA so that he'd pass out from the gas and he wouldn't have to experience any more of the horror of this day. The trouble was that the gas had dissipated, and he was left to hide in abject terror under the aircraft. Now this officer was going to make him fight again. His stomach flipped over at the thought.

Simmons mentally surveyed the somber situation that confronted them. The engineering spaces, some of the most important areas of the ship, were still in American control. It might not be for long, however, unless he could somehow relieve the pressure on Taylor and his men. The island seemed to be in the hands of the enemy and at this moment they were probably steering the ship toward North Korea and captivity. He thought of trying to capture the island, but in the meantime he could very well lose the engineering spaces. He would certainly lose the ship if that happened. Their only chance lay in joining forces with Taylor now, and capturing the island later.

Should he tell Taylor to stop engines? The ship would go dead in the water and any enemy planes about would think the attack had failed. They might then attack the ship, and even a few hits with a MiG's cannon shells could start fires that could get out of control and ultimately sink the *Truman*. A mental vision of exploding ordnance caused him to cringe. He couldn't rely on Hastings's one F-14 to defend the ship perfectly even if he was still around. They would reach the North Korean coast in maybe two hours. The battle for the *Truman* would be over by then, one way or another.

The voices floated over to them once again. Simmons knew they weren't American voices. He dropped to the deck and waved MacKenzie to get down. Simmons sighted along the deck, peering under the various trucks and aircraft to get a bearing on the enemy soldiers. He spotted three pairs of the peculiar black shoes the North Koreans wore. They seemed lightweight and rubber soled and were vastly different from the bulky boondockers the American sailors wore. The North Korean shoes appeared to be in a circle, then they all turned as their attention was taken up by someone else. Two pairs of American boondockers suddenly were thrust into the middle of the group. It was the two sailors saved by the North Korean officer!

Simmons swore under his breath. He had forgotten about them. Was there some way to get them back from their captors? He counted four North Koreans just before the group suddenly turned and headed aft in a direct line to Simmons and MacKenzie.

Simmons looked around in a panic. They couldn't stay where they were. In seconds the North Koreans would walk right over them. He spotted one of the weapons elevators that stuck out from the sides of the hangar bay and motioned MacKenzie to head for it. They scrambled on all fours and quickly took cover to one side of the elevator.

Simmons could hear the light footsteps of the North Koreans mingled with the heavier steps of the American captives and the frenzied breathing of MacKenzie. They flattened themselves on the side of the bulkhead and waited for the enemy soldiers to walk by on their way aft. They could hear an occasional foreign word as the footsteps drew even with them. Simmons brought his M16 up to bear while MacKenzie just clutched his with both hands, the barrel pointed uselessly straight up.

Two North Koreans guarding the two captive Americans marched by just feet from where Simmons and MacKenzie stood in frozen silence. MacKenzie's breathing was drowned out by Simmons's pounding heart. Simmons waited for the other two enemy soldiers to show up, but the group was a full ten feet past him and the two others were nowhere in sight. Where were the other two North Koreans?

A noise suddenly came from beside him, a puffing of air and then perhaps a moan. Simmons didn't look; he knew that MacKenzie was the source of the sound. The two North Koreans turned around and looked about in a puzzled manner. Their gaze swept the hangar bay bulkheads, investigating the passageways and offices for the source of the noise. Simmons couldn't wait any longer.

He opened fire on the closest North Korean and put half his clip into the man's side. He fell limply to the deck. The other North Korean swung his gun barrel about to bear on Simmons but was hampered by the captive sailors, who were in the line of fire. The two manacled sailors stood and gaped for a second, then broke and ran for a truck about fifty feet farther aft in the hangar bay.

The second North Korean got a bead on Simmons and opened fire just as Simmons hit the deck. The enemy burst slammed into the bulkhead, missing the still-standing MacKenzie by an inch. Simmons shouted to the young sailor to get down, but his warning was lost in the exchange of fire between Simmons and the North Korean who was rapidly backpedaling to get to the port side and some cover.

Both bursts of fire went wild and the North Korean found cover behind an F-18 on the port side of the hangar bay. One advantage as far as Simmons was concerned was that the enemy soldier didn't have a line of sight to him or MacKenzie. Simmons's eyes flicked to the running sailors, who were just about to reach the cover of a truck. An

AKR opened up from deep in the forward part of the hangar bay. In an instant it was joined by two others. The hail of gunfire cut down the two fleeing Americans in midstride, the bullets shattering their bodies unmercifully and flinging them to the deck in a heap.

"NO!" screamed Simmons, his shout drowned out by the rattle of gunfire. They never had a chance, he thought as rage ran through him. Handcuffed with their arms behind their backs, they couldn't even run normally. Somehow, someway, he would kill these North Koreans who saw fit to shoot unarmed, bound Americans in the back. He willed himself to calm down enough for rational thought. If he and MacKenzie could get below one deck, they could come up on the other side of the hangar bay and surprise them.

Simmons looked about and groaned. The nearest passageway to get below was on the other side of the weapons elevator, the side exposed to North Korean gunfire. They couldn't go aft or they would be cut down like the other sailors.

The bulk in Simmons's pockets suddenly registered in his mind. He had grenades, six of them. He quickly examined them. They all seemed to be the fragmentation kind, not a smoke grenade in the bunch. They'd just have to do. He glanced at MacKenzie, who was cringing in the corner. Simmons grabbed him by the front of the shirt.

"Listen to me. I'm going to throw two grenades into the hangar bay. Right after they detonate—and I mean *right* after—we're going to head around the corner and get to a ladder that goes below decks. You follow me." He shook MacKenzie violently. "Did you hear what I said?"

MacKenzie swallowed hard and nodded his head. Simmons let him go. There wasn't much time. If he was thinking of how to outflank the North Koreans, he was sure they were thinking of doing the same to him. He crouched down on the deck and pulled two grenades out of his pockets. He pulled the pin on one and threw it as far forward as he could. The AKRs started up again, the bullets ricocheting off the bulkhead near Simmons's right arm. He pulled the pin on the second grenade and flung the grenade around the corner. Simmons and MacKenzie pressed their backs to the bulkhead and waited for the blasts.

The first grenade went off with a hollow roar. The AKRs immediately went silent as the North Koreans ducked for cover. The second grenade went off, the blast much closer. Simmons yelled for the young sailor to follow him. He turned and ran around the bulkhead into the remnants of the blast and smoke created by the grenade.

Pieces of metal and small particles of nonskid coating showered Simmons as he made a headlong dash around the weapons elevator. He pointed his M16 in the general direction of the North Koreans and fired a short burst in an effort to keep them ducking. In only a few giant strides he found sanctuary in the passageway behind the weapons elevator.

The AKRs started up again, sending rounds that punished the forward bulkhead of the elevator. Simmons bounded down the steps to the second deck, then turned around to urge MacKenzie to hurry along. Simmons stopped dead in his tracks. MacKenzie was nowhere to be seen.

The officer ran over to the ladder he had just come down and stared up at the hangar deck. Was MacKenzie lying bleeding to death in the hangar bay? There was no time to wonder about it. He had to quickly flank the North Koreans before they moved to some other location. He would find out about MacKenzie later.

Simmons ran forward past sick bay and came upon a crew's galley. He entered cautiously and searched the space for the telltale green fatigues of the North Koreans. Seeing none, he ran over to the port side and tiptoed his way up the ladder to the hangar deck. He peered out the door leading to the hangar bay. There was a roaring noise of escaping steam from the starboard side of the hangar bay. Fragments from one of his hand grenades had put some small holes in the catapult steam chambers. Had the chambers been fully charged they might have exploded with great force and taken care of any North Koreans unfortunate enough to have been close to them.

Simmons carefully searched the area for the three enemy soldiers. He located one right away. He was spread-eagled on an F-18 wing with his back toward Simmons. He had his AKR pointed over the leading edge of the wing to cover the starboard side of the hangar bay.

That side of the hangar bay had become nearly obliterated by the escaping steam. Simmons craned his neck in vain to locate the other two North Koreans. He brought his M16 to his shoulder and got the one North Korean he could see in his sights. He hesitated. There it was again. Shooting a man in the back. He lowered his weapon as a new thought struck him. If he shot the North Korean, the others might be able to tell where the shots came from. But if he used a grenade . . .

Simmons leaned his M16 against the bulkhead and took a grenade out of his pocket. He pulled the pin and gingerly lobbed the grenade under the wing of the F-18. Was it any better to blast the soldier apart rather than shoot him in the back? Simmons shook off the thought and pressed his back to the bulkhead. He heard the North Korean begin to move around on the F-18's wing. After what seemed like an eternity the grenade went off.

A thunderous secondary explosion was right on its heels. Uh, oh, thought Simmons. What was it? JP-5? Ordnance? He took a peek through the doorway and saw that the aircraft's port side had disappeared. The rest of the F-18 was rapidly becoming engulfed in flame. The North Korean was nowhere to be seen. Simmons imagined that he had been blown to bits. The thought churned his stomach.

He looked at the steam-enshrouded starboard side and decided that he had to go through the steam to find the other North Koreans. He stepped through the doorway and turned left to get to the forward bulkhead of the hangar bay. The AKRs opened up when he was halfway across to the starboard side. He flopped to the deck and then realized they weren't shooting at him.

Who are they firing at? MacKenzie? Was he still alive? Simmons fought the almost overpowering urge to jump to his feet and charge into the steam. He got up into a crouch and quickly got over to the starboard side of the hangar bay.

The mist encircled him and he found it hard to breathe. Panic rose in him. No, this isn't the engine room, he told himself. He forced his eyes wide open to keep his mind focused on reality.

The AKRs spoke again. This time they were very close by, no more than twenty-five feet in front of him. The steam cut his visibility down to only a few feet. It swirled and eddied, sometimes giving him a glimpse ahead, sometimes engulfing him completely.

Simmons caught a flash of yellow ahead. There was a truck not ten feet in front of him. He made it to the side of the truck just as the AKRs opened up again. The North Koreans were both on the other side of the truck and using another vehicle for cover to fire aft at someone. The steam seemed to end there and the two enemy soldiers had good visibility to see into the rest of the hangar bay.

Simmons got out a grenade, quickly pulled the pin, and tossed the grenade between the two trucks. He turned and ran as fast as he could back through the steam. He thought he heard some words spoken in panic just before the detonation. The blast seemed muted compared to the one before, as if the steam somehow suppressed it. Simmons hit the deck and waited for secondary explosions. There were none.

He got to his feet and cautiously went to the side of the truck. He peered around it, expecting to see the remains of two North Koreans, but only one body was visible. Two AKRs lay on the deck. A trail of blood led off down the starboard side of the hangar bay.

So, he's got no weapon and he's wounded. Maybe now he feels like those sailors who he shot in the back. Simmons looked around the second truck and gazed aft. He grimly checked his M16. Time to pay back for those sailors, and MacKenzie too.

Simmons proceeded aft along the starboard side of the hangar bay, alternately tracking the blood trail and looking in all directions at once for more enemy soldiers. He got to the end of the bulkhead on one side of the aircraft elevator opening and stopped. The blood trail went past the opening in the direction of the same weapons elevator that he and MacKenzie had hid behind just moments ago.

Simmons summoned up his courage and sprinted past the opening to the bulkhead beyond. The blood trail led past the hangar deck control office, one of the deck division's offices, and the entrance to the passageway that Simmons had nearly flown down to get to the deck below to flank the North Koreans. Simmons followed the blood trail as it curled around the weapons elevator.

The trail inexplicably stopped. Simmons stooped to one knee and looked all around him. No one was there. It was as if the North Korean had dropped off the side of the ship. He bent down to examine the blood more closely. The soldier had been bleeding quite a bit at that point. The drops were quite densely packed. Could he have doubled back?

The North Korean hit Simmons as if he was shot out of a cannon. The lieutenant caught the flash of metal swishing past his ear as he flew backward and hit the deck, his M16 sliding away to rest ten feet from him. The enemy soldier leaped at him, brandishing a bayonet, as Simmons caught his first glimpse of his adversary.

The grenade had wounded him in his leg, but to Simmons he seemed to be covered with blood. Simmons lashed out with his foot at the North Korean's wounded leg and connected solidly. The man screamed with pain and dropped to the deck. Simmons got up on all fours and jumped on the man's back. He wrapped an arm around his neck to get a stranglehold, but the man wriggled out of Simmons's grasp and swung the bayonet viciously. The soldier missed, but Simmons fell on his back in an awkward attempt to get away from the North Korean's slashing attack.

The soldier jumped on Simmons's chest and drove the bayonet at him. Simmons got a hand on his arm, but it slipped out of his grasp. The tip of the bayonet slammed into the OBA canister.

Pain immediately shot through Simmons's chest. He let out a roar of agony and frustration. The North Korean tried to pull the bayonet out of Simmons's OBA, but Simmons knocked his hands away in a frenzy. He pushed on the North Korean in an effort to shove him off his chest, but the enemy soldier hung on. He got his hands on Simmons's neck and began to squeeze. Simmons gripped his wrists and tried to wrench them loose, but the Korean was very strong. Simmons could feel the enemy's thumbs sink into his neck, searching for his vital airway to crush the life out of him.

A short burst of automatic weapon fire riddled the side of the North Korean, and he immediately slumped over dead on Simmons's right shoulder. Simmons rolled free, gasping for breath, and crawled away from the dead soldier. He got his breath back and looked up to see MacKenzie, his M16 drooping by his side and a stricken look on his face.

"I had to shoot him, Mr. Simmons! I *had* to!" He was about to cry. "I didn't want to shoot him! I didn't want to!"

"Shut up! You want everyone to hear you?" growled Simmons. He was very glad to see MacKenzie again. He went over to the young sailor and put his hands on the fireman's shoulders. "You saved my life," he said in a hoarse voice.

MacKenzie calmed down a bit, then suddenly noticed the bayonet still sticking out of the officer's OBA canister. His eyes grew wide. "Mr. Simmons! Are you all right?" he asked in a hushed voice.

Simmons grabbed the bayonet and worked it out of the canister as he grimaced with pain. The tip of the bayonet must have nicked him in the chest. Simmons dropped the bayonet on the deck and grabbed MacKenzie's shoulder to steady himself.

"OBAs save lives in more ways than one," he mumbled to himself. He shook his head to clear it. Where had the North Korean come from? The passageway, thought Simmons. He must have hid in the passageway. He looked at the young sailor next to him. "By the way, where were you?" he asked.

MacKenzie jabbed a thumb over his shoulder. "When they started shooting I went on the, uh, what do you call it?"

"The sponson?" asked Simmons incredulously. MacKenzie nodded. Simmons had never thought of it. It was at once the best and the worst hiding place. The sponsons were the narrow decks protruding from the sides of the ship; they were used for refueling at sea and similar operations. Out there MacKenzie would have no retreat except to jump over the side. On the other hand, who would ever think to look for anyone there?

"Why didn't you follow me?"

MacKenzie's face fell. "I guess I didn't have the guts, sir."

How could Simmons chew out this guy? He had saved his life. He took a deep breath to steady his insides. They had to get on with it. They had to join Taylor.

MacKenzie took a few steps toward the dead North Korean. "Why is he covered with blood? Did I—"

"No," said Simmons quickly. "He covered himself with blood from the wound in his leg, maybe to scare us, or to psych himself up for more combat."

Simmons fell silent. Such madness. How were they to defeat such a fanatical enemy?

 # Chapter Nineteen

Simmons leaned against the hangar bay bulkhead, gathering his strength and resolve. He loosened his OBA to see his chest wound. The bayonet had pierced the canister but only dented the breastplate underneath. It was that sharp protrusion that had caused Simmons the pain. Blood had also stained his shirt down the middle.

He considered removing the OBA but quickly decided against it. It had saved him once, it might save him again. Would it stop a bullet? Simmons had no wish to find out, but it was the only sort of body protection he had at the moment. He took a handkerchief from his pants pocket, ripped it in half, wadded up both halves, and shoved one wad into the canister slit. He couldn't let its caustic contents drip all over him. He shoved the other wad under the breastplate of the OBA to protect his chest from the sharp dent.

His eyes wandered to the fire that still engulfed the F-18. It wasn't dying down, but it wasn't spreading either. They couldn't take the time to put it out. He looked at MacKenzie and motioned him to follow.

They descended a ladder amidships on the starboard side of the hangar bay and went to the second deck. They entered the crew's mess and proceeded cautiously forward, stepping over corpses as they went. The lights were blown out and the area was filled with smoke. In the dim light Simmons could see three or four bodies of North Koreans. Taylor had fought well in defending the ship. He wished he had done half as well.

MacKenzie started to cough at the smoke. Simmons jumped in surprise, then turned and chewed out the young sailor for making so much noise. If there were any enemy soldiers around, both MacKenzie and he would be dead in seconds.

They approached the next space forward, where the lights on the starboard side had survived the battle, and Simmons saw bullet-scarred bulkheads and blast marks from a North Korean grenade that had gone off on the port side.

The next space forward was a medical area, which was shrouded in darkness. Gunfire had shattered the overhead lights but he could distinguish several bodies clad in blue. A grenade had made its mark on the access trunk that led to the third deck.

The sounds within the huge ship floated over to them. Simmons put out his hand and touched MacKenzie's chest to stop him, and they both listened intently in the darkness. They heard voices over the machine gun fire that seemed to be on the deck below. He had trouble placing their direction, but two things were certain—they were North Korean, and they were headed their way. They had to move quickly.

He motioned to MacKenzie and together they descended to the third deck. Halfway down the ladder, the door on the third deck opened and two North Korean soldiers stepped into the access trunk. Miraculously they didn't look up but began to closely inspect the hatch leading to the fourth deck. Simmons and MacKenzie froze and dared not even breathe.

They stood motionless for a few seconds until a bell went off right under Simmons's chin. The OBA alarm! He had forgotten about it!

Simmons opened fire immediately; a second later the North Koreans whirled and fired. The blast from Simmons's M16 slammed into the enemy soldiers, causing their aim to be wild and flinging them backward through the doorway. Simmons let out a breath—he hadn't even had time to crouch down to evade the enemy gunfire. He quickly shut off the OBA alarm.

He bounded down the remaining steps and cautiously peeked out the doorway, only to look directly into the eyes of another North Korean. The enemy soldier was peering around a set of nearly destroyed lockers that Taylor had used for cover just minutes before. The soldier was in the crew compartment about ten feet away from the access trunk when he spotted Simmons. He opened fire immediately and the American had to jerk his head back instantly to avoid the blast from the soldier's AKR.

Simmons ripped a hand grenade out of his pocket, pulled the pin, and promptly dropped the grenade on the deck in front of him. He fell to his hands and knees immediately in a frantic search for the live grenade. Precious seconds ticked by as Simmons skittered back and forth in a panicked search of the dimly lit access trunk. MacKenzie hadn't seen him try to use the grenade and stood dumbfounded at the lieutenant's actions. Had the man lost his mind?

Simmons's hand finally closed around the grenade. In a single motion he lifted it and threw it through the doorway into the crew compartment. It careened off the bulkhead and disappeared behind the lockers. Simmons turned to get away from the doorway, but only managed to fall over a stupefied MacKenzie.

The explosion came quickly. The force of the blast was concentrated along the walls of the confined compartment, and it seemed to Simmons as if his head were in a vise. The deck shook beneath them, and then it was over, leaving only clouds of smoke in the unventilated spaces.

Simmons reeled from the ringing in his ears and the ache from the concussion of the blast. He shook off the pain and sprang to his feet. He asked MacKenzie if he was all right, his voice sounding strangely muted. MacKenzie nodded nervously. Simmons inched his way back to the doorway and quickly looked into the space. Smoke swirled toward him as he fought to see through the darkness; the grenade had blown out the emergency light over the doorway. After a few moments he was able to make out several North Korean bodies that were piled near what was left of the lockers. He gazed past the bodies into the bunk room and saw no one.

The shouting of some orders in a foreign tongue came to them, and after a second getting his bearings Simmons placed the voice on the port side. North Koreans came to the doorway on the far side of the crew compartment and immediately opened fire on Simmons and MacKenzie.

They had to get out fast! Simmons went halfway up the ladder to the second deck and caught a glimpse of a dark green uniform in the doorway above. They were cut off by North Korean soldiers. Only one place to go, thought Simmons. Down to the fourth deck!

He glanced at the hatch that led to the fourth deck and groaned. It was securely dogged down. He shouted to MacKenzie to keep him covered and he jumped on the hatch. MacKenzie alternated between firing into the crew compartment and firing up the ladder to the hatch leading to the second deck, while Simmons feverishly worked on the scuttle's handwheel. It was a tough job—someone had really jammed it shut— and took a full thirty seconds as they both waited for a hand grenade to greet them.

He threw open the scuttle and leaped through, only to slip on the ladder and fall in a heap on the deck below. The barrel of an automatic weapon was shoved into his face.

"Shit! I almost shot ya, Lieutenant!"

The sound of automatic weapons' fire from above made the sailor cringe, but Simmons quickly gathered up his M16 and climbed the ladder to give MacKenzie covering fire. Simmons sprayed the two doorways in the access trunk with M16 fire, then backed partway down the ladder to let the young sailor climb onto it. They both grabbed the scuttle handwheel and let it slam shut, then spun the handwheel to close the scuttle as tightly as possible. Simmons breathed a sigh and marveled that he was still alive, then descended the ladder into the now stifling engine room. The air was so hot it was painful to breathe; Simmons estimated the temperature to be about 130 degrees Fahrenheit. Taylor had never restored the ventilation, he thought dully.

He looked up to a welcome sight. Chief Taylor and seven sailors were waiting to greet them. Taylor's stern, sweating face broke with relief at the sight of Simmons and MacKenzie. Simmons shook Taylor's hand enthusiastically.

"I'm mighty glad to see you're all right," said Taylor.

"You did a hell of a job keeping the North Koreans from reaching the engineering spaces," replied Simmons. He hesitated, then asked the question uppermost in his mind. "How many men did you lose?"

Taylor's face fell. "Over twenty, I guess." A pause. "It's hard to take." He glanced at the officer. "How about you?"

It was Simmons's turn to feel despair. "I lost them all." He was amazed at how easily he said it.

Taylor's eyes widened in disbelief. "Oh, my God," he said with hushed sympathy.

"Except for MacKenzie, they're all dead."

They stood in silence for a few moments, then Simmons tried to inject a little hope into their situation. "Maybe there's a couple of guys still left up in the island." His voice sounded lame.

Taylor glanced back at the hatch. "I wonder how long it'll take them to get through."

The gravity of the situation hit home. They were on the fourth deck in the forward engine room trapped from the decks above by North Koreans and unable to go forward or aft due to the lack of doorways in the bulkheads on this deck. The ship was constructed that way for damage control purposes; if one engineering space was flooded or on fire, then it wouldn't propagate to the other engineering spaces. But the setup provided no maneuvering room for Simmons and his men.

A glance about and a quick head count made Simmons even more depressed. Including Taylor, MacKenzie, and himself, he had only ten men to battle the North Koreans.

And how many North Koreans were left? Of the one hundred fifty that the three helicopters had deposited onto the *Truman* there were perhaps forty to fifty remaining.

He had the men check their weapons—there wasn't much ammo left. Simmons checked his pockets—one grenade. He glanced about again, noting the plentiful cover his men would have for their last stand. Maybe they could get ten to twenty North Koreans before succumbing to their superior numbers.

He would make the most of the engine room arrangement, which had the entrance ladder from the third deck on the starboard side. The North Koreans would have to make a sharp left turn and go around a bulkhead to get to the rest of the engine room. To the right of the ladder in the engine room was the secondary conning station. He would put some men there and maybe catch the enemy by surprise.

The engine room consisted of two levels. The upper level, or fourth deck, had the central control station, where the watch controlled the machinery in the space. The lower level had the two massive steam turbine engines that turned the outboard screws that propelled the ship through the water. Entrance to the lower level was by means of two ladders, one on the port side, and one on the starboard side that was an extension of the entrance ladder from the third deck. Simmons cringed as he thought of enemy soldiers swarming into the engine room; the Americans had no place to go but down to the lower level.

He thought about somehow sabotaging the main engines. Maybe he could use the old trick of a monkey wrench in the main reduction gears. That would permanently prevent any propulsion from the forward engine room. However, the reduction gear inspection covers were secured with padlocks, the keys to which were kept in a safe in the engineering logroom. The chief engineer was the only one with the combination to the safe. Simmons could forget that notion.

They could scuttle the ship by opening an inspection plate in the seawater intake to the main engine condensers. Seawater would flood the compartment and there would be no stopping it. But even with the entire forward engine room flooded, the ship would still sail along on the propulsion provided by the aft engine room and nuclear reactor. Besides, it would take half an hour to take off the myriad bolts that kept the inspection plate in place. He and his men probably had only a few precious minutes before the North Korean attack. His thoughts of sabotage ended there.

Simmons thought of surrendering. They had fought almost to their last breath. They were almost out of ammo. Almost.

Almost.

But they could still fight. He thought of the sailors in the hangar bay and rage ran through him once again. Maybe they deserved a last stand. Maybe everyone on the carrier deserved everything he could give, even if it was his life and the lives of the men with him.

Simmons straightened and gathered his men around him. They didn't once mention surrendering, he thought. Simmons gazed into each man's face as he deployed them around the engine room. They were all grim but determined.

They knew what their chances were.

It's a gamble, thought Pak, but a necessary one. He would fling all his remaining men, except for the half dozen in the island, into the final attack on the forward engine room. The Americans still had the capability of scuttling the carrier, and he could not let that happen.

He shook his head in wonder. He had totally underestimated the Americans. They had fired on the helicopters on the flight deck to disable them so they couldn't take off. That had severely limited the number of men Pak could get aboard the ship. Their fighter aircraft had swept his men from the skies, and that abominable black man in the khaki uniform had orchestrated a brilliant defense of the inside of the ship. He had chosen his defensive areas well and had used a few choke points to bleed Pak's force of men. And he had made Pak fall for that trap in the machine shop. Pak was sick at the thought.

Pak gave the hatch leading to the engine room a worried glance, then looked over his men. They were ready, all forty-eight of them. There would be no finesse to this attack; he would shove all his men down the hatch as quickly as possible, and overwhelm the remaining Americans. He couldn't use any hand grenades for fear of damaging the engine room controls. Maybe they would get lucky and the Americans would run out of ammunition, or surrender. Again they had chosen their defensive terrain well.

Pak spotted the officer in the hangar bay who had been ready to execute the two Americans. That officer would have the honor of leading his men into the engine room, he resolved grimly. He would learn firsthand what these Americans were made of.

Pak stepped over his dead and glanced up the access trunk to his men on the second deck. Two Americans had just fought their way down to join the others in the engine room. He had caught a glimpse of khaki and silver bars on one of them. The American officer was joining his men for a last stand. Pak never thought he would feel such respect for the Americans; they had been the objects of unremitting scorn all his life.

Now, he knew better. It would be a shame to have to kill them.

Simmons's breath rasped in his throat as he stared at the dogs on the hatch. At least they would have some warning; the North Koreans would have to undog the hatch to get below. They probably wouldn't come through the narrow scuttle. If they did, his men could easily pick them off one at a time. No, they would open the large hatch and rush us all at once.

Simmons's speculation was confirmed an instant later. The dogs on the hatch began to slam open two at a time with loud jarring noises. The men jumped and took careful aim on the ladder. Simmons pulled the grenade from his pocket and put his finger through the ring.

The attack came with horrifying quickness. The hatch flew open, followed by a hail of gunfire that sent bullets ricocheting around the engine room. The sailors ducked in surprise and three enemy soldiers slid down the ladder to the metal deck. They immediately charged to their left, toward the still-crouching sailors. The doorway to secondary conn opened and two sailors emptied their weapons into the backs of the charging North Koreans.

Another hail of bullets from the hatch above slammed into secondary conn, but the two sailors had retreated safely inside. The North Koreans now flowed from the hatch in a seemingly never-ending stream. Simmons's men opened up on them and managed to get seven or eight of them before most of the sailors ran out of ammo. They darted from their cover past central control to the port side of the engine room.

Simmons caught a glimpse of the two sailors in secondary conn raising their hands in an attempt to surrender, and the North Koreans gunning them down with vicious bursts from their AKRs. Rage welled up in him. He pulled the pin from the grenade, flipped the grenade toward the biggest concentration of North Koreans at the base of the ladder, then ran past the control station, and dove behind a bulkhead.

The blast seemed to shake the entire vessel and rattled the deck plates under Simmons. The grenade blew out the overhead lights and left the starboard side of the engine room in darkness and enshrouded in billows of smoke.

Simmons jumped to his feet and shouted to his men to get to the lower level. He gave a glance toward the entrance ladder and saw a horde of enemy soldiers leap over their dead comrades to continue the attack. Simmons got to the ladder that led to the lower level, and with bullets pinging around him he managed to get below with the rest of his men.

Panic-stricken, he looked about for a place to hide. His eyes immediately locked on to a watertight door on the aft bulkhead between the two massive steam turbines.

The escape trunk! He had forgotten about it! That narrow, vertical passage led to the deck above to allow men to escape the engine room in case of an engineering casualty. It might also allow Simmons and his men to escape the North Koreans.

"Quick, Chief! In the escape trunk!" he shouted over the cracking of automatic weapons' fire. The sailors ran for it in a desperate race to delay their execution. The North Koreans opened fire from above, killing one sailor and wounding two others.

Simmons and Taylor emptied their weapons as MacKenzie and the two others dragged the wounded sailors into the escape trunk. The fire from above stopped for a few seconds as the North Koreans maneuvered for a better line of fire. Simmons and Taylor took full advantage and ran for the escape trunk.

The thought occurred to Simmons in a burst of déjà vu. It was a horrifying gamble, but there was nothing left to do. They squeezed their way into the escape trunk and slammed the door.

"MacKenzie! Any ammo left?"

The young sailor stopped scrambling up the ladder and looked down at the officer. "Yeah, but—"

"Gimme it! Quick!"

MacKenzie reluctantly lowered his weapon to Simmons.

"C'mon, Lieutenant! Let's get the hell out of here!" shouted Taylor.

"Get these people up the ladder, Chief!" Simmons shouted back as he grimly cocked the M16. He peered through the doorway and saw the North Koreans make their first cautious moves down the ladder to the lower level. He quickly scanned the overhead with its maze of pipes covered with white lagging material; the pipe he wanted was bigger than the rest.

He spotted it after a moment and opened fire on it, seconds before the North Koreans opened fire on the escape trunk. A burst of fire slammed into the door and made Simmons duck, but he continued to fire on the pipe, sending shredded insulation in all directions.

His M16 stopped firing as the clip ran out, and his hope disintegrated. He heard a faint whistle from the pipe, but it wasn't enough. He desperately searched his pockets for a forgotten grenade, but he had none.

So close, he thought. So—

The pipe gave way with a tremendous explosion. A wave of steam swept across the engine room, searing all in its path. Paint peeled, metal railings and deck plates expanded and warped under the intense heat. Main steam, driven at extreme temperature and pressure, flew at the North Koreans, boiling them in seconds. With skin melting, eyes exploding, blood gushing from their ears, nose, mouth, and eye sockets, only to be instantly vaporized by the searing steam, they died.

Simmons slammed the door shut and gagged in horror as he listened to the steam drown out the screams of the North Koreans.

Chapter Twenty

P ak lay on the deck in shock. He made a move to raise his hand, but it shook too much so he left it still.

My men! The pride of Communist Korea—*all dead!* His mind turned numb at the thought. The American officer had sacrificed himself and his men just to kill as many of Pak's men as he could. He had been told that the Americans would not fight like that; he was told that they would surrender easily. How wrong! And Pak's force had paid the price. The Americans had fought like demons. They had fought the way Pak's force was supposed to have fought.

Outnumbered, outgunned, with no possibility of reinforcements, they had fought to the last man. How ironic! Pak and his men were supposed to be the heroes. Instead they had made heroes of the Americans. No matter what happened now, the stand the Americans had made in the engine room would become legend.

Pak raised his hand again; it didn't tremble as much this time. He pushed himself to a sitting position and his eyes fell on the hatch that led to the graveyard beyond. Steam hissed from the seams in the gasket, and Pak was beginning to feel the heat of the engine room through the tiled deck.

He got to his hands and knees, and suddenly realized what was in front of the hatch. He grew sick and vomited, more at the thought of what he had done than at the sight. A severed right hand and three fingers from a left hand were hanging from the edge of the hatch.

Pak had been near the ladder when the main steam line had exploded, and he had made a panicked exit to avoid being incinerated. He had slammed the hatch and dogged it down without seeing who was behind him, and had thrown himself on the deck in despair. He had deserted his men; worse yet, he had slammed the hatch on the man behind him.

More irony! He had become the coward and the American officer the hero! The American had rallied his men and had died with them, while Pak had run away. There was only one recourse.

He looked about for a weapon and found an AKR a few feet away. A quick burst and . . .

The mission popped into his mind, and he suddenly realized the possibility of completing it. The American resistance had ceased, and Pak still had half a dozen men in the island. If the aft engines kept turning, he could still get to Nampo; he could still complete his mission.

He struggled to his feet and hefted the AKR. He would complete the mission and deal with himself later.

The roaring of the steam grew louder as the nuclear reactor's computer sensed the drop in line pressure and increased the reactor's output to compensate. When the main steam line pressure continued to drop, the computer automatically shut down the reactor and the roaring began to fade.

The heat pressed in on Simmons, who was leaning exhaustedly against the escape trunk door. His mind had stopped functioning at the thought of what was happening on the other side of the door. *And what the bodies looked like* . . .

He gasped and jerked back as the door became hot enough to burn him. He opened his eyes and saw the paint start to bubble on the inside bulkhead. The groaning of metal told him that the door was deforming under the intense heat and pressure; it might not last long.

Simmons dragged himself to his feet as memories and horrible visions struggled for his consciousness. He savagely shoved them aside. Not now! I'll have my moment later, when I have time to let the reality of it all hit me. Not now when men are counting on me!

He turned to climb the vertical ladder, but the small porthole in the escape trunk door caught his eye. It was miraculously unbroken in spite of all the automatic weapons' fire the door had endured. He stared into the glass, drawn by the horrific reality that lay inside the engine room. Gratefully, he saw nothing but dark, swirling mists, the lights having exploded under the extreme heat and pressure.

The groaning of the metal increased and spurred him to start his climb to safety above. One thought occurred over and over. *And now I'm the reason for the horror. . . .*

He got to the top few rungs of the ladder and friendly hands dragged him from the escape trunk. Simmons sank to the deck in exhaustion. He sat with his head in his hands and didn't hear Taylor's weary voice order the sailors to set up fire hoses to cool the hatches to the engine room. After several minutes Taylor touched Simmons's shoulder.

"You all right, Paul?"

Simmons looked up after a second's hesitation into Taylor's concerned eyes. He knows what I'm going through, thought Simmons. And what I will go through. The thought reassured him and gave him strength. He nodded to Taylor.

The sailors returned from the other side of the ship after setting up the fire hoses on the main hatch, where Pak had been moments before. They had seen the severed hand on the hatch, but none of them drew any conclusions from the ghastly sight and were too sickened to mention it.

Simmons took a head count. Seven of them left, including the two wounded sailors. How many had they started with? His mind stopped. He couldn't think about that now. Time enough later.

He dragged himself to his feet, trying to distract himself from his thoughts by physical movement. He straightened himself, let out a sigh, and looked at Taylor. Simmons was the officer again.

"I'm going up into the island to see if I can get one of the radios working, and maybe get some help. Judging by the number of enemy soldiers that hit the engine room, I don't think there are many North Koreans left up there. There still might be some in the lower decks, so be careful."

Taylor nodded in agreement.

"I'll steer the ship from there," continued Simmons. He thought about the construction of the engineering plant for a moment. The carrier actually had two independent engineering plants, fore and aft. The forward reactor fed the forward engine room and the two engines within it. The second, or aft, reactor fed the aft engine room. The two independent systems were separated that way for damage control purposes, so that the loss of one plant would not affect the other plant. The loss of the *Truman*'s forward plant would cut their speed not quite in half.

"The aft engines should keep turning," said Simmons. Taylor nodded in agreement. "Get everybody back to the aft engine room," Simmons continued. "The only thing we can do now is hold the last engine room and the bridge, and hope for the best."

"OK, Lieutenant," Taylor said.

Simmons turned to the young sailor next to him. "MacKenzie, let's go."

They stopped by the armory to rearm, then quickly but cautiously retraced their path back to the island. Simmons slowly began to climb the ladder to the flight deck level, with MacKenzie trailing behind him. He strained his ears to pick up any sound, but he heard only the wind as it made its way through the hatches and passageways in the island. He had to dodge piles of corpses here and there; most of the dead were American sailors. They had met the same fate as the sailors in the hangar bay, shot in the back while fleeing the onrushing enemy.

The number of corpses increased as they proceeded up the ladder until they reached the flight deck level, where the bodies were two and three deep. Black streaks lined the wall of the passageway, the result of a hand grenade. Simmons's stomach started to churn as he gazed at the mangled bodies heaped in the passageway. There were many more North Korean bodies visible. His men must have fought furiously until the superior numbers of the enemy overwhelmed them. He could hear MacKenzie choking behind him.

My God, is anything worth all this? Could anything be *that* important to cause people to murder each other like this? Why didn't the North Koreans leave us alone? Simmons's thoughts grew bitter.

The attack was over and the crew of the *Truman* had won, but at what cost? He began to wonder what would have happened if he had decided not to resist the North Koreans. All his men would still be alive, but the Communists would be in control of the ship. What would they have done with the ship and the crew? His mind refused to go any further, and he stopped with the thought that he had done only what he had to, no matter how horrible the results.

Voices intruded on his thoughts. North Korean voices were coming from one of the levels above him. Some of the enemy were still in control of the island, thought Simmons, and they were probably steering a course for a North Korean port even though the last engine room was in American hands. He had to take the rest of the island. There could be only a few North Koreans left.

"Mr. Simmons, let's get out of here," whispered MacKenzie in a fearful voice.

As Simmons turned to give MacKenzie a dirty look he noticed the personnel elevator on the other side of the passageway. An idea hit him. Why not outflank the enemy—they would never expect someone to come from the elevator.

"Come on," said Simmons.

MacKenzie started to object, but Simmons grabbed him by the arm and shoved him toward the elevator. They stepped inside and the door slid silently shut. Simmons decided to go up to the bridge level, then work his way through the rest of the island. He pushed the button for the 09 level. The elevator went smoothly into motion and he stepped back from the door. He brought his M16 up to chest level, then turned to MacKenzie.

"If you see enemy soldiers when the door opens, don't hesitate. Open fire immediately, OK?"

MacKenzie swallowed hard, gave Simmons an anguished look, and nodded quickly. Simmons looked up at the flashing lights above the doorway just as the 06 light went out and the 07 light came on. He began to have doubts. Suppose there were more enemy soldiers than he thought? His heart started to pound.

The 07 light went out and the 08 light came on.

Suppose the North Koreans weren't surprised and they were waiting for them? Would a hand grenade greet them as the door slid open? Simmons began to reach for the emergency stop button when the 09 light came on and the elevator came almost imperceptibly to a stop. Half a heartbeat later, the doors slid noiselessly open.

An empty passageway greeted them. They exhaled with relief and cautiously stepped out of the elevator and glanced both ways. To the left was a head, and next to it was the closed door of an officer's stateroom. To the front and right of them was the ladder leading to the lower levels of the island. To the immediate right on the same side of the passageway as the elevator were several rooms with the doors half open. The passageway ended with an officers' head, and to the left was a passageway leading to the bridge.

Simmons decided to check this level for enemy soldiers prior to checking out the rest of the island, and he whispered his intentions to

MacKenzie. They slowly proceeded to the right, after checking out the head to their left, and immediately came upon the first doorway on the right side of the passageway. Simmons held the M16 close to his chest and put his back against the bulkhead, the right arm next to the doorway.

He took a quick look in the room, then jerked his head back and let his mind register what he had seen. Just as a TV picture is constructed line by line from a stream of electrons, Simmons's mind began to fill in the details of the room.

It was a senior officer's stateroom by the looks of it, and it was empty. They slowly went past the doorway and came upon another doorway. Simmons looked through the doorway, and again quickly stepped back. That stateroom also was empty. He glanced at the words on the door. It was the captain's sea cabin.

The sound of voices startled them, and they were both instantly put on guard. Simmons put his back against the bulkhead and slid silently toward the next doorway, which led to the chart room. The voices were definitely coming from the next space, but he couldn't tell whether they were Korean or American. Simmons nervously gripped his M16 and braced himself for a quick glance into the chart room.

He stuck his head into the doorway, then quickly yanked it back to safety. His right index finger reached for the trigger of the M16 as his mind filled in the details of what his eyes had seen. There were four men standing with their backs to the doorway. They were wearing green fatigues.

An incredible rush of anticipation came over him. The danger of the situation never entered his mind as a sense of invulnerability washed over him like a wave.

Simmons charged into the chart room, firing a long burst at the four North Koreans in the space. He caught all of them in the back. They were flung about the room and landed on the deck in disarray, their bodies oozing blood, and life.

 # Chapter Twenty-one

MacKenzie heard the sound of someone coming in spite of the deafening blast of Simmons's M16. He had followed Simmons up to the door of the chart room and watched the officer disappear into the space, but he didn't have time to see how Simmons made out. He was sure that someone would be coming from the bridge to investigate the gunfire.

He almost called to Simmons to alert him to the sound but quickly decided against it. The North Koreans might think that one of their own people had opened fire, and they wouldn't expect to find Americans on this level of the island.

The passageway entrance was close to him, not more than five feet away. He gripped his automatic rifle tightly and pointed it in the direction of the entrance.

Two North Koreans suddenly came stumbling through the doorway and froze in amazement at the sight of the American sailor standing so close to them.

MacKenzie didn't hesitate. The burst of fire caught the lead soldier in the chest and the second man in the side of the head. The force of the bullets threw the two soldiers back until they rebounded off the bulkhead and fell to the deck. MacKenzie took his finger off the trigger and the tremendous din of the M16 ceased.

He heard the faint tinkle that the last few ejected shell casings made when they hit the deck, but took no notice. His eyes were riveted on the entrance in anticipation of the next enemy soldier who would enter. That soldier would be forewarned and wouldn't die as easily as the first two.

MacKenzie turned slightly and inched his way toward the entrance. He was in a quandary. If he looked around the corner he could very well have his head blown off. But if he didn't, a hand grenade could greet him in the next few seconds.

Where the devil was Simmons? He had disappeared into the room and hadn't come out yet. Maybe he was dead. MacKenzie hastily revised that thought; he hadn't heard the distinctive sound of AKR gunfire from the direction of the chart room.

A barely perceptible sound registered in MacKenzie's mind and he instantly knew that someone was coming down the passageway. He had better act fast if he was going to beat him to the punch.

He threw himself across the doorway toward the opposite bulkhead, firing as he moved and sending a brutal stream of lead up the passageway. He fired blind, not knowing whether a soldier was there or not. There was a soldier, and the surprised North Korean didn't have time to react. MacKenzie's stream of bullets was accurate and caught the soldier across his midsection. The Korean grunted and pitched forward face down on the deck. His weapon flew in front of him and slid up the passage toward MacKenzie.

The young sailor was surprised at the accuracy of his instincts during combat. He became flushed with pride at his killing of two North Koreans and the wounding of a third. He was an effective fighter now, able to carry his own in combat. The paralyzing fear he had felt in the hangar bay had left him. He still felt fear, but now he thought he could control it so that he could function in any situation.

MacKenzie stood and slowly made his way past the wounded soldier toward the bridge. He cautiously entered the bridge and found to his great relief that it was clear of enemy soldiers. He quickly looked about at the unconscious sailors who littered the deck and spotted the captain, who was stretched out near the aft bulkhead. MacKenzie grinned. He hadn't expected to ever see the dignified Capt. Ralph Sturdevant in such an undignified position. He was flat on his face with an arm extended as if he had been reaching for something. MacKenzie briefly wondered if Sturdevant had tried to warn the crew but was struck down by the gas. He shrugged off the thought and scanned the bridge once again.

He felt exhilarated. The battle was over and they had won; they had beaten the North Koreans at their own game. Then he wondered what would happen to the North Korean that he had left in the passageway. Would he be sent back to North Korea? If I was the one lying there in the passageway, by this time I'd be dead. His exhilaration turned to bitterness.

MacKenzie reentered the passageway and walked up to where the wounded soldier was lying on the deck. The Korean had pushed himself over onto his back and defiantly stared back at the young sailor. MacKenzie finally had what he wanted for most of his short life. He had the advantage over someone. He had been waiting for this moment for a long, long time.

He stared at the wounded North Korean. The man was obviously in excruciating pain. He rolled slightly from side to side and moaned and worked his legs back and forth in the most pitiful manner. So, this is what combat is all about, thought MacKenzie. Moments ago he had felt hatred and almost paralyzing fear at the thought of the North Korean invaders. Now, looking at this one helpless enemy soldier, he felt no fear or hatred at all. Only pity.

MacKenzie leaned his back against the bulkhead and let out an exhausted sigh. Supreme advantage over someone wasn't what he had expected. The sight of the blood streaming from the North Korean's stomach sickened him, and the gurgling sounds from the man left MacKenzie weak. He had the urge to help him but didn't know how.

When MacKenzie could no longer stand to look at the wounded man he turned and slowly walked back down the passageway toward the chart room to find Lieutenant Simmons.

There was a groan in the passageway and then all was still.

USS *LANSDALE*

"Main control, bridge."

The answer came very slowly, or so it seemed for Comdr. Michael Packard. He looked up from the intercom and surveyed the bridge. Everyone seemed to be on their toes, as alert as they could be. The OOD was anxiously scanning the horizon with binoculars, as were the surface lookouts.

"Main control, aye."

The fuzzy voice almost startled Packard, but he pressed the transmit lever immediately. "This is the captain. Can you get me any more speed?"

The voice returned from the depths of the ship. "Maybe a little, Skipper, but I'm dragging the boilers down to 550 psi already."

The answer confirmed the captain's suspicion that there weren't too many more knots in the ship he commanded. "Well, do what you can."

"Aye, aye, sir."

Packard turned to the enlisted man standing next to him. "I'll talk to the crew now," he said.

"Yes, sir," the man answered and walked over to the 1MC. He flipped a switch and blew the bo'sun's pipe to announce to the crew that the captain was about to speak.

Packard stepped up to the microphone. "This is the captain speaking. You're probably all wondering where we're going in such a hell of a hurry." He paused to heighten the suspense a little. "The USS *Truman*, along with her escort vessels, have experienced a total communications failure. The reason for this is still unknown. We have been ordered into her operating area with all possible speed to find out what happened." He paused again and listened to his voice echo around the ship.

"As soon as we enter the *Truman*'s operating area we'll go to general quarters. This is a precautionary measure in view of the international situation in this part of the world. We have no information that the *Truman* was attacked, but we must guard against that possibility. In any event we'll find out in the next hour or so. Should we have to go into combat I will expect every member of the crew to obey orders quickly and diligently. That is all."

They had been steaming along at thirty-plus knots for an hour and a half now. Some of his officers had been grumbling about the delay in informing the crew of their destination, and he hoped this little talk would silence their complaints. He moved over to the intercom again and pressed the lever. "Combat, bridge," he said.

"Combat, aye."

"This is the captain. Keep me informed of the distance to the Chinese coast or any of their islands."

"Aye, aye, Captain."

Now all he had to do was wait, which had always been difficult for him.

Packard was the commanding officer of the USS *Lansdale*, a modified *Gearing*-class destroyer. It was originally built at the end of

World War II but was modernized in the sixties to include new antisubmarine weapons. During the seventies most of the destroyers in its class were decommissioned or sent to the naval reserve force; the *Lansdale,* however, was selected to undergo another conversion. This time it was to carry sophisticated passive electronic surveillance equipment, "eavesdropping" equipment, which could gather information on radar or communications stations.

The *Lansdale*'s conversion was a result of a decision made in the Pentagon following the capture of the USS *Pueblo* in 1969 to put intelligence-gathering equipment on combatant vessels. The purpose was obvious. A ship such as a destroyer could defend itself much better than a ship such as the *Pueblo*. A destroyer was twice as fast and much more heavily armed than a so-called environmental research vessel, the official designation of the *Pueblo*.

Officially the *Lansdale* was a combatant vessel, but its real mission was electronic intelligence, or ELINT. The *Lansdale* was on just such an ELINT mission off the coast of mainland China when the message ordering them to the CTF 78.1 operating area was received. The *Lansdale* was ordered to visually locate the *Truman* and render any assistance necessary. Packard's ship was the closest surface unit to the *Truman*'s operating area and therefore would be the first to arrive, a fact that caused butterflies in Packard's stomach. All other units, except possibly aircraft, were at least six to eight hours away. Whatever lay ahead for Packard and his crew, they were on their own.

An hour and fifteen minutes later, a voice came over the intercom with the expected pronouncement. "Bridge, combat."

Packard leaned over to the intercom and pressed the lever. "Bridge, aye."

"Tell the captain we've just entered the *Truman*'s operating area."

"This is the captain. Thank you."

"Combat, aye."

Packard turned to face the OOD. "Sound general quarters," he ordered.

The officer gave the captain a crisp "aye, aye" and ordered the bo'sun's mate of the watch to sound general quarters. The man went to the control panel, flipped up the protective cage, and pressed the button that sounded a gong about twice a second, the panic-inducing alarm that sent men scurrying about the ship to their battle stations. The bo'sun's mate made the necessary announcement over the 1MC and the watch was changed to the general quarters personnel. Tension was evident among the crew members on the bridge as helmets and life jackets were donned. Reports of the combat readiness of the ship started to arrive at the bridge with satisfying quickness.

"Captain, main control reports all boilers on the line, the propulsion plant is split fore and aft, and double A & D is set," proclaimed one of the numerous telephone talkers.

"Very well," replied Packard as he gazed out the window of the bridge with his back turned to the rest of the crew.

Another telephone talker spoke immediately after the first one. "Captain, DC central reports condition Zebra set at 1155."

Packard's eyes shot up in surprise. He glanced down at his watch, did some mental arithmetic, and came to the conclusion that it took only two minutes to button up the ship. That was the fastest time ever for his crew. The possibility of going into real combat must have something to do with it, he thought. Reports from all over the ship came tumbling in. Gun mounts, missile batteries, deck division, CIC—all manned and ready. Packard and his crew settled down to wait.

Ten minutes later, the navigator spoke over the intercom. "Bridge, this is plot."

The OOD walked over to the intercom. "Bridge, aye."

"We're at the last known position of CTF 78.1."

"Bridge, aye," replied the OOD and informed the captain of their position.

Packard mumbled acknowledgment. "Keep the lookouts on their toes," he said to the OOD. "Tell them to look for floating wreckage in addition to scanning the horizon."

Packard was beginning to get nervous. The *Truman* was nowhere to be seen. It could have sailed off in any direction. It couldn't have sunk without a trace, he thought; there would be something floating about. He forced himself to settle down and let their highly sophisticated home act its role as a detector.

"Bridge, combat."

Packard was the first to the intercom. "Captain, aye."

"Captain, ELINT has two CHICOM X-band radars that just lit up on the coast north of us. Surface search only, no fire control stuff yet. They're probably wondering what's going on. We've got some S-band in the general direction of North Korea, but it's pretty faint. Nothing positive on it yet, but it's probably airborne radar. No infrared at all.

And we've got nothing, I mean nothing, at HF, VHF, or UHF in our vicinity. Really weird."

Packard pushed the lever on the intercom. "The *Truman* has to have a Hawkeye up and probably a CAP, too. Nothing from them?"

"No, sir, nothing. But they could be out of range."

I have a bad feeling about this, he thought.

"Captain!"

Packard whirled to look at one of the telephone talkers on the bridge.

"Comm's just picked up a survival beacon!"

A chill ran down Packard's spine; someone was in the water. "Any voice contact?" he asked.

The talker repeated the question into his microphone, listened for a second, then replied, "Not yet, sir, but we're getting personnel data."

Was it the *Truman*'s crew, or . . . Packard went to the intercom. "Comm, bridge."

"Comm, aye."

"This is the captain. I need to know who's on that beacon."

"It's a weak signal, Captain. We're at maximum range, but we've made out two names so far, a Lieutenant D. Carver and a Lieutenant F. Majewski. Computer lists them both as naval flight officers."

An aircrew in the water! A plane shot down! "I need to know what kind of plane it was," said Packard after a second's thought.

"Working on it, Captain."

"Give me an intercept—we'll pick them up."

"082 degrees true, sir."

Packard turned to the OOD to give him the course change, but he was interrupted by one of the phone talkers.

"Captain, we've got more survival beacons. Four . . . no, five. Bearing 095." The *Truman*'s CAP?

"ELINT has weak signals that look like a Phalanx radar!" someone else spoke up.

The task force had to have been attacked, thought Packard. Otherwise the Phalanx wouldn't have been activated.

Another phone talker spoke. "Combat reports surface radar contact, bearing 015, range 12 miles, speed 15 knots." Anxiety masked all other emotion in the young man's voice.

Surface lookouts, along with everyone else on the bridge, immediately focused their attention in the direction indicated by the telephone talker.

The aircrews in the water will have to wait, thought Packard. He ordered a course change to head directly for the contact, and moments later one of the lookouts shouted the discovery of smoke on the horizon.

Now it begins, thought Packard. What are we heading toward? A sick ship, or a real shooting war? "Combat, bridge," he said.

"Combat, aye."

"This is the captain. Are there any other contacts? Any at all?"

"Not yet, sir." The reply was definite. Something was burning just over the horizon. Nuclear-powered ships do not make any smoke. There was one nonnuclear-powered ship with them, though, the *Oldendorf*, not too gently referred to as the task force's weak sister. That one was a gas turbine ship, though, and it wouldn't make smoke either.

His thoughts evaporated immediately as one of the lookouts shouted, "It's a carrier!" He took another look in his binoculars and added, "It's a nuke!"

That was the *Truman*; it had to be, thought Packard. "Ask the comm center if they've contacted them yet," he said to one of the telephone talkers. The man nodded and proceeded to comply with the captain's order.

Packard turned to the OOD. "Set a parallel course and take us alongside."

"Aye, aye, sir," was the reply.

Packard looked through his field glasses and the huge carrier swung shakily into view. He rested his elbows on the shelf below the bridge windows, and his view of the *Truman* steadied up. His eyes traced the plume of black smoke down to its source on the flight deck. The smoke boiled upward with such ferocity that he caught only glimpses of the actual fire. The object being consumed was hidden altogether.

"Captain, comm center doesn't get any answer." It was the telephone talker again.

"Very well," mumbled Packard. Something puzzled him about the ship, something not noticed by the rest of the bridge personnel.

As they drew closer to the huge vessel Packard looked for detail, any detail, any clue that would tell him what had happened to the *Truman*. At first glance it looked as though a fire had broken out on the flight deck, and that it had somehow affected communications. That possibility was defeated almost immediately in Packard's mind. It wouldn't explain the lack of communications with the two escort vessels. And where were they?

"Bridge, combat."

Packard walked over and pressed the lever. "Bridge, aye."

"Contact course seems to be drifting slowly to port. . . ." The CIC officer hesitated.

Packard sensed the mood of the officer even though they were in two different parts of the ship and their only contact was by intercom. "Let's have it, Lieutenant. What's bothering you?" demanded the captain.

"Well, Captain, it's almost as if no one's at the helm."

That was it! The CIC officer had put into words what had been bothering Packard from the first moment he had spotted the carrier.

Packard ran back to the forward window and hurriedly brought the binoculars up to his eyes again. The *Lansdale* was drawing very close to the *Truman* and he could see the flight deck in greater detail. His eyes searched quickly for the damage control party that would be fighting the fire. His effort was in vain. There didn't appear to be anyone on the flight deck. He thought about the CIC officer's remark about no one being at the helm. If no one was at the wheel, then there must be no one on the bridge.

He stopped. It was a chilling thought.

Where was the crew?

# Chapter Twenty-two

S immons sat on the deck of the chart room with his back against the bulkhead, and gazed dispassionately at the four North Korean bodies. Moments ago they had been living, breathing. Now what were they?

Simmons's mind ignored the question and instead proceeded to objectively analyze his actions of a few minutes ago.

So, this is how it's done. The adrenaline gets flowing and you feel as if nothing can stop you. In the engine room and now. And afterward you begin to think. If the pain is too severe, you get numb. The way I am right now. . . . The numbness will wear off after awhile and I'll have to confront all this, but maybe for now I should just be grateful.

He knew now what his father had meant when he said that he didn't have time to think about it. *I figured some other guys would get it but not me. If I had gotten shot, I'd have been really surprised.*

Yeah, Dad. Me too.

He heard someone running but didn't bother to turn around. A breathless MacKenzie entered the chart room.

"Mr. Simmons, there's a ship approaching. I don't know if it's North Korean or what." He gave the lieutenant a quizzical look. "You've got to take a look at it!" he nearly shouted. "Dammit, sir!"

Simmons blinked his eyes for the first time in several minutes and turned to face MacKenzie. "What ship?" he asked hoarsely.

MacKenzie let out a sigh and all but dragged the lieutenant to his feet. "It's off the starboard beam and coming on fast. Hell, I just got into the navy and I don't even know our ships, sir, much less theirs." He picked up both M16s and tried to hand Simmons his, but the lieutenant made no move to accept it.

Simmons looked at the two North Koreans MacKenzie had killed. With a blank expression on his face, he headed up the passageway toward the bridge. He walked in a daze, his body going through the motions as if by habit while MacKenzie dutifully followed two steps behind. Simmons walked past another now dead North Korean without looking at him. MacKenzie couldn't resist a glance, although he quickly forced his eyes away and got closer to Simmons.

Simmons entered the bridge and was led over to the starboard side, where MacKenzie handed him the binoculars and pointed at the steadily growing spot on the horizon. Simmons automatically raised the binoculars to his eyes and the spot instantly grew into a full-sized ship. He cleared his throat and lowered the glasses as MacKenzie waited expectantly.

"Well, what is it?"

"It's one of ours," replied Simmons, the fatigue evident in his voice.

MacKenzie started to talk about how wonderful it was that help was on the way, but Simmons was past caring. The horrendous events of the day had taken their toll; he was emotionally and physically drained. He longed for forgetfulness, oblivion.

Simmons stood numbed and watched the ship grow steadily closer, then eventually pull alongside the *Truman*. Something in his mind commanded him to function. He had to play the drama out to the end. After all, he had other people to think about; the rest of the crew was depending on him. He turned to MacKenzie. "Get on the helm and try to keep a steady course. I'm going to talk to them by radiotelephone."

MacKenzie had been watching Simmons with rising anxiety, but he suddenly grinned with relief. Simmons was acting like an officer again. MacKenzie gave him a crisp "aye, aye" and was at the helm in an instant.

Simmons went to the aft bulkhead and examined the RT set. It was one of the new ones with no cord connecting the telephonelike handset with the main body of the device, much like a cordless telephone. He picked up the receiver from its captive housing and hesitated.

A voice suddenly boomed from the loudspeaker. "Kingpin, this is Satan One. Over."

Some RT procedures came back to Simmons as he listened to the call being repeated over and over. Their code word seemed to be Satan One.

He pressed the lever hidden in the handle of the handset and said, "Satan One, this is Kingpin. Over."

"Kingpin, what happened? Over." The relief in the voice was evident as it came over the loudspeaker.

Simmons's mind froze at that simple question. *Now I'm the reason for the horror. . . .* The screams of the North Koreans echoed in his mind as he fought to control himself. He gritted his teeth and began the explanation that he knew he had to give.

"We got gassed, Satan One, which knocked out most of the crew. Then North Korean helicopters started to land on the flight deck. We just barely fought them off, and I think there are still some North Koreans loose in the ship."

He walked over to the inboard side of the bridge and looked out on the flight deck. Most of it from the island aft was ablaze. The first helicopter that they had shot down was responsible for most of it, but the fuel truck that had exploded near the port side elevator had sent flaming gasoline toward the fantail.

"Half the flight deck is on fire, along with another fire in the hangar bay. I'll need some people to fight it, and some armed sailors to make a sweep of the ship to search for—" He stopped in midsentence and gazed down at the torn bodies of the two sailors murdered by the MiG during the strafing run. He had forgotten about them. He thought that they had taken cover.

"Kingpin, what's the matter?"

He had never expected this. No one had ever warned him that if he joined the service he might have to kill people someday. No one had ever told him that one of the horrors of war is that innocent people get slaughtered just because they're in the way. Or that you become like an animal in order to survive. Anger rose in him. Why didn't they tell him? *Goddamn them!*

"Kingpin, do you read? Over."

He spun around and hurled the handset at the RT box in frustration. The device missed MacKenzie's head by an inch, bounced off the bulkhead, and clattered to the deck. Simmons covered his face with his hands and began to sob, "Goddamn them! Goddamn them all!"

They had forced him into his decision to resist the North Korean attack. The nameless, faceless symbol in Simmons's mind of military men with their sense of honor and duty had trained him to make him react the way he did. He had made the decision to defend the ship without realizing the consequences. Who could have told him that so many people would die as a result of his decision? Who could have described to him the horror of a grenade blast in a confined area? Who could have warned him that he might make mistakes that would get his men killed? *They* could have told him, but they had chosen to omit those "minor" details. It might make men hesitate to kill the enemy, and hesitation was not allowed. You must kill quickly, efficiently and without thinking. Time enough to get sick to your stomach later, when it was safe.

Frustration swept over him and he wanted to lash out in some way at "them," to take revenge for using him in their game of world power. He quickly realized that there was no way to do it. "They" in reality was a huge system spawned from the necessity to deal with human evil on a monumental scale, and in the process it dealt evil of its own. Man's methods of defending himself were too massive for one man to change. There was nothing left to do but attend to his own survival.

"Damn it, Kingpin, what's happened?"

Paul Simmons straightened himself, took his hands away from his face, and gave a quick glance at MacKenzie, who was in the process of letting out yet another sigh of relief. Simmons walked over to the radiotelephone, picked up the handset, and pressed the lever.

"Satan One, this is Kingpin. This is Lieutenant Paul Simmons in temporary command. I'm going to stop the ship dead in the water so we can transfer personnel. Most of the rest of the crew is unconscious except for some engineering personnel. I desperately need people to fight fires and search for enemy soldiers. Please acknowledge. Over."

There was a pause as the crew on the other ship digested his statements.

"Kingpin, Satan One. This is Captain Packard of the USS *Lansdale* speaking. Did I understand you to say that the North Koreans attacked you with gas and that they tried to hijack the ship?" The incredulity in his voice was unmistakable.

"That's right, Captain," replied Simmons.

Another pause, this one shorter than the last. "Kingpin, can we transfer our people while underway? I don't like the idea of going dead in the water in this area."

"Negative, Satan One. I don't have anyone to man high wires, and there's almost no one in the engineering spaces. Should we have an engineering casualty we just might drop everybody overboard. Besides, I've got a fireman at the helm." Simmons looked at MacKenzie and almost smiled. MacKenzie gave him a lopsided grin.

"OK, Kingpin, but let's do it quickly," was the reply.

"Roger, Satan One. Let me know when you've got your men assembled," said Simmons.

"Kingpin, how many casualties do you have?" asked Packard.

Simmons shut his eyes in physical pain at the thought of how many sailors had been wounded or killed during the day. "Over a hundred, I think. I . . . don't know," he mumbled.

Another pause. "We'll send over all our corpsmen, Kingpin," said Packard. His voice was quiet with sympathy. "Did you say *Lieutenant* Simmons?"

"That's right, Captain."

"Sounds like you did a hell of a job, Lieutenant. Well done."

Yeah, well done, thought Simmons bitterly. The conversation was over and Simmons replaced the handset in its cradle, then turned to MacKenzie.

"I'll take the wheel; you go below and tell Chief Taylor that we're going to take people on board from a destroyer to help us fight fires and look for North Koreans. Tell him that he should put rope ladders and whatever else he can find over the side to help these people get on board." MacKenzie turned to leave, but Simmons called after him. "And for God's sake be careful! There's probably still some enemy soldiers around," he admonished.

"I'll be careful, sir," MacKenzie promised, then disappeared around the corner. He entered the elevator and proceeded below decks.

"Kingpin, this is Satan One. Over."

Simmons left the helm and picked up the RT handset. "Satan One, this is Kingpin. Over."

"Kingpin, we've got our people ready and standing by. Over."

"Satan One, I'm stopping the ship now."

"Roger, Kingpin. We'll keep station on you. Out."

Simmons hung up the RT set and walked over to the engine order telegraph. He rang up STOP on the two aft engines and hoped someone was still in the engine room to receive his signal. The answering pointer swung around and matched the bridge pointer with a clang of bells. Simmons nodded to himself in satisfaction.

Nothing to do now but wait, he thought. Aircraft carriers take an extraordinary amount of time to slow down.

USS *LANSDALE*

"Sonar contact!"

Captain Packard swung around to look at the phone operator. Alarm ran through him.

The young sailor put his hand to the earphone over one ear, then shot a glance at the captain. "Bearing 095!"

"Let's go to ASW stations," said Packard to the OOD. The captain received an "aye, aye," and the OOD relayed the order to the bo'sun's mate of the watch, who made the announcement.

"You think it's North Korean, sir?" asked the OOD.

"It sure as hell isn't one of ours," replied Packard. "Let's get out there, mister."

"Aye, aye, sir." The OOD turned to the helmsman. "Right full rudder! All ahead flank!"

The destroyer picked up speed and swung away from its parallel course with the *Truman*. Packard picked up the radiotelephone.

USS *TRUMAN*

"Kingpin, Satan One."

Simmons picked up the RT handset. "Kingpin," he said.

"We've picked up a sonar contact on our starboard beam. We're going to check it out. You'd better get to flank speed ASAP. Out."

"Roger, Satan One." Simmons went over to the engine order telegraph and rang up flank speed on all four engines. He stopped and looked at the position of the telegraph's levers. The aft EOS answered with a clang of bells as the answering pointer swung around smartly to indicate flank speed. The forward answering pointer remained still. Was it so easy to forget that the forward engine room contained nothing but corpses?

Simmons turned away from the engine order telegraph to stare out the side windows of the bridge. So, the North Koreans still had some tricks up their sleeve. He watched the *Lansdale* steam away from the side of his ship.

CH'OLLIMA 4

Captain Pang Chin-u stared through the periscope at the two American naval vessels in the distance. He had been told that it would be obvious when to attack. No orders were needed from higher command, and he need not contact the officer in tactical command on the American carrier. If Captain Pang's boat had to attack, that officer would probably be dead.

Pang and his crew had slipped out of the Pipa-got submarine base on the west coast of North Korea, and had hugged the Chinese coast to get around behind the American task force. His aging boat and his training crew were not up to a prolonged battle with the Americans, but with luck he would be able to carry out his orders to sink the American carrier if the helicopter attack had failed.

The American carrier was heading southwest. If the North Korean attack on the ship itself had been successful, then the ship would be heading due east toward the North Korean mainland. The ship was on fire, but Pang couldn't tell what had happened to the helicopter strike force. He surveyed the scene carefully. No helicopters in sight. But his countrymen might still be fighting for control of the ship.

Pang scratched his head quickly and glanced at his watch. The attack should have been over long before this. Minutes ago the carrier had been joined by an American destroyer, and together they were steaming away from North Korea. If he was going to attack he had better do it quickly. That destroyer would detect him any minute now.

Captain Pang snapped the periscope handles to their upright position and ordered the periscope retracted. His orders came tumbling out in a rush. "Load torpedo tubes one through four! All ahead flank!"

His crew's eyes grew wide, then the men rushed to obey. Pang ordered the periscope up to get a firing solution.

His heart went into his throat. The destroyer had turned toward them!

USS *LANSDALE*

Captain Packard knew it was a race. He had only one antisubmarine weapon aboard, ASROC. It was a pretty potent weapon but it had limited range. He had to get within range before the North Korean sub let loose with its torpedoes.

"Captain! Sonar says the contact is flooding forward tubes!"

Packard shook his head in frustration. The North Koreans were getting ready to fire. He went over to the intercom. "Combat, bridge."

"Combat, aye."

"This is the captain. Let's go active and get a firing solution."

"Combat acknowledges going active sonar."

Until now Packard's ship had been using only passive sonar, which were just listening devices. Now he would start his sonar pinging to get a much more accurate fix, which would then be fed into his ASROC weapon system before launch.

"Range 12,000 yards!" called out a phone talker.

A race it was. The *Lansdale* had to get to within 10,000 yards before it could launch its ASROC.

All he could do was wait.

CH'OLLIMA 4

Captain Pang gaped at the American destroyer through his periscope. There were no evasive maneuvers, nothing tricky or sophisticated. The American was coming straight at him, as fast as he could. This would be over very quickly, with one of them surviving and the other going to the bottom of Korea Bay. He hadn't expected such a direct attack. Americans weren't that bold, were they?

Pang grimaced at the charging destroyer, then stepped back from the periscope.

"Open outer doors on tubes one through four!" he ordered.

USS *LANSDALE*

The range wound down slowly as Packard stared impatiently at the sea in the direction of the contact. The range became 11,500 yards, then 11,000, then 10,500. His mind ran quickly over the North Korean sub threat. They had some ex-Soviet Whisky-class boats on this side of Korea, but they were old and used only for training. When submerged and running on batteries, they were also pretty damn quiet.

"Range 10,000 yards!"

"Launch ASROC!" commanded the captain. He went to the forward bridge windows and watched the missile leap from its launcher and start its ballistic trajectory toward the enemy submarine. "Secure pinging!" Packard commanded.

A few seconds later he got the message he had dreaded. "Captain! We have high-speed screws, bearing 010!"

CH'OLLIMA 4

Pang slapped the periscope handles up and ordered the periscope down. His boat had done all that it could. Four of his Russian-made 533mm torpedoes were on their way. With luck one of them would hit the destroyer, so that he could go after the carrier later, if he could catch up to it.

But now he just had to survive. He had seen the flash and the smoke coming from the launcher in the bow of the American destroyer. He knew all too well what that meant.

"Left full rudder! Dive to 50 meters!" That was perilously close to the bottom, but he had to risk it.

A plan came into his mind, and he realized he was ideally set up for it.

USS *LANSDALE*

"Right full rudder!" ordered Captain Packard. He had to get his ship on a maximum velocity vector with respect to the torpedoes' course, so he turned the ship ninety degrees away from the torpedoes' line of bearing. This was done in the hope of confusing their homing devices. The quick change of course would also put great turbulence in the water to create a false position for the torpedoes to home in on. He had some other actions to take as well.

"Launch decoy aft!" he ordered. The acoustic decoy would make shiplike sounds and hopefully draw the torpedoes to it.

"Torpedoes appear to be in passive mode. Constant bearing, decreasing range!" said a phone talker.

Those four words—*constant bearing, decreasing range*—were the most frightful words in the navy. The torpedoes were coming straight for them. Packard's heart fluttered.

CH'OLLIMA 4

"The American missile has hit the water!" The trainee hadn't expected to go into combat. Indeed, none of them were expecting it, but the orders had come and they had to be obeyed. Now all their dreams of glory were gone, blown away by the storm of war.

Actually it was the American torpedo that had broken the surface of the water, thought Pang. With the rocket motor jettisoned, the torpedo was lowered to the sea by parachute. Once in the water its motor is activated and it hunts its quarry.

Well, let's give it something to home in on, thought Pang.

"Launch decoy from aft signal ejector!" His crew jumped to it. "Right full rudder. Ahead one third," he ordered.

His mind ran on quickly. The American would have turned one way or the other to put the maximum distance between them and the course of his torpedoes. If the American had turned right, then Pang should be at this moment facing the American's course at a right angle. He should be able to get off another shot at the destroyer, but it would have to be blind. He couldn't risk his periscope being seen by the destroyer. With torpedoes going off nearby, probably due to the American decoys, the American crew might lose contact for a minute or two.

"Captain! The American torpedo has been detonated by our decoy!" The crew let out a shout.

"It's not over yet," said Pang, but he smiled for the first time since leaving Pipa-got.

USS *LANSDALE*

"High-speed screws, bearing 240 and drawing left!" The enemy torpedo would miss them. Packard could hear the bridge crew exhale with relief.

"ASROC detonated at 8,000 yards, but sonar thinks we missed," said one of the bridge crew.

"Where is the contact now?" asked Packard. The phone talker relayed the question into his sound-powered phones.

"Sonar says they lost it."

Packard shook his head. This sub captain is a real pro. He had only an old Russian diesel boat, and he was making life very difficult indeed.

"Captain, we're getting detonations to port!"

Packard nodded. His decoy worked. Now where was the enemy sub?

CH'OLLIMA 4

Pang had the boat drifting slowly up to a depth of fifteen meters. One of his phone talkers spoke up.

"The target is at bearing 015. Bearing changing rapidly to port."

Pang gave a quick smile of anticipation. He didn't have range information because he was using only passive sonar, but the bearing information told him that he had guessed correctly. The American ship had turned to its right, and now he was headed toward the destroyer's port beam. He eyed the large clock that was near the periscope. He'd have to launch in about forty-five seconds.

"Have they got the forward tubes loaded yet?" He hoped that it was impatience that showed in his voice and not the fear that gnawed at his insides.

"They have tubes one and two loaded, and they're working on the other two." His lieutenant was afraid that the captain would be angry at the bad news.

"We'll have to go with just two torpedoes then," sighed Pang. This crew had been assigned for training, not real combat. They had done well up until now, but their lack of experience was beginning to show.

"Flood tubes one and two!" ordered the captain.

After half a minute, a crew member shouted, "Tubes one and two are flooded!"

"Open outer doors on tubes one and two!" said Pang.

USS *LANSDALE*

"Captain! Passive sonar contact! Bearing 275! There are sounds indicating they're opening outer doors!"

Packard whirled to the intercom. "Combat! Go active, get a fix, and launch two ASROC, ASAP!"

"Combat, aye, aye!"

Packard nervously trained his binoculars in the direction of the enemy sub. This captain was good enough to make Packard fear him. Somehow he had evaded the first ASROC and had gotten in close to the ship. None of this should be happening. The *Lansdale* should be on an ELINT mission, not shooting it out for real with a North Korean sub. The carrier task force was supposed to provide ASW capability, but with their crews unconscious there would be no launch of Viking ASW aircraft or LAMPS helicopters from the *Oldendorf* to deal with the submarine threat.

"Captain! High-speed screws bearing 250! Constant bearing, decreasing range!"

"Secure pinging! Right full rudder!" Packard ordered. He would have to try to keep the torpedo on the outside of the tight turn to starboard that he had just ordered. Hopefully he could just steam in circle; the enemy torpedo would be on his port quarter trying to catch up to him until it ran out of fuel. It was one helluva gamble.

Packard watched two ASROC missiles leap from their launchers and fly on their deadly mission.

CH'OLLIMA 4

"The American will probably launch his ASROC at us again just as before. Launch another acoustic decoy from the aft ejector and take us down to 50 meters," said Pang to his second in command. The man nodded and rushed to obey.

A few seconds later, a phone talker said, "Splash in the water close by!" The American had launched sooner than expected!

"Quickly! Get that decoy launched!" shouted Pang. Seconds later Pang got the word that the precious noisemaker had been launched out the aft ejector.

Pang and his green crew endured the wait badly as they heard the sounds of the approaching torpedo mingled with the sounds of the decoy. Some cried, some broke down completely, others stood in stony silence and waited for death.

"Stop engines! Silence in the boat!" Pang knew he'd never outrun the American torpedo; he'd just have to hope that the decoy made more noise than his boat.

The detonation came suddenly, rotating the sub nearly on its side. Pang and his men were tossed around the sub's insides as the boat heeled over. It gradually rolled upright and they picked themselves up from the deck and looked at each other in surprise. The torpedo had exploded close by, but it had gone after the decoy, not the sub.

Pang straightened himself and grunted at the smiles from his crew. Quite a change from a few seconds ago. The crew began to chatter excitedly at their extension of life, until one of the phone talkers gave the captain a frightened look.

"Splash in the water 150 meters to port!"

The words hit Pang's crew like a cannon shell. Even this inexperienced crew knew what it meant. They all fell into shocked silence.

Pang had to do something. "Right full rudder! All ahead flank!" Maybe a miracle would save them.

"Have they reloaded decoys yet?" Pang's question was like a thunderbolt across his crew. Perhaps there was still a chance.

"Aft ejector almost reloaded!"

Pang became very calm upon hearing the last message. His inexperienced crew still had not gotten the decoy reloaded. The sound of the American torpedo's pinging came to him through the hull before one of his men blurted out that the torpedo had gone active. The torpedo had acquired his sub and was in its terminal phase. The decoy would do no good now.

A phone talker spoke up. "Torpedo's speed is increasing!"

Pang estimated that they had twenty seconds left. "Tell them to hurry with the decoy," he said in a quiet voice. He turned his back on his crew and thought about his wife and three children.

USS LANSDALE

"High-speed screws fading!"

All eyes obediently went in the direction of the torpedo that was chasing the *Lansdale*. Packard took a deep breath to settle his insides. His tactic had worked. The enemy torpedo had run out of fuel. He eyed a phone talker. "Tell combat to give us an intercept course."

The young sailor relayed the command into his sound-powered phones. Another sailor spoke up.

"Sonar says ASROC two detonated at an estimated 3,000 yards."

Packard rubbed his face in an attempt to fend off fatigue. Three thousand yards sounded about right.

"Captain, sonar says they have sounds of a collapsing pressure hull on the same bearing as the ASROC detonations."

Packard closed his eyes and tilted back his head in relief. The *Lansdale* had gotten the sub.

 # Chapter Twenty-three

USS *LANSDALE*

Captain Michael Packard had his crew patrol the area for half an hour while looking for indications that the North Korean sub had really met its end. The sonar crew was kept on their toes and no other contacts were detected. Some diesel fuel was seen but no debris. Packard wanted to linger in the area until he had irrefutable proof that the sub had gone down, but he felt an urgent need to rejoin the *Truman*. The carrier desperately needed corpsmen and firefighting parties.

The *Lansdale* set sail at flank speed to rejoin the huge carrier. After a few minutes the carrier came into view on the horizon and steadily drew nearer as the thirty-knot *Lansdale* rapidly overtook the *Truman*, which was going fifteen knots. The destroyer approached the carrier at an angle, about 120 degrees relative to the *Truman*'s bow, with Packard intending to pull along the carrier's starboard side.

Packard heard one of the phone talkers gasp. Packard whirled to look at him.

"Sonar contact!" Another sub! "High-speed screws, bearing 090!"

"Fire ASROC along the line of bearing of the torpedoes!" commanded Packard. He had just ordered a snap shot of a couple of ASROCs in the general direction of the enemy sub so that the North Korean captain would have something to worry about. Maybe if he was lucky he'd get the bastard.

Packard looked at the phone talker. He expected to hear the young sailor say those four horrifying words again. *Constant bearing, decreasing range.*

"High-speed screws bearing drawing left!"

Left? Packard's eyes shifted in the direction of the port side of the ship. His gaze locked onto the carrier, which now loomed in his vision. They're firing at the *Truman*!

"Fire decoys starboard!"

The thought of torpedoes hitting the *Truman* seemed to twist Packard's insides. The whole damned crew was unconscious! The few that were still awake weren't enough to take care of the damage and fight the fires that would result from the torpedoes. The largest carrier afloat could very well be sunk by one lousy North Korean submarine!

Packard watched the decoy hit the water and knew it wouldn't be enough. The phone talker confirmed his estimate. "High-speed screws, bearing 065!"

The torpedoes were already past the decoy. Packard ordered another decoy to be launched, then lapsed into silence.

The decision was there. The one he didn't want to make.

His ship was still traveling at thirty knots, hurtling headlong into a space between the massive carrier to port and the torpedoes to starboard.

CH'OLLIMA 5

Captain O Ch'ol-kay stared transfixed into his periscope. He had heard the sounds of his companion submarine's fight with the American destroyer. His boat had been deployed south of Captain Pang's position and had with some difficulty intercepted the carrier in its flight southward. With Pang keeping the American escort vessel busy, he had an unimpeded line of attack on the American carrier.

His crew had excitedly gone about the business of launching four torpedoes from the bow tubes when they heard the thrashing screws of the American destroyer.

Captain O Ch'ol-kay stayed with the periscope view much too long, fascinated by the vision of his torpedoes, the American destroyer, and

the American carrier all heading toward the same point on the surface of Korea Bay.

He felt a surge of admiration run through him for the American destroyer
captain. He was flinging his ship between the torpedoes and the carrier.
He was sacrificing himself and his crew for the sake of the carrier.
The American was performing bravely.

The North Korean captain suddenly saw smoke and two missiles
quickly fly away from the bow of the destroyer. An antisubmarine missile
launch!

USS *LANSDALE*

Packard thought of his crew and felt the misery of command as he
had never felt it before. How many will die as a result of my next
order? Command at sea was never for the faint of heart.

"Tell sonar to go active!" said Packard a little too loudly. The phone
talker obeyed immediately, not knowing the import of the captain's
command.

The OOD's head shot around. "Captain! The torpedoes—" He cut
the sentence off after seeing the look on his commanding officer's face.
The normal toughness drained from the OOD's eyes, leaving him with
a strained look. He slowly turned back around to stare out to sea.

"Captain, torpedo bearing is drawing left more slowly," said a member
of the bridge crew.

Packard gripped the bridge railing until his knuckles were white.

"Torpedo bearing is 025 degrees and slowly drawing right." The
phone talker sounded puzzled.

The OOD came up to Packard, his voice sounding plaintive. "Maybe
more decoys, Captain?"

Packard could only nod his head. He was afraid to trust his voice.

"Sonar requests to secure pinging, sir," said a phone talker.

The OOD shot Packard a desperate look. The captain stared him in
the eye. "Tell sonar to keep pinging with the max repetition rate."

The phone talker repeated the command. Packard expected a panicked call over the ship's intercom, but there was none.

They know, he thought. He straightened and looked into the eyes
of his bridge crew. There were some orders to give. For insurance.

"Right full rudder! Stop the starboard engine!" Packard waited a few moments for the engine room crew to get the starboard engine stopped. "Starboard engine back full!"

The USS *Lansdale* now had one engine full forward and one engine full reverse. The effect twisted the ship as fast as possible to starboard and in the process created an unbelievable amount of noise. The USS *Lansdale* presented its starboard side to the onrushing North Korean torpedoes.

"Captain! Torpedoes have just begun pinging and their speed is increasing!" said a phone talker.

The OOD gasped in despair and Packard braced himself for the impact. The enemy torpedoes had just locked on to his ship.

"Captain! Torpedoes have constant bearing, decreasing range!"

CH'OLLIMA 5

"Emergency dive! 50 meters! Left full rudder! All ahead flank!"

Captain O Ch'ol-kay slapped the periscope handles upright, then hesitated. He flipped them down again and peered through the glass. The American destroyer was skewing around in the sea to form a physical barrier to the torpedoes. The captain slapped the handles upright again and ordered the periscope retracted.

"Launch decoys!" he ordered, then settled down to await the arrival of the American torpedoes.

"Splash in the water 600 meters astern!"

That would be the American missile-turned-torpedo, thought the captain. The acoustic decoys are right in line with it. That torpedo shouldn't be a problem.

But where was the second one?

USS *TRUMAN*

Lieutenant Paul Simmons stared in horror through binoculars at the four approaching torpedoes that trailed white streaks in the dark blue sea. To his astonishment the *Lansdale* raced toward the torpedoes. Simmons could see the white streaks bend slightly toward the destroyer. Packard was attracting the torpedoes to his ship!

Simmons looked about quickly as a feeling of helplessness ran through him. There was nothing he could do to take the heat off the *Lansdale*.

There was a muffled explosion followed by a geyser of water 500 yards short of the ship. A premature detonation! Simmons found new hope.

A second explosion occurred much nearer to the destroyer; it began to roll the ship to port but it still was a premature detonation due to the decoys fired between the destroyer and the oncoming torpedoes.

Two explosions occurred in quick succession and Simmons knew that the *Lansdale* had been hit. Water spray and smoke enveloped and quickly obscured most of the destroyer. Simmons strained his eyes to see the ship's fate.

Emotion welled up in him as he stared at the stricken ship alongside. Captain Packard had sacrificed himself and his ship to save the *Truman*.

Simmons watched in horror as the *Lansdale* began to roll to starboard.

CH'OLLIMA 5

The sound of the torpedo explosions carried clearly through the water to the North Korean sub. The crew cheered as they heard the torpedoes detonate. The men had no way of knowing whether their torpedoes had hit anything, or if they had been detonated by the American acoustic decoys.

Captain O Ch'ol-kay leaned against the bulkhead as his boat dove rapidly. Another explosion rattled the sub, this one much nearer than his torpedo explosions. His crew sobered quickly.

The captain nodded to himself. He had expected that one. It was the first American torpedo that had hit the water. His decoys had detonated it about five hundred meters astern. His concern was for the other American ASROC. His crew hadn't detected it yet.

As if on cue, a phone talker spoke up with tension in his voice. "Splash in the water!" He hesitated. "Directly above us!"

"Launch decoy!" commanded the captain. After a few seconds, "All stop! Make your depth 40 meters!"

The torpedo from the *Lansdale* began pinging almost immediately after hitting the water and quickly dove after the now quiet submarine.

Captain O Ch'ol-kay heard the pinging and immediately ordered his boat to flank speed and left full rudder. It was all in vain; the North Korean crew heard the pinging get louder and louder as the torpedo homed in on its quarry.

The last vision of the captain was the horror-stricken faces of his crew as the torpedo detonated beneath the submarine. The blast snapped the hull in two, instantly flooding both halves and sending fifty-four North Korean sailors to the bottom of Korea Bay.

USS *TRUMAN*

Simmons held his breath as he watched the rolling of the *Lansdale* to starboard slow and finally stop. He estimated the list at about twenty degrees. She was still underway, though; that was always a hopeful sign.

Simmons let out his breath and never felt so helpless. He'd have to wait until the crew of the *Truman* recovered from the gas attack to render any assistance at all to the *Lansdale*. Simmons wanted to ask Captain Packard what damage he had sustained from the torpedoes, but he held back. Packard would be busy as hell right about now.

The speaker behind him came alive. "Kingpin, Satan One."

Simmons flew over to the RT handset. "Kingpin."

"Lieutenant, we've taken two torpedo hits, one in the bow and one in the aft engine room. They probably detonated early, but the blasts put a couple of holes in our side. It's a damn good thing they detonated to one side of the ship and not under the keel, or else we'd be on the bottom by now. Forward engine room seems OK, so that leaves me with one screw and a top speed of about fifteen knots. So, don't go running away from me, y'hear?"

"Captain, we lost the forward engine room during the battle," Simmons explained, "so we're limited to about the same speed. Can you control the list?"

"DC central says they've got it under control. They can shift some fuel around to take off some of the list. My people think they got the sub, but they're not sure. Our passive sonar is still working, and the area is clear of contacts. Even at fifteen knots any other subs would have a hard time catching up to us, as long as they're not in front of us."

"Uh, Captain . . . ," Simmons hesitated. "How many casualties?"

There was silence for a while. Simmons could imagine a captain in agony at the loss of some of his men.

"I would guess about thirty or so."

Simmons lowered his head in sympathy. "Captain, . . . tell your men . . . thanks." It was all he could think to say. His heart went out to the men of the USS *Lansdale* and their brave captain.

Packard's voice was quiet. "You're welcome, Lieutenant. Out."

Simmons hung up the handset, then sank down to the deck in exhaustion and stretched his legs out among a host of prostrate sailors. So many lives lost, he thought. And for what? How futile all of this is.

He tried to force the miserable thoughts from his mind, but he had little success. He stood and gazed out the forward windows of the bridge at the expanse of sea that lay in front of him. He would have to set sail for Japan; that would be the nearest naval base. Satan One could navigate for him and give him headings over the radiotelephone, as long as she stayed afloat.

He detected movement out of the corner of his eye, but he didn't react to it. He knew it wasn't MacKenzie and he didn't care to make the effort to turn to see who it was. A flash of green sent warning signals through his mind, and half a second later a burst of fire confirmed his suspicion that it was an enemy soldier.

Simmons hit the deck at an awkward angle in a desperate attempt to avoid the North Korean bullets. The fire ripped a line along the front bulkhead, smashing plexiglass panels, and came toward Simmons with terrifying speed.

Inexplicably the machine gun stopped just as the stream of bullets drew next to him. Simmons took full advantage of his stay of execution. He was on his feet in a flash and leaping at the North Korean. Recognition fluttered through his mind in the instant before his body smashed into his attacker. It was the North Korean officer who had prevented his men from being murdered in the hangar bay.

Pak had been searching the hangar bay for his men who had been guarding the captured Americans, and had found to his rage that his men had been killed. He spent several minutes mourning his fallen comrades and, as a result, had missed most of the battle between the *Lansdale* and the two North Korean subs. However, on his way up to the bridge he had seen the *Lansdale* take the torpedo hits. He had expected the American destroyer to sink quickly, but the ship hung on and continued to steam alongside the carrier.

He hadn't known about the subs, but it didn't surprise him that Kang had secret contingency plans. He knew then that he and his men had lost the battle, but he also knew that to be captured would be the ultimate disgrace. They were the elite attack group and he was their leader. He, like the Spartans in ancient Greece, was expected to come back victorious, or not come back at all.

Pak was surprised upon entering the 09 level to see the dead North Koreans, evidently killed by Simmons and MacKenzie; the North Korean colonel knew that his men no longer controlled the bridge. A simple plan had formed in his mind. He would seize the bridge and try to ram the other American vessel. He had expected to find such an important location heavily guarded, but was surprised to discover that there was only a lone American officer present.

He had fired his weapon point-blank, but the American started to move even before he fired. His gun jammed just as he was about to kill him, and Pak was faced with the prospect of hand-to-hand combat.

Then he made his mistake. He stopped to free up his weapon instead of discarding it and immediately finishing off his adversary.

As Simmons came at Pak, the North Korean froze momentarily. The American officer in the engine room! He had survived his own brilliant trap for Pak and his men!

Simmons hit Pak with a lowered shoulder and everything his 190-pound frame had to offer. The two of them slammed into the bulkhead with a thud. Pak immediately fought back and swung the barrel of his gun toward the small of Simmons's back, but the blow had a diminished effect due to Pak's lack of leverage. Simmons backed up a step and instantly received a knee in the chest. He straightened slightly and lashed out with his left hand toward Pak's face. The North Korean bent forward to duck the blow and Simmons's right fist came up and smashed into his face. The uppercut snapped Pak's head back and he again rebounded off the bulkhead.

Simmons swung again with his left, a blow that the dazed Korean managed to avoid. Pak moved a step to his left and gripped his gun with both hands. He swung the weapon viciously like a club and aimed a blow at Simmons's head. Simmons saw it coming but couldn't move fast enough to avoid it completely. The gun barrel glanced off the top of Simmons's head and sent him sprawling to the deck.

Pak closed in. He aimed another blow at the prostrate American, but it missed its mark as Simmons wriggled away. Simmons got to his hands and knees and crawled around the helm to buy time to recover from the attack. He jumped to his feet and whirled around to see Pak lift the gun high over his head to bring it down on the dazed American.

Simmons threw himself at Pak and got in just under the descending weapon. His momentum carried him and the lightly built North Korean to the deck, where they grappled with each other in a frantic fight for survival. Twisting, clawing, kicking, they rolled about the deck, each trying to get the upper hand.

Pak gouged at Simmons's face and in a furious assault with his fists he managed to wrench free of Simmons's grasp. The North Korean quickly glanced around the bridge and immediately his eyes locked on to Simmons's M16, which was leaning against the rear bulkhead. Simmons followed Pak's gaze and a second later they were both scrambling toward the weapon. Pak had half a body length head start and got to the weapon first.

Simmons leaped to his feet and put his entire body into a kick aimed at Pak's head just as the North Korean swung the barrel around to aim it at the American. Simmons's foot crashed into Pak's face, sending the North Korean in one direction and the rifle in another. Simmons picked up the M16, cocked it, and pointed it at the now groggy enemy soldier.

Pak groaned and lifted his head from the deck to see Simmons pointing the M16 at him. He gingerly touched his mouth and glanced at the blood on his hand, then he slowly stood and squarely faced his adversary.

"It's over," said Simmons, then realized that Pak might not understand English.

"And you have won," replied Pak and gave Simmons a stiff salute.

The American's eyebrows went up in surprise at the well-spoken English from the North Korean. "Looks like you'll be a prisoner for a while," said Simmons.

Pak's face changed as the numbing reality of defeat swept over him. He had never even considered it before today, but now he was faced with the unspeakable. He handled it the only way he could.

"No prison for me," he said with determination in his voice, and he suddenly turned and ran, crouching low to the deck. Simmons raised his weapon, but the helm partially blocked his line of fire. He fired anyway, more in an effort to discourage Pak's flight than in a real attempt to hit him. The blast hit the helm and the rear bulkhead but missed Pak as he ran down the passageway to the middle of the island. A second later, Simmons was after him and caught a glimpse of the North Korean as he scrambled down the stairway toward the flight deck.

Simmons took the stairs three at a time in an effort to catch the quick enemy officer. Pak got to the flight deck level and jumped through the doorway. Simmons pursued doggedly, with one thought on his mind: Pak would rally whatever remaining North Koreans there were and continue the fight. He had to stop him!

Simmons got out onto the flight deck and instantly spotted Pak silhouetted against the smoke and flames of the still burning helicopter. Pak was running at top speed toward the conflagration on the deck. Simmons saw that he had a clear shot at the fleeing North Korean and stopped to bring his M16 to bear. His finger curled around the trigger. He hesitated.

Fire! Dammit! His mind commanded his body to shoot, but he suddenly realized he couldn't do it. He groaned and lowered his weapon.

Pak's furious pace toward the burning helicopter never slackened. Instead of circling the flaming hulk as Simmons expected, Pak leaped headfirst into the roaring blaze and endured a horrifying death.

 # Chapter Twenty-four

PYONGYANG, NORTH KOREA

Kang dropped the curtain in front of the window. The view had begun to be a very difficult one for him; thoughts of continuance after that day had only deepened his despair. Life would go on, the people would go on with their lives, but Kang's name would become only a memory to them. After a few years it wouldn't even be that. Kim would see to that. Kim Woo Chull would rule, now that Kang had led himself to his end. With opposition from Kang disappearing, Kim could easily take over the presidency and become North Korea's dictator. To Kang it did not matter that Kim had won, only that Kang had lost. Kang had led them to disaster, and now Kang would pay the price for defeat, the ultimate disgrace.

His mind was caught up in the turbulence of random thoughts as he walked away from the window. Did someone leak the plan to the Americans prior to the attack? How could Pak have failed?

The MiG pilots were sure—all the helicopters were shot down and a thousand of North Korea's best men were killed. First reports had indicated that complete surprise had been achieved and that the attack force had encountered only minor opposition from one of the escort vessels.

The expected news of final victory was delayed for some time, but Kang was confident. How could they fail?

The first hint of disaster had come from the decimated MiG-29 squadron. They had been attacked by hordes of American planes, had fought valiantly and shot down thirty planes, but were beaten off by the much more numerous enemy aircraft. Kang had received a report in his command post that there was a launch of eight U.S. aircraft from the *Truman* just prior to the gas attack. There were twenty MiGs in the North Korean squadron. He had made a mental note at the time to confront the squadron leader with the truth after news of Pak's victory.

Kang slumped into the armchair behind his desk and put his head into his hands. His world had ended with the look on the command staff's faces; words were unnecessary. Kang knew all was lost. Agony filled him as he relived the moment, and his hands drew into fists tight with rage. What had happened to Pak? He had staked his life on Pak's success and Pak had failed him.

Kang released his fists and placed his hands flat on the desk in front of him. He gazed about the room. His command post was dark now; its staff had been dismissed hours ago. His eyes lingered at the place in the darkness where he knew his war medals lay encased in glass. He had been on the rise then and nothing could stop him. He had come such a long way to be stopped just short of his goal. He embodied the Communist ideal in his country and had accomplished much in the old regime. When the old regime got in his way he eliminated it. In the ensuing chaos he sensed an opportunity that would never come again. He would bring America to its knees.

Kang groaned to himself. He had had a second motive. The attack on the carrier, named *Truman*, was his chance for symbolic revenge on the long-dead American president for his part in the murder of his family in 1950. He had come so very close to succeeding with his revenge; some helicopters had actually landed on the carrier's flight deck. Then the Americans had sprung their trap, but what kind of a trap was it? Kang had no idea. He would never know. Not that it mattered.

The Americans had even gotten away from his contingency force, not one but two submarines! There was no contact from them, and his staff presumed that they were both sunk. MiG-23s, MiG-29s, helicopters, a thousand crack troops, cruise missiles, and two submarines had failed to even halt the Americans. What did they have that was so powerful?

Kang got to his feet with a sudden thought. He went over to a filing cabinet against one wall and fumbled in his pants pocket for the key. He unlocked the file and immediately went to a secret compartment underneath one of the drawers. The folder was old and yellowed now and beginning to crack at the seams. He returned to his desk and turned on a small lamp. The light hurt his eyes and he blinked quickly until they adjusted themselves. He opened the folder with trembling hands.

There were ten sections, one to each man. The pictures were still intact. The sections contained two pictures, one invariably taken by the U.S. government, and the other taken by his agents. One picture when they were alive, and one when they were dead. This was the proof demanded by Kang of his agents when they carried out his revenge on the B-29 crew that had murdered his family.

Kang thumbed through them one by one. Captain Reynolds, handsome, smiling on one side of the page, and swollen and distorted from a drowning death on the facing page. Kang knew each one by heart, having memorized each detail over the years. The severed head of the copilot killed in an auto accident. Sergeant Wood's mangled and broken body at the bottom of a ravine. Body after body passed before his eyes yet one more time until he got to the last section, where there was only one picture. The flight engineer had died before his agents could kill him.

Kang flipped the folder shut and snapped off the light. He had always renewed his hatred of the Americans by looking at those pictures, and at the same time he had felt a curious emptiness at the culmination of his revenge. The feeling was the same this time. The dead American bomber crew hadn't been enough—he had always wanted more. Kang had gloried over every U.S. defeat at the hands of his country—the hijacking of the USS *Pueblo*, the various planes shot down, Americans hacked to death in the DMZ. But each time the satisfaction was short-lived and left him with an insatiable thirst for more. Always more. And now there would be no more.

He let out an exhausted sigh and wandered over to the window to draw back the curtain. His eyes swept over the city once again and failed to see a single civilian. His vision naturally followed the retreating daylight until he found himself staring at a statue jutting boldly above the horizon. It was silhouetted against the sky by the last vestige of light offered by the waning day.

It was Ch'ollima, the winged horse. The legend had provided much inspiration to his people and he had chosen that name for the code name of the attack to provide the same inspiration for Pak and his men. Instead, the name had presided over a disaster, a farce that Kang had engineered. He could never face the Presidium or the people with this incredible defeat.

Kang dropped the curtain for the second time and quickly walked back to his desk. He settled in his chair and felt in the darkness for the desk drawer. For the second time in his life Kang had lost something very dear to him. He briefly relived those violent moments in August of 1950. The sight of the torn bodies of his mother, sister, and brothers slipped through his mind and made him cringe. He thought of the few years they had had together, and suddenly realized he could not remember their faces. He could only remember the sight of their death caused by an errant bomb.

He yanked the drawer open and felt inside. His hand immediately closed on the automatic that had been with him since the fifties. He pressed the muzzle of the pistol to his temple and pulled the trigger.

PEARL HARBOR, HAWAII, THREE DAYS LATER

The U.S. Naval Hospital in Pearl Harbor was filled with the heroes of the *Truman* and a few from the *Lansdale*. Virtually everyone who had resisted the North Korean attack was wounded, with Chief Taylor and Fireman Apprentice MacKenzie notable exceptions. The hospital staff jumped to their tasks and treated their charges like gold.

The leader of the *Truman* heroes was treated the best of all. Lieutenant Paul Simmons had even received a phone call from the president himself. Simmons had quickly learned about the other aspects of the battle, such as Machinist's Mate Third Class Johnson's initial fight with the North Koreans in the second deck galley. He had survived the grenade blast but would need months of recovery to get back on his feet again. He wouldn't get much I & I for a while, thought Simmons with a smile.

The navy gave them all a few days to recover a bit, then they decided to give in to the insatiable appetite of the news media for every aspect of the story of the decade. Simmons's hospital room was a madhouse, with a news conference held at bedside and much brass, including CINCPAC, in attendance. After an hour of give-and-take with the news media the doctors and nurses shooed everyone out, including the brass, and left Simmons to get some sorely needed rest. He closed his eyes and began to drift.

She strode into the hospital room with no warning. He became aware of her presence and opened his eyes, sat up, and just gaped at her for a few seconds.

"Eva!" Simmons finally managed. He sat up straighter in the bed as she came over to his side. He wanted to hug her unmercifully, until she screamed for relief. She was the best sight he could have wished for. She didn't bend over so that he could kiss her, but stood upright and rather formally shook his hand. He was disappointed and it showed on his face.

"How did you get here?" he asked.

"They still have planes, you know," she replied.

"No, I mean the nurses," he said.

She shrugged. "I guess they didn't see me." She regarded him closely. "So, how are you, Paul?" she asked softly.

He stammered a bit. "OK, I guess, you know," he started, then launched into the list of his wounds as he had done for so many of the navy and the media alike. "I've got a severely sprained left shoulder," he gestured to the massive bandages that hid the ice packs. "And I got some bullet fragments in my left side. . . ."

Eva let him go on for a while and studied his face. She noticed with amusement that his speech still slowed perceptibly whenever he looked into her eyes. He knows, she decided after a bit. He knows that this is good-bye for us. I hope he got as much as I did from that one night together.

" . . . so I'm not in too bad a condition," he concluded.

"I'm staying with Ron," she said abruptly. "He needs me now."

Simmons nodded his head slowly. "How did it change?"

"When he came back from the battle, he called me right away and told me to get on a plane to Hawaii. He said he would be there in a few days. He never did anything like that before." She lifted her eyes to stare off into space. "He said he was different," she said in a low voice.

"I heard he had a perfect day," said Simmons.

There's that word again, she thought. "Maybe being perfect is not all it's cracked up to be," she mumbled.

"What?" he asked.

"He seems vulnerable now—not the granite facade that he used to be. Maybe the combat did it. He might even tell me what happened someday," she said in a wistful tone. They both fell silent.

Ron Hastings walked into the room and stood next to his wife. Simmons tensed. What now?

"Why don't you leave us alone for a moment?" Ron asked Eva. She gave Simmons a worried look and wordlessly left the room. Hastings watched her leave, then turned to face Simmons. Here it comes, thought Simmons.

"You're quite the hero now, aren't you?" Hastings said.

"You didn't do so bad yourself."

Hastings nodded slowly while keeping his eyes on the lieutenant. He gestured quickly over his shoulder. "I won," he said. It was a simple statement of fact.

"Yes, I suppose that's very important to you," replied Simmons.

"For her? Damn right it is." He regarded Simmons silently for a moment. "I don't even know why I'm here," he mumbled to himself. He turned to go.

"Thanks," said Simmons. He meant it.

"Don't thank me. I almost left you to that MiG," said Hastings over his shoulder.

"But you didn't."

Hastings turned to face Simmons once again. "Next time I won't save you," retorted Hastings.

"I think you will," said Simmons. He extended his right hand.

Hastings ignored his offer of a handshake and got a sour look on his face. "Don't push your luck, Lieutenant." Then Hastings turned on his heel and walked out the door.

Simmons's father came to visit. It wasn't like Eva and Ron Hastings's visit; Simmons had advance warning. Simmons vowed that this time when he talked to his father it would be different, not like his last leave that seemed to have occurred so long ago.

"Hello, Son," his father said with a considerable amount of kindness.

"Hi, Dad. Where's Mom?" he asked as he glanced behind his father.

"She couldn't make it," Joseph Simmons replied. It sounded lame. Just as well, thought Simmons. "Dad . . . I want to ask you something." The elder Simmons's eyebrows went up in a question.

"When I was home on leave last time, what did you tell the family about me?"

His father suddenly seemed defensive. "What do you mean?"

"You know what I mean."

His father nodded slowly. "I just didn't want them to badger you about what had happened in the engine room."

"Maybe I wanted to talk about it. Maybe I wanted to talk to *you* about it," said Paul in a plaintive tone. "As it was you set it up so that no one would talk about it." He lowered his eyes. "Least of all you."

His father looked stricken. He hadn't expected this from a son he was intensely proud of.

The next question was even more unexpected. "What happened in Vietnam?"

His father began to stammer. "I . . . I . . . "

"How many survivors were there? What did they feel like afterward? How did you feel?" asked Paul in a rush.

His father settled down a bit and got a faraway look in his eyes. "I don't like to think about it, Son. It was the worst thing that ever happened to me." His son's eyes were insistent. He took a deep breath.

"We were in a skinny little offshoot of the Mekong River, so it was easy for the VC to get some sampans to cut off our retreat. We couldn't go forward or back. We just had to shoot it out with them. I saw men dropping. . . . " He stopped for a minute as he fought to control himself.

"We had four PBRs with a crew of five each. The VC got two of the boats with mortars and shot my boat full of holes with small arms' fire. Just before we sank we boarded one of the sampans and got into a full-fledged firefight at point-blank range. I lost most of my crew because we boarded that sampan." He stopped suddenly.

"You made a decision that cost a lot of lives," said Paul in a low tone. His suspicions were confirmed. His father had gone through something very similar to what he had just endured.

Joseph Simmons began again. "I called in an air strike on my own position. The fourth boat was blown out of the water by our own planes." He seemed suddenly tired. "Two of us survived. The other guy lost a leg. I didn't get a scratch."

"I thought one of the Purple Hearts was for—" began Paul.

"No. I got a few minor wounds before that." Joseph Simmons sank into the one chair in the room. They lapsed into silence and idly listened to the bustle of nurses in the corridor attending to the *Truman*'s heroes.

"How did you feel?" Paul Simmons's question was like a thunderclap in the quiet room. His father gave him a quick look, then resumed staring at the floor.

"They gave you a medal, Dad. Did you feel like a hero? Were you proud of it all? Like you had gone through something very hard to do, but you stuck it out and did the right thing, and won in the end?"

His father groaned and passed his hands over his face. Suddenly Paul Simmons felt sorry for him. He was sorry he had ever brought it up. He had resurrected it all for selfish reasons, to find out whether his father had experienced the same feelings he had, and would face.

His father had obviously not come to terms with his feelings, but had buried them beneath a hero's facade. Keep telling yourself you're a hero to soothe the reality and finality of all the death you've seen. Maybe the medals were good after all. You could construct a wall of them to keep out your emotions. Paul also understood why his father had made a point of telling the rest of the family not to talk about the engine room disaster. It might force him to confront his own feelings about what happened so long ago in a river valley halfway around the world.

Paul gazed at his father again. What a change from a moment ago when he had entered so full of pride for his son. Maybe it was time for both of them to face what was ahead. Paul asked his father one more question, his emotion overflowing as his voice cracked.

"Or did you feel guilty?"

Epilogue

F or conspicuous gallantry and intrepidity in action at the risk of his life above and beyond the call of duty while serving aboard the USS *Harry Truman*. Lieutenant Paul Francis Simmons, United States Navy, organized and led a party of the ship's company that successfully defended the ship against a boarding attack. The ship, having undergone a chemical gas attack that had anesthetized more than ninety-five percent of the crew, was boarded by troops of the Democratic People's Republic of Korea in a helicopter assault.

"Lieutenant Simmons immediately assessed the situation and organized the remaining conscious crew members into an effective fighting force and, although outnumbered almost seven to one, surprised the first wave of attackers and inflicted heavy casualties upon them."

President John Dawson paused for a breath but did not look up from the citation he was reading. They were on the south lawn of the White House—president and vice president, members of Congress, most of the Dawson administration's cabinet, high-ranking naval officers, and the men who were being honored. Members of the press corps jostled for optimum viewing position while the birds chirped excitedly from their perches in the surrounding elms and oaks. It was late summer, the hottest part of the year, and the sun proved it by beating down unmercifully on the gathering. A breeze would spring up now and then, providing some fitful relief from the heat, but the winds vanished as soon as the president began to read the citation, as if nature was holding its breath so it wouldn't miss a word.

"Despite these casualties, enemy forces occupied various parts of the ship, but did so only by sacrificing large numbers of their forces. Lieutenant Simmons then led an attack on two helicopters that had landed on the forward part of the flight deck and disabled them, thereby preventing the enemy from landing reinforcements.

"After losing all his men to enemy fire from helicopters and aircraft above him, Lieutenant Simmons worked his way below decks and defended the engineering spaces by annihilating the remaining enemy forces in a fierce battle in the forward engine room.

"Lieutenant Simmons then proceeded to the island and with one other man secured the bridge from the enemy in desperate hand-to-hand combat. He then assumed command of the *Truman* and despite having only a few men left who were conscious and unwounded he sailed the ship to Japan.

"Lieutenant Simmons's determination to resist the attempted hijacking of his ship by vastly superior forces and with only a handful of men sustained and enhanced the finest tradition of the United States Naval Service.

"Consequently, in accordance with an act of Congress and for the actions described in this citation, Lieutenant Paul Francis Simmons, United States Navy, is awarded the Medal of Honor."

Dawson spoke the last three words slowly, as if they were sacred words in a religious rite. He turned to his left and gingerly lifted the medal from the open box. He turned back around and raised the medal while Simmons bowed his head slightly to enable the diminutive chief executive to slip the ribbon over his head. When the medal was in place, Dawson lifted it to study it. In the middle of a five-pointed star supported by an anchor was Minerva, the Roman goddess of wisdom, repulsing discord.

"Well, Paul, it isn't very big, but it's the nation's highest award," said Dawson in a low voice amid the clicking of camera shutters and the whine of film advances. He let the medal fall on the officer's white uniform and lifted his gaze to smile at Simmons.

The president extended his right hand and after a short pause Simmons gave the president a perfunctory handshake. Dawson could almost hear the navy brass exhale with relief.

"You've given us all something to cheer about. Congratulations, Lieutenant," said the president.

"Thank you, sir," mumbled Simmons in an almost inaudible voice.

At first, Simmons had refused to accept the medal, but he was finally convinced to take it by an obscure chaplain assigned to the Pentagon. The chaplain had stressed the good that had come from the lieutenant's actions. One fanatic general could have caused a war that could have cost hundreds of thousands of lives. All that had been averted by Simmons's ragged, historic defense of the *Truman*. In addition, the perpetrators had perished. It is a curious fact, said the chaplain, that much good can come from so much evil. It is the state of the human race to be immersed in confusion and paradox but still have its ideals so well ordered. You are only human, Paul Simmons, said the chaplain, so let a grateful nation honor you as if things are really black and white, instead of the horrible smear of gray that is reality. The lieutenant relented in the end.

Simmons turned his attention away from the president and surveyed the crowd as they broke into enthusiastic applause. Some of the crew from the *Truman*'s escort vessels were present. Remarkably, no serious casualties had been sustained on either the *Truxtun* or the *Oldendorf*, only a few broken bones and a host of bruises when sailors fell down ladders as they succumbed to the gas. The rudder on the *Truxtun* had taken a set to starboard and the ship went in circles for eight hours until the crew awoke and found to their surprise that the engines were still running. The USS *Oldendorf* sustained some damage from the cruise missile attack but no one was seriously injured. The *Oldendorf* apparently caught only the fringe of the gas, because most of the crew was awake three hours after the attack.

The USS *Lansdale* made it all the way to Japan on one engine and with a fifteen-degree list. Captain Michael Packard was wrong about the number of casualties he had recounted to Simmons just after the battle with the North Korean subs. He had said thirty; it was forty-six dead, twelve wounded, two missing. The *Lansdale* had paid a severe price to save the *Truman*.

Captain Packard had received the Navy Cross for his sinking of the two enemy subs and his action to block the enemy torpedoes from hitting the *Truman*. He had been hailed as a hero, but the death of so many of his men sobered him and he took no joy at receiving the U.S. Navy's second highest award.

Simmons scanned the line of people who had already received medals and citations. There was the grinning, nervous Fireman MacKenzie, and the rocklike mass of MMCS Alvin Taylor proudly displaying a new award on his chest. There were also the relatives of the one hundred seven officers and men of the *Truman* who had been killed in action, with tearful wives and mothers holding small cases, Purple Hearts within.

Captain Ralph Sturdevant, who had been an admiral selectee, was noticeably absent. He had been the subject of a several-month-long inquiry, and while no charges were filed, the navy couldn't bring itself to promote him to admiral after his ship had been boarded. The navy suggested that he retire, and he did.

There were also a lot of people Simmons didn't know; he had no idea that so many people had been involved in the battle. Lieutenant Majewski and the rest of the crew of Eagle One, the *Truman*'s Hawkeye radar aircraft, were in line. They had miraculously survived being shot down by the squadron of MiG-29s, although Simmons could spot the lumps of a cast or bandages under the uniforms of a few of them. And the surviving members of an air force squadron led by Maj. Scott Litwinko, which had been based at Osan, South Korea, were also in line.

Next to them were the surviving members of Blackline flight, headed by their commanding officer, Comdr. Ron Hastings.

Simmons glanced at Eva, who stood next to her husband. She smiled at him and he was surprised at her warmth and vigor. He had come to a stunning realization in the intervening months since the attack on the *Truman*; he didn't need her as he thought he would. And now she didn't need him as well. She had made that clear in the hospital in Hawaii. She seemed determined to make her marriage work.

He gave a quick, guilty glance at Ron Hastings, who returned a hard look. His face softened after a second, and he gave Simmons a slight nod.

They'll make it, thought Simmons. Together, they'll make it.

He hadn't wanted to look at his father; he was afraid of what he would see. His father loomed in his peripheral vision and Simmons knew he was staring at him. Simmons glanced over when he could stand it no longer and nearly broke with emotion. His father stood erect with tears of pride streaming down his cheeks for all to see. His mother was blinking back tears of joy, his brother was just grinning, and his little sister was jumping up and down.

In the months since the confrontation between Paul and his father in the hospital room in Hawaii, a bond had arisen between them, each understanding the other and appreciating the crises of their lives more fully. Not a lot of words were said on the subject, but the feelings were there and communicated in subtle ways, as men tend to do.

Paul was embarrassed by the memory of the emotional scene in the hospital. Father and son had embraced each other and wept as the stored-up emotion in both of them came pouring out. They had continued to embrace as the nurses walked in. That one moment had saved Paul's sanity. Just knowing that someone else had the same feelings had made all the difference.

Paul glanced at his father again. The elder Simmons knew what it was all about—this business of making heroes—and he was proud of his son anyway. Maybe it's too ingrained in our nature to feel any other way, he thought.

And now I've survived once again, mused Paul. To what end? What kind of feelings am I going to have now? He glanced again at Eva. He owed her a lot—everything. She had revealed the reason for his guilt feelings after the engine room accident, and now he was better prepared to deal with them, and with the feelings he had after the battle for the *Truman*.

Did Pak know? Is that why he killed himself? He couldn't face it—day by day, year after year, knowing that he survived and his men had died.

People talk about how different the Asian mentality is. Maybe they're not so different from us after all. Mentally disciplined men such as Pak and Kang had taken the ultimate escape route, but he would not. He would live and suffer with the memories and the feelings, and somehow learn to come to terms with them.

Someday.

U.S. Navy Enlisted Rating Structure

CHIEF PETTY OFFICERS		
Master Chief Electrician's Mate	EMCM	E-9
Senior Chief Machinist's Mate	MMCS	E-8
Chief Boatswain's Mate	BMC	E-7
PETTY OFFICERS		
Storekeeper First Class	SK1	E-6
Quartermaster Second Class	QM2	E-5
Disbursing Clerk Third Class	DK3	E-4
NON-RATED MEN		
Fireman, Seaman, Airman	FN, SN, AN	E-3
Fireman Apprentice	FA	E-2
Fireman Recruit	FR	E-1

The ratings listed here for chiefs and petty officers are examples only. There are some sixty different ratings, most of which are represented from the E-4 to the E-9 level.

Chiefs are normally addressed as "Chief" or "Senior Chief" or "Master Chief." Because of this, the chief engineer, who is an officer, is not addressed as "Chief."

Petty Officers may be addressed as "Petty Officer So-and-So" or as "Ess Kay One So-and-So." Firemen are addressed as "Fireman So-and-So." Formerly, petty officers and non-rated men were frequently addressed by their last names only, but this practice has been gradually abandoned of late, the use of the title with the last name being deemed more respectful.

Glossary

Aegis Greek for "shield." This is a task force threat management system that coordinates the radar and sonar data from the ships in a task force, including the data from a highly capable phased-array radar, which is collocated with the Aegis control rooms.

AK-47 A Soviet automatic weapon made famous by the Vietnam War

AKM A newer Soviet automatic weapon derived from the AK-47

AKR Designation given to a Soviet 5.5mm machine gun with a firing rate of eight hundred rounds a minute

angels Code for aircraft altitude in thousands of feet

APC Armored personnel carrier

ASROC Antisubmarine rocket. This missile has either a Mk 46 acoustic homing torpedo or a nuclear depth charge as its warhead. It is the primary submarine defense for many of the U.S. Navy's destroyers and frigates.

ASW Antisubmarine warfare

AWACS Airborne warning and control system. This is an airborne radar plane (Boeing 707-320B airframe) that provides early warning of airborne threats. Its mission is similar to that of the navy's Hawkeye radar plane.

bandit Enemy plane

bingo alarm Or the bingo fuel-set. This is a low-fuel indication in a fighter plane.

BMC Chief boatswain's mate

CAG Naval slang for the air wing commander on a carrier

CAP Combat air patrol

captain's mast A meeting before the ship's captain where an offender is judged and sentenced

CDO Command duty officer

centering up the T (dot) This refers to the alignment of symbols in a pilot's heads-up display that allows him to fire missiles and guns with extreme accuracy.

Chief engineer Officer in charge of the engineering department aboard ship. On a carrier, normally he has the rank of commander.

CIC Combat Information Center

CINCPAC Commander in chief, Pacific

Circle William Designation marked by a *W* inside a circle, denoting hatches and especially ventilator systems that must be closed in the event of chemical, biological, or nuclear warfare

COMSEVENTHFLT   Commander, Seventh Fleet

COMSTA   Communications station

CTF   Carrier task force

DC Central   Damage control central. This is the area in the bowels of the ship where battle or fire damage is assessed and repair parties are coordinated by the damage control assistant to the chief engineer.

double A & D   Double acceleration and deceleration. Throttlemen in the engine rooms increase or decrease the speed of the ship's engines at a certain rate during normal operations. During general quarters that rate is doubled.

E-2C   Called Hawkeye, it is the carrier's radar plane and it is used for early warning of threats to the task force.

ECM   Electronic countermeasures

E division   Electrical division. They are responsible for electrical generation and distribution aboard ship.

ELINT   Electronic intelligence. That intelligence gained by electronic means, such as with radio receivers, and radar

EM1   Electrician's mate first class

engineering logroom   This area has the desks of the engineering department officers, typically the main propulsion assistant, electrical officer, damage control assistant, and the chief engineer.

engine order telegraph   Abbreviated EOT, this mechanism sends engine forward, reverse. and speed commands from the bridge to the engine rooms, or the EOS in the case of a nuclear carrier.

EOS   Enclosed operating station. The watch standers in control of an engineering plant stand their watches in an air-conditioned space that is located inside one of the reactor rooms.

ETA   Estimated time of arrival

expanded metal   Sheet metal slotted and stretched to make a heavy-gauge screen with large diamond-shaped openings

F-4   U.S. Navy/Air Force fighter plane designed in the late fifties and upgraded ever since. It is a fixed-wing, dual-seat aircraft capable of more than Mach 2, or twice the speed of sound.

F-14   U.S. Navy's premier fighter plane, used for high-level intercept of airborne threats to a naval task force. It is a large, swing-wing, two-seat aircraft capable of more than Mach 2, or twice the speed of sound.

F-l5   U.S. Air Force fixed-wing, single-seat fighter plane capable of Mach 2.5

F-l6   U.S. Air Force fixed-wing, single-seat fighter plane capable of more than Mach 2.

F/A-18   U.S. Navy fixed-wing, single-seat fighter-bomber capable of approximately Mach 1.8

FEAF   Far Eastern Air Force

field day   General cleanup of a space

five by five   Jargon to indicate that radio reception is very good

flash (message)   The highest priority message in the military. It must be transmitted from its source to its final destination in a matter of only a few minutes.

Flogger   NATO code name for a MiG-23

Fox one/two/three   Launch of a Sparrow/Sidewinder/Phoenix missile

Fulcrum   NATO code name for a MiG-29

GQ   General quarters. These are the stations manned by the ship's crew when the ship is going into combat or when the captain wants maximum watertight integrity. Sometimes GQ is called when a fire breaks out that could spread throughout the ship, or when the ship is in danger of losing watertight integrity from a storm.

hatch   Any opening in a deck that is watertight when secured. The term *watertight door* should be used for such openings in bulkheads, and *hatch* should be used only for such openings in decks. Many sailors, however, use the word *hatch* to describe any opening with a watertight seal. Therefore, some dialogue in this novel has the word *hatch* meaning an opening in a bulkhead.

Hawkeye   See E-2C

heads-up display   This display is projected on a transparent screen in front of the pilot so that he can keep the target and firing symbols in view at all times. See "centering up the T (dot)."

HF   High frequencies, or 3 to 30 megahertz. These frequencies can bounce off the ionosphere and propagate great distances, and as such they are not limited to line-of-sight propagation.

HICOM   High command network. This is used by fleet commanders to communicate between fleets and nearby commands.

IFF   Identification friend or foe. Aircraft have transponders that are activated by radars and that will identify the aircraft to the radar as friendly.

IP   Initial point. This is the point at which a bombing run commences.

IR   Infrared or heat. The portion of the electromagnetic spectrum below visible light in frequency. Infrared is used in targeting for some missiles and "smart" bombs.

JP-5   Jet fuel

KGB   *Komitet Gosudarstvennio Bezopasnosti*, the very powerful Soviet secret police and intelligence agency

KORCOM   Korean Communist

LAMPS   Light Airborne Multipurpose System. This is a combination of ship board equipment and helicopter avionics that extends the ASW capabilities of destroyers and frigates by allowing the helicopter to detect and engage enemy subs while at a great distance from the ship.

list   The amount in degrees that a ship is leaning from the vertical

main control   This is the station, normally in the forward engine room on nonnuclear ships, where the engines and energy-producing systems are controlled.

MCRD   Marine Corps Recruit Depot in San Diego, California. M Crud to the navy people

M division   This division is responsible for the main engines, and the steam turbine end of the electrical generators.

MiG-23   Soviet-made fighter plane, NATO code name Flogger. A swing-wing aircraft capable of exceeding Mach 2, or twice the speed of sound.

MiG-29   Soviet-made fighter plane, NATO code name Fulcrum. It is more modern than the MiG-23 but still somewhat behind the latest western technology.

MM   Machinist's mate. The mechanical technicians aboard ship

MMCS   Senior chief machinist's mate

MM3   Machinist's mate third class

MPA   Main propulsion assistant. Usually a lieutenant commander on a carrier, he assists the chief engineer by being responsible for main engines, reduction gears, drive shafts, screws, and associated spaces.

naval flight officers   These nonpilots man other stations in naval aircraft. For example, see RIO and TACCO.

NAVCOMSTA   Naval communications station

OBA   Pronounced oh bee ay, it stands for oxygen breathing apparatus. It is a self-contained source of oxygen worn by sailors and used in firefighting aboard ship.

1JV   Designation for the sound-powered phone circuit connected to the bridge

1MC   Designation for the ship's public address system

OOD   Officer of the deck. He has command of the bridge and all ship's movements during a watch.

Phalanx   Designation for the ship's last-ditch defense against low-level airborne threats. It is a six-barreled Gatling gun that is capable of firing three thousand rounds a minute.

phased-array radar   A radar using an array of transmitting and receiving antenna elements that have their signals individually phase-shifted to form a beam, or be "pointed" in a selected direction. This radar has the advantage of being able to track many targets by electronically shifting the antenna beam,.rather than having to move the entire antenna.

Phoenix   High-speed, long-distance, air-to-air missile used by the U.S. Navy. In midcourse it uses semiactive homing, with the aircraft's radar illuminating the target. In the terminal phase of the flight it has fully active homing, meaning that it uses its own internal radar for guidance.

plan of the day   This one- or two-sheet paper gives information to naval installation personnel and ship's crews, identifies the command duty officer and officer of the day, gives the uniform of the day, and relays other pertinent information.

POET   Primed oscillator expendable transponder. This is a small expendable radio frequency active device, ejected from the ECM dispensers on fighter aircraft, that mimics the radar return from an aircraft to decoy an oncoming radar-guided missile away from the aircraft.

PriFly   The area on an aircraft carrier containing the air traffic controllers

QC   Quality control. These are technicians that monitor audio transmissions at a communications station.

RATT   Radioteletype

repair party   This is a group of sailors who are responsible for damage control in a designated part of a ship, typically during general quarters.

RHIP   Rank has its privileges

RIO   Radar intercept officer. The rear seater in dual-seat aircraft

RT   Radiotelephone

SAM   Surface-to-air missile

S-band   The band of radio frequencies from 1.55 to 5.2 gigahertz. Propagation of these signals is limited to line of sight; these frequencies are typically used for radar and satellite communications.

screw pitch controls   Newer naval ships, such as frigates and destroyers, have variable-pitch propellers, or screws, the control of which is typically on the bridge.

Seasparrow   Surface-to-air missile used aboard naval destroyers for air defense. Traveling at Mach 2.5, this missile has semiactive radar homing out to about eight nautical miles.

secondary coming station   This station takes over responsibility for a ship's conning movements if the bridge is knocked out during a station battle.

Sidewinder   U.S. air-to-air missile with infrared homing

SIF   Selective identification feature. This is a code added to the signal from a plane's IFF transponder that identifies the plane and its altitude-to-ground radars.

Silkworm (HY-2G)   Chinese coastal defense cruise missile that is relatively obsolete by western standards

splitting the plant fore and aft   Most naval vessels have a fore and an aft plant, each consisting of one or two main engines and a nuclear reactor or several oil-fired boilers. The steam from each plant can be cross-connected so that both plants supply steam to both sets of main engines, but they are always split during general quarters, resulting in two independent plants for damage control purposes.

sponson   A small deck projecting out from the side of a ship, typically used for refueling at sea stations, or for supporting guns in the older carriers

TACCO   Tactical coordinator. In a Hawkeye radar plane he vectors carrier aircraft to intercept threats to the task force. See naval flight officers.

tactical information display   This display is in the rear cockpit of an F-14 and is monitored by the RIO, who gets a display of the plane's radar or a 360-degree display of air traffic.

tally   Short for tallyho. This designates a sighting by an aircraft crew; for example, "Tally two at 3 o'clock."

TAO   Tactical action officer. He mans the CIC and controls the ship's engagement of hostile forces.

UHF   Ultra high frequencies, or 300 to 3,000 megahertz. These frequencies are limited to line-of-sight conditions and are typically used for aircraft voice and data transmission.

undog (a hatch)   The act of releasing the small metal cams, or dogs, that seal a watertight door or hatch

UNREP   Underway replenishment

vampire   Call over comm nets indicating that surface-to-surface or air-to-surface missiles are heading toward the ship

VC   Vietcong

VHF   Very high frequencies, or 30 to 300 megahertz. These frequencies are normally limited to line-of-sight conditions.

watch your six(o'clock)   A caution that an enemy plane is behind you

WestPac   Western Pacific area

X-band   The band of radio frequencies from 5.2 to 10.9 gigahertz. These frequencies propagate in a line of sight and are typically used for radar and satellite communications.

XO   Naval slang for the executive officer, the ship's second in command

ZDK   Request to retransmit a message

Zebra   As a material condition aboard ship this indicates the closing of all watertight doors and hatches.